OUT OF THE BLUE

HIGH STAKES

.

DEE J. ADAMS

Edited by Melissa Johnson
Cover Art by Croco Designs
Digital Formatting by Author E.M.S.

DEDICATION

This one is for my Aunt Carol and Uncle Thom...
My pseudo parents who have supported me through thick and thin.
Thanks for being there when I needed you and especially for always
believing in me. Love you both with all my heart.

This also goes out to Malcolm and Beth, my favorite brother (okay...my
only brother!) and SIL. Thanks for being so awesome! Don't know what
I'd do without you guys. You're lifesavers on multiple levels. Lots of
mushy hugs and kisses! Mwah! Love you!

Dear Reader,

I'm so happy to finally bring you Brendan's story. The poor guy went through so much in *Against the Wall*, that I wanted to give him his happily ever after as soon as I could. Like any good hero, he has to work for it, but the reward is worth it.

I especially loved giving Seger Hughes a cameo in this book. Seger has his own story in *Dangerously Close* (the third book in the Adrenaline Highs series). Since Brendan has been working for him for a few years, it seemed apropos to give Seger his two cents in this story.

Finding love isn't always easy, but with a lot of understanding and compassion, Casey and Brendan manage to find their way. I hope you enjoy their journey in *Out of the Blue*.

Thank you for taking the time to read any of the books in this series or my Adrenaline Highs series. There are a lot of books out there and I'm thrilled you chose one of mine.

I love to hear from readers, so feel free to email me at deej.adams1@gmail.com.

Best,

Dee J. Adams

ACKNOWLEDGMENTS

There are always a ton of people to thank when it comes to writing a book and because I missed someone the last time, I have to thank Robena Grant for being first eyes on my last book, *Always Dangerous*. Robena, thank you so much for all your insight and thoughtfulness. You rock, lady!

A huge thank you to Ashley Argota for helping me with the songwriting portion of this book. I gave Ashley a cameo because she's my LoveBug and I adore her. She is also one of the most talented young ladies I've ever worked with and oh my god the girl can sing. Check her out, you won't be sorry.

Thank you to Lynn Marshall for always being there with good advice and—for this book—the very talented Andrea Rimmer. (Andrea specializes in prosthetics and she has her own story in Lynne's book, *A Mother for His Adopted Son*, a Mills and Boon Medical Romance.) I loved that the person I needed to help a character was alive and well and living in my good pal's wonderful book!

As always, my most heartfelt thank-you to my editor, Melissa Johnson. Melissa you keep me on track and make the whole process practically seamless and tremendously enjoyable. You are Supereditor... (yes, a new superhero!) and I love you.

Last, but never least, thank you to Sean and Katelyn for being my biggest supporters and favorite people in the whole world. I love you guys.

Any mistakes are my own.

CHAPTER 1

THE EARLY MORNING SUN slowly rose over Diamond Head as a cool breeze lifted Casey's long hair off her neck. Her balcony suite afforded her the spectacular view of brilliant blues and greens of the churning Pacific Ocean. It also offered the perfect spot to watch a few gorgeously tan and fit males as they jogged by. *No complaints here.* If anything it added value to this pretty—albeit lonely—room.

It felt liberating to be able to look and not feel guilty. Hell, not only could she look, she could touch as well. After a week at this dream hotel and fantasy suite, she'd decided it was about damn time to touch.

She was on her honeymoon, for God's sake. May as well find a guy to dirty the sheets with since her ex-fiancé wasn't there to do it. Her heart raced and her stomach twisted just thinking about him.

Jerk.

Asshole.

Bully.

She had a mile long list of all the names she had for her former almost-husband. The sad part was they weren't really new names. She'd chosen to overlook his less-than-stellar qualities, because that's what a person did when they loved someone. They took them for the good and the bad.

Or not.

Really, she should have seen it coming. Casey sat on the comfortable chaise on her balcony, keeping her eyes peeled for the day's distraction. She popped the top on a tube of body cream and slathered some on her legs.

Maybe breaking up was for the better. "Hell, no *maybe* about it, Case. He did you a favor." Who wanted to be married to a guy who didn't consider her feelings or ambition? Who wanted a guy so overprotective that he had to know her every move, every minute of the day? Who wanted a man telling her how to dress or what to eat? Or more importantly what she should and shouldn't do with her life?

Not too many people took her ambition seriously and Casey had tried not to let it bother her. But how long could a girl go without support from her parents and especially her fiance?

Now she finally had a shot at something spectacular and where was she? Alone on her honeymoon.

She gazed at the interior of her plush suite. Soothing ocean colors accented the walls and spotlighted the king sized bed with its thick white comforter. A large mahogany desk and matching dresser and night tables furnished the room, and a big Jacuzzi tub sat inside the open partition to the bathroom, begging to be used. Time to say good-bye to the high life. Jeff's family had money to burn, while she was a teacher and her parents lived modestly on a steel salesman's income. She had no problem trading the finer things in life for her independence. The fact that she hadn't acquired this freedom on her own terms pissed her off something fierce.

The first notes of "Old Time Rock and Roll" by Bob Seger disrupted the calm of the crashing ocean and Casey checked the screen. Her mother. Ugh. She wiped the excess lotion on her hands on a nearby towel and took the call anyway. "Hi, Mom. What's up?"

"Casey? Oh... I didn't think you'd be up so early."

Then why did you call if you didn't think you were going to talk to me? Because she wanted to leave another scathing message without interruption. "Surprise. You got me. Did you need something, Mom? I'll be home tomorrow." Apparently going three days without getting chastised for not being married wasn't possible.

"I realize the week is almost over, but it's not too late to apologize to Jeff and make things right."

She snorted, but her gut twisted at the idea. "Mom, how many times do I have to tell you, he broke up with me? Why am I apologizing when I did nothing wrong?"

"Casey, why are you so difficult now? You used to be such a sweet girl. Jeff just wants to take care of you. He wants—"

"He wants to own me, Mother. He doesn't want to take care of me. The fact that you keep calling and sticking up for him is total..." bullshit, but she couldn't say that word to her mom.

"Honey, you've never been practical about what you want in life. Think of what you're giving up? Jeff and his family can take of you for the rest of your life. Your future is secure with him. You won't have to worry about money or status. You can quit your teaching job at that...that school and concentrate on having kids and being a good wife and mom."

Gah! Casey wanted to scream. Her mom sounded exactly like her grandmother. A woman's job was in the home. Who still thought like that? "Mom, I'm not you. How many times have I told you that? I'm only twenty-four. I want different things than you did at my age." The phone jostled.

"Casey, this is your father."

She rolled her eyes. Round two.

"We've all been very patient with you for the past week, but enough is enough. When you get back here, you've got a lot of work to do to get back in Jeff's good graces."

Unbelievable. They never listened to a word she said. "I'm fine, Dad, thanks for asking." Casey kept her tone neutral. "Don't worry about picking me up from the airport. I'm sure if Zoe can't do it, I can take a taxi." No use repeating the fact that Jeff had broken off the wedding. "Hello? Dad, are you there? This connection is the worst. Dad? I can't hear you? Da—" She disconnected the call herself. Enough of that bullshit. Tension streamed through her in tight knots. Her folks made it harder and harder to stay calm. Knowing they sided with Jeff was worse than a knife to her back. They'd never seen his nasty side. She hadn't either until about two years into the relationship. Maybe if they knew about his temper, they'd cut her some slack. But she wasn't going to have that conversation over the phone so it would have to wait.

This Hawaiian vacation sucked harder than the rip tide that had kept the crowds from the water the last few days. She scanned the almost empty beach, watching the occasional runner jog past. She'd spent the past three days talking herself into doing something completely out of character. Something her best friend would be completely on board with.

For once in her life she planned to be a little reckless and very spontaneous... If you could call psyching yourself up for three days "spontaneous."

Being bold was not one of her strong suits. Her high school years had been awkward and painful. As the tallest girl in class, she'd been the butt of too many jokes. The few dates she'd gone on were with boys she considered friends. Seemed as if any of the boys she *really* liked didn't return the feeling. She hadn't met her best friend until college and that came about because they'd been roommates in the dorm. Vic gave Casey the self-assurance to embrace the qualities she'd been born with and slowly a more confident woman had evolved.

There! She saw him and her heart did that little trip and double skip as she took a second to admire his six pack—and no she wasn't talking beer—broad shoulders and muscular chest. He'd secured his shoulder length hair into a low ponytail. The man was gorgeous and he'd been alone every morning for his beach run. Casey planned to rectify that. On this last full day—and night— she was not going to be alone.

Casey grabbed her towel, took a last look in the bathroom mirror and adjusted *the girls* in her bikini top. The new light blond streaks she'd added to her brown hair two days ago still surprised her and she ran a quick hand through the long straight tresses before heading out of her hotel room.

Jeff had always frowned upon her coloring her hair. *If I wanted a blonde, I'd be dating a blonde.* His parents had been grooming him for public life since his early years and their teachings had stuck like his mother's neat dark chignon. Well, Jeff could kiss her ass. How many years had she let that man dictate her life? Too many. Those days were over.

Happily.

She had a fresh start with an exciting future only a week away. She didn't need Jeff or any other man telling her how to dress or wear her hair or what to do for a living.

Casey took the stairs, her heart picking up pace with her stride as she crossed the paved terrace of the hotel's beach café toward the sand. The sun had barely kissed the beach and cool sand oozed between her toes. Palm trees swayed in the morning breeze and the din of the spectacular blue ocean waters crashed next to her. She absolutely believed the ocean held healing powers. Maybe she'd needed the extra waves and wild wind to push Jeff out of her psyche. Didn't matter to her either way. She was glad he was gone and she could hold her head up high. Everything happened for a reason. Including spotting her current target.

Tossing her small colorful bag near the spot where Mr. Gorgeous stopped every morning after his jog, she debated her next move. Did she wait here or in the water? The storm off the coast had wreaked havoc on the shore and all water sports had been cancelled for the last three days. It was almost as if Jeff had conjured up bad weather to punish her for going on their honeymoon alone. Well screw him. Her sister and maid of honor, Zoe, would've been the perfect "my wedding fell through, but I'm going to party on the honeymoon anyway" pal, except she'd come down with food poisoning at the last minute, leaving Casey by herself.

Maybe this was why. So Casey could get lucky without any regret or any guilt from her sister.

Casey glanced up and her heart nearly stopped when she saw Mr. Gorgeous already headed back in her direction. Had she been daydreaming that long? She still hadn't decided where to be. Stay here on the beach or be casually enjoying the water ten feet away?

He got closer and closer, his arms and legs pumping, sweat glistening off his tan skin and all those muscles rippling everywhere. Sun glinted off his dark hair and showed fiery red streaks.

Oh. My. God. He was part ginger. *Love it.*

Doing her best to look like this was a regular morning, Casey strolled out to the water and let the cool tide crash in around her ankles. A bit chillier than she expected, but maybe the storm waters had dropped the temperature. The beach was still mostly empty so she hoped MG—as she'd come to think of him—would stop at his usual spot to check his watch and take a breather.

Casey took a step off the foot and half shelf and let the water hit her at the knees, refusing to be one of those wimps who cringed at cold water. She turned to make sure MG was in his spot and hid a smile that even though she'd encroached somewhat on his territory, he stayed true to his morning routine. She was even more thrilled when he looked up and waved. She cocked her head, letting her hair fall to the side in a move that showed off the length. Her heart thumped harder since this little excursion was working much faster than she thought it would. He waved harder and even called out to her, his eyes wide as if—

A hundred pounds slammed into Casey's back. At least that's what it felt like as a wave of water threw her forward. The shock of impact had her gasping, which was a huge mistake since she only took in salt water. The force of the wave tumbled her onto the gravely beach then back out to the ocean. Casey scrambled for purchase, for air. Water tumbled her every which way but up. Her lungs seized as she sputtered, choked and coughed while still trying to find any air among the salt-water intake.

Dead.

She was most certainly going to die in three feet of water. She felt every rock and shell as the water pounded her against the sand. Her arms, stomach and legs burned with the impact. As quickly as the water scraped her against the bottom, it took her out just as fast. The roaring in her ears deafened her so much that she only heard the rapid beat of her heart pounding a death song in her head. No matter how much she flailed against the tide, she couldn't find the right direction and water surged into her nose and mouth. Her lungs burned like the Tiki torches she watched outside her hotel room every night. She wasn't going to last another five seconds.

A hell of a way to die on her honeymoon-for-one.

CHAPTER 2

IF BRENDAN HAD JUST looked up a few seconds sooner, he might've warned her in time, but he'd barely gotten a word out when the wave hit.

He didn't bother looking for a lifeguard since it was still too early. He just sprinted to the water as the waves tossed her like a rag doll. She flailed under the pounding surf and Brendan fought the water to reach her. Just as he wrapped his arm around her waist another wave struck them sideways and tossed them both into churning white foam. Brendan managed to keep his internal compass steady and got to his feet, dragging the girl with him before another wave did more damage. She was tall, all legs and long hair that tangled around her face. Didn't she know there was a yellow flag warning on the beach?

She didn't have much fight as he lifted her more securely in his arms and trudged to what he assumed was her towel on the beach. She continued to gasp, cough and spew water and Brendan empathized. It sucked to get taken out by a wave. She was in the worst phase of it, too, trying to expel the water while getting in enough air to satisfy her lungs. Brendan set her down and watched helplessly as she tried to breath. He clapped her back a few times even though he knew he wouldn't do much good. He just hated being helpless. Hated it with a passion.

He passed her the towel and she coughed up more ocean water then wiped her face and blew her nose into the corner. Minutes passed as they sat together, as she slowly pulled enough air into her lungs to breathe instead of gasp and cough.

Her long hair was plastered to her shoulders and back and the morning sun highlighted incredible smooth skin over miles of tone muscle.

"You okay?" Brendan finally asked. It might be good to sound like a normal human instead of a drooling idiot. Those legs of hers were enough to suck the brains right out of a man's head. He took a second to shake out his hair…and maybe clear his head.

"I…" She coughed again and held up a finger as she tried to clear her throat. "I will be," she finally uttered in a raw voice.

He sat with her a few more minutes as she cleared her throat and coughed some more. He noticed two bottles of water where he'd picked up her towel and opened one before handing it to her.

She sipped gratefully then reached for the second and pushed it at him. "Here. For you." Her voice was still raw, but she managed the words without coughing so he considered it progress.

Since he was parched after his run, he accepted her offering and slugged half the contents in one shot. He caught her watching him as he recapped the bottle.

"Thank you," she said. She cleared her rough throat and pushed wet hair off her face. "Seriously. I have no idea how that happened, but thank you. You saved me."

Now that she had the towel in her lap and hair pushed back, he saw the crazy blue-green of her eyes. His pulse skipped then steadied, then skipped again when she smiled at him. Brilliant white teeth. Plush lips. Full and inviting and very kissable if he let himself think about it, which he couldn't since he'd just met her and didn't even have a name. That problem he could remedy. He had to talk over the waves that crashed nearby.

"I'm Brendan. And you're welcome. Glad I was here to do the saving." Wasn't that an understatement? He took a quick glance at the rest of her, noticing the flat stomach and sweet, sweet curves.

She stuck out her hand. "Casey…and I'm glad too." Her palm was cool and Brendan thought of the ways he could heat it up. Heat her up. "Any chance I could say thank you with breakfast. On me. All you can eat." She blinked. Salt crystals lodged in her long dark lashes and sparkled in the sun.

All you can eat. On me. His mind went to a very dirty place and he smiled at her offer. His mini vacation had been a complete surprise and he'd been lonelier than a lost dog, so her invitation sounded perfect.

"I guess it's a good thing I like breakfast," he said. He wasn't picky either. He'd eat any meal. On her. He huffed out a breath, glanced at the aqua ocean and tried to clear his filthy mind. He blamed his older brothers, mostly Danny since his revolving door of women seemed never-ending.

"Something funny?" she asked.

"Nah." He drew a line in the sand with his index finger. "Just thinking how my day suddenly got better." No lie there.

That brought a breath-stealing grin to her full lips. What a mouth she had. God, he pictured all the things she could do with that mouth and his lungs nearly seized.

She nodded. "It's the second sharp turn my morning has taken. The first was getting clobbered by that wave."

"Which reminds me. Didn't you see the yellow flag?" He pointed toward the lifeguard stand fifteen yards away. "You probably shouldn't have been in the water at all."

Her smile faded. "A yellow flag doesn't mean you can't get in the water. It just means the current is strong. I was barely in knee deep so I didn't think I was in danger." She stood up and reached for her towel, water bottle and small beach bag, her movements brisk.

"Hey, wait a minute." He stood next to her, surprised at her height. She had to be close to six feet tall. He only had about three inches on her. "Is something wrong?" He gave her his best pout face. The one his mother caved to almost every time, the one his brothers ribbed him about because he "got away with murder with that look."

She wouldn't meet his gaze. Gone was the *I want to eat breakfast then you for dessert* look and in was the *I can't even look at you much less touch you* stink-eye. Long seconds passed before she shook her head and sighed. "No, nothing's wrong. I just..." She waved her hand in the air. "Forget it. It's not important." She started walking toward the hotel and Brendan kept her long-legged pace.

"How about we meet down here in thirty minutes? It'll give us time to shower off the salt." She faced him under the awning of the beach café, her cheeks flushed. "For breakfast," he added when she seemed confused.

Her face flamed hotter. "Right. Breakfast. I'll... I'll meet you back here."

Before his impromptu ocean escapade, he'd been covered in sweat from his run. Usually his runs happened on treadmills in whatever hotel his boss occupied, so this spectacular scenery was a nice change of pace. "Perfect."

She continued toward the hotel and Brendan followed. "Are you staying *here?*' she asked. Her eyes rounded in surprise.

"I am." Something had definitely changed her mood and he pretended not to notice. "You too?"

"Me too."

He couldn't tell if she sounded more distressed or aggravated. Damn. He'd never seen her until now. "How long have you been here?" he asked.

"All week. I'm leaving tomorrow." Apparently not soon enough by the tone in her voice.

"So I guess we'll have to make the most of..." He almost said today, but noticed her mood swing so amended his word. "Breakfast."

She nodded, but looked completely uncomfortable with the idea. So what had he said that upset her? She excused herself to the right side of the hotel, while Brendan headed left. He'd have to work on her at breakfast and get the smile back.

Twenty-nine minutes later, Brendan stood in the lobby. He'd thrown on a pair of cargo shorts, white T-shirt and cross-trainers. He hated not wearing his boots, but this was paradise and it was too hot to wear jeans.

He spotted Casey as she exited the elevator. It was virtually impossible to miss her. Wearing a tie-dye sundress of blues and greens, she could've been modeling for a catalogue. Hell, she probably was a model. Sure, he'd noticed her features when he'd scooped her from the water, but she'd also resembled a drowned rat. The transformation stunned him. She seemed larger than life as her colorful dress set her apart from the dark maroon carpet and white walls. She had every bit of his attention when she looked at him with those amazing aqua ocean eyes.

The one thing he knew for certain: He wanted a fresh start. Something had happened to turn her off and he wanted to flip that switch. So when she approached him with that leery look on her face, Brendan ignored it and hit her with his best smile.

"Hi. Brendan St. John." He stuck out his hand the same way she'd done on the beach. "I don't think I've seen you around."

Casey glanced to the right then to the left then slowly put her hand in his. "What are you doing?"

"Starting fresh," he said, enjoying the softness of her skin. They'd both been full of sand and salt after their aquatic acrobats. "Contrary to what my brothers may think I'm not a total bonehead. Something happened before we came inside and I have no idea what it was. I just want a second chance."

A ghost of a smile crept across her lips. "Oh, no, it was nothing, it was me." She blushed as a raucous family of five walked by dressed in beachwear. "Are you okay with the restaurant here?" She pointed toward the corner of the hotel where the main restaurant served breakfast, lunch and dinner.

The place wasn't cheap, but nothing at this hotel was. He wouldn't be staying here if his boss hadn't been footing the bill. "Sounds good." Who was he to decide if she could afford the place or not? Maybe her little frilly sundress had very deep pockets.

Since it was still an early hour, they were seated immediately at a table for two and ordered breakfast. Brendan had dodged the place mainly because of the linen birds. All the napkins at every table were folded in the shape of a bird and he felt guilty sticking his boss with the price tag. Not that his boss couldn't afford it, but it seemed excessive when he could grab a coffee and breakfast at the diner down the street for a fraction of the price. Seriously, it seemed crazy that people took so much time folding something that people were going to undo the second they sat down.

Birds aside, Brendan couldn't keep his gaze off her. In fact, maybe his brothers were right and he was a bonehead, because he'd never guess that the wet fish he pulled from the sea would turn out to be this gorgeous girl.

"You're staring," she said with a shy glance.

He took a sip of his orange juice and felt his cheeks flush. "Sorry. You..."

She waited then prompted him with her head cocked. Her hair fell to the side in a silky wave so shiny he itched to touch it, to run

11

his fingers through it, to wrap it around his fist and hold—

"I...what?" she asked.

He exhaled and did a mental shake to clear his head, then picked up that little bird napkin and spread it across his lap. "You surprised me."

"How?" Damn she was smooth. Cool and in control as her steady gaze pinned him to his spot.

"I don't know. I just didn't expect to meet anyone and all of sudden...there you are." It was like winning the lotto and not knowing you entered. *Thank you, very much, yes, I'll take some of that.*

"Are you here on vacation?" she asked, smoothing her finger over the rim of her tea cup.

"It started out as business, but it's turned into a vacation I wasn't expecting when my boss's plans changed." He'd been a little put out at first because he'd been expecting to keep busy. He didn't have anything against paradise, but spending time on his own wasn't his idea of fun. He didn't have a brother to explore with or a girl to keep him occupied in other ways.

"That doesn't sound bad." She took a sip of her chai latte and Brendan didn't see any rings. Not that he expected to find one, but it was good reassurance just the same.

"It's not. I just hadn't planned for so much down time." He liked to keep busy, keep moving. He wasn't great at standing still and even in paradise he'd learned that he still watched his back. Would he ever really get over being kidnapped? Years had gone by but sometimes anxiety still threatened to eat him alive. "What about you? Vacation or business?"

She laughed and the sound carried very little humor. She leaned forward and lowered her voice as a group of people walked behind her to their table. "You want to know the truth?" When he nodded, she looked around and moved even closer. Brendan caught a whiff of her perfume, something flowery and fresh. It made his mouth water. "I'm on my honeymoon."

Brendan pulled back and looked around the spacious room, sure to find a giant guy with beefy arms crossed over his beefier chest and ready to murder him for having breakfast with his bride. So much for the lottery win. So much for the plans to spend more time with her. Didn't it always happen this way?

Casey shook her head and her smile faded as she set her hand on his arm. Her warmth sent a hot sizzle through his bloodstream. "No worries. The wedding never happened, so technically this isn't really a honeymoon. It's just a honey. Or a moon." She shrugged. "Or a vacation for one. Take your pick."

Brendan had too much information to process. Honestly, he wasn't sure he heard her right. "You mean to tell me that some douchebag had a shot to marry you and bailed? Clearly he's nuts." His relief returned in increments and those failed possibilities were back on the table.

Casey cocked her head again and a small grin played on her magnificent lips.

Brendan returned the smile and took her hand. "So why did Mr. Douche bail? Any idea? Please don't tell me you caught him with one of your bridesmaids." That would suck a huge wad.

"Nope." She shook her head. "It comes down to this. He gave me an ultimatum and when I didn't do what he wanted, he cut me loose. Simple as that."

"What was the ultimatum?" Brendan wanted to know what could possibly cause a man to let a woman like this go. Granted, he didn't know her, but so far nothing struck him as whack job. She was adventurous enough to set foot in a rough ocean, which although not extremely smart, lead him to believe she wasn't a sissy. She hadn't cried like a baby after he'd pulled her out of Mother Nature's clutches and she'd offered him water when she could've used the second bottle herself. So yeah, off the top of his head, she didn't seem like the kind of girl any sane man would dump.

"It doesn't really matter," she said, gesturing the problem away. "The longer we were together the more controlling he became."

"How long *were* you together?"

"Total? Four years. But the last two were pretty miserable. This was just the final straw. After a couple of days when I realized I was more broken up about the work of returning everyone's gifts than I was about losing my fiancé, I realized I was better off without him. I can't imagine what being married to him would've been like. He did me a huge favor."

The most random thought hit Brendan. His brother, Blake, had fallen in love with his girlfriend at first sight. Brendan had secretly scoffed at the idea. Love at first sight? Seemed highly unlikely. But the second Casey had looked at him with her ocean eyes, Brendan had a sense of what his twin felt when he met his girlfriend, Abbey.

He rubbed his thumb over her knuckles, feeling a spark of something new and wonderful streaking through his veins. "I think he did me a favor too."

CHAPTER 3

CASEY COULDN'T FIGHT THE optimism glowing in her chest. Sitting in a four star restaurant with beautiful white linen table cloth and the ocean breeze drifting in through a nearby window, she couldn't deny the opportunity happening in front of her.

Those first few minutes at the beach had mortified her beyond her wildest imagination. Number one, she'd had to be rescued, number two, she'd been covered in seaweed, salt and snot—not a good combination—and number three, she must have looked like a class A bimbo to get caught up in a wave so close to shore. *Way to make a great first impression, Case.* She'd managed to get over it and even get an invitation out—mission accomplished!—until he mentioned the yellow flag warning. Then it was like getting clobbered with her own stupidity. She wanted to disappear, to hide in her room until her flight took off.

Here she was, free of Jeff, supposedly an independent woman, and she needed to be saved in three feet of ocean water by a total stranger.

Casey would've completely forgotten about the invitation to breakfast if Brendan hadn't reminded her. In the thirty minutes it took to get ready, Casey had psyched herself up. She'd showered, put on her favorite dress, fixed her makeup in record time and headed downstairs, intent on overcoming the embarrassment and keeping her original plan.

She tried to keep her heart from beating out of control. Brendan St. John wasn't only a gorgeous specimen of a man, he was sweet and fun and everything she'd fantasized about. She still couldn't believe they'd been staying in the same hotel and hadn't run into each other before she'd made her move on the beach.

He'd taken out the ponytail and his long hair hung thick and wavy away from his face, showing off his amazing eyes. Lord have mercy, they were as blue as the Hawaiian sky. Intense. Sexy. Full of life and sparkle.

A girl could fall for a man with eyes like that.

Not that she was doing any falling. Not for a long time to come. No way, no how. Not her. This delicious man in front of her was strictly temporary. Strictly rebound. And what a perfect rebound man at that. He had everything she wanted. A body to die for, a smile that melted anything in its path and a sense of humor to keep her grinning for weeks.

They watched each other for way too long and Casey felt another blush creep into her face. Was she the only one feeling these sparks, the only one to get a tickle where she hadn't been tickled in far too long?

This guy was nothing like Jeff. For starters, her ex had never understood her sense of humor. She found herself constantly explaining her puns to him, which took the fun right out of any jokes. Jeff kept his blond hair super short and his eyes were completely different. Literally. One blue and one green.

Boy did she not want to be thinking about Jeff right now.

Conversation. She needed something brilliant to say.

"So what does your boss do? Is he staying here too?"

Brendan shook his head, his gaze never wavering from her eyes. "Nope. He's got a house on the North Shore."

She didn't know too much about the island, but figured anyone who had a house in paradise probably had some money to play with. "So instead of having you stay there with him, he put you up here?" She took a sip of her chai latte and enjoyed the spicy sweetness. "Tiny house?" Okay, she was fishing, but didn't really care.

He snorted. "Not even close. I think he just wanted private time with his wife. She used to travel with him constantly, kind of like the way Linda McCartney always traveled with Paul. But she's been working a lot lately so they're catching up on alone time."

"That's sweet. Sounds like a nice boss." It was odd how he compared him to Paul McCartney though. Unless...

Nodding, Brendan sipped his OJ. "He's actually a great boss."

"I see that. What does he do?"

"He's a musician...like Paul." He smiled and made it clear that there was more to the description.

Casey returned the grin. "What? You're going to leave me hanging?" Then she put a few pieces together. His boss put him up in a five-star hotel while he stayed in a house on the North Shore. "He's more than just a musician, isn't he? He's someone famous? Like Paul?" she added, because he seemed to be the comparison of the conversation.

Brendan's eyes crinkled together as he nodded. "You could say that. Yeah." He took another drink and had Casey on the edge of her seat. "I can tell you the perks are pretty amazing."

She flicked her napkin across the table. It was very unladylike and Jeff would've had a fit, but Brendan laughed and dodged her lame assault. "So, who?" she finally asked, looking around self-consciously when she realized her loud voice carried through the room. Something moved in her peripheral vision and she did a double take, but didn't see anything. The oddest sensation crept up her spine, but after a final glance she faced Brendan again. "Who?" she said more softly.

Brendan sighed. "You might not even like him or his music. It's no big deal." He waited another few seconds until Casey thought she might explode with curiosity. "Seger Hughes," he finally said.

Casey's jaw nearly hit the table. "Are you kidding me? You work for Seger Hughes?" She'd had a crush on him for years. Well, she had a crush on the new version of him. The older version hadn't appealed to her at all, but the new and improved Seger had lit her up with his soft ballads and hard muscles. "What do you do for him?"

"I'm his assistant. Gofer. Whatever. I'm the whatever guy." Brendan sat back as two servers set dishes in front of them.

Casey almost didn't care about breakfast anymore. She'd give her right arm to be Seger Hughes's gopher. "How long have you worked for him?" She picked up her fork and attempted to eat her omelet.

"A few years. It's not always a full-time gig. It depends on his touring schedule."

His boss must have rubbed off on him because he even talked like a musician. "You have to tell me... Is he as nice as people say?"

Brendan nodded. "He is. I got lucky when I found that job."

"How *did* you find that job? I'd kill to work with someone as talented as that man."

Brendan dove into his French toast and swallowed before answering. "It was total luck and timing. His old assistant was a friend of a friend and planning to move back home because of family issues. I happened to be in San Francisco at one of his tour dates and met up with my pal's buddy. I ended up getting VIP passes, hanging with the band after the show and meeting Seger. He was complaining about losing Doug and wondering where he was going to find a replacement and Doug said, 'Please, this job is so easy a monkey could do it.' Then he looked at me and said, 'Hell, even Bren could do it.' Next thing you know, he's showing me the ropes and explaining what he does for the man. And boom, suddenly I have a new job."

"Wow. That is *serious* luck and timing." Nothing that exciting had ever happened to her. Unless she counted the formal dinner Jeff took to her when his dad had won his Senate seat. But Jeff had kept her next to him with an iron arm all night and she hadn't had a chance to talk to any of the high profile people who'd supported his dad.

"It beats bartending," he added. "That's my other gig. I still fill in when I'm not working for Seger. My friend's parents own a restaurant and they plug me in when I'm not on the road."

She nodded, but wanted the good stuff. "So what do you do for Seger?"

"A lot of everything. I handle his day-to-day needs when we're on the road. Make sure his guests are taken care of at each venue." He shrugged. "Doug was pretty much right. A monkey could do the job. But like I said, the perks are good." He gestured to the surroundings and Casey nodded her agreement.

"What do you do?" he asked.

Casey sipped her tea. "I'm kind of in between things at the

moment." She was full of understatements today. "I was teaching music at a private school, but I'm not sure I'll be going back." She liked the kids, but working in a classroom all day felt claustrophobic. She needed new scenery to keep creative. Teaching was slowly leaching her drive to succeed in music.

"Music?" His beautiful eyes widened. "What do you play?" He took another bite of his breakfast and Casey enjoyed the way he dove in with gusto. Everything about him screamed masculine.

She dug into her omelet again before it got cold. "Piano, mostly, but guitar too."

"No shit." He spread his arm out wide. "I play guitar and synthesizer."

Who would've known they had music in common? She'd have pegged him for a jock all the way.

"So how come the school gig isn't working out?" He took a big bite after the question and Casey loved the way his square jaw chomped his food. God he was gorgeous from the top of his ginger laced head to the bottom of his size-giant shoes.

She met his gaze and hurried to answer. "I'm just hoping something different comes along. I'm not sure I'm cut out to teach kids." Her *something different* was definitely coming, but she had to keep that news under wraps.

They discovered they were both from Los Angeles and talked high schools and colleges. Turned out they actually knew a few of the same people, friends of friends in a local band. They lingered over breakfast until they got the evil eye from the restaurant manager, then they slowly walked toward the lobby area.

"So what's your plan for today. Your last day, right?"

She nodded and got that strange sensation on the back of her neck. She looked around the lobby, but didn't see anything out of the ordinary. She faced Brendan. "Last day." She looked him square in the eyes. "Last night too." Maybe that came off a little desperate, but his smile flashed bright white and she suddenly didn't care.

"It's still early. Want to snag a couple chairs by the pool and hang out for a while?"

Her girl parts cheered with pompoms. "That sounds like a decent plan." No reason to sound too excited about the idea. "I'll get changed and meet you at the pool." Casey casually walked toward the elevator, squashing the urge to skip, bounce, or run so that she could spend as much time with Brendan as possible. Just knowing she'd get to stare at his chest for the next hour or two made her skin tingle.

Once out of the elevator, Casey hurried down the hall to her room and stripped off her clothes as she pawed through her suitcase looking for her special honeymoon bikini. Virgin white. Haha. Yeah, that was a joke, but whatever. She wanted to wow this boy. She wanted to make sure that the next one or two hours morphed into ten or twelve. She not only wanted this whole day, she wanted this man for the entire night.

CHAPTER 4

ONE OF THE BEST days of Brendan's life turned into one of the best nights. Hanging with Casey poolside was as good as a lottery win and smoothing sunscreen on miles of her silky skin pretty much turned him into a drooling fool. Casey made it fairly clear she wanted him, which meant they spent the whole day getting to know each other. And touch each other. A whole day of foreplay so to speak. About eight or so hours of buildup to the main event.

They'd parted ways to shower—again—and change for dinner. On the off chance they ended up coming to his place, Brendan picked up his dirty clothes, tossed them into the closet and slid the door closed. Then he straightened up the bathroom. He caught a glimpse of himself in the mirror and froze.

No matter how much he tried to avoid looking at his ear, it was always the first place his gaze landed when he saw his reflection. He didn't know why. It wasn't as if one day—by some miracle—he might discover he had a whole ear.

He was fairly certain Casey hadn't noticed it yet. His hair covered it pretty well. Of course it was a matter of time. Then she'd ask. He either had to tell her the truth or lie about it. Or...

He pulled out the prosthetic ear from his toilet kit. He hadn't had it for long. The prosthesis overlapped his partial ear without the need of surgical inserts or medical adhesive. He never would've gotten it if it wasn't for next week. Hell, he never expected to make the cut, so when he got in, he couldn't turn down the opportunity. He'd thought long and hard about what he wanted the public to know about him. Cameras would catch his bad ear in a minute and he'd be forced to come clean. Then people would speculate and he didn't want to put his family through it. They'd been through enough already. Flashes of the kidnapping swamped him, made him sweat. With the exception of his older sister, the whole family had been held for ransom and beaten severely. The scumbag behind the abduction had used them as leverage so that Jess would get what he wanted from her boss. To prove his ruthlessness, one of his goons had cut off part of Brendan's ear and sent it to Jess.

Brendan shook off the memory and exhaled hard. So maybe he should put the ear on and save himself the aggravation with Casey.

Or maybe he should let her see who he really was. Wasn't that the real test anyway these days? "Screw it." Brendan tossed the prosthetic back into his bag. He'd save it for next week when he really needed it.

Brendan thought the night called for something special so he took Casey to a classy seafood place down the main strip. A giant aquarium in the center of the front entrance housed all kinds of fish of colorful shapes and sizes. They had drinks at the massive oak bar while they waited for a table. If he wasn't looking right at her, he watched her in the mirror behind—and between—all the liquor bottles. Muted lighting set the stage for great possibilities. They ordered their own dinners, but tried a bite of each other's. They talked about his brothers and compared notes on big sisters. She asked a lot of questions about his parents, but didn't share too much about her own.

A band played and a small hardwood floor provided a place for people to dance. Brendan was ready for any excuse to touch her, so when Casey finished the last bite of her shrimp, he stood and held out his hand.

"Dance with me?"

Her eyes widened and sparkled. "Really?" She didn't hesitate more than that before taking his hand and rising to her feet. "I can't even remember the last time I danced."

It wasn't the first time she'd mentioned something that gave him insight to her past. "Don't tell me the ex didn't take you dancing? What did you see in this guy?" Maybe he shouldn't have asked, because he'd meant to keep things light.

She shrugged a glossy shoulder. "He didn't start off bad. He was just never into dancing. Not his *deal*."

Apparently treating her right wasn't his *deal* either. "Okay, I'm only going to say one more thing, then I'll shut up. Any guy who doesn't take the opportunity to hold his girl in his arms and sway to the beat of good music is very whacked." He would've used stronger language, but figured that might piss her off, so he kept it clean. Once on the dance floor, Brendan pulled her close. "Did I tell you I was almost picked as one of the professionals on *Dancing With The Stars?*"

Her eyes rounded and her jaw dropped open. "No way! Really?"

Brendan shook his head. "Nah. I'm kidding."

She laughed and smacked his chest playfully before he set one hand on her waist and the other in her hand in a classic dance pose and led her around the dance floor. "I hardly watch reality TV, including the dance shows. Don't have time," she said, following his moves.

"I don't have the inclination," Brendan agreed. "Most of that shit makes me sick. I don't like watching people humiliate themselves on national television."

Her smile faded. "Not everyone gets humiliated. Depends on the show. I think some shows really open doors for people. Look at Kelly Clarkson and Carrie Underwood."

He nodded, loving the warmth of her palm on his shoulder. "Very true. It's not that I'm against it, I guess I'm just not one to watch the drama."

"So if an opportunity came along for you to make your dream come true, you wouldn't go for it."

He couldn't lie since he was doing exactly that. He shook his head. "No, I would definitely go for it. I just don't understand the bug-eating, make-yourself-miserable shows that exist. The dance shows and singing shows are entertaining in a way that Kardashians are not."

She smiled at that. "I have to agree."

The band struck up a slow song and Brendan set Casey's hands around his neck. He wrapped his arms around her waist and pulled her even closer. She aligned perfectly with his height and looking into her gorgeous eyes and wicked smile made his pulse race faster. Her fingers toyed with the ends of his hair and the tingle traveled straight down his spine and to his groin.

"You're a great dancer," she murmured, her face close to his.

He wanted to dive in for a kiss, but liked the anticipation of waiting. "You can thank my mom," he told her, brushing a long chunk of hair over her shoulder. "None of my big brothers would let her practice with them, so I got stuck with it."

Her smile sent another bolt of heat and lust below his belt. He'd have to consider calling it a night soon or risk walking back to the hotel with a massive hard-on.

"Aw. That's kind of sweet," she said. "I'm sure your mom really appreciated it."

"Well, I *am* the favorite." He said it like it was a no-brainer and loved the laughter that washed over him.

After another dance, Brendan paid the bill and they strolled back toward the hotel with the stars twinkling overhead. He linked their fingers, and her sidelong glance and soft smile promised heaven was just around the corner. Warm sultry air seemed to intensify the heat bubbling between them.

"Feel like dessert?" he asked as they walked by an ice cream shop.

"I'm so full. I couldn't eat another thing, but if you want something we can stop." She slowed and tugged him back toward the shop's entrance.

Brendan took the opportunity to back her up against the glass wall, their hands locked together at their sides, his body pressed against hers. "I definitely want something." Her chest rose with deep breaths and she licked her lips and it was all Brendan could do to keep from throwing her over his shoulder and hauling her back to the hotel. This whole day had been about seduction and he didn't want to blow it now. He wanted this to be a night neither one of them would ever forget.

"What would that be?" Her whispered words barely registered in his sex-starved brain. He couldn't even remember the last time he'd had sex. He'd been so busy on this last leg of Seger's tour that he'd hardly had time to think about sex. While a lot of the crewmembers still let rock groupies lead them around by their dicks, he'd lost interest in those girls a long time ago. And, yes, even though Casey knew about his boss and his job, she wasn't anything like the fan girls Brendan was used to. Casey cocked her head, waiting for his answer.

"I think you know what I want."

"Then maybe we should head back to the hotel and compare notes."

"Yeah." He nodded slowly. "I think maybe I just want to give you one thing to think about before we go." He saw the question in her eyes, but he didn't give her a chance to say anything. He just moved in slowly and let his lips glide over hers. The bustle of the crowd behind him faded away and he concentrated on the softness of her mouth, the lush, smooth caress of her lips against his. She tilted her head a fraction and molded their lips closer together.

Heat spread through Brendan's veins like wildfire and he pulled away before his hard-on got too massive. He really didn't want to walk the rest of the way back with a giant boner.

"We can skip the ice cream. I've found something much sweeter I'd rather eat."

Casey licked her lips and Brendan nearly lost his resolve and dove back for another luscious kiss, but he stepped back instead and they continued toward the hotel...at a much faster pace. Brendan couldn't get there quickly enough.

The night crowd packed the streets and weaving between people slowed their progress. The smile she shot him as they waited for the walk signal at the street corner had him grinning like a dope. He glanced at the timer ticking down the seconds until they crossed. Fifteen and counting. Down the street, a tour bus zoomed closer and Brendan stepped back a bit to avoid the draft. Casey slipped her arm under his and locked them together. Just as he looked over at her, he caught the surge behind him in his peripheral vision. The wall of people behind him stumbled forward and smacked into his back. The force sent him forward over the curb.

Right in the way of the oncoming bus.

Road kill.

The second the thought flashed in his head, Casey's grip tightened on his arm and he was hauled around, his momentum

25

catapulting him toward the sidewalk. Weight rolled over his back as he landed halfway on the sidewalk and half in the street. The bus plowed by, missing his foot by inches, the driver laying on the horn as he passed.

Brendan ended up on all fours, breathing hard, his palms and knees stinging from impact. What the hell had just happened? "Shit," he breathed. "Casey!" He glanced over to find her sprawled next to him on the cement, breathing as hard as him, her eyes wide open and shocked. The guys who'd plowed into him were the first to offer a helping hand and sincere apologies.

The biggest of the men—and probably the one to send Brendan flying—wore a Hawaiian shirt full of orange and red palm trees with a pair of khaki pants. Somewhere in his fifties, the man looked like the ultimate first timer, his face beet red as if he'd had way too much sun during his visit. "I am so sorry, man," he said, looking over his shoulder. "Someone slammed into me and I went right into you. You okay?"

Brendan helped Casey to her feet as he got up himself. He was glad he'd worn jeans tonight if only to protect his knees. "Yeah," he said. "I'm okay. Casey, you all right?"

"Yeah." She rubbed her right palm and Brendan took a look at it. It was as red as his, but not bleeding.

"Maybe we should get some ice at the hotel," he said.

"I'm so sorry," the guy said again.

"Not your fault," Casey said, giving him a smile.

Brendan looked behind the group of people standing around, but no one looked suspicious. Not that he knew what he was looking for or even why.

"You sure you're okay?" he asked her.

She nodded, reassured him with a soft smile. "Yeah. Wow. That was scary."

"Yeah," he agreed. "Little bit." He looked around again, shaking off the feeling of being watched by more eyes than just the people in the vicinity. In all the fuss, they'd missed the crossing so they had to wait for another cycle. "You know you totally just saved my ass, right? If you hadn't swung me around, I'd be splattered on the hood of that bus." He gestured down the street where the bus's tailpipe blew out exhaust.

Her grin widened. "Hey, look at that. Technically this makes us even. I guess now we can thank each other equally tonight."

A second ago, he'd been freaked out at the close call and now she had him smiling. Not too many people had that ability. The light changed and Brendan checked the street before crossing. He was done dancing around this subject and the hotel was right in front of them. There was no pain in his knees or palms that would keep him from Casey tonight. "Your place or mine?" he asked.

"Yours," she said without missing a beat.

Good thing he cleaned up the room earlier. His pulse raced faster as they walked up the pathway. Rope lighting wrapped the surrounding trees and illuminated the historic hotel.

His dick didn't care that they were still in public and the closer they walked to his room, the harder he got. Brendan punched the button for the elevator and they stared at each other as it ticked down. There was nothing he wanted more than to get this woman to his room, strip her of her clothes and touch every inch of her with his hands and tongue.

The door dinged open and Brendan led Casey inside. He waited until the car started moving before he pinned her against the sidewall.

"Do you have any idea how much I want you?" He hoped he didn't sound like a crazed stalker, but the hours of talking and innocent touching had his brain at the end of sanity.

"I'm not sure," she replied. Her skin pebbled under his touch as he stroked her bare shoulder. "But I think it might be almost as much as I want you."

No words had ever sounded better and Brendan quit stalling. This time when he tipped her chin up, he planted a kiss on her lips that she wouldn't forget. It didn't take much coaxing for her to open to him and he slid his tongue inside the warm cavern of her mouth and tasted her for the first time. She tasted like the peppermints their server had brought with the check. She tasted hot, delicious and just like a woman should.

Brendan roamed his hands down Casey's sides and discovered all those sweet dips and curves for the second time.

She moaned into his mouth, grabbed his shoulders and pushed

him against the wall next to them. The kiss hit another level as she straddled his thigh and circled her tongue around his.

Coherent thought scrambled into the abyss as Brendan let her have him. God it was sexy when a woman took control.

All too soon the elevator bell rang and Casey pulled back. She dragged him from the car, but stopped short. "Which way?" Her eyes nearly glowed with heat and lust. Brendan tugged her left and all the way down the hall to his ocean facing room, searching his pockets for his card key to expedite the process. The card slid in on the first try. Pure luck at this point because his brain was about to explode with the possibilities.

He got it open, tugged her in behind him and pinned her against the door before it had a chance to close.

She welcomed his onslaught with her own. Her busy hands ran across his shoulders, down his arms, around his waist and held him tight. Not a chance in hell she didn't feel how badly he wanted her. He snugged up tight against her lower stomach, loving the way she pressed against him. With every new spot she touched, his blood surged hotter, faster.

Bed.

He needed the damn bed because he wanted her on her back. Wanted to take her dress off one inch at a time and explore every new piece of skin.

"I want to see if I missed any spots with that sunscreen today." He trailed his lips along her jaw as he pulled her with him to the bed.

"I have tan lines to prove you were very thorough in your application." Her voice sounded husky. Needy.

The beast inside him roared.

"Not that I don't believe you," Brendan whispered before brushing his lips across hers. God damn, her lips were as amazing as they looked. Soft, full, warm and welcoming. "But I'm going to have to take a look for myself." The desk lamp he'd left on gave him just enough light to appreciate all her smooth skin.

She nodded, chasing his mouth for another kiss before murmuring, "Of course. I completely understand."

Everything in him rejoiced with her reply. "How about I start at the top and work my way down?" As he spoke, he slowly removed the flimsy shoulder strap holding up her Hawaiian print dress. The rolling ocean waves had seemed almost alive with every move she made. The slinky fabric had been teasing him all night as it draped and shifted over Casey's curves. It slid beneath his fingers like silk. His lips followed the path of that little scrap of material as it eased down her arm. "So soft," he whispered against her skin. And he wasn't talking about the material. God, she smelled like a goddess. Like something heavenly and innocent.

Next came the other strap and he guided Casey's arms up so he could take his exploration farther. He eased around her back and pushed her long hair aside to trail his lips along her neck. She dropped her head forward and a low purr rumbled from her throat.

"I love that sound." He spoke as he trailed his lips down the open expanse of her back, stroking his fingertips in little circles along her shoulder blades. Goose bumps rose beneath his touch and he grinned.

"You're smiling," she murmured.

"How can you tell?"

"I can feel your lips on my back. You're smiling."

Brendan straightened and moved in front of her, the bed at their side. Casey lifted her thick lashed lids and met his gaze. Like this morning, Brendan felt as if he was being pulled under by the riptide. She was taking him down with just that sexy look. Her aqua eyes sparkled even in the dimness of the room.

He cupped her face, brushed his thumb along her cheekbone then leaned in and kissed her. Casey didn't hold back. She wrapped her arms around his neck, opened her mouth to his questing tongue and nearly sucked the life out of his lungs. She was fire in his arms, alive and warm and totally on board with this whole seduction.

Considering he'd waited all day for this, Brendan had to admit his patience was about gone. He tucked his thumbs into the tight elastic top of her dress and eased it down over her breasts. God, she was beautiful. Pert breasts with dusky pink nipples standing at attention just begging for him to touch, to taste. Brendan kissed her again, just to let her know he was as interested in her mouth as the rest of her, because shit, she had the finest mouth, he'd been dreaming about it all day…dreaming about a lot of things all day.

Brendan cupped her breasts and finally left her lips. He bent and licked one of those sweet peaks into his mouth. She threaded her hands into his hair and moaned as he sucked her. Blood rushed south with the speed of a flash flood. Brendan couldn't remember the last time he ached for someone this badly. The need to claim her, to sink inside her nearly burned him alive.

He got to his knees as he continued to pull her dress down over her hips. He tasted every new inch of silky skin during his descent.

Just to torture them both a little more, he kept her underwear in place as the dress pooled at her feet in a soft hiss of material. His mouth hovered at the bikini line she'd been so concerned about this morning. Brendan ran his hands along her hips, down her mile long thighs and back up again. Standing topless over him, she was like an Amazon goddess.

"Turn around," he said softly. "I need to check my work."

Her heavy lidded eyes flashed with heat and her chest rose and fell with heavy breaths. "If you must." Casey turned and Brendan got a face full of super-fine ass since she had ditched her white bikini bottoms for a crazy-sexy black lace thong. Glory hallelujah.

"Jesus," he whispered. "You absolutely have the finest ass I have ever seen." She looked over her shoulder at him, her smile as sexy as the curve of her ass. "And," he continued, stroking a gentle finger along the tan she told him about. "I see my attention to detail paid off. No burns for you." Brendan couldn't stop himself. He'd never really considered himself an ass-kisser. Not in any way, shape or form, but this ass was priceless. Easing the thong down, he followed the path with his lips and tongue, stroking the smooth globes with his hands and his mouth.

He was pretty sure he didn't have a drop of blood left in the head above his shoulders because it all resided in the one below his waist.

Maybe Casey had similar issues because she turned, giving him a flash of her clean-shaven self before getting on her knees on the bed. She motioned him forward.

Brendan didn't have to think twice about that invitation. But before he got on the bed, Casey set her hands on his jeans and went to work with the button and zipper.

Pop. Hiss.

Done.

With her gorgeous eyes on his she pushed her thumbs into his waistband and took everything down. No slow going for this lady. She knew what she wanted.

Brendan thanked the Good Lord it was him.

CHAPTER 5

CASEY GLANCED UP AT Brendan after she got his jeans and boxer briefs down. She'd only ever been with Jeff and had no one else to compare him to. Until now. *This* was what she'd been missing? Had that been part of Jeff's issue? Small penis syndrome? Talk about going from one extreme to the other...

"Wow. That..." She struggled for words. "That's...truly impressive. I think I won the jackpot."

Brendan flashed her a sexy grin and joined her on the bed. Okay, he didn't so much join her as take her down, laying her on her back as his mouth made love to hers. God his kiss was spectacular. Not too dry, not too wet...the perfect amount of tongue action. His hands stroked over her flesh, making her want him that much more. So much delicious skin to touch, and every smooth inch of it pressed along every inch of her.

"I'm not too sure about that," he mumbled as he traced kisses along her jaw. "I was the one that hit the jackpot. I didn't realize that plucking you out of the water was going to lead me—lead us—to this."

"I didn't either." Except that might've been a lie. She'd certainly hoped for this, but Brendan surpassed anything her imagination could've conjured up. Jeff didn't come close in comparison. If she'd only known. But she hadn't, because Jeff had been her first and only. He'd systematically removed her from most of her friends and tried to make himself her whole universe. Why hadn't she seen it while it was happening? Why had she bought into his negative comments and given in to almost his every whim? To be loved? To be accepted? Well, bullshit to that.

Obviously the universe had a lot more to offer than Jeff. Duh.

"Hey." Brendan's sexy whisper brought her gaze to his and she stared into his mesmerizing blue eyes. "Where are you?" He eased some hair off her cheek and she tingled at the sweet gesture.

"Sorry. Right here. Where I want to be." She stroked her fingers along the smoothness of his square jaw and realized he must have shaved right before their dinner. He smelled so good—like spicy, sexy man—she wanted to inhale him, to keep his scent in her head for the rest of time.

When she moved her fingers toward his hairline to cup his head and bring him closer, he reared back. "What? What's wrong?"

"Nothing." He took her wrist and eased it back on the pillow next to her head, trapping her against cool sheets before giving her what she wanted. His mouth. Then he went one better and covered her with the strength of his hard body. She opened her legs to accommodate his hips and loved the weight of him pressing her down. "You have one seriously sexy mouth," he said before diving in with another kiss.

Jeff had always said her mouth was too plastic looking. That he loved her in spite of it. She'd purposely toned down any lipstick because she knew Jeff didn't like when she played up her lips.

Hearing Brendan say those words sent a rare jolt of confidence to her budding self.

Casey vowed that she'd never let a man tell her who she was or what to do for the rest of her life. Starting now, she was going to be in charge of her destiny. In charge of her happiness. She'd let two good years blind her to a man who wanted her under his thumb. She'd come up with one excuse after another to justify his nasty behavior, but no more. No more temper tantrums, no one breaking her things. No man in her face, making her feel small.

With a new sense of freedom—and maybe even pride—Casey surged up and took Brendan to his back. He probably could've stopped her if he wanted, but he went with the flow. A little groan vibrated from his chest as she rubbed against his giant erection, causing a sharp intake of air for herself when she connected with her clit.

"That's it," he coaxed. "Right there." He held her hips as he moved beneath her, a series of strokes that rubbed her clit harder and slicked them both up with her arousal.

"Oh, God," she breathed. He wasn't even inside her and the friction was unbearable. "You need a condom." Preferably before she went crazy and impaled herself on him without one. Though she'd been on the pill for years now, the dangers of unprotected sex still mattered. Brendan might be nice and gorgeous, but she didn't know his bedroom habits and refused to take any chances.

"Yeah. Box. Bedside table." He pointed with his left hand and she crawled toward the drawer. Brendan's lips didn't stay idle and he sucked the nipple that had presented itself while she scrounged one-handed for the condoms. She moaned and stilled, letting him have her while each fresh lick and suck pulled at an invisible string from her clit. She'd never burned like this before. Never needed relief—release—to this driving extent.

There! She found it. She pulled a strip from the box and used her teeth to rip the top one open, but she hesitated once she had it in her hand. Though Brendan knew her recent single status, she didn't want him to think that she had blinders on. And dammit, maybe now was the perfect time to assert her new confidence, even if she snuck into it backward.

"Just so you know, I'm healthy. I had a physical a couple of months ago, so…all clean." Okay. *Awkward.*

Brendan gave her a soft smile. "It's all right. I'm clean too. To be honest, it's been a while since I've done this."

That struck Casey as total bullshit and she narrowed her eyes. "Why? I mean, you're single, cute, fun. You work for a rock star. I'd think you'd have your pick of women and then some."

"Yeah, I discovered that whole rock-n-roll scene really wasn't *my* scene. I'm not much for having a different girl in every port. It's a little too sleazy for me."

A man with scruples too. He was too good to be true.

"What about having a girl in this port?" she asked mainly because she wanted to bring the fun back.

In response, Brendan rolled them and put her beneath him where she enjoyed all that heavenly masculine pressure pressing her into the bed. "I think I'll always remember this port. And this night." He kissed her, his lips gliding over hers, his tongue sneaking out to lick a path across her bottom lip. "And this girl."

Casey moaned as she opened her mouth to him. She stabbed her hands on either side of his head to hold his hair back as they kissed. Her fingers brushed over his ear and…

Whoa! What…?

Brendan yanked back, breathing hard.

"Hey, what? What's wrong?" Now it was her turn to ask. Except she thought she knew. Something was wrong with his ear. She hadn't even noticed until just now when she felt it. "Brendan?" He sat back on his heels in the middle of the bed. Moonlight illuminated his wide eyes. "Bren. It's okay." She mirrored his pose so that they sat across from each other, both breathing hard, both slick and a strip of condoms lying between them.

For a guy who seemed so full of confidence until now, he looked totally unsure.

"You want to talk about it?" she asked.

"Not if I don't have to," he said, his gaze never leaving hers, his voice resolute.

"Okay." She had secrets, too, so she couldn't hold it against him. "That's okay. Did I hurt you? Is that the—"

"No." He didn't shout the word, but the finality was there.

As was her curiosity. "Can I see it?"

For a second she thought he might say no. For a fleeting moment she thought he might call an end to this whole night and that would crush her. To her surprise, he pulled his hair over his ear and gave her a better view. The bottom two-thirds of his ear looked as if it had been sheared right off.

"That looks like it hurt." She didn't give him pity because he wouldn't want that. She checked the other ear and noticed multiple stud piercings. "On the bright side, you're saving money on piercings."

CASEY'S REACTION WASN'T WHAT Brendan anticipated. He didn't see revulsion, or pity. Just curiosity. Then a joke. One that actually made him smile and that was the last thing he'd expected.

"My sister said the same thing," he admitted, letting a smile creep on his face. She grinned back at him and something shifted inside him. He hadn't planned for tonight, hadn't planned to like this girl as much as he did. She was real. It was the only way to describe her. Well, along with beautiful and fun.

She watched him, didn't seem fixated on his ear the way some people did when they noticed. He felt a little obligated to give her something for that alone. "It did hurt. A lot. Bled a lot too." He'd never forget the warm stickiness of his blood dripping down his neck to pool on his shoulder then trail down his shirt. The relentless throbbing that drummed in his head for hours after the scumball had sliced his ear.

She waited for more, but he didn't know where to start or how to tell her. No one wanted to be a victim. No one wanted to admit to being helpless and unable to defend themselves. "I think it just adds to your mystery." She scooted closer, wrapped herself around him as he sat on his calves.

The turn of events had taken the steam out of his hard-on. Literally. But now with Casey rubbing up against him, her breasts teasing his chest, the blood was beginning to flow south again.

"I don't mind mystery." She kissed him softly, stroked her hands up his chest, down his arms and around to his back, staying clear of his ear. The fact that she gave him that space made his heart open up a little more.

Most women didn't get it. Or him. They didn't understand how private he was when it came to the topic. Not everything was a subject for discussion.

The kiss only took a second to turn molten hot. With her tongue in his mouth, Brendan moved forward and laid her down again, intent on showing her how much he appreciated that she didn't press him about the topic.

Oh yeah…he definitely planned to show her.

Once he had her beneath him, he wasted no time in moving south, dragging his lips and tongue down the silky softness of her chest. She didn't have big breasts, but God, she didn't need them. Besides, he was more than happy with every curve. He continued down to her abs and stomach. She was long and willowy and fulfilling every fantasy he had about doing it with an Amazon.

Finally, nestled in the juncture of her thighs, he seized what he wanted. His dick got harder when he tasted her and harder still when she moaned his name, and damn that was sexy as hell.

"Oh, God, yes. Brendan. Bren—oh God. Right there. Don't stop."
She slowly came apart beneath his tongue and fingers, and
Brendan had never felt a bigger desire to please, to give. His dick
throbbed with the need for release, but he ignored it, focusing on
every breath Casey took and every sound she made. He brought
her right to the edge and backed off, ensuring that when she
finally went over, she'd fall so hard and so long she wouldn't ever
forget this night.

Her legs tightened around his head and Brendan thought he'd
finally discovered heaven. At least heaven on earth. It wasn't as if
he'd never gone down on a woman before. So what made Casey
special? So far…everything.

After bringing her up and letting her down three times he dove
in for the finale. He'd be surprised if he had any hair left by the
time she climaxed, but he didn't care. She chased this last one,
almost as if she wouldn't give him the chance to leave her hanging
again. The idea made him smile even as he lashed his tongue
repeatedly over her clit while he pumped inside her with two
fingers.

She tensed beneath him and a keening cry wailed from her lips.
She bucked against his mouth as her internal muscles clenched
around his fingers. He lapped at her sweet honey and a sense of
fulfillment made his chest tight.

Finally, when she went limp, he kissed the inside of one thigh
and rested his head on the other. Jesus. That was—

"Oh my, God," she finally murmured, still breathing hard.
"That was…that was…"

"Amazing?" he finished for her.

"No. I mean, God, yes, but it was better than amazing." He
lifted his head to find her watching him. She beckoned with her
index finger then patted the spot next to her. "You. Here. Now."

Damn that was sexy. "If you're sure." He crawled over her,
taking a detour for her mouth. She didn't seem to mind as she
wrapped her arms around his shoulders and took his kiss like she'd
been starved for days. But she rolled him where she wanted him—
on his back—before coming up for air.

"You realize I have to reciprocate, right?"

"You don't *have* to," he said. Because honestly, he'd be happy to just saddle up with a condom and go for gold. In his current state, he'd go off like a canon with one push inside.

"Oh, trust me," she said, and her smile made his dick twitch. "I am so going to reciprocate." She cocked her head a fraction. "In fact, unless I'm mistaken, it seems like you might be okay with that idea."

Yeah, she was talking about the major twitching down below every time she rubbed against him. "Oh shit," he hissed, because she wrapped her hand tightly around his deprived dick.

"Hm. Not really the response I was hoping for." She set her lips on his chest and worked her way down. "Maybe you don't want my mouth on you. It's hard to tell."

Words escaped him. He might've mumbled something or not, he wasn't sure, because her hand kept pumping as her tongue licked and her teeth nibbled a path straight to his dick. She smoothed the drop of pre-come around the engorged tip and he groaned.

"Hm," she said, her lips against his very sensitive and slick flesh. He felt the vibration all the way to his balls and he nearly lost it. "This looks very delicious."

"Case, I'm not going to last," he ground out. He lifted his hips to prove his point. He needed to pump, needed to move.

"Yes, you will," she replied. Then she took him into her mouth. The snug, wet heat drove him to the brink.

"Jesus, Casey." He couldn't breathe. Couldn't think. Could only feel the need to come. The urge to give her everything.

"Feed it to me," she said before going down again.

Mindlessly he lifted into her mouth while she continued to stroke the base of his dick. He wasn't sure what drove him over the edge...her dirty talk or her tight grip on him, but his climax loomed seconds away. Sweat coated his skin as he barely held onto control.

"Casey. Gonna come." It was all he could say as he gripped the sheets in a white-knuckle hold.

"Mm." She hummed on him and that was it. He hit the peak. It was like every nerve in his body exploded to life in a rush of euphoria. She pulled off just as he came. She hadn't needed to keep him on any edge, because he'd done that all by himself by making her wait for *her* orgasm. Maybe she realized that.

After the last shudder, Brendan was totally wasted. He cracked one eye open as Casey cleaned her hand on tangled sheets before crawling over his chest and snuggling into the crook of his arm. He wasn't sure if she did it on purpose, but she picked his good side and that only made him more content to hold her close.

He had no clue what to say. He hadn't even been inside her, but he'd had one of the most explosive orgasms of his life. "Five minutes," he said.

She adjusted her head to see him. "What's in five minutes?" Her lips were slightly swollen and it made his dick twitch with fresh anticipation.

"I'm going to put one of those condoms on and make you come so hard you're going to see stars."

She wrapped her lean thigh over his as she trailed her hand down his stomach. "Five minutes, huh. Let's see if I can't make it four."

CHAPTER 6

CASEY NEVER EXPECTED ANYTHING—or anyone—like Brendan St. John. She didn't know men like him existed. It only proved how sheltered she'd been. How much she'd allowed herself to be kept down. The realization angered her more than she liked. Maybe that was the reason she wanted so much tonight. She wanted to experience everything he had to offer.

He grabbed her wrist before she wrapped her hand around his semi-hard erection. "Not so fast." He rolled her to her back and covered half her body with his. She loved the smile on his face, the mischief in his eyes. "You're going to kill me tonight, aren't you?"

Her heart swelled at the idea that she might wring him dry. With Jeff, it was over once he came. He gave her hers, she gave him his and boom, lights out. She'd never been given the opportunity to go all night.

Casey considered his question and finally shook her head. "I solemnly swear not to kill you. That would suck for me."

He laughed. "Suck for you?" His brows quirked in a cute slant. "What about me? I'm the dead one."

"Well, yeah, but look how good it was at the end."

He laughed again before his smile dimmed and he stroked his thumb across her cheek. "I couldn't think of a better way to go."

Oh, the man knew how to sweet talk. "Now you're just sucking up."

"Is it working?" He didn't bat an eye or crack a smile.

She laughed and her heart soared. It was crazy to be this happy with a virtual stranger. God, she'd known this man for sixteen hours. What was she doing?

"Hey? There's that look again. What are you thinking?" His fingers stroked across her temple in a sweet caress and made her feel special, appreciated.

"I don't know. This is nuts. I've never been this crazy or spontaneous. Never this..." She had a hard time coming up with the word. "Independent." That was it. She'd completely lost her independence with Jeff. This night was a major turning point in her life and she owed it all to Brendan. "Thank you."

His eyes narrowed. "What'd I do?"

"You gave me something I haven't had a very long time."

"A mind-blowing orgasm?"

She smiled. Should've seen that answer coming. "Okay, you gave me two things I haven't had in a long time." His smile was as good as a lotto win. "You gave me freedom."

He sobered as he watched her, his gaze soulful and intense. "I think I want to give you *freedom* all night long."

She loved his sense of humor. With the exception of his ear and the mystery behind it, he seemed so lighthearted and honest. As much as she wanted to know what happened, she didn't want to ruin the night by killing the mood. "You're a funny man."

He shrugged a broad shoulder. "Seriously." His smile faded. "I know we just met and things are happening fast, but I want to see you when we get back to L.A."

Whoa. Not what she had in mind. She had no plans to date anyone for a long time. She wanted to find herself first. This day, this night with Brendan was about finding her independence. It was about being spontaneous and enjoying a part of life she hadn't in the last couple of years with Jeff.

Besides, any type of relationship with Brendan was bound to end badly. He was the rebound guy, the guy to have fun with, the man to screw so she could wash Jeff from her mind.

The longer she waited, the more his face darkened. "Sure. Why not." She hated lying, but it wasn't as if she'd ever see him again. Hopefully he wouldn't ask for her number tonight. Los Angeles was enormous and they lived in different parts of town. They'd never seen each other before this trip and they wouldn't afterward.

Brendan let out a huff of air. "You scared me," he said. "I

thought you were going to come up with some bullshit excuse why we shouldn't see each other back home."

"And miss out on more of this?" She grabbed his ass and squeezed. He did have a spectacular ass. Tight, round, very fine. She could see herself falling for a guy like Brendan and she wouldn't put herself in that position. Tonight was a confidence builder and nothing more.

From now on she planned to follow her gut. No more bending to anyone's needs but her own.

Even pulling off Brendan at the last second of his blow job had been for her benefit. Though she was never a huge fan of going down on a guy, she knew how important blow jobs were to men. Jeff had drilled that into her.

She'd despised the way Jeff held her down when he climaxed, forcing her to take his come down her throat. It should be her choice to participate in something that intimate. She shivered, remembering, and Brendan cupped the side of her head.

"You okay?" he asked.

"Yeah." Why couldn't she get Jeff out of her head? He was killing her. "How about we take a few minutes to just lie here? That okay with you?"

His eyes narrowed and his concern was right there, right on the surface. "Sure. Of course." He moved to his side and pulled her against him, her back to his front. He felt so solid holding her tightly to him as she used his bicep for a pillow. He stroked his palm soothingly down her side from her waist to her hip, down to her thigh and back up again, mesmerizing her with his gentle touch, just as he'd done today at the pool when he'd smoothed on sunscreen.

Her chest tightened and her eyes stung. It was crazy to be feeling this kind of emotion after one session of oral sex with a relative stranger. She'd just never had this kind of intimacy. Casey snuggled up even closer against Brendan's front.

She felt his semi-hard erection grow against her ass, felt his need for her in the way he purposely stroked along her stomach and eased his hand over her breast to play with her nipple. He may as well have flipped a switch. In just that span of seconds, she wanted him again. Wanted to feel him inside her even though she'd already come harder than she'd ever had.

She tried to turn, but Brendan kept her pinned against him.

"Stay," he whispered. It wasn't a command like she was used to, but a plea. "I like you this way." He nibbled her ear and fresh electric streaks tore straight to her center. She pushed against his penis, loving the way Brendan aligned himself between her butt cheeks and thrust. "Do you know you have the sexiest ass on the planet?" His tongue stroked behind her ear in an erogenous zone she didn't know she had and Casey pushed her breast into his hand as she arched her back. "God, Case, you're driving me crazy."

Casey swallowed back the lump in her throat and fought the tightness in her chest. Everything he said built her up. It was as foreign as her missing confidence. "We can't both have the sexiest ass," she said to keep the conversation light.

"I agree. So you win. Gimme half a sec." Brendan sat up, hunting for something, then came back to her, tucking up again to push his very full erection between the tight crease of her ass. No more semi anything, the man was one hundred percent ready to go. He pulled her hair back and set his lips on her neck and beneath her ear, sending hot sparks shooting to all points south.

At the same time he started pumping against her, his hand trailed down to cup her mound. He pushed so hard from the back that it rubbed her against his strong hand and very wicked fingers.

"Gimme one more sec," he whispered in her ear.

She heard the rip of plastic, felt him shift behind her and then once again he returned.

"Lift your leg, Case." He lifted her thigh over his as he tucked up beneath her. "That's it. Just like that." The large head of his penis just barely kissed her opening. It was torture to feel him there, agony waiting to be filled. He cupped her with his hand, stroked a finger over her clit and made her gasp. She was already so wet and he slicked that moisture around and around her clit until she wanted to scream.

"Please, Brendan. God, please." She wanted it. Needed it. Needed to feel full and wanted.

"Shh," he soothed. He pumped two thick fingers inside her and she didn't know whether to press down on them or push against the erection throbbing between her thighs. He moved up a fraction

43

and gave her the tip. God he was big, stretching her, filling her and he'd barely gotten started.

"So tight, Casey. God, you're so tight." He pushed up again and gave her a little more and Casey could barely breathe. "Lift up," he coaxed softly and she lifted her thigh higher over his. "That's it." He pushed up some more and they both groaned. His fingers continued to circle and Casey pressed against them.

"God, more. More, Bren."

"Easy, easy." He pushed in farther and Casey gritted her teeth as she sank down on him more.

"All of it. Bren, give me all of it." His fingers were driving her to the brink of insanity. She needed to come desperately. Sweat slicked her skin as they moved against each other. Brendan's lips were never far from her skin. He licked her neck, bit her ear lobe, nibbled on her shoulder, all while stroking her with his free hand and owning her clit as he teased her with his dick.

One more adjustment and he pushed up again. Casey squeezed his wrist, keeping his hand between her legs as he started to move out of her. She didn't care how he moved as long he kept his fingers circling her clit, driving her to the edge.

His thrusts stayed steady, taking her on a ride in time with his circling fingers. "I love how you feel against me, Case. So strong. Sexy." His lips glided along her shoulder and Casey wanted his mouth.

She turned her head and he was right there, right with her as he held her chin and kissed the living hell out of her at the same time he pushed in and out of her, driving her headlong into another climax.

Everything centered on Brendan. He was all over her, his skin hot, sweaty and smooth, his breath warm on her cheek, his lips never far from hers. Instead of being freaked out, Casey couldn't get close enough. She pushed her ass against him, demanded more and he gave it with harder and harder thrusts.

They were both breathing hard, sweating up the sheets, sliding along each other in a slick, sinful ride. Every nerve stretched tight and Casey chased that orgasm with a vengeance.

"So close, Case. I'm so close."

"Me too. Oh God, me too." She gripped his wrist tighter and

rode both his dick and his fingers. Over and over, each stroke took her higher. The pleasure was unbearable, unspeakable. Every move rocked her closer to release, closer to euphoria.

"C'mon, Case. Come with me." She heard the strain in his voice, the effort it took to hold back. Maybe that's what threw her over the edge. His consideration.

Casey hit the peak and froze. Every muscle tensed as all her cells exploded and blew apart into tiny fragments. Each fresh vibration shook through her limbs with unprecedented satisfaction, a blissful haze so complete, her mind went blank.

Vaguely, she heard Brendan groan and the pulse of his orgasm throbbed inside her as he continued to pump a few more times. His grip on her shoulder was like iron but Casey didn't care. She liked the hold he had on her.

After all, it was only temporary.

THE SOUND OF THE ocean whispered in Brendan's head. Morning light busted through the curtains and he opened slit eyes. He didn't move, he just breathed in Casey's scent on his pillow. Fresh flowers and sunshine mixed with sex. A heady combination. His dick perked up thinking about a morning session deep in Casey's warm, wet heat.

He grinned remembering the night before and all the times they'd turned to each other. All the whispered pleas, the dirty words, the sweat. He'd been bewitched with the smile on her face as she rode him. Mesmerized at the rapture when she closed her eyes and came. It was her desire as much as anything that had caused his orgasm during that round.

Five times was a record for him. He didn't even know how his dick was upright at the moment. The stupid thing didn't know when to take a break. Every muscle ached in a *fucked-all-night* kind of way. He couldn't remember the last time he'd been this sore from a night of sex. Casey must be hurting too.

"Case? Casey?" He turned his head and his smile faded at the empty spot next to him. "Casey?" he called louder. She must be in the bathroom. But even as he had the thought, the room seemed too still, too quiet.

Brendan sat up and wiped a hand over his face and through his hair as he looked around. "Casey?"

Not a peep. Not a sound. Her clothes should've been in a pile on the floor. Maybe she left a note…except he didn't see one on the desk or the night table. Tossing the sheets back, Brendan saw no sign of her at all. He checked the bathroom, disappointment heavy in his chest. Nothing.

Okay, so maybe she went to get them some breakfast. *She could've ordered room service.* The voice in his head pissed him off. *She bugged out, dude. The only person you're going to get lucky with this morning is yourself.* "Fuck that."

Brendan pulled on his running shorts and shoes, fighting the urge to get angry. It was later than he usually ran, but he wasn't going to forgo his normal routine just because of a night of crazy awesome sex.

There had to be a reason Casey bailed without a word. Maybe she left a note for him at the front. Yeah, that made sense. With his confidence back, Brendan stopped at the front desk and asked. The attendant typed a few things into her computer before looking up at him.

"I'm sorry, Mr. St. John. No messages."

Okay. Now he was getting pissed. "Can you tell me which room Casey…" Shit! He didn't even have her last name! Seriously? How the fuck did he not get her last name? He clenched his jaw.

"Casey…?" She waited, but shook her head, reading his dilemma. "Even if I had her full name, I can't tell you, I'm sorry. You could use a house phone, the operator could connect you to her room, but she can't do that without a last name."

Brendan went for a long shot. "Have you been working all morning? Maybe you checked her out. She's really tall, long straight, blondish-brown hair, beautiful blue-green eyes." Jesus, he sounded like a sap.

Her eyebrows lifted. "Oh, yes! I saw her this morning. I didn't check her out, but my colleague did a couple of hours ago. I remember wondering how long it takes to grow hair that long."

Brendan's heart stalled. "Seriously? She checked out?"

She gave him a sad smile. "Sorry about that."

He didn't budge, couldn't believe it. They'd never even

exchanged numbers. He had no idea how to reach her in Los Angeles.

"Is there anything else I can do for you?" The woman's question brought him out of his thoughts.

"No, that's it. Thanks." Anger built in increments as he walked to the beach. Brendan started his run hard. All he could think about was the unparalleled night he'd had with a woman who came into his life from out of nowhere. Then she'd disappeared just as quickly. He had one more day in paradise. How the hell would he manage it without going out of his mind?

He pumped harder as sweat rolled down his face and chest. How could she do that? Hadn't they clicked? She wouldn't have let him do all the things he did to her the night before if she didn't like him. Anger pushed him harder as he hit the halfway mark and turned back for the hotel.

Damn, he'd liked her. Liked her too much.

Why had she bolted?

Because of his ear? He doubted it. If it disgusted her that much she never would've let him lay a hand on her. Okay, so maybe she was scared, but he couldn't guess from what. Last night had been totally consensual. Of that he was certain.

He slowed and finally stopped, his heart beating out of control. "You're the rebound guy, dipshit."

Brendan bent over and sucked wind, trying to get air into his fried lungs. He'd been used and used hard. Okay, so it wasn't as if he didn't get anything out of it, but her disappearance still hurt. Would it have killed her to leave a note? Something like... *Hey Bren, sorry to fuck and run, but you were just the thing I needed to get over my ex, so thanks and have a great life.* At least with that he'd have known where he stood.

He'd track her down that's all. He'd track her down just to tell her what a shitty thing she did. Not a word. Not a one single good-bye. But shit, how did he find her without a fucking last name? How would he tell her what a low-life move she'd made? All she'd had to do was tell him she didn't want to see him again. He'd have been hurt, but he'd rather that than wander around the hotel, looking for her and having to piece together the clues about why she hadn't wanted a relationship.

Relationship? He was losing his mind.

Brendan started running again. He needed to clear his fuzzy head. How did he find her without a last name? He'd call in the big guns. His twin brother, Blake, loved to find people. In fact, he did it for living, working for a private investigator as he earned his hours for his own PI license. They had contacts up the wazoo. They knew how to get information the average guy couldn't.

Brendan felt better with his new plan of action. He slowed his pace as he neared the hotel, his lungs heaving and his heart heavy. Whether he wanted to admit it or not, Casey had hurt him. Less than twenty-four hours with that lady and he already felt the loss like a knife in the chest.

He shouldn't feel this devastated. He had a great night. *Unparalleled* his brain repeated. But he had big plans after next week and it's not like he could ask her to wait for him when he disappeared for six weeks or so. If he was lucky enough to last that long where he was going.

So yeah, the run had cleared his head. He'd still look for her, but he'd wait to do the search after this next adventure he had planned. An adventure he never would've participated in if his brothers hadn't convinced him to do it.

Brendan looked out to the spectacular ocean and all people in the water. The sun glistened like an orange beach ball low in the sky. The winds had died down and it was just another day in paradise.

Would he have ever met Casey if she hadn't been in the water yesterday?

Brendan sucked in air and blew it out hard. He'd find her one way or another.

CHAPTER 7

CASEY ZIPPED UP HER bag on the sofa and looked around her apartment. The coffee table looked barren without the usual mass of magazines and glasses littering the top. Vacuum wheels lined the runner where she'd sucked up any crumbs and dirt on her path from the kitchen to the den. Everything looked neat and in order. Hopefully, if everything played out the way it was supposed to, she would be back in six weeks to pack up her stuff and start a new life. Her sister promised to pick up her mail and cover any bills that needed to be paid during Casey's absence.

God willing she'd be gone the whole damn time. Honestly, if she was home to pay bills then it meant she'd lost the chance of a lifetime.

Of course, she'd already accomplished that when she'd walked out on Brendan last week. God, it still hurt...had been the hardest thing she'd ever done. Harder than splitting up with Jeff, so what did that tell her? In the dim dawn light, Brendan had looked so freaking beautiful next to her, his lips almost turned up into a smile even as he slept. She'd wanted to touch him one last time, run her fingers over his muscled bicep or across his jaw. But she couldn't chance waking him up. She didn't want the good-bye. She only wanted the memories they'd created during the past day and night.

One night vs. four years, and the one night won hands down. Of course, dealing with the guilt wasn't something she'd planned on.

The notes of "Old Time Rock and Roll" filled the silence. Casey found her phone in her purse and checked the screen. Parents. Her intestines knotted as she answered.

"Casey, I'm so glad we caught you," her mother said. "It's not too late to forget about this idea, honey."

"Mom." The warning in her voice should've been enough, but it wasn't.

"Honey, you're better than this reality show. You don't need these people to tell you if you're good enough. You write lovely songs. You can play them for your students and everyone can enjoy them that way."

Casey wanted to scream, but she kept her voice level. "Don't you want me to be successful, Mom? Isn't that why you sent me to college and made sure I had a good education?" Sometimes she wished she'd gone to school somewhere other than San Diego. Maybe then she'd have put down roots farther away from her parents. "Because you want me to succeed?"

"Of course we want that," her father said. He must have been on another extension. "Within reason," he added. "These shows are the death of this country. And what if you lose your job because of this? Will your school even take you back if you don't win?" He had a point because the school's director had told her they could only hold off so long before finding her replacement. The longer she lasted on the show, the more chance she had of losing her regular job.

"Look, Dad, I'll deal with my job, but don't exaggerate the show. Yes, some of them are stupid, I agree, but some can really help people find their dream."

"But it costs your pride, honey," her mother said. Ever the optimist.

"Let me get this straight, Mom. Reaching for my dream embarrasses you?"

"You always do that, Casey. Stop putting words in your mother's mouth."

"Dad, I'm just trying to understand why you're both so against this. I get that you've never been into reality television." Or any television for that matter unless it was reruns of any of the old shows that played on obscure cable channels. Granted her parents were older than most of her friends' parents, but for a couple of sixty-four year olds they acted more like they were in their eighties. "I understand you want me to be happy and you don't think this is the way to go about it. All I'm asking is that you two try and understand where I'm coming from." She heard her mother's muffled sobs. *Oh, for God's sake.*

"Now look what you've done," her dad said.

"Casey," her mother said through tears, "Your father provided a stable roof over your head and gave you everything you needed growing up. Is it so hard to respect his wishes?" Classic Mom. Defer to Dad and please him at all cost. "We may not have had a ton of money, but at least we can hold our heads high because we do the right thing."

Meaning that participating in this show was the *wrong* thing? "Mom, at some point you and Dad are going to have to trust that I can make my way in life without making every decision according to your plan. I'm sorry that you..." She cut herself off before she said something stupid. "I'm sorry that you're unhappy and I'll talk to you when it's over. Bye." She disconnected before they said anything else, closed her eyes and took a deep breath.

Someone knocked on the door and Casey checked her watch. Zoe was right on time. That was a miracle in itself. Her sister never ran on schedule unless it involved work.

Casey swung the door wide and froze at the sight of Jeff filling the frame. First her parents and now *him*? Wearing one of his thousand-dollar gray suits, he looked like his father, the politician. He was only an inch taller than her, but he was wide, with massive shoulders and giant arms. The look on his face was enough to send her heart slamming against her ribs, but she refused to show any emotion.

Of the four years they'd been a couple, she'd been walking on eggshells around him for the past two, his temper growing worse as time went by. Well, she didn't need to worry about that anymore because she didn't care how angry he got. He had no power over her anymore. The relief of that gave her a fresh sense of freedom despite the cloudy look on Jeff's bulldog face.

"How was our honeymoon," he asked without any preamble. He cocked his head to the side in a defiant gesture she'd learned to recognize as his fighting stance. Usually he got that look right before he broke something. His two-toned eyes glared at her.

She was dying to tell him that the honeymoon was great. That she'd fucked more in one night than she had in the last five months with him, but common sense told her to keep that tidbit to herself.

"It was very relaxing, thanks." She didn't back up, didn't invite him in. She watched his jaw clench and knew he was battling back his true feelings.

"Look, Casey…" He ran a hand through his blond hair, seemed as if he struggled to find words. "This whole thing…got out of hand."

Really? Ya think? "You mean the whole ultimatum thing? Or the canceled wedding part?" She was dying to hear what he had to say and at the same time she didn't give a shit.

"Look, I love you."

She almost laughed. She could count on both hands the number of times he'd said those words over the years.

But he continued, "That's not something I can turn off. I still want to marry you. You had your little rebellion. You took a vacation. I get it. We can still get married. We'll just do something small or elope."

Not for all the money in the world. She couldn't wait to test this new proposition. Nodding, she considered his words. "I guess we can talk about it after the show."

His eyes turned infinitesimally harder before he dropped his gaze to the ground and shook his head. "You're not still planning on doing that piece of shit reality show are you?" He met her gaze. "You're going to embarrass yourself and me. I can guarantee you're going to regret putting yourself out there like that."

The only thing she regretted was four wasted years with him. "I guess we'll agree to disagree. So if your ultimatum still stands, then nothing's changed." Was this his idea of crawling back to her? What a joke. Just like their relationship.

His nostrils flared and his cheeks reddened. "I'm only going to say this one time. Do not go on that show." The guy didn't know when to give up.

"Or what, Jeff? You're not going to marry me? Oh, wait. Been there, done that. Why do you care anymore? We're not together. I'm not going to embarrass you."

Every visible muscle tensed. "Of course you're going to embarrass me!" he hissed. "All my family and friends know you and know we were engaged. All the people I work with. They're all going to laugh at me when they see you on this joke of a show." He took a step toward her and Casey eased the door closed a little more before he stopped. "It's not like you have a chance at winning. Be real. I've read your stuff. You're not that good of a songwriter."

Just one of many knives he continually stabbed in her heart. She should be used to his cut downs, but they still hurt. "They can't be that bad if I made the show." She'd had to give them a sample of her work. That was only one part of the interview process. She had no idea how she managed to keep her voice so calm when all she wanted to do was wrap her hands around his thick neck and squeeze.

"I guess everybody gets lucky sometime," he mumbled.

Son. Of. A. Bitch. "I'm going to do you a favor, Jeff."

He glanced up, the hope—or maybe expectation—in his eyes fascinated her. He got that look when he thought he'd won.

"I'm going to make this crystal clear so you won't stress about it in the future. I will *not* change my mind about marrying you and I am *not* changing my mind about the show. You can tell anyone in your life whatever reason you want about why we split. I really don't give a shit. But the one thing *you* are *not* going to do is *tell me* how to live my life. I did that for four years and now I'm done. You almost managed to suck the life right out of me, but I realized it in the nick of time. I guess it's a good thing you gave me an ultimatum. I might have married you otherwise."

Casey tried to close the door, thrilled that for once she got the last word in. Except before it clicked shut, Jeff put his foot in the crack. A second later, he shoved the door open wide with a beefy forearm. The force threw her backward as he stalked inside. Her frustration at being a second too slow morphed into rising panic as she backed up.

"Oh no." He shook his head.

Casey knew that voice, the body language, and it always scared the shit out of her, just as he always wanted it to. "Get out." She needed her phone. Needed to call for help. How could she think that because they weren't together anymore, he wouldn't want to intimidate her? God, where was Zoe? Jeff would never do something with a crowd. He was always Mr. Cool when he had an audience. He saved his tantrums for when he had her alone.

He'd never hit her before, but he'd destroyed property, a lot of property, mostly belonging to her. But he always replaced it with something newer and better. Always apologized and promised to work on his temper.

Yeah, like that ever happened.

But now, the cold, calculating hatred in his eyes scared the backbone right out of her. "I'm not going anywhere until I get what I want," he said, closing the door behind him. "You know I always get what I want, Casey." He locked the deadbolt and a shot of paralyzing fear cut straight through her middle.

Casey spotted her phone on the coffee table next to her purse and suitcase and backed up toward it.

"Where you going, baby?" Jeff taunted as he stalked closer. "Think you're going to call someone?"

"Get out of my apartment." She'd only been here a couple of weeks before the honeymoon trip and it hardly reflected her personality, but it was still her space. Just as she reached for her phone, Jeff sprang at her, knocked her back on the sofa with a hard forearm to her chest. Air rushed out of her lungs as her pulse spiked. Before she scrambled up, he straddled her on the cushion, towering over her like a beast with fangs, pinning her tight. "Get off me," she gritted out. Beating at his chest one-handed, she wasn't nearly strong enough to do any damage.

"I think you miss me, baby," he said softly.

It was the calm that scared her. The vile intent in his eyes as his gaze raked over her pumping chest. He caught her third strike and locked her wrist into his meaty paw of a hand. Her other hand was trapped next her side by his thick thigh.

"Casey, Casey, it's me. Remember me? Remember how much you love making me happy?"

"Past tense, Jeff. We're finished." She saw what he was thinking by the way he settled his groin in front of her face. "Get the hell off me."

"I think you need a reminder of the good times, baby." He unbuttoned his suit coat and exposed the tented fabric of his pants.

"I don't want this, Jeff. Get off me." Casey struggled beneath him, angling to get her trapped hand free. Where the hell was Zoe? She looked toward the door willing her big sister to save her.

"Oh you want it, baby. I know you do." With his free hand, he undid his button and the hiss of the zipper followed. "I've got your breakfast right here, Casey. Open up."

Gritting her teeth, Casey wiggled her hand free at the same time a knock sounded at the door. Jeff's head snapped to the side and Casey grabbed his family jewels and squeezed at the same time she pushed him off her lap. He crashed into the coffee table on his back.

"Casey?" Zoe's worried voice sounded outside and a second later, her sister's key fumbled in the lock. She stormed in just as Casey scrambled away from a raging Jeff. "Hey!" she said, powering forward. Casey loved her big sister's spirit. It didn't matter that Casey had six inches on her sis, because Zoe rocked a giant personality.

Every inch of Casey trembled in a mix of shock and immeasurable relief. With shaking hands, she reached for the phone that Jeff had knocked over when he fell. "I'm calling the cops." She hated her fractured voice.

Somehow, Jeff had got his pants zipped and he stood, looking hardly any worse than when he barged through her door. "Don't bother." He straightened his tie and tipped his head to the side, cracking vertebrae in his neck. "I'm leaving. For now." He pointed a finger at her. "We're not done, Casey. You can count on that." He stalked past a gaping Zoe and she slammed the door on his back, her loose dark curls bouncing with the effort.

"What the hell was that?" she asked, turning slowly back toward Casey. "Oh, honey," Zoe said as she got a good look at her. She must have been a wreck because Zoe reached her in a heartbeat and enfolded her in a sisterly embrace. "What happened?"

"He knocked on the door. I thought it was you and opened it before checking. He forced his way in and..."

"That good for nothing pig." She gave her a big squeeze before pulling back and meeting her gaze. "You should call the cops anyway and report it."

"They're not going to do anything. I don't have a mark on me.

He just scared me." Though he would've done way worse if Zoe hadn't come when she did. "C'mon, let's get out of here." On shaky knees, Casey gathered her suitcase and purse and followed Zoe out the front door, locking it behind her. "I'm sure glad I gave you a key."

"Me too." Zoe stopped, forcing Casey to stop behind her. The afternoon sun hid behind some fluffy clouds and a light breeze drifted through the trees. Not a bad day if Jeff hadn't ruined it.

"What's wrong?"

Pointing to the street, Zoe stood taller. "He's still here."

Casey darted a glance to the black Hummer parked two buildings away. Maybe she should call the cops. But even as she lifted her phone, the engine roared to life and Jeff peeled out. "Don't come back!" Casey yelled to the departing vehicle.

"Seriously," Zoe said, resuming their walk. "Are you okay? What'd he say? What'd he want? What was he doing when I came in?"

Casey hadn't told anyone about the extent of Jeff's personality. Her family knew she was having second thoughts, but she'd never expressed her fear of his dark side. The few times she'd talked about it, no one believed her because he acted like such a nice guy with people around. They thought his need to touch her in public was cute. They saw a man with his hand on her waist or around her shoulder, but didn't realize the ironclad force of his hold. They watched him shower her with gifts, but didn't know it was because he forced her to swallow his come or because he yelled at her for some inane reason like folded laundry.

Unsure how to answer Zoe's questions, Casey was as honest as she could be. "I'll be okay after I stop shaking. He said he wanted to get back together and of course he doesn't want me to do the show. As far as what he was doing when you came in... I think he was about to rape me."

Zoe turned abruptly. "What? Jeff? Rape you?"

"I'm telling you, Zoe. You don't know the guy. I don't think anyone does. I spent four years with him and the last two were nothing like the first two. Look, don't tell Mom and Dad. They're still hoping we'll work things out and they spin everything like it's my fault."

"Why don't you tell them?" Zoe asked, unlocking her car with the key fob. A double chirp sounded. "They don't want you unhappy, you know."

"I know, but they see financial success as happiness. They don't get it. Honestly, how does it make me look to admit that I let a man treat me this way for so long? I just want to put it behind me."

Zoe opened the trunk of her white BMW. "I get it, but I don't like it."

Casey shoved her stuff inside and took a deep breath, keeping an eye on the corner of the road, making sure that Jeff didn't come back for a repeat performance. She didn't think he would. Not with witnesses. Casey hugged her sister. "Thank you for coming when you did. You saved me."

Zoe squeezed her tight. "That's what big sister's do." She patted Casey's back. "C'mon, let's go pick up Vic. Don't want to be late for this thing."

The *thing* that could change her life.

CHAPTER 8

BRENDAN TOSSED HIS RAZOR into the toilet kit and zipped it up just as someone pounded on his door. "I'm coming. Hang on!" He checked his ear before leaving the bathroom—a habit ingrained for several years now—then tossed the kit into his duffle bag and crossed the living room. "You're early," he said to his brothers as he opened the door. He made a last sweep of the apartment to check he didn't forget anything. Nothing obvious glared at him. The place seemed hardly lived in since Blake had gotten serious with his girlfriend. Brendan figured those two would be moving in together any day now, and he'd have to find a new roommate.

Eric sauntered in, head down as he punched something into his phone. "Had to get gas. I expected more of a line." That was Eric. Oldest brother, always making sure everything happened according to plan. He'd come straight from work and wore a dark suit with a blue dress shirt and matching tie.

"Besides, I'd rather be early than late," Danny said, bringing up the rear.

That got a laugh out of Brendan. "Since when? You're the King of Late." He checked out the faded jeans and worn gray T-shirt his brother wore. As usual, Danny did what he wanted and not what was asked. Brendan shouldn't be surprised.

Eric's focus lifted from his phone. "Since we went to a party last week and he was too late to get dibs on Laura."

"Lori. Her name was Lori," Danny cut in. Of course it was. Because Danny did everything according to how it might affect him getting a woman. Not that he ever had problem getting women, but whenever he *couldn't* get a woman, look out. The game was on. Danny loved the chase.

"Laura, Lori. Whatever. Now he's all about getting to places early so he doesn't miss anything." Eric scowled at his phone.

"Wonders never cease," Brendan muttered. He gestured to Danny's clothing. "I see you dressed for the occasion."

The sarcasm wasn't lost on Danny and he looked down at his attire. "What? This is what I always wear."

Brendan rolled his eyes. "I know. That's my point. You could've worn something a little less...used."

"It's not like we're going to be on camera," Danny said.

"At least not yet," Eric added, shifting his gaze from his screen as he pocketed his phone.

"No, I told you guys they changed the opening to include the drop off. That means America gets to meet you too, D-hole. Right now."

Eric's brows slanted in annoyance. "Hey. Respect," he said, punching Brendan's shoulder, but he didn't have much heat behind it... At least not as much as it could have or would have if Brendan had said *E-hole*. Eric took his role as the oldest brother very seriously and basically took any opportunity to lord his bulk over his little brothers as often as possible. Not that any of them were *little* any more, but Eric did have a bit more muscle than the rest of them.

"What?" Danny looked panicked as he turned to his Eric. "You didn't tell me this. When did this happen?"

Brendan held back a groan. "I told you both a couple of weeks ago when Mom had us over for dinner."

Eric squinted as he thought back. "Did you really? I don't remember." Not that it mattered since he wore a suit.

"Because you had your head buried in your phone like you always do." Brendan made a last run through of the apartment. "Okay. I'm good to go. Blake should be back from his trip tomorrow."

"We know," Danny said, but he had his eyes on Brendan's shirt, a faded denim with navy stitching. "Hey, what if I borrow the blue shirt Mom gave you for Christmas. That would work for this drop off."

"Packed it." Brendan grinned at the disappointment on Danny's face.

"Blake's got to have something I can borrow." Danny strode to Blake's room where they all knew he'd find something in the closet. Since he started dating his girlfriend, Abbey, Blake's wardrobe had taken a turn for the better and they all benefitted from it.

Eric glanced at Brendan. "Hey, did you find out who the judges are yet?"

"Not yet." Brendan moved by him to grab a hoodie off the counter. The producers had been hush-hush about all aspects of this show. Brendan was practically going in blind.

"Whoa!" Eric grabbed his arm and pulled him back and Brendan knew from the trajectory of his stare exactly what he was looking at. "Danny, c'mere," he called. "Check it out." His eyes narrowed. "When did you do that?"

Danny came into the room, throwing one of Blake's new shirts over his head, a moss green pullover that Abbey said set off the red highlights in Blake's hair. "What? I'm busy raiding a closet. Dude, I have to ask Abbey to buy my clothes too. Blake's got some nice shit in there." He looked between them both. "What? What's wrong?"

"Check it." Eric pointed to Brendan's ear...his new *prosthetic* left ear.

"Whoa! You got it? When? Why didn't you tell us?" He lifted Brendan's hair and inspected it more closely. "That is one fine piece of work. You can't even tell. Do you like it? Can you feel it?"

Brendan slapped his hand away. "Get off me. I picked it up right before I went to Hawaii. It was ready early."

"Ha, see! I told you that chick liked you. What was her name? Annie, Audrey?"

"Andrea, dickhead. Andrea Rimmer."

Danny nodded. "That's it. She was hot. You get a vibe from her?" Danny waggled his brows and Brendan just rolled his eyes. A picture of Casey suddenly popped in his head and soured his mood in an instant. "No, I didn't get a vibe from her. I was only a job." A job to her and one night stand to Casey. Still pissed him off.

Eric still had his gaze locked onto Brendan's new ear. "Looks good, bro." He gave him a half smile. "Just not sure why you're doing it now. It's been a few years. I didn't think it bothered you anymore."

"It's not that it bothers me as much as it bothers other people. Makes them uncomfortable. I don't want to freak anyone out with the real me. I especially don't want the questions. If I don't wear the prosthetic, someone might connect me to Jess's movie and I don't want to anyone on the show to think I'd use it as leverage for votes."

By the time his sister's movie had been released, she had married her husband and changed her last name. The movie about their ordeal had used fictional names so the St. Johns were still relative unknowns if no one counted the national news of their rescue, but even that got buried pretty quickly because of a big news day with someone trying to get into the White House and a downed plane in the ocean.

Eric nodded his understanding. "Is it uncomfortable? I mean to go from not having one to wearing it all the time... Seems like a stretch."

"It's not a big deal." But Brendan actually had the same worry. What if he rolled over in the middle of the night and it fell off? What if cameras caught it somehow? Screw it. He'd rather risk it than go in knowing what the outcome would be. "Remember, I'm a bartender at Stanley's. Not a word that I work for Seger Hughes. If they find out, I could be disqualified."

"Why?" Eric asked. "He has nothing to do with it, does he?"

"No, but just the fact that he's in the music business...they might think that gives me an upper hand. I don't know, but I don't want to risk it." He picked up his duffel bag and headed to the door. "Let's go. I don't want to be late."

The three of them headed to Eric's gray RAV4 while the early summer sun peeked out from the clouds. Danny glanced over his shoulder. "What did you end up telling Seger to get the time off? I mean, if you make it through the whole thing, you'll be gone six weeks. Isn't he going to miss you?"

"He's taking a three month break to write and spend time with Ashley at home. The timing couldn't have been better. He needs me less when he's at home than on the road." Brendan tossed his bag into the back seat and followed it in. "I told him Jess needed me for a couple months while she's in pre-production for her new movie." Brendan shrugged. "He was fine with it."

"Wow. I wish I had a boss like that," Eric scoffed. He worked in a law office and Brendan got the impression he hated it.

"And what happens when he sees you on the show?" Danny asked, bringing up the elephant in the room.

"He hardly watches TV and he hates reality shows with a passion."

"I thought you did too," Danny said.

"I do. Did. Used to." Brendan felt the need to explain. "Look, this thing is huge. The prize money alone is enough to go for it, but a record contract on top of it? Trust me, I never thought I'd be here or get this far and I have no clue if I'll make it to the end or even win the damn thing, but I know I have to try. It's my future."

Eric glanced at him in the rearview mirror. "I promise we won't screw up. At least, not intentionally."

"Very reassuring," Brendan mumbled.

"REMEMBER," CASEY SAID FROM the passenger seat as her sister pulled into the television lot. She looked between Zoe and her best friend in the back seat. "Don't screw up."

"Seriously, Casey…" Zoe said, winding her way slowly through the parking lot. Her sister looked exceptionally hot—as in smoking hot—with her makeup and hair done to perfection. Casey had been so wigged out about Jeff that she hadn't noticed until they'd gotten in the car. Same with Vic. Sometimes Casey felt like the odd woman out when she was seen in public with these two women. It didn't matter that she towered over them both because they had bucket loads of confidence. Maybe that's why they connected so quickly once Casey introduced them four years ago. "How could we screw up?"

"I don't know. Just don't say anything embarrassing or be ditzy. That goes for you too," Casey said, pinning her best friend with a pointed glare. Vic had straightened her normally wavy—

and natural—strawberry blond hair. She had her mother's Irish looks from her creamy skin to her brown eyes.

Vic smacked her lips together to even out her pink lipstick. "I haven't seen you this nervous since your engagement party."

"Haha," Casey said, smoothing her hair. The reality of marrying Jeff had set in the night of her engagement party. She'd had more jitters than a cat trapped in a dog pound. Just like then, the actuality of what she was about to do set in. In just a few hours, she'd be on national television, vying for the chance of a lifetime. Her stomach turned over and her palms slicked.

Zoe parked the car and the three of them made last minute adjustments to their makeup before heading to the four-story building next to a row of stages. Would she be on one of those sets? What would it look like? She had so many questions rolling around in her head and none of them would be answered until she was already in the hot seat.

Casey hefted her tote bag and rolled her suitcase behind her, praying she'd make it long enough to warrant all the packing.

"Don't worry," Vic whispered as they reached the door. She flipped her hair over her shoulder where it fell in a sheet of strawberry gloss. "You're going to do great. I think you're going to win this thing."

"If only." Casey's heart slammed out of control and the show was hours away. How would she survive once the cameras started rolling?

A placard pointed straight down the hallway in front of them indicating the *Write Your Ticket* offices just ahead.

"Okay," Casey said a minute later, as Zoe put her hand on the knob. "Let's do this thing."

Zoe gave her a wide grin, opened the door with a flourish and Casey led the way inside with her back straight and a smile on her face. Who knew when the cameras might be rolling? Half a dozen desks littered the large office space with closed-door offices scattered around the perimeter. A mammoth copy machine sat against the far wall with a large corkboard hanging near it.

A young woman sat at the first desk to her left and Casey stopped in front of her. "Hi. I'm—"

"Casey Turner!" The girl stood up and put her hand out. With her boy short hair and lower lip piercing, she struck Casey as a rebel. "I'm so happy to meet you! I'm Olivia. We've been expecting you. Today's the big day. It's so awesome!" Okay, an excited rebel. "Why don't you follow me and I'll take you to the introduction room."

"The introduction room?" Vic asked.

"Yes. It's where we shoot everyone introducing themselves. We'll get the three of you together then get each one of you separately."

Casey's stomach flipped. Not a minute wasted. The phrase *be careful what you wish for* suddenly branded itself in her brain. She'd wished, hoped and prayed to be picked as one of the contestants on this show. Now that it was actually happening, her stomach was flopping around more than a guppy out of water.

Olivia walked to a room on the other side of the expansive office. "Casey, you can leave your bags here. A PA will bring them later when we get to the house. Everything'll be safe. You can keep your purse if you want."

She wanted. "Okay." She left her bags in a neat pile near the door.

"So," Olivia said. "You're scheduled to be the first person in the house which means you're first for everything today. We'll start the three of you in hair and makeup then go in for introductions, then Casey goes into the house. One of the PAs will take you down the hall to get started."

"Hair and makeup?" Casey had no idea they were going to this extent for the opening.

"Yes." Olivia smiled and lifted her brows. "We want everyone looking their best for the intros." She looked between the three of them. "Although I see you guys won't be taking much time in there. You're already gorgeous." Olivia blushed and took them out the door on the other side of the room. They walked down a different hallway and into a virtual maze before cutting right into a brightly lit room where four women waited in different stations.

"This is the makeup department," Olivia said, pointing to two women on the left. "And this is the hair department." She gestured to the women on her right.

One by one the ladies introduced themselves. Lucia and Jani made up the hair department and Erin and Michelle did makeup. Casey figured there wasn't much to do with her long, straight hair, so she sat down in Erin's chair for makeup.

Twenty-five minutes later, Casey, Zoe and Vic were escorted to another room where a camera and lighting setup surrounded a small set with three silver metal chairs and red backdrop.

The hot seats.

Olivia turned to the three of them. "Okay, ladies. This is where you say good-bye. After we shoot the three of you together, Casey will shoot a section by herself then we'll take her out a different door and get the two of you by yourselves. From here on out, everything is on camera. I'll give you a minute alone while I make sure we're all set to go." Olivia left them and Casey's knees started shaking like a bowl of Jell-O in a massive earthquake.

"Oh my, God," Casey muttered. "I can't do this."

Zoe glanced at Vic and they each huddled closer. "Yes, you can," her sister said. "This is your dream coming true."

"Not if I don't win," Casey whispered. "Then I'm just a huge public failure, exactly like Jeff said."

"Hey!" Vic squeezed her hand. "Cut it out." The seriousness in her eyes caught Casey's full attention. "Jeff is a dickhead. That's been established." Vic probably knew more about Jeff than anyone. She hadn't been a fan for over a year. Jeff had slipped his usual cool and told her to *shut the hell up* during a conversation about politics. Vic never forgot it, so she'd been thrilled when the wedding had been called off. "You are a great songwriter and you're about to show it to the rest of the country. Just go do what you're good at and don't think about anything else. You got it?" Vic was always good at cutting to the chase. "You got this far so there's no reason you can't win this thing."

Casey glanced between her sister and best friend. They believed in her. Hell, she believed in herself. She just needed a little extra kick-start to get going. "Okay," she said, psyching herself up for the next week or two or six or however long she'd manage to stay in the game. "I can do this." She took a deep breath. "Thanks for being here. Thanks for agreeing to do this. I know it's asking a lot." They'd lose their anonymity too, because of this. They'd be on national TV once a week for as long as Casey managed to stay on the show.

"No sweat," Vic said with a wink. "I could use more Instagram followers." Working for a PR firm, Vic was all about publicity. Her bosses were all for this weekly side gig in case it brought more attention to their business. They made crazy money handling some very high profile celebrities.

"I owe you guys so huge. I don't know how, but I'm going to repay you and it's going to be big. Bigger than big. It's going to be giant." The doorknob turned and Casey's heart stuttered along. It was happening too fast. "Oh my, God."

Zoe and Vic snatched her closer for a group hug.

Vic's lavender perfume mixed with Zoe's vanilla and she breathed in their confidence. "You got this, girl," Vic said. "We're here for you no matter what."

Casey didn't get a chance to say anything because Olivia was back and she had a couple of men with her.

"Okay, ladies, this is Don and Michael. They'll be helping us today. Don will set you up with RF microphones and Michael will be shooting you. Our producer, Karen, will be right in and she'll be running everything from here." She smiled and looked at Casey. "It was great meeting. Good luck!" She left, closing the door behind her.

Casey's mouth went dirt dry exactly as her pits began to sweat. Great. Don attached a little microphone to her collar and clipped the small box on the belt of her dress. It only took him a couple minutes to outfit the other two. As he did that, bright lights flipped on from different directions and all three of them swallowed back tension. Casey knew Zoe and Vic were nearly as nervous as she was. "What does RF stand for," Casey asked.

"Radio frequency," Don answered. "Not so much wireless as battery powered," he explained.

The door opened and a woman walked in. She wore gray suit pants, a fitted white button up shirt and high gray pumps. Her shiny dark hair shone almost blue in the bright lights. She went straight for Casey. "Casey, nice to meet you. I'm Karen Sales, the producer. "I'll be asking the questions." She gestured to the seats. "Casey, you can sit on the end here," she said, indicating the far left seat.

"I'm just going to ask a few questions and I want you to answer as honestly as you can."

"Sure," Casey said.

Karen signaled to Michael and the red light flashed on the camera in front of them. "Casey, let's start with you. Tell us your name, a little bit about yourself and introduce us to your outside team."

"I'm Casey Turner. I'm twenty-four and from Los Angeles and…" A blank. Already she had nothing to say. How the hell was she going to write songs if she couldn't even say more than ten words at a time? "And I recently went on my honeymoon alone." *Holy shit!* What had she just done? *Hurry! Something else!* "This is my big sister Zoe and my best friend Victoria."

"You can call me Vic," Vic said, smiling for the camera. Casey wouldn't be surprised if Vic scored some major press with her introduction to America. She was the stuff cover girls were made of. Not to say that her sister was anything less than gorgeous, they were just polar opposites. All three of them. They were a triangle, circle and square, each very different and with strong personalities even if Casey's was just emerging.

"Casey, tell us about your solo honeymoon. What prompted that?"

"Uh…"

"Her ex gave her an ultimatum," Vic volunteered. "When she didn't cave, he called off the wedding."

Casey almost had a coronary. She was sure her face registered Vic's declaration like a bomb, but she couldn't do anything to stop the fallout. Holy shit, there was going to be fall out. Vic obviously didn't care how Jeff was going to take this news because she'd never been a fan of the guy. Maybe Casey had inadvertently blurted out the honeymoon part, but *her* information hadn't needed to be shared with America. This was the exact thing Casey had wanted to avoid and it was all out in under thirty seconds.

"Vic," Casey said a little too sharply, her eyes as wide as the camera lens catching all of it.

Vic had the courtesy to blush. "Oh. Sorry. TMI. My bad." Except Casey saw in her eyes, she wasn't feeling *bad* at all. She'd totally nailed Jeff to the wall on purpose.

"We love TMI," Karen said, her dark eyes sparkling with enjoyment.

"I'll bet," Zoe mumbled. She glanced at Casey, a knowing look in her eyes. This was the kind of thing Vic did purposely. She played the ditz when in reality she was super smart. She used her looks to get what she wanted and she surprised people for shock value. Usually the shock value wasn't anything of this magnitude.

Didn't matter that Casey was still sitting down, thanks to Vic, she'd totally stepped into the shit. She prayed the show hired an editor who would have mercy on her soul.

Right.

CHAPTER 9

"OKAY, BRENDAN, IT WAS nice meeting you and your brothers. We're going to talk to them for a few more minutes while you head to the house. You'll see them next week for the second episode." The producer, Karen, smiled as he gave his brothers a partying two-fingered salute and headed out.

He couldn't believe he was really doing this. He'd already been told the order of people entering the house and he was last. He didn't even have names. The list only had contestants listed by number. The fact that he was last—number eight—didn't make him feel especially positive. The show was a six week trial run, with someone being eliminated at the end of each week. So was he the only one who noticed the extra contestant?

Actually, he felt more like he was about to walk into a trap. He was the last to see the house, the faces and the setup. The last to soak up everything before the show started in earnest. A definite disadvantage. No time to size people up. No time to get a feel for the place or the people.

Brendan left the room and stepped into a large hallway where a man greeted him with an outstretched hand. Wearing black jeans and black boots, the guy had enough product in his dark slicked back hair to oil a garage door. "Hi, Brendan. I'm Miles Griffith, the executive producer." Brendan had heard his name throughout the interview process, but had never met him. Miles was a well-known music producer getting his feet wet in television. Kind of like Simon Cowell without the accent. "We're all really excited to have you on the show."

Miles gave him a strong handshake, but never stopped talking.

"I just wanted to remind you that this opening is live for the East Coast and will be essentially live for this coast as well. Just be cognizant of that fact and watch your language. We wouldn't want to get in trouble with the FCC on our first night." He flashed a straight bright smile as Brendan regained his hand.

"Sure," Brendan said. He hoped he sounded calmer than he felt. The idea of *live* hadn't actually hit him until this second. A healthy dose of paranoia swirled in his stomach.

Miles led him through another maze of hallways and opened a door to a room on the right. "I believe this is yours, correct?" he asked, pointing to Brendan's duffle bag. "Go ahead and grab it and we'll head straight to the house."

Sweating palms had never been one of Brendan's favorite things. He wiped a hand on his thigh as he hefted the bag over his shoulder.

"Nervous?" Miles asked and they continued down the hallway. Pictures of the studio lot from the sixties lined the walls. Old Hollywood at its finest.

"Little bit, I guess." He didn't see a reason to lie about it.

They reached a heavy door marked Stage Eighteen in red lettering and Miles put his hand on the thick metal handle. "Okay. This is the spot. Once you're inside, walk up to the front door and wait until you hear your name. Then go ahead and walk into the house. Remember, we have cameras set up in all rooms except the two bathrooms."

"Right. Cameras." What the hell had he gotten himself into? A huge wave of regret mixed with the paranoia and stirred in his gut like acid. He never should have gotten into this mess. He hated reality TV like cats hated water and now he was about to be the ultimate hypocrite.

"Okay then." Miles beamed. "Break a leg." He opened the door and Brendan hesitated before walking into the cool darkness of a soundstage. Too late to back out now.

The whole thing was lit to look like the outside of a house. Painted hunter green, the craftsman styled home had a heavy wood door with bronze handles. The large porch spread out on either side where lush greenery disguised the outer edges that became nothing but a black void, essentially a large wraparound tunnel where the cameras must be filming the interior. As instructed, he walked to the front door and listened, unsure if they knew he was there or not. His heart thundered and his mouth went stone dry. He looked over his shoulder, about ready to retrace his steps when he heard, "Please welcome our final contestant, Brendan St. John."

Suck it up. Do it.

Brendan opened the door and walked through. The large entry way looked like a regular house with new hardwood floors and a thick red oriental carpet in the foyer. Bright turquoise paint covered the biggest wall in the great room with a brown wall opposite and two different sitting areas in between. Farther inside what seemed to be a large sunroom, he saw a group of people, all holding drinks and all looking as if they'd already won the damn show. Brendan saw everyone had dropped their luggage near the front door so he did the same as he entered.

He scoped out the competition as he moved forward. Four men including him and four ladies, but he couldn't see one woman very well since her back was turned and a couple of guys blocked her.

Focusing on the people closest to him, he did his best to smile.

The host of the show, Steve Bardell, walked toward him with an outstretched hand. The guy had Hollywood looks and a smile to match. His thick dark hair looked Beverly Hills perfect. "Brendan, nice to meet you. What do you think of the house?"

Brendan took another look at the large rooms that seemed to flow into one another in a subtle color scheme of tans, deep browns and turquoise. A big fireplace served as the center focal point.

"It's beautiful." What else was he going to say?

"Hopefully it's beautiful enough to spark some creative songs from you and your fellow contestants." Steve turned to the others in the room. "Now that we're all here, let's make the introductions official. Brendan this is Jack, Mitch, Dante and Kirby and over here we have Courtney, Lisa, April, and Casey."

Brendan locked eyes with Casey just as she turned. Everything stopped. Wearing a slinky black dress with a slit up the thigh and sexy heels that put her in his height range and showcased her long legs, she looked just as beautiful as she did the day he met her. He

71

didn't think her eyes could get any wider. Did he have that same look on his face? He worked really hard to look unaffected, to pretend that he didn't know her, but acting wasn't his forte. Never had been.

He mumbled hellos to everyone and shook hands with the people nearest him. He didn't want to touch Casey. He knew he'd feel the same spark she ignited in Hawaii. He saw it in her eyes and didn't need to feel it in her touch.

"Now that the contestants have met, it's time to meet our judges," Steve continued, forcing Brendan to concentrate on his words. "Please welcome Grammy- and Tony-nominated artist, Sara Bareilles, and Grammy winners Garth Brooks, Sarah McLachlan and Rob Thomas."

Shit. The surprises kept coming as the four entertainers strode into the house via the front door. Steve talked to each one individually, but Brendan lost track of his words as his gaze settled on Casey. She flashed her amazing ocean eyes in his direction then quickly looked back to Steve who picked up a crystal bowl with cards inside as the judges disappeared as quickly as they'd come in. "In here, we have our first game." He shook the bowl. "Each card has the name of a celebrity singer who will appear on the show. A little while ago, we had a random draw to see who would go first using contestant numbers one through eight. Contestant number one was our first pick so Casey if you could come up and choose a card."

Brendan swallowed as Casey set her drink down and walked over. Her hair flowed around her like silk and her skin had a healthy glow. She pulled a card from the bowl.

"Now open the front side flap," Steve instructed. "And read the name."

She slid the flap up, her fingers shaking as she did. "Kanye West." She looked at Steve like everyone else and Brendan forced his mind on the current process and not Casey's mouth.

"Great. Now, our next contestant has the opportunity to either pick Kanye from you or they can choose to draw. That next contestant is Jack." Steve held out the bowl and walked over.

Jack looked around before he picked his card and when he lifted the flap, his eyes widened and his jaw dropped open. "Carrie

Underwood." A total look of wonderment passed over his face. "Holy sh—I mean, wow. Carrie Underwood!" He lifted the card so everyone could see her name.

The group oohed and awed. "As each new name is revealed," Steve explained, "each of you will have a choice to either pick a name you've heard, or take a name from a contestant who's picked, forcing that contestant to pick again. Did I mention that the celebrity you choose now will be the person to sing your first song this week? Keep in mind as long as someone has to choose a name, you run the risk of losing your celebrity for the first week." Steve looked around the room.

Holy shit! Jack already had Carrie Underwood in the bag unless someone took her. But who else might be in there?

A sudden flop sweat had Brendan wiping a hand down his face. What if his boss's name was in that hat? Oh shit, what if he lost his job *and* his place on this show because he never mentioned the connection to Seger in his application? Instead of working his intestines into a knot, he blew out a breath and concentrated on the game.

Lisa picked next and she drew Kristen Chenoweth. Clearly there wasn't a bad name in the bunch. At least not yet. So why did people have the option to take a celebrity away from someone? There had to be a trick somewhere.

Brendan went next and he chose to draw from the hat. He picked Rihanna. He couldn't believe his luck.

April chose Ed Sheeran. Courtney chose Pitbull. Dante chose Ryan Tedder. Only one person left to draw and Mitch sauntered up to Steve and his magic hat of celebrities. He pulled his card and lifted the flap. A massive grin split his face before he looked up. "Seger Hughes," he said, showing his card the way all the others had done before him.

A wave of heat spread through Brendan like wildfire. He was dead on so many levels once Seger got here. And what about Casey? Brendan locked gazes with her. She could easily reveal his secret. She had to know this was a surprise to him too, but maybe not by the way she stared at him with cold ocean eyes.

"Now, I know some of you might be thinking that the first person who chose a name got shafted from having a choice since we didn't know any of the celebrities before we started. Which is why…" Steve looked to Casey. "Casey, can pick her choice of any artist she wants, leaving one of you," he looked out to the group, "with Kanye."

Casey licked her luscious lips as she gazed around the room at all of the contestants.

"Now, Casey," Steve went on. "You can hold onto Kanye if you want. That's your prerogative. Or you can choose to pick anyone else's celebrity. Your choice." Steve paused. "Oh. One more thing," he said. "One of your celebrities isn't really here." He smiled at the confusion of the group. "I mean, one of those names in your hands isn't actually on the show which means if you're holding that celebrity in your hands once Casey makes her decision, then you, too, will be off the show."

"What a minute," April said. Her fine platinum blond hair swung around her face as she shook her head. "You mean we won't get to compete? We won't even stay for the week?"

"April, if you're holding the old maid, you won't even stay for the night. We have six weeks and seven contestants. Ball's in your court, Casey. What's it going to be? Are you going to trade Kanye for someone else? Or will you take your chances with him?"

Casey's hand shook as she thought it over. She eyed everyone in the circle before stepping forward. She walked right toward Brendan, but turned at the last second and stood in front of Mitch. "I'd like Seger, please."

Mitch clenched his jaw and the tension in the room ratcheted up a notch before they traded cards and Casey went back to her spot in the circle.

"So, Casey, tell us why you traded for Seger."

Brendan thought his heart might pound through his ribs it was beating so hard. What if Casey outed him right this second before he even got a chance to prove himself. God, what if he was holding the wrong card and got booted that way?

"I've always liked Seger, but mostly I'm not a huge Kanye fan. I thought what he did to Taylor Swift was bad enough, but then after his comments about Beck, he lost me completely. I want to work with some I respect."

"I understand," Steve said. "Just so you're all aware, as the weeks go by and as the contestants dwindle down, so too will the celebrities. Each week we'll showcase a different genre and your celebrity will have to sing the song you write for that genre. So on the country week, the person with Carrie Underwood is going to be in fat city. Likewise the person with Kristen Chenoweth on Broadway week is going to be in a sweet spot. Just realize," he added cryptically, "that the celebrity specializing in that genre might already be knocked off the show." He looked around the group. "A lot of variables to consider for the duration of your stay."

Brendan looked around the room and realized all of them had been kept in the dark about this turn of events. They'd known they'd have to write a new song every week, but there'd been no mention of celebrities singing them and no mention of different genres.

Shit. Things just got very real.

CASEY DIDN'T KNOW HOW she was keeping herself together when inside she wanted to curl up into a ball and hide from the world. Too much was happening at warp speed and she could barely keep up.

Brendan.

Pick a card.

Trade a card.

Celebrity spin the bottle.

It was crazy. She barely had time to process one thing when something else happened.

"Okay," Steve said, clearly ready to drop another bomb.

God, what if she'd just picked the losing card? What if Seger was the no-show? What did Brendan know about it? He had to know something since he worked for the man. Wasn't that a conflict of interest? Shouldn't having a job in the music industry prohibit him from being here? She could've sworn she read that in the rules, but the bright lights were making her fuzzy and keeping a straight thought seemed impossible.

"When I name the celebrity and if you're holding their card, you'll be picking up your bag and walking out the door." The tension in the room jacked up even more and Casey almost hoped she was the one to get ousted. She hated this...hard. Steve looked around at all of them. "The no-show celebrity is..."

They waited that interminable reality show wait where bad music played and the camera panned to all the contestants. A few people fidgeted. Perspiration broke out under Casey's arms.

What seemed like five full minutes later, Steve finally opened his mouth. "Kanye West."

Casey slapped a hand over her mouth. It would've been her. Relief warred with knowledge that she'd made the cut and actually had to perform... With Seger Hughes.

Mitch's face turned all sorts of red as it dawned on him that he was out. "Are you kidding me?" The anger in his voice echoed in the room. "Are you fu—are you serious?" He stalked up to Casey full of steam, his face flushed and his muscles taut.

Casey had a sudden flashback of Jeff approaching her and backed up a step. In an instant, Steve and Brendan showed up and flanked Mitch, ready to grab him if he tried anything.

"Easy, Mitch," Steve said. He seemed to be enjoying the whole scene. This was reality TV at its best.

Mitch faced Steve, anger blazing off him like dumpster stink, his dark eyes spitting mad. "Easy? You think it's funny to mess with our lives, to yank our chains?" He shot daggers at her with his vicious stare. "Thanks," he seethed. "For nothing!" He stalked out, snatched his bag and slammed the door behind him.

Casey might've been relieved if the room hadn't suddenly started spinning. Her legs got shaky and she moved to the nearby brown leather sofa before she fell on her face. She should be celebrating the fact that she'd at least be here the first week with a singer she loved, but her insides quaked too hard to enjoy the accomplishment.

"You doing okay, Casey?" Steve asked, his fake concern making her a little more nauseous.

"I'm fine." Not to mention a big fat liar. She wasn't fine at all. Seeing Brendan was the first shot to her confidence and having a mini flashback to this morning with the way Mitch advanced on her was just the icing on her crappy cake.

Steve turned back to the camera and started talking and Casey didn't hear a word he said. Something about celebrating with all the food they'd brought in. Taking the time to get to know each other before the week got started. The group shifted and a faint din rose as they all seemed to talk at once.

Brendan took the spot next to her and a chill raced down her arms. He hadn't lost one bit of sex appeal since their time in Hawaii. He smelled delicious and looked even better in a denim shirt with fancy navy stitching. The material molded to his chest and showcased his spectacular muscles.

"You left." He said it simply with the tiniest hint of an edge, but she saw the hurt in his beautiful eyes. He was talking about Hawaii. She'd never meant to cause him any pain. She thought he even might appreciate the lack of an awkward morning after. Still the place was full of cameras and microphones and Casey had to be careful. His comment could've been because she'd left the circle just now to sit down.

"I just needed time to process." That was the truth. Her night with him had been scary in the most amazing way. His attentiveness, his drive to please her had been just what she needed and something she'd never had. One night with a stranger should not have affected her the way it did.

"Process?" He didn't damn her with the word. He didn't make it an accusation. He seemed like he was really trying to understand her and that made her chest even tighter. He nodded slightly, then pegged her with his gaze. "So did you? Process, I mean?"

She felt his warmth and wanted the heat of his hand along her back. She remembered how secure he made her feel in Hawaii as they'd walked the crowded streets. "I'm getting there. It was a lot to take in."

They still could've been talking about this whole reality show scenario.

He nodded. "Yeah, I guess so." He looked like he wanted to say more, but he wiped a hand over his mouth and jaw instead almost as if he censored himself before saying anything. The gesture brought Casey's gaze to his ear. His fully formed ear...

"Hey, what happened to—" Shit. She stopped herself just as his pleading eyes caught her gaze. Obviously he wanted to hide the fact that he had a mangled ear. She couldn't blame him. In an environment like this it would be big news. Before he or anyone else eavesdropping asked, she hurried on. "Oh, forget it. Not important."

"Getting cozy already?" April walked over with two glasses of something bubbly and handed one to Casey. Her smile was all high school. "This is for you. I owe you for not handing Kanye to me." She shivered as if the idea creeped her out. "I'm kind of glad Mitch is gone. He's too hot-headed to be locked in here for so many weeks."

"Thanks," Casey said, lifting the glass in a salute. She sipped the champagne and avoided any discussion of Mitch. The sweet bubbly drink tasted too sweet and tickled her nose, but she drank it anyway. From now on anything they said was recorded and edited and she didn't want to give anyone ammo. Besides, she wasn't about to trash talk someone—that included a bully like Mitch—without knowing how it might come back at her. None of them knew each other, with the exception of her and Brendan, and, of course, Brendan and Seger. Which led her to the next observation.

"I think the weeks are going to fly by, especially as we get knocked out." She didn't even want to think about the anxiety of writing a new song every week for the duration of her stay. They still didn't know what genre they had to write this first week. She sipped more champagne knowing it was a mistake to overdo it. She hadn't eaten much today and it was going to hit her hard if she didn't watch herself.

After a minute of small talk on the sofa, Casey, April and Brendan joined the group around the long tableful of food. A smorgasbord fit for royalty. Jumbo shrimp with cocktail sauce, spanakopita, trays of fresh fruits and vegetables, chicken skewers and rice all vied for space, and on the end, an array of desserts looked mouthwatering. Mini cupcakes of all kinds, cake-pops, brownies, cookies... It was enough to cause a sugar coma just looking at it all. Casey had a little bit everything, sticking mostly with protein and washed down a chocolate cake-pop with more champagne.

Food helped her mood. The champagne didn't hurt either. She

loosened up enough to get past the whole Mitch incident and even managed to talk with people besides Brendan.

Steve had gone one by one and introduced the contestants a little more thoroughly to the audience so that everyone had a better and bigger picture of who they were, which meant the rest of them could talk quietly and eat while he interviewed his prey. He snagged her in the middle of the group and asked her questions about her day-to-day life. He touched on her teaching, but thankfully didn't hit on her solo honeymoon. She wasn't sure if he had that information yet, but figured it was a matter of time before it bit her in the ass.

After the thirty-five minutes it took to talk to everyone, Steve motioned for their attention. "Before signing off on our live broadcast, I want to thank all the people watching, but mostly I want to thank our contestants. It's going to be a fun couple of months here at *Write Your Ticket*. We hope you all will tune in every week at this time to see how our songwriters and celebrities fair during the week. Until next time, I'm Steve Bardell. Good night!"

Finally, the live portion ended. Casey felt a small reprieve knowing thousands of people weren't watching them at this exact moment. Granted, she still had to watch her mouth and her step because cameras were rolling twenty-four seven, but it wasn't like they could show every minute of everyone's stay here.

Steve set his mic down and looked around the room, his smile devious. "If you all would follow me," he said. He seemed very happy with whatever bomb he planned to drop next. He led the way out a thick door that spit them outside. The walls of the house had been built into the stage. Fresh air felt good on her heated skin. The sun had set and stadium lights illuminated a big yard. Huge green fences blocked out the surrounding lot and adjoining neighborhood. A gorgeous, new, black two-door BMW coupe sat on display in the middle of the yard. Zoe would've gone crazy for that car. Her sister was a BMW maniac.

Steve pointed to it and gestured everyone to follow. "This sweet machine can be yours," he said, turning to the seven of them. "All you have to do is sit in it."

"What do you mean, 'sit in it'?" Courtney asked. She seemed

the most cynical of the group so far. Her hour-glass figure hinted at a serious boob and booty job. So far she'd questioned everything and rarely smiled.

"I mean, that all of you will pile into the car and the person who stays in the longest wins it."

"Driver's seat!" Jack called, setting his drink on the nearest table and running to the car.

"Shotgun!" Both April and Dante called it at the same time and started running with Courtney right on their heels. The rest of them followed.

"How does this pertain to writing songs?" Brendan asked as he peered inside. The two-door coupe barely had seating for five and there were seven of them.

"It doesn't," Steve admitted. "It's just one of the few games we've devised so you guys can get to know each other better." He opened the passenger side door wide, and Dante dutifully pulled the seat forward so the rest of them could climb in back. "I think you ladies might want the guys to sit down first. Unless you want one of *them* on *your* lap."

Jack didn't budge from the driver's seat and Casey already chalked him up as someone to watch. She didn't trust people who blindly followed without asking questions.

"April called shotgun, so she can sit in my lap," Dante said. His freckled face made him look fourteen as opposed to twenty-three.

Brendan got in next to Courtney and Lisa. He barely fit in the tiny space. He patted his lap and Casey realized it was either his lap or another female she didn't know. *Not* sitting on his lap might look more suspicious, so Casey sucked it up, eased in and settled on Brendan's hard thighs.

CHAPTER 10

PERFUME FROM FOUR DIFFERENT women quickly overpowered the new car smell, and Brendan had no idea why he'd stepped foot in this damn claustrophobic hot box in the first place. He didn't need a car and, though it was nice, he wouldn't be caught dead in something this small. He liked bigger machines. He liked knowing if an accident was going to happen, then he was in something big enough to take a beating.

But as Casey settled her very nice ass on his lap, he knew why he'd done it. Turned out he was more of a masochist than he thought. Yeah, she'd made it very clear what she thought of him and their one night together, but it didn't change the fact that he was insanely attracted to her. Still. Even after getting shit on.

So what was wrong with him? Lust is blind? Apparently.

He had weeks in front of him where he couldn't talk to her the way he wanted to.

Plus, what if she exposed him and his relationship with Seger? Hell, she'd already nearly blown his prosthetic ear. What happened when Seger saw him? His boss hadn't said one word about being on the show. Of course, Brendan hadn't said anything either, but he'd been under contract to keep his mouth shut. Seger had probably signed the same confidentiality agreement.

Casey shifted and reminded him that her fine ass graced his lap. "I'm totally crushing you," she murmured.

"I'm fine," Brendan assured her. He was better than fine. He could stay like this all day if he had to. All night. He loved the weight of her, the way her long hair fell like silk in front of him.

"How long do you think we'll last in here?" Lisa asked from her corner of the coupe.

"You guys may as well call it quits now because I'm not letting this car go to anyone else." Jack stroked his hands around the wheel as if it were a woman. His attitude turned Brendan off. At least Dante seemed like a decent guy...unless his shy smile was just a con. Jack continued, "This baby is mine."

Brendan refrained from the eye roll and kept his poker face. He had to remember cameras were on them at all times...probably one or two hidden in the car's interior.

"Don't count on it," Courtney said, leaning toward the front seat. Her very round breast brushed his arm. "My car is on its last legs and I need this for survival."

"I guess we'll be fighting it out," Jack said with a smile.

A couple of hours passed and the seven of them exchanged small talk. Where they were from and how they got into songwriting. Brendan did his best to think about anything but the woman on his lap. Virtually impossible. He remembered everything about her. Her scent, her curves. The dirty words she'd whispered in his ear. His reaction below the belt made complete sense, it was just a very big nuisance and shitty as hell timing.

Casey shifted one too many times and Brendan figured he knew what was wrong since he was having the same issue.

"Gotta pee?" he asked softly.

"Like a racehorse," she muttered.

Courtney and Lisa laughed and agreed with "Me too" and "I know."

So all that food and drink had been on purpose to assure a quicker ending to this little contest.

"You guys can fight it out. I'm done." Casey shoved forward. "April, Dante, I don't care how you do it, but get your butts out of that seat so I can crawl out." What ensued next was nothing short of keystone cops. After opening the passenger door, April had to shove over to the console and Dante moved completely over the front dash as Casey bent over to flip the seat forward. The extra pressure on Brendan's lap not only exacerbated his bladder issue, but his hard-on issue as well.

"Ditto that." Brendan took the opportunity to wrap his hands around Casey's waist and help lift her forward out of the back seat. She scampered out of the car and didn't stop. Brendan hauled himself out and stayed on her heels, reveling in the cool air and hoping he made it to one of the two bathrooms.

Casey found the first one and slammed the door, leaving Brendan to rush past the rest of the rooms until he found—thank God—the other bathroom. A few minutes later, they met in the living room. With the urgency past, they just watched each other. They couldn't say what they wanted to say, not blatantly, not without risking their spots on the show. If anyone thought they knew each other beforehand, it might end their chances of staying.

"Want to look around the place?" Casey asked, heading toward the luggage near the front door. "We may as well take dibs on the bedrooms as long as they're sitting in the car." She rolled a bright pink suitcase away from the wall.

"Sure. Sounds like a plan." Brendan passed her as he went for his duffel bag. He inhaled her subtle flowery fresh scent, which made his dick perk back up again. "I don't even know how many rooms this place has."

"I think just two. Girls in one, boys in the other."

He watched her and thought about the last room they were in together. His hotel room. "Wonder if the beds are as soft as the one I was in last week on my vacation."

A flush stained her cheeks and Brendan knew exactly what she had racing through her mind. The same thing running through his. Bare, slick skin, erotic touches and wreck-the-sheets sex.

"Guess there's only one way to find out." Casey turned and Brendan followed, still not sure how he felt about having to set aside the conversation he wanted for who knows how many weeks.

The frustration killed him.

THE CROWDED BAR SHIFTED and moved around him like a living animal. He caught the bartender's eye and signaled for another whiskey. Anything to dull the raging anger boiling in his blood.

Casey.

Just hearing her name made him angry. He wanted to hurt her, hurt her so badly that she'd never get over it. She'd ruined everything. No one was going to look at him the same way again. She'd ensured that after tonight. No one watching would ever forget it.

The thought of it made his skin tight. Made his palms itch and his fists clench. She wasn't going to get away with it. He just hated having to wait for the damn show to finish before he got his revenge.

But then an idea came to him. A great idea.

He had connections. A lot of connections. So why wait until the show ended? Why couldn't he give the American public something to talk about?

He downed the rest of his drink as the bartender brought another. Yeah, watching Casey become the victim of a terrible accident on the set would be a reality show moment no one would forget. He couldn't wait to make that happen.

The whiskey burned going down and it was just what he needed to dull the pain. He picked up his phone and scrolled through his contacts then punched the number he wanted. "Hey, it's me," he said, when a voice answered the call.

"Hey, man. How are you? I saw what happened. You okay?"

He took another sip of whiskey as he caught the eye of a pretty blonde from the mirror behind the bar. He wasn't in the mood. Shifting on the stool, he leaned on an elbow. "I'd be better if you helped me get rid of a problem."

His friend laughed. "You know me. Always up for a little challenge if the price is right. What'd you have in mind?"

"Not sure." He scanned the bar, watching the well-dressed people hoping to get lucky. "Maybe a little accident on set if you know what I mean?"

There was the tiniest of pauses. "Anything's possible. Show business can be a very brutal industry. Lots of accidents happen on set."

He liked that answer. "I'm hoping so. I'm sure hoping so."

"I'm guessing we're talking about the pretty girl that did you wrong. It's a waste of a beautiful face, have to admit."

"Lots of pretty faces, my friend. She's just another one in the crowd and she's going to regret dicking with me." He took another drink as his buddy laughed.

"I love it when you go all psycho. It's creepy shit, bro."

He took offense at the words, but it wouldn't do him any good to lose this opportunity. He wasn't psycho. Hardly. He was just pissed. Pissed enough to go to the trouble of ridding the world of Casey Turner. "So can you make an accident happen on that particular set?"

"Like I said, anything's possible if the price is right."

It paid to have people in the right places.

Chapter 11

"**Rihanna. Shit. It took** me all week to wrap my head around the fact that Brendan actually met her. I still can't believe that lucky little prick got to work with her." Danny shook his head while he stuffed his ID back in his wallet and rolled up the window as the RAV4 went through the gate.

Eric couldn't believe it either. They'd all fantasized about her at one point or another growing up. He pulled into a parking spot at the studio lot, cut the engine and replaced his ID as well. "I'm waiting to see if he gets paired up with Seger. I guarantee that neither one of them knew the other was going to be there."

Danny snorted. He put the visor down, opened up the mirror and ran a hand through his hair. "What were the chances? Seriously? It's crazy. I can't believe Bren didn't just give his songs to Seger to begin with." Next, he pulled off his shades and cleaned one of the lenses with the bottom of his button up shirt. At lease this time, he'd worn something other than a ratty T.

"He said one of the roadies already tried and Seger shot him down cold. Bren didn't want to take the chance."

"I know, but…" Danny shook his head. "He must be good if he made it this far."

"Yeah… I don't think he realizes that." Their little family band usually performed covers for their own enjoyment. None of them had realized Brendan created original music until he told them about trying out for the show. Eric opened his door. "C'mon, let's get this over with. I'd like to say we won't have to do it again, but if Bren keeps writing songs like the one Rihanna performed last night, then we might be here for the duration."

Danny grinned. "That would be the shit, you know, little brother making it with a big time contract." His smile dimmed. "He sure deserves it after everything he's been through."

Danny deserved it too, but Eric didn't bring up. They'd all dealt with the same issues of being kidnapped, beaten and held hostage. Brendan and Danny had suffered the worst, but Danny always denied it, always gave props to his youngest brother for surviving.

Still, Eric agreed. Brendan deserved as much success as he could handle. "Gonna be a sad day when little bro has to give us a job." Eric had worked his ass off in school and had followed in their dad's footsteps as a lawyer. Too bad he hated it. The pressure to be like his dad weighed on him like a two thousand pound gorilla. Pressure to be as good a lawyer, pressure to be a good role model for his little brothers. Pressure to be as successful in his chosen field as his sister was in hers. So far, he had zip to show for it. Though he didn't begrudge any of his siblings' success, he couldn't help but think he'd taken a wrong path in his life. He just didn't know how the hell to get on the right road at this point.

A white BMW pulled into an empty spot by the door as the guys got closer. Two women got out, a brunette and a strawberry blond. Eric felt the light jab Danny gave his shoulder blade as the four of them neared the door of the building. Yeah...like he hadn't spotted them already.

Taking a few quick steps to reach the door first, Eric held it open for both women. One word described them both. Hot, hot, hot.

He was glad he still had his suit on from work. Women liked power suits. Okay, so maybe his suit was just a regular suit, but it said something about him. Hopefully something good.

The brunette had curves for days and they outlined the tiniest fucking waist he'd ever seen...the ultimate hourglass. She glanced at him as she breezed by, her vanilla perfume climbing up his nostrils and making his gut clench. "Thanks." Wearing a slinky form-fitting lavender dress with a slit up the side, her body said party, but her demeanor screamed all business.

Danny stood on the other side of the door as the ladies filed in before them.

"Thank you," the strawberry blond murmured as she passed. Though Eric held the door, she gave Danny a once over, hot enough to melt iron. Her teal dress fit just as snuggly as her friend's and showcased the perfection of her round, tight ass.

"My pleasure," Danny replied, giving her his patented wink. Eric lost count how many women that wink had reeled in. Sometimes he wished for the same free spirit that inhabited his little brother. Danny never stressed about the future. He lived one day at a time and took whatever random job came his way. Whether it was stunt, modeling or courier work, he did enough to get by and seemed damn happy with his life.

Eric followed everyone inside and enjoyed the scenery as the two women strode ahead in their stilettos.

It didn't take a genius to figure out they were probably here for the same reason. Eric just wanted to know which contestant belonged to them. As the four of them walked down the long hallway to the production office of *Write Your Ticket*, Danny slid him a wide-eyed glance that said *how's* that *for a nice view?*

Once at the production office, the brunette opened up the office door and gestured for them to go first. "Fair is fair," she said, a sexy smile playing about her beautiful lips.

Eric held the top of the door, coming into close contact with the most amazing blue-gray eyes he'd ever seen. "I wouldn't dream of it," he murmured. "Ladies first."

A blush stained her cheeks. "Well…" She glanced at her friend, the strawberry blond with porcelain features. "That's very…gentlemanly of you."

"He's nothing if not a gentleman," Danny added, his gaze totally focused on the very toned beauty standing next to him. The four of them created a bottleneck at the door and the brunette ducked forward into the office.

"Thank you." This time she sounded a little less business and little more party.

Her friend followed her with another full once over at Danny and a smile. "Thanks again."

"My pleasure," Danny said.

Eric smacked his arm after both ladies had stepped away. "I opened the doors, dipshit."

"Same difference," Danny said, taking the spot behind the strawberry blond. He glanced over his shoulder and waggled his eyebrows. "Thanks, man."

Shaking his head, Eric couldn't hold back a grin. His brother was an admitted hound dog, but he did have a good sense of humor and a heart of gold. As aggravating as Danny could be sometimes, it was hard not to love the guy. "Anytime, bro, anytime."

The same lady from last week waited at the desk and smiled as they approached. Eric couldn't come up with her name then spotted it on the plate at her desk. Olivia. "Zoe and Victoria." She looked down at a list. "And Eric and Danny, right?"

"That's us," the strawberry blond said.

"Yep," Danny agreed.

So they had a name for the women, they just didn't know who was who.

"You can all have a seat right over here," she said. "I'll let our producers know you're here." Olivia walked through a maze of desks and disappeared around a corner leaving the four of them together.

"Which contestant is yours?" Danny asked, always ready to jump into the fray.

The woman looked at each other before the brunette met Danny's gaze. "My sister. Casey."

Danny's brows pulled together. "Casey. She's the tall one, right, with the long hair. Second place finisher last night."

"That's her. What about you? Wait. Let me guess." She glanced between the two of them. "You belong to last night's big winner, Brendan."

Eric and Danny both nodded. "Is it that obvious?" Eric asked.

She fluffed her thick, dark hair and those loose curls bounced around her shoulders. Eric wanted to feel those curls between his fingertips. "The hair and eye color is a dead giveaway," she said. "The family resemblance is very striking."

"It's a curse," Danny said with a familiar grin. Eric called it his hunting grin. Little brother was on the prowl for some action and by the way his gaze kept going to the strawberry blond, it was very clear which lady he preferred.

Olivia returned. "Eric, Danny, we're ready for you now."

"We'll be right there." Danny stepped in front of the strawberry blond. "I'm Danny. And you are?"

"Victoria. My friends call me Vic." Which meant Casey's sister was Zoe.

"Well, I sincerely hope that you consider me a friend."

"Hard to say." She gave him a sexy smile and Danny ate it up. "I mean I don't know you so that makes it hard to be friends." She gave Eric a once over that brought heat to his face. Shit, she was man-eater.

Danny didn't seem fazed. His brother was the polar opposite of the rest of the men in the family. Four out of five St. Johns liked monogamy. One woman at a time. Hell, their parents had been together since high school and their dad had never so much as looked at another woman. Danny seemed to juggle a handful at any given period. "True, very true," he conceded. "I say we rectify that. Dinner? Tomorrow night? You and me? How about it?"

Bingo. It never took him long to pounce when he found something he liked.

"Oh. Uh. Wow." She shook her head in a little confused bob, a victim of the steamroller that was his brother. "I..."

"Here," Danny said, pressing his case. He grabbed a notepad and pen from the desk and scribbled his name and number down before ripping it off and handing it to her. "Call me when you decide." He gave her another one of his patented winks. "We'll have fun."

Eric grabbed Danny's arm and led him from total destruction. "Nice meeting you, ladies," he said. Although technically he hadn't met either.

"Same here," the brunette, Zoe, said at their backs.

Chuckling at the forlorn expression on Danny's face, Eric shoved him forward good-naturedly. "Down boy," he murmured. He followed Danny into the same room they'd been in a week ago when they'd dropped off Brendan for the opening of the show.

"Hello, guys. Nice to see you again. I'm Karen. We met last week. Thanks for shifting times. We had a little scheduling glitch so we had to double up the interviews this week."

"Is that why we ran into those other two outside?" Danny asked.

Karen nodded. "Correct. Why don't you have a seat and we'll get started so you two can get out of here."

Eric grabbed a chair and Danny sat next to him. It took a second to get used to the bright lights glaring into their eyes. Karen sat next to a cameraman and after a nod he pressed a button and a red light flashed on the camera.

"So, guys, what did you think of your brother's first song last night?"

Eric jumped in first. "I thought it kicked all kinds of ass. Not only did it suit Rihanna's voice perfectly, but it had lyrics that said something valuable." Truthfully, he'd been completely blown away by the song. He knew he had a talented brother, but shit...Brendan had set the bar amazingly high last night.

"Danny, what about you? What'd you think?"

"Well, first, Rihanna is hot. I gotta say that."

Eric shook his head and elbowed him in the arm. "The song, man, she's talking about the song."

"I'm getting there. Don't get your panties in a twist." He wiped a hand down his jaw. "Let's be honest, Bren's song beat the others by a landslide. I know I speak for Eric and for our whole family when I say we're really proud of him."

"Do either of you have any predictions about his closest competition?"

"Casey's song was really good," Eric admitted. She'd come in second by a tiny margin. Seger knew his way around a song that was for damn sure. "I think if Bren has anyone to worry about it might be her."

"What did you guys think of the sparks flying between your brother and Casey all week?"

Eric was afraid they'd go there. The show wanted as much drama as possible. Although he couldn't say for certain that something was cooking between Brendan and Casey, he didn't want to fan the flames. It was nobody's business what happened between them. "I guess I didn't see it. Brendan didn't do or say anything out of the ordinary with her. Danny, did you notice anything?" They'd already discussed the possibility of this topic and agreed on their approach.

Danny shook his head. "Not really. I was too busy watching Casey, April, Lisa and Courtney."

Karen lifted tired eyebrows as if she'd dealt with Danny's kind of smooth talk for years.

"One last question for you both before we bring Brendan in. We'll give you a few minutes to decide on your clues for Broadway week. What's the one thing you'd like our audience to know about Brendan? Something that might sway votes his way in the coming week."

Eric glanced at Danny and knew exactly what his brother was thinking, because the same thing was running through his head too. They could play the sympathy card, but they'd never share the once in a lifetime event that had shaped all their lives. Brendan worked hard to put the incident behind him and the whole family respected it. He never brought it up, never used it as an excuse for anything. Eric still couldn't believe Brendan had finally taken the plunge with a prosthetic ear, but he understood his brother's need for privacy, especially since he had the same issues.

"Brendan is a very low profile kind of guy. He probably wouldn't want us to tell you that doing this show is way out of his comfort zone. He's risking his privacy to be here because he's a songwriter at heart. Sometimes a person has to do things they don't want to do to live their dream."

CHAPTER 12

CASEY WOKE UP, HER eyes gritty. The dim bedroom came into focus, the line of three beds next to hers all decorated with different solid colored duvets that matched the walls and furniture. Two weeks ago, she'd grabbed the first bed, purple. The others had sorted between green, red and yellow.

Now, two of those beds were empty.

She turned on her back, the muted purple wall decorated with colorful abstract art screamed at her to wake up and write despite it being—she checked her phone—five-thirty in the morning. She hadn't been sleeping well and now the pressure was mounting with two second place finishes in as many weeks. She was the only one to land in the top two spots both weeks and it marked her as a serious threat.

Her spirits lifted thinking about the coming week. She'd picked Seger again and couldn't wait to come up with a new song. Seger proved to be one of the most versatile artists simply because he'd revamped his own sound so drastically. Really, every artist on the show had the ability to sing anything, but having Seger on her side gave her more confidence.

She still wished for a minute alone with the guy without cameras rolling. She wanted to know what he thought about his assistant being part of the show. Casey was fairly certain that Seger didn't know anything about her where Brendan was concerned. She didn't get any type of weird vibe from him at all.

It had been an awkward time, trying to figure out how far she could go during collaborations. Artists tended to be picky about their music. She definitely was. But how far did she push when it came to an icon singing her song? The celebrities realized they had to let the contestants pen the song, but they weren't banned from helping with the music. It made the process more of a collaboration, which made the songs stronger.

Casey chuckled to herself remembering Zoe and Vic's clues as to this week's genre. *"When you give a birthday present or shower gift or a Christmas gift, you have to do it,"* Zoe said. *"When a TV show finishes its episode or when someone pounds on the door,"* Vic had added. Casey had literally scrunched her face up into a ball. *What?* It took a few minutes to figure it out. Rap.

It was still going to be interesting to hear Seger Hughes sing a rap song. Hell, she hoped she could *write* a rap song. Though she loved all kinds of music, she had to be honest that rap wasn't her favorite genre. Not even close. So how did Seger feel about it? So far, anyone stuck with a genre and an artist that didn't *excel* in that genre had lost their spot on the show.

Tossing the covers off and sitting up, Casey looked at Lisa sleeping soundly in the third—yellow—bed, her blond hair streaming across the pillow. They were the only two women left. Those of them lacking the Y chromosome seemed to be dropping fast.

Casey pulled her notebook from the small nightstand next to her bed and stared at the blank page. Rap. Rap. Rap. What the hell did she know about rap? She scribbled absently as words tussled in her head, searching for space, for continuity. When she looked down, the initials BSJ stared up at her.

Brendan.

A flush heated her face. It didn't matter that Lisa won last week's show, Casey considered Brendan her biggest competition. It kind of sucked. The man didn't seem to have a talentless bone in his sculpted body.

The toughest part was looking into his eyes and knowing what he wanted to talk about. It was the thing she wanted to talk about *least.* Yes, she'd walked out. She never dreamed she'd see him again so was it such a crime? He had as good a night as she did, so...

Lisa rolled to her back and started snoring. No way to work with *that* soundtrack in the background. Casey quietly got up, made a pit stop in the bathroom to brush her teeth and snuck out.

Wearing her white sleep shirt and shorts, she padded to the designated quiet room with her pen and paper hoping to get some words down before the day started for real.

Casey opened the door and stopped short when she saw Brendan already sitting at one of the two small desks. Her brain and heart fought a battle. Her brain said, *walk out the door*, but her heart wanted her to sit on his lap, take the pen out of his hand and kiss him senseless.

His eyes flashed up then filled with heat. His long hair hung to his shoulders in messy waves...the rumpled look suited him. "Good morning," he murmured, his voice early morning rough and so very sexy. He probably would've sounded exactly like this in Hawaii if she'd stayed long enough to find out.

It took her a second to find her tongue. "Hi. Sorry. Didn't realize anyone was up...or here." Her brain won this round and she took a step back.

"Wait!" Brendan stopped her, his hand out. "There's room if you want to share." He motioned to the other spots. A leopard print beanbag with a lap desk, a black leather recliner and a small white desk across from the maroon one Brendan currently used. The house was big on crazy color schemes.

Casey hesitated. She sometimes hummed when she came up with new songs and she didn't want to give anything away. Hell, she wasn't even sure she could concentrate long enough to come up with anything with Brendan in the same space.

"C'mon," he coaxed. "I won't make a sound." He gestured with his head for her to come back. Those pleading blue eyes were hard to resist.

As usual, he cracked the wall she kept trying to build, and her lips quirked up. "It's not you I'm worried about."

His straight white smile made her heart stutter. The man was all sorts of delicious. "Noisy songwriter, I take it?"

She tipped her head from side to side. "Possibly." What the hell. She couldn't work with Lisa snoring in their room and any other part of the house might have one of the other guys. At least she liked Brendan's company. Casey moved into the room and crashed onto the beanbag. They worked quietly for a while as she toyed with words, phrases and music. She thought about the early rap years and music by Will Smith to the hardcore beats by Eminem. What made those songs so appealing? The heart and soul of the story they told. So what story could she tell?

Breaking free. Living life. Getting out. Finding me.

Hm…maybe…if she flipped it.

Living life. Breaking free. Getting out. Finding me.

"I like that," Brendan murmured, turning to her.

Casey met his gaze and felt a hot blush stain her cheeks. "Was I humming?"

He nodded. "Kind of catchy." He repeated the familiar tune running through her head. "Go ahead. Do it again. I've got something for it."

Humming the music, Casey started at the beginning and Brendan joined in with a harmonizing riff. They watched each other for changes, signaling higher or lower as they continued. The sounds blended together in a perfect storm of notes. They hit a snag and both laughed at the misstep.

Brendan grabbed her wrist and pulled her up. "C'mon. Come with me."

"Where?" Casey laughed as he dragged her down the hall and into the music room. Piano, keyboard, guitar, bass, drums…if it played music it occupied space. The show had cameras everywhere to ensure they caught every step in the process of each new song as it and the writer evolved.

Brendan grabbed the guitar and started playing the tune they'd been humming only he turned the beat into a ballad. Casey caught on and sat behind the piano, picking up the third line and nodding her head in time with the music.

Again, they watched each other for changes. Then from out of the blue, Brendan started singing: *"Remember that night not long ago. You took my hand we danced long and slow. Your kiss was like something I've never known. And I wanted to make you my own."*

A full body chill raced down Casey's spine and she jumped in with a chorus. *"But life rarely happens like we want it to. We stumble and fall, stumble and fall. What if I said I'm sorry now. I never meant to hurt you. I never meant to hurt you. We just stumble and fall, stumble and fall."*

Brendan shook his head, the pain in his eyes guaranteeing that she'd hurt him when she'd left without a word. *"I want to hold your hand again, kiss your lips again. I want to walk in paradise with you by my side. Forget the world and call you mine again. Don't run and hide. Don't run and hide."*

Casey's throat tightened with emotion. *"But life rarely happens like we want it to. We stumble and fall, stumble and fall. What if I said I'm sorry now. I never meant to hurt you. I never meant to hurt you. We just stumble and fall stumble and fall."* She looked away and slowed the beat. Brendan followed her lead and together they played the last haunting notes.

Pressing her lips together, Casey blinked back the sting in her eyes. Guilt swamped her like the wave that morning in Hawaii. A few moments later, the sound of Maroon 5's "Daylight" filled the room and she looked over her shoulder.

Brendan stood by the sound system, which contained thousands of songs, basically any type of music ever created. The music was there for inspiration or recreation, whatever the contestants needed. He held his hand out just like that night at the restaurant. Casey took it and waited. He put her arms around his neck, his hands around her waist and pulled her close.

She forgot how solid he was. How warm and strong. But this was still a mistake. "What are you doing?" she whispered. "All of America is going to be watching this when they edit the show together."

"So what? Dancing's not against the law." He turned her, pulled her back in and swayed as the music drifted around them.

"They're going to make a big deal out of it. They're going to put us together and pit us against each other. They'll speculate and—"

"I don't give a shit," Brendan murmured against her ear. Tingles shimmied down her spine. He felt so good, his quiet strength wrapped around her as they moved to the music.

The audience might not hear his whisper since the mics that were running twenty-four seven were out of earshot at the moment.

The more they swayed against each other, the more she felt his interest crop up low against her stomach. His hand moved down the center of her back and he rested the tip of one finger right at the top of the divide between her ass cheeks. An erogenous spot she'd never realized she had until their night together. He'd touched that spot and she'd nearly gone off like a rocket.

She gasped and clenched her jaw, fighting the streaks of instant lust that shot through her like fireworks on the Fourth.

Brendan had swayed them right into the corner of the room so no one saw where his sly hand rested or how his wicked finger circled and pressed into the one little spot that drove her crazy. At this point the pretense of a dance had gone out the window. They just held on tight, heads next to each other. His warm breath wafted against her ear as they stood.

"Bren." She barely got his name out. She wanted to rub against his front. Rub against the finger teasing her in back. In response, he pressed his thigh between her legs. Oh God. She wanted more. Needed it and there was no way in hell she was going to get it.

"Want you so much." His soft words barely penetrated her dazed mind. No way any microphone could pick up those words. Hell, she barely heard them.

"Can't," she murmured back. Even though she wanted to more than anything. She wanted to feel him deep inside her, pushing, filling her, giving her all the satisfaction she could handle and more.

"I know." He sighed and pulled away, looking into her eyes, searching for something. She had no idea what. "Hey, Case?" His voice was still whisper soft.

"Yeah?"

"Can I kiss you?"

A full body chill broke out on her skin. It wasn't as if he hadn't kissed her before, but the audience didn't know that. Clearly he was checking for permission because of the thousands—maybe millions—of people who would be watching when this aired. He was so sweet to ask.

This was the shit they hated about reality shows. The private stuff that should remain private since the show was supposed to be about their musical talent. The relationship between two people shouldn't matter and no one else had a right to know.

What about her parents! They'd flip their lids if she kissed a guy on national TV. Blatant displays of affection should be behind closed doors. Decent people did not kiss in public. And Jeff...he'd lose complete control if she kissed someone for the world to see so soon after their breakup. Not that she really cared what he thought, but—

"Case?" He was still waiting, his gaze sincere and molten hot at the same time. Screw what other people thought. She got to live her life her way and at the moment she wanted his kiss as much as she wanted to win the show.

She nodded, a barely-there shake of her head, and his smile warmed her from the center of her chest. He moved in so slowly, so movie perfect. Women across the country were going to fall in love with him after this. Well, they could suck it, because she got first dibs.

His lips hovered right over hers before gliding whisper soft across her mouth. A sweet, innocent kiss. As if it was a first, when they'd already devoured each other multiple times in paradise.

After eternal seconds of teasing her lips, he went in for the real deal, coaxing her lips apart when she gasped into his mouth as that hidden finger delved right between her ass cheeks. He took her fully, laying claim with his tongue, taking her sanity and her breath with one red hot kiss sure to melt panties in all fifty states. Stroking deep into her mouth, he didn't hold back. He tasted like toothpaste and Brendan, like the best part of morning. On and on their tongues tangled in a glorious wet reunion. When he finally pulled away from her, Casey was dazed, breathless and in dire need of release.

Brendan removed his roaming hand and held her steady, both hands on her waist. His blue eyes were on fire, his breathing as unsteady as hers.

"Nice to meet you, Casey Turner," he said. His voice sounded low and sexy and she wanted to inhale him in one bite. "I hope we can become great friends, and maybe more."

Casey couldn't tear her gaze away from his intense eyes. Long seconds ticked by and she wondered if he might kiss her again. Hoped he'd pull her close enough to absorb all his heat and the incredible feeling of confidence and lust he sparked in her.

"Breathe," he whispered, a half grin lifting his lips.

She blinked and took in much needed air.

"I guess we should get back work," he said, shifting away from her.

She nodded. "I guess so." She swallowed, exhaled an unsteady breath and realized he still had his back to the camera for a very good reason. "Here," she said, ducking past him. She grabbed his guitar and handed it to him as he turned, effectively blocking the erection beneath his nylon workout shorts.

"Thanks." A blush stained his cheeks and she wondered if the audience would see it.

"Sure." She backed up toward the door. "I'll just head back to…" She pointed outside. "You know…the quiet room."

He nodded. "Okay. See you later." His very blue eyes tracked from her toes to her mouth and sent another delicious chill down her spine. Casey bit her bottom lip to keep from saying something stupid like, *"Wish you could fuck me later too."*

CHAPTER 13

CASEY DIDN'T GET OUT fast enough. Jack barreled into the room effectively pushing her back inside.

"Making beautiful music together?" Jack asked, heading to the keyboard. Brendan didn't know if he meant that in the literal or figurative sense, but he didn't care either way. "Don't mean to break up a party, but it's my designated time so," he gestured for them to scram, which meant Brendan had to give up the guitar and leave.

Casey must have guessed his predicament because she held out her hand. "Here, I'll set the guitar back in its stand." Since she blocked his body from the camera, Brendan took her up on the offer and together they walked from the room with Casey shielding him for the most part.

"Thanks," Jack called from behind them as Brendan closed the door.

They ended up back in the quiet room, but Brendan felt anything but quiet. He wanted to shout, to dance, to celebrate. Having Casey on board for that kiss meant he had a shot with her. She disappeared in Hawaii, but at least she hadn't said no to him now. The first thing on his agenda the minute the cameras were off was to find out what exactly she needed to process. He wanted to hear it from her.

Damn, he'd opened a can of worms with that kiss on national TV. He'd done the exact thing he hated about these shows and he hadn't given a thought about it in the heat of the moment. All he'd wanted was to taste Casey again, feel her lips under his, her tongue stroking against his. *Well, mission accomplished, dickhead.*

"You excited for this week?" Casey asked from her spot on the beanbag. Her cheeks still had a pretty blush and Brendan hoped it was because of their kiss. "You're going to love Carrie. She's great. I had so much fun with her last week."

Brendan had barely stayed on the show last week, coming in second to last with Ryan Tedder, so he was glad to have one of the top celebrities this time around. "You're on a roll," he reminded Casey. "Two second place finishes."

"Look who's talking, Mr. I Won the First Week Right out of the Box." Her smile absolutely wrecked him. She could give a dead man a boner with that smile.

Brendan forced his mind back to the conversation and shrugged. "Beginners luck. After last week, I'm not sure it means anything."

Casey shook her head. "I don't think so. I think you're loaded with talent." She cocked her head. "Why didn't you tell—" She stopped and her eyes widened.

Figuring she'd been about to blow the fact that they knew each other before the show, or even worse than that by mentioning Seger, Brendan jumped in to save her and himself. "Why didn't I tell you that I'm a great songwriter while you were sitting on my lap in the car? Modesty."

She laughed and he saw a silent *thank you* in her eyes. But her smile faded and she glanced down at the paper in her hands. "Guess we should get back to work."

No matter how much he'd rather talk and flirt with her, they did have songs to finish. "Guess you're right." Brendan turned back to the music he'd been working on before Casey's humming had distracted him. He couldn't use anything they'd just created together, but the notes kept pushing their way into his brain. The song was by no means finished, but what they'd riffed together in just a few minutes could eventually be a great tune with some TLC.

Brendan concentrated on the lyrics he'd started for Carrie's song. Though he didn't expect them to win with a rap song, he knew Carrie was more versatile than people gave her credit for. She had a powerful voice and a great stage presence. If he could come up with decent lyrics and half decent music, he could make it through this round and head to week four. He didn't expect to win, not with Ryan, Seger and Rihanna still in the mix. This would've been Pitbull's week to shine if he'd still been in the competition.

He smiled thinking about Ryan belting out the show tuned he'd penned last week. He hadn't expected the rocker to sell it so effortlessly. More than half this competition depended on the performer and a few of them were more than versatile enough to handle all the genres coming their way...including Carrie Underwood belting out a rap song for him this week. Pitbull had even pulled off a great ballad on week one, but April's lyrics and music hadn't been sharp enough to keep them in the running.

No doubt, each week the pressure mounted as singers got knocked off and the competition dwindled. Week three, which meant halfway through. Brendan still had three chances to land Seger...if they both lasted that long. That was bound to be an interesting week. They'd have to pretend they didn't know each other and Seger wasn't a fan of lying. Yep, it was going to be interesting.

Brendan worked on his song for three days before he met Carrie. Casey had been a hundred percent right in that the singer was absolutely genuine on every level. Meeting a lot of celebrities had become the norm while working for Seger, but Brendan still managed to get star struck when meeting other performers he admired. Performers like Carrie Underwood. She was beautiful and talented and there was nothing *not* to like about her. Brendan showed her the lyrics and his palms sweated as she looked over the sheet. He knew the words by heart and watched as she soaked them in.

I'm gonna take it from the top and tell you all about how.
He turned me inside out and left me upside down.
Everything was kickin', I was cool as ice.
I met him and I thought yeah, man, paradise.
But the love he gave was conditional and it disappeared with the moon.
So I'm telling you I ain't fallin' in love, no, no not anytime soon.

Don't tell me lies. Get outta my way.
Don't look at me like you want me to stay.
'Cause I know the deal. You ain't for real.
You don't give a damn about how I really feel.

I don't want that knife in my back. I won't bow down to your ways.
No, I don't want that knife in my back. I won't go drowin' in your waves.
A solid shot is what got to my chest and I swear this time is the last.
'Cause next time I see you I'm not gonna flinch, you'll just be part of my past.

The chorus then repeated, followed by a bridge:

Why did I think we had a shot? Why did you make me fall so hard?
Now all I've got is this broken heart. And nothing to show but this big ass scar.
How do you know if he's for real or the one?
How do you tell if it's a lifetime or fun?

The song ended with a final repeat of the chorus.

After what felt like an eternity to Brendan, Carrie lifted her gaze from the page and stood taller, her head cocked to the side. "Got music to this beauty?"

He thought his heart might bust through his ribs as he nodded his relief. He sat at a synthesizer in the music room and pounded out the beat. Carrie caught on and showed him a side to her Brendan didn't know existed. She turned as "street" as any versatile performer could.

When they finished the first go-round, Brendan had a great feeling about this week's show. The crowd was going to eat up Carrie's rap. For her part, she seemed ecstatic to show the audience how limitless her talent seemed to be. They worked for three days on the song and it only got better as she helped him tweak the music.

Before show time, the contestants met to shoot a section of the show to talk about their week. Likewise, they'd meet at the end and discuss the performances and reminisce about the person and celebrity voted off. Everyone sat in the same semicircle according to how they entered the show. That meant Casey sat virtually opposite him in the circle and they basically stared at each other the whole time.

Not a hardship. Brendan figured he could look at her for a very long time and not get tired of the view.

Five of them remained out of the original seven and by the end of the night, there'd only be four. Brendan didn't include Mitch since he had been booted before the show got started. He figured Dante, Jack and Casey had the best chances of winning with Rihanna, Ryan Tedder and Seger singing their songs. But all the performers had shown their talent by jumping genres and giving their all to stay in the competition.

Though the cameras never turned off, there were obvious things that the group had figured would never make airtime. Waiting for the producer to stage this chat session was one of those times. They all laughed in camaraderie that went along with the pressure. In just a few short hours, one of them would be history.

Something squeaked overhead and Brendan glanced up at the lights. The whole rack swayed gently, but Brendan didn't see anyone overhead. Not that he usually did, but clearly guys had to work on the lighting and they probably did it when the group was in the yard, playing one of the stupid games the show rigged up to keep everyone competing against each other. Brendan also decided those stupid games took them away from their composing and created more stress and panic.

Yeah, because that made for good television.

Miles sat down next to the cameraman. He looked his normal Hollywood cool in an ice blue button-up shirt and navy slacks. "Okay, let's get started." He motioned to the cameraman and the red light flashed on.

Something dropped behind Casey's seat, but Brendan only saw it peripherally since he had his eyes on Miles. Whatever it was didn't make a sound as it landed on the area rug beneath them. For a second, Brendan wondered if he had some kind of floater in his eye and nothing had dropped at all. But then he heard another noise above and watched the lighting rig shake again. Earthquake? He waited for the usual vibration under his feet or the walls to shake, but neither one of those things happened. A nasty smell of fumes—something burning—hit his nose and everyone seemed to notice it as they looked around.

"How about we move out from under the lights for a second?" Brendan said getting to his feet. A flash and crack happened over their heads and everyone jumped and ducked simultaneously. Another high pitched squeak rent the air and something else dropped behind Casey as she got to her feet. Brendan didn't wait for her to move. He dove, tackling and rolling, protecting her head with his hand and tucking her close as a crash sounded exactly where she'd been seated.

Glass from the light shattered and covered the chair and carpet. A small fire exploded on the ground, sending foul smelling fumes into the set.

"Everyone out," Miles ordered, pointing toward the yard.

Brendan's heart beat wildly as he helped Casey to her feet. "You okay?" He scoped her for injuries. *Damn, that had been close.*

She nodded, her eyes wide and her face pale. "Yeah. I think so."

He looked up at the lighting rig again to see a dangling rope and a support beam hanging limply from the grid. Then he hurried them out to the yard, keeping her hand locked tightly in his, watching as crew members fired extinguishers at the downed light.

Once in the yard, Brendan turned and took a closer look. Casey's eyes were still wide and freaked out, but he figured his were too. "You're sure you're okay?"

Taking a few deep breaths, she gave him a hesitant smile. "I am thanks to you. How'd you know that light was going to fall?"

"I wasn't sure. I thought I saw something fall behind you a minute before the light flashed. Then the whole rig shook. I didn't like the sound or look of any of it. It wasn't like we had an earthquake. That's what I thought it was in the beginning, but nothing else moved."

"Well, thank you for being so observant. That was almost a very big disaster."

Very big didn't begin to describe it. That light would've crushed her in a heartbeat. Brendan's stomach rolled over. She eased a chunk of hair behind her ear with a shaky hand and the urge to pull her close and keep her safe bolted through him. Screw it. He didn't care what America thought. "C'mere." Gently, he tugged her into him and wrapped her up in his arms. She went without a fight and it only made him more determined to have the conversation he wanted. They needed to have a serious talk about Hawaii and their morning after. Or the lack of one in their case.

CASEY DIDN'T EVEN KNOW how she managed to shoot the episode that night. After the show, they got together again in their usual semicircle, although this time they sat outside in the warmth of a Southern California night. Instead of overhead lights on a grid, the crew had set up stands weighted down with sand bags so they were still lit up like a halftime show of the Super Bowl.

She figured the only reason she'd lasted tonight's cut was because Seger was so damn good. Casey knew she'd messed up on the piano. Her mind had been on the accident, on the way it felt to be in Brendan's strong arms when all hell broke loose. She felt even worse because Seger had hugged her instead of yelling at her for screwing up.

The celebrities had something at stake in this game too. The winner won a hundred thousand dollars to donate to the charity of their choice. They wanted to win as much as the contestants.

But Casey knew better than to point out her screw-ups. Seger and she were the only ones who really knew what happened and she wanted to keep it that way.

The show said farewell to Lisa and Kristin Chenoweth, which meant Carrie Underwood was still in the running with country music looming in the future. It also meant Casey was the lone female left on the show. She'd have that giant room with four beds all to herself. Technically it gave her an extra quiet room all to herself.

After the show recap ended, Casey wanted to stay glued to her seat, but she knew the crew had to clear the set, and the contestants weren't allowed to be in contact with anyone but each other and a few of the producers.

Someone came over and shadowed her from the bright light. She knew his scuffed brown boots. She knew a lot about him because she watched him so much. Like the way he ran his hand through his hair when he concentrated on lyrics. Or the way he sucked on his bottom lip when he riffed on the guitar. She glanced up and met Brendan's gaze.

He held out his hand. "How 'bout I walk you inside?"

She didn't need the escort, but she wasn't going to pass up holding his hand. Especially when she needed his comfort. She loved how the lights hit his hair and brought out the red streaks. Even his stubble sparkled with red highlights when his face caught the right light. Standing over her, Brendan looked so strong, so confident. She remembered his mile-wide shoulders has he hovered over her, pumping inside her and driving her to one explosive climax after another. A damp spot wet her underwear as she took his hand and stood. "Thanks," she murmured.

"You hungry? Thirsty?" he asked with a sidelong glance.

She loved the narrow-eyed gaze he gave her. The concern she saw nearly melted her wet underwear. "What did you have in mind?" She could really use a nice glass of wine, but the house didn't have any alcohol stocked. They'd checked.

He led her into the kitchen. "I've got just the thing for a tough day." He flashed a sexy smile and Casey held her breath at the spectacular sight. After pulling a stool out from the counter that ran along the long galley kitchen, he gestured for her to sit. She did. He searched a lower cabinet, grabbed a small pot and set it on the stove.

"A little milk," he murmured as he snatched a carton from the fridge. He turned, holding up the milk and a packet of hot chocolate. "You do like hot chocolate, right?" He shrugged. "I mean, who doesn't like hot chocolate?"

She bit her bottom lip through a smile, feeling warm and fuzzy all over. With a nod, she confirmed his question. "I do. It's one of my favorites. I just usually only have it when I'm really cold."

He pursed his lips together and looked around the kitchen. "I could turn up the AC? We could freeze the house. Might be fun."

She loved his out-of-the-box suggestion and grinned. "I don't think that'll be necessary. Besides, it might bring one of the others, and I like the size of this party just the way it is." A big admission on her part—on a couple of levels—and one she refused to regret. She knew they'd edit this into the show, but she didn't care. She wanted Brendan to know how she felt. Her little way of letting him know that she liked him despite leaving him in Hawaii.

The heat in his eyes had her catching her breath a second time. The man was as potent as a narcotic. He gave her his back as he poured milk into the pot and turned on the burner. He found two mugs and set the hot chocolate packets on the counter before turning back to her.

"So... How are you? For real?" His gaze flicked to hers. "You okay?"

He might've been talking about the light accident or the fact that she'd botched tonight's show or the fact that she was the lone female left standing. So many things to choose from. Casey chose to pick the accident and nodded. "Thanks to you, yes. I'm glad you're observant. Tell me something else about you," she said.

He went back to the stove. "Like what?" He stirred the milk and poured the contents of the packets into the mugs.

"Like...how old are you?" She caught the extra sparkle in his eyes. Yes, they were covering different territory than in Hawaii. They hadn't talked about age.

"Twenty-three," he said. "You?"

"Twenty-four." She liked being a little older than him. "When's your birthday?"

"June twenty-second. When's yours?" he asked.

"No way! I'm December twenty-second. Our birthdays are exactly six months apart." Kind of cool. She especially liked the sexy smile he shot her way. She'd learned about his big sister and three older brothers—one of them being his twin—during their poolside conversation in Hawaii. She also knew they were in a family band of sorts, but she wanted more. "So what got you started playing the guitar?"

A half smile lifted his lips. "That was my dad's fault. He was a closet musician himself. A drummer. My mom accused him of having kids just so he could force us into playing instruments so he could have the band he always wanted."

Envious of the fondness in his voice and eyes, Casey wished she had a similar relationship with her parents. "How old were you when you started playing music?"

"I don't know...maybe five or six. My dad threw instruments

in all our hands at a very young age. We had a rocky start." He grinned, reliving a memory.

"You obviously took to it. Did everyone else get as good on their instruments as you did?" she asked.

Brendan chuckled. "Well, we didn't suck *all* the time."

His endearing reply made her smile. "So you were kind of like the Jackson Five?" Any Michael Jackson fan knew how he started.

Nodding, Brendan glanced up. "Exactly. Just like Michael." He did a suggestive bump and grind and grabbed his crotch for good measure. Then he pulled off a very impressive spin move and moonwalk before holding the tip of an imaginary hat.

Casey burst out laughing. "Look at you! Fancy." She leaned her elbows on the granite counter and relaxed. "What music did you start out playing?"

Brendan stirred the milk. "My dad was big on the oldies. Boston, Credence Clearwater Revival. Van Halen."

She snorted. "My parents were into the *original* oldies. Bach, Beethoven. Mozart. All I got was classical." It was all she'd learned in the beginning.

The milk sizzled and Brendan filled each mug, stirring the contents together. "And a pinch of cinnamon," he murmured, tossing in the spice. He walked around the counter, handed her one of the mugs and took the seat next to her. Their thighs touched from the knees up and Casey's heart thumped harder with the contact.

"Where did you learn to make hot chocolate this way? It's so old fashioned," she mused, trying to focus on anything except the warmth he radiated. She took a sip and about died. "Oh my, God, this is so good."

Brendan took his own taste. "It's better with marsh-mellows and a touch of nutmeg, but I couldn't find either. My mom taught us that perfect hot chocolate needs milk, not water. Plus, you pick up a few things when you're working a bar."

"I'll have to remember that." She took another sip, enjoying their alone time and the way Brendan looked at her over his cup. His blue eyes still had all that heat that melted her. Could the camera pick that up or was she the only one who saw it? "What else did your mom teach you?" She loved getting to know him better.

"She taught me to go after what I want." His meaning was crystal clear, but Casey chose to misinterpret it. What she couldn't ignore was his warm palm sliding from her knee and up between her legs.

She opened her legs a fraction, giving him silent permission. No way the camera could see what he was doing. Their bodies blocked all camera angles. "That's why you're here. Why we're all here," she added. Her voice sounded oddly low and she cleared her throat.

He gave her a barely there smile because he probably understood her dodge. "Did you think you'd make it in?" he asked, taking a sip of his hot cocoa. He looked cucumber cool as he sipped his drink and circled a sensitive spot with his thumb—midthigh—that had her wanting his hands all over her.

"I hoped I would," she admitted. Casey had to focus on the conversation. "I didn't have the support I'd hoped to have when I first mentioned the idea to important people in my life. But ultimately, not having that support made me stronger in the end. So I guess it's a good thing."

His smile faded and he set his cup down. His warm palm cupped her upper thigh. "I was very lucky in that respect. My family was very supportive. I'll admit, they talked me into it, but I didn't tell them until after I'd sent in my video."

"Why?"

"We're not big fans of the limelight. I just thought this was a good way to chase a dream."

"You don't think being a songwriter puts you in the limelight?" Casey asked. She couldn't help the skepticism in her voice.

"It's the singers who are usually in the spotlight. Not the songwriter."

"You don't see yourself ever singing one of your own songs? Like Ryan?" She shifted a fraction and he took advantage of her parted thighs. Their gazes locked and she couldn't miss the extra heat in his eyes.

He licked his lips. "Maybe. I don't know. I just like the idea of creating music and hearing the finished product from someone else. I never considered myself a performer."

"But you sing your songs as you write them, just like we all do. You have perfect pitch. You don't think that makes you a performer?"

"Maybe to an extent. I don't know. Let's just say I don't see myself playing to tens of thousands of people like all the singers here do. Sure, I can carry a tune, but I think it takes more than that to make it to the top."

"Like what?"

"A larger than life personality helps." He shrugged. "Not sure I've got that in my back pocket."

He was so wrong. He actually had a lot of larger than life qualities, but listing them on television might get her tossed from the show.

"Why are you smiling?" he asked, taking another sip from his mug.

Instead of saying what she wanted to say about one particular larger than life quality of his, Casey answered his question. "I think you have a wonderful personality."

"Oh yeah?" He leaned in close until his warm chocolate breath wafted against her lips. His index finger hovered right at the crease of her thigh and she barely sucked oxygen into her lungs.

"Absolutely," she whispered. "Of course it's not going to stop me from winning this thing."

He pulled back, his eyes sparkling. "Is that a challenge, a throw-down maybe?"

"Not at all." She sipped her drink. "Just a fact."

"Really?" His hand disappeared and he turned her stool so they faced each other. He locked his legs between hers. Another ripple of sexual awareness shot through Casey from her thighs—where his warm hands palmed her—to straight up her center. "How about a little wager?"

"What kind of wager?" Casey kept her drink in her hands to keep from touching him the way she wanted. Even if part of her wanted to torture Jeff, she really didn't love the whole country weighing in on her relationship with Brendan.

"If I win, you go out with me when it's over," he said.

"And if I win?" she asked.

"You go out with me when it's over."

She laughed, nearly spit out her drink. "That's the same thing. What's the point?"

His face turned serious. "The point is that we go out after this. Without the cameras, without the audience. You and me with nothing in front of us or behind us."

She shook her head. "There's always going to be stuff behind us." She meant Jeff, but maybe he was thinking about Hawaii. Or possibly the show. Not that it mattered. "Neither one of us can change our pasts."

"True, but we can move on and choose our path for the future."

She agreed with that. "Isn't that why we're here?"

He nodded. "It is. Yes, it is." He lifted his mug and gestured she do the same. "Here's to forgetting the stuff behind us and moving forward. Here's to making new friends and keeping them around for a long time."

Casey clinked her mug into his. "I'll drink to all of that."

Chapter 14

WEEK FOUR BEGAN WITH another stupid challenge, although this time the prize actually appealed to Brendan. A seventy-inch flat screen TV. That baby was as sleek as any machine he'd ever seen. But as he'd done with all the other prizes up for grabs, Brendan intended to tank the contest. He kept his eye on the main prize and kept his focus on the weekly song. Sure the daily and weekly prizes were awesome, but winning them took time and effort...things he didn't have if he wanted to write a great song.

Not that he felt confident he'd win this challenge anyway, not when it involved karaoke. Ugh. That little pastime had never been his favorite.

The remaining celebrities, Ryan Tedder, Carrie Underwood, Rihanna and Seger, served as judges and the best/most entertaining contestant won the TV. He didn't expect to win, nor did he want to. Casey, Dante and Jack, the other remaining finalists in the house, all had better singing voices, which worked fine for him.

A glass floor had been built eight feet over the pool and made a spectacular stage for them to perform. Underwater lighting flashed all different colors and lit up the outside and their performances from beneath their feet along with the standing lights around the yard.

For once, the producers let them practice the challenge before actually taking part in it. Maybe they realized the dangers of a completely cold performance at this stage of the game.

Thanks to his brothers' clues, he already knew who his celebrity singer would be and had the night to think of something before he got the official word tomorrow. Getting those clues gave them a leg up on writing something that might fit their intended singer. Guessing wrong meant potentially starting over or giving a major tweak to the existing piece. Brendan laughed softly to himself, thinking back on Danny's clue.

"Wet dream."

Eric had simply nodded. "Paradise."

Rihanna. He knew for two reasons. First, When Danny had been about fifteen, he'd woken up because of a wet dream about Rihanna and he'd never lived it down. They'd all been camping in the backyard and his confusion and subsequent wet spot had given them all a lesson in the male reaction to mental stimulus. Second, she was from Barbados, which they all considered paradise. So, yeah, it helped having brothers who'd always carried a torch for Rihanna and Brendan was pumped that he'd be working with her a second time.

Now he just had to get through this damn karaoke night and get to work.

Dante picked Andy Grammer's song, "Honey, I'm Good." He'd even worn a black leather jacket, maybe in hopes of summoning Grammer's success. The rest of them couldn't help but bop to that number-one hit. Jack picked "Animals" by Maroon 5 and showed off his tattoo sleeve with a black tank top. His performance had them all chair dancing. Casey chose Megan Trainor's song, "Dear Future Husband." Wearing tight black leggings, black stiletto heels and a flowing hot pink shirt, she looked like the rock star she should be.

As each person sang, the rest of them sat on stools behind them so the camera caught everyone's reactions. Because they'd all grown closer over the last few weeks, there wasn't much animosity as they each performed. If anything, Brendan felt a sense of support from his fellow contestants. This challenge was about winning a TV, not the week, and since this was more for fun, they enjoyed the music and took the opportunity to cut loose.

At one point during Casey's song, she strutted to the opposite side of the stage and stomped to the beat of the crescendo in her sky-high heels. A spotlight hit her and she looked like a goddess when she finished the song, one hand high in the air and her hip cocked, grinning so big that Brendan's heart fell hard and fast right then. He'd never known anything like the immeasurable pride filling his chest. No, she might not belong to him, but he wanted her to. He wanted to sit down at a piano with her and make music then he wanted to take her to bed and make love.

She was a shooting star and he liked that he knew her before, because this was just the beginning for her. The audience was going to go crazy. This one little karaoke song might very well launch her into the big time.

Casey walked back, breathing hard, and held out the mic as he stood for his turn.

"You have to do that move tonight," he told her. "That was awesome."

"No way!" She shook her head, laughing. "That was just for us. I'm counting on the fact that they won't have time to edit it in the show." She put the mic in his hand. "Go on. Your turn. Don't forget to give the camera an ass shot. It's looking mighty fine in those jeans." She sat on the stool he vacated and flipped her hair over her shoulder with a twinkle in her eyes.

Brendan forced himself to look away from her dazzling smile and walked out to center stage. The longer he knew Casey, the more she surprised him. Or maybe she was psyching him out.

He nodded for the music. He'd purposely gone old school with his choice for a couple of reasons. One, he'd stick out as the only singer that hadn't picked something contemporary, which would probably throw him out of the contest. Two, he picked an artist that meant something to one of the judges. "Old Time Rock and Roll" by Bob Seger was one of Seger Hughes all-time favorite songs. In a little known fact, Seger actually took his name from Bob Seger over two decades ago when he'd started his career. Brendan had learned that pretty quickly because his wife called him by his real name...Mel. His boss's Bob Seger collection was the other giveaway. Picking this song assured a loss with Seger mainly because his boss hated when people tried to cover his idol. In Brendan's mind, it was just another little way to make sure he won Seger's vote honestly and not because of any relationship they had. With little chance of winning this challenge, Brendan let loose with all the heart and soul a Bob Seger song deserved.

The small audience of judges, producers and crew seemed to enjoy the show and when he finished, he got the same round of applause and level of excitement as everyone else who performed. Maybe he hadn't stunk up the place after all. He just had to recreate it later tonight.

The group broke for dinner since tonight's show was going to be a live event. Again. The live shows were doing well enough to warrant them weekly and though Brendan couldn't say he was getting used to them, at least they didn't terrify him as much. Casey informed him during the meal that the song he picked also happened to be her ringtone. Brendan took that to be an omen.

Less than two hours later, they returned to their backyard stage. The sun had dropped and the lights looked incredible coming from beneath them in the pool.

"You going to do your stomp?" Brendan asked Casey as they took their spots.

"No. I told you that was just for us before. I don't even know what I was doing."

"But it was great. Look, if you don't do it, I'm going to steal it. I'd hate for you to lose because I took your moves." Whereas Casey had looked like a sex goddess the way she owned the stage, Brendan would look like a class-A geek. It worked if he wanted to lose.

"Be my guest," she said.

Steve came over and stood at the edge of the stage. "Okay, we're about ready to start. Remember, we want to see you guys do exactly what you did for the rehearsal. Cameras will be expecting the same performance."

"Awesome," Brendan muttered. "I *will* get to see you do it again."

"No, you won't. I don't care what the cameras are expecting. I'm not doing it," Casey whispered.

"Rebel," he whispered back.

"Getting there." The conviction behind the soft-spoken words surprised him and she looked ahead as if waiting for someone to contradict her. He wanted under her skin. Wanted to know what demons she had chasing her. The woman he met in Hawaii was a

117

total rebel. Damn, he wanted this shit to be over already so they could pick up where they'd left off.

The show started for real and Steve introduced them and the songs they planned to sing. Dante lit the place on fire, Jack kept it burning and Casey blew it up. As she said, she didn't do her stomp, but she still delivered an amazing performance, strutting across stage, her longs legs looking even longer in those massive heels. With her hair flowing all around her, she rivaled any and every rock goddess. All that pride he'd felt during the rehearsal filled him up a second time and nearly burst his heart.

He'd bet money that Dante and Jack were relieved they didn't have to follow her. The only reason he didn't mind was because it ensured his loss. Still, his palms slicked up and his pulse raced as his turn neared. Brendan tried to shake off the nerves and remind himself that this performance didn't mean much. He was happy to lose the karaoke contest since not obsessing over it had given him more time for songwriting this week.

Not one of those platitudes made him any less nervous.

Casey handed him the mic as they passed each other on stage. "Dare you," she mumbled. She was talking about that stomp on the raised part of the stage opposite them.

He laughed. "It's on." In that minute, the sparkle in her eyes meant the world to him. This was the woman he'd fallen for in Hawaii, the playful woman with a truckload of confidence and enough personality to fill a freight train. The woman who just put her heart and soul into a song and probably won a giant flat screen because of it.

The lights nearly blinded Brendan, but he smiled for the camera. "This is an oldie, but a song I think most of you will recognize." The first few piano notes hit the air and Brendan dove into the song like a flat screen TV depended on it.

Right before the crescendo of the song he moved to the corner of the stage where Casey had done her stomp and he did a similar version. The roar of appreciation from his fellow contestants had him thinking he had a shot at winning that giant flat screen after all. Just as the music slowed, the floor shifted beneath Brendan's feet. Losing his balance, he looked down as a giant crack split the floor and the whole piece split, buckled and broke. Chaos erupted.

It was a slow motion disaster as everything on that end of the stage slid into the water. The amps and all the cables at the end hit the pool in a show of sparks brighter than the finale at Disneyland. Screams and shouts rent the air as Brendan lost his footing and slid, following all of it in.

Electrocuted. He was two seconds from getting fried. The microphone flew in the air as he reached for the edge of the stage and caught it. He got no traction on the glass. Every centimeter his fingers slid put him that much closer to his death. Sweat coated his skin and his pulse jumped like the wires bouncing with electricity over the water. The light show underwater combined with the sparks over the pool and created a surreal attraction.

A hand grabbed his wrist. His feet dangled inches from the high voltage water.

"Brendan!" Casey's voice reached his ears over the din of the music and buzzing electricity. "Hold on!" She started tugging. His weight would surely drag her down with him. He gulped in air to warn her off when another hand grabbed his other arm and both people hauled him up.

Dante helped Casey reel him in and Jack was right there to aid Casey. Relief surged through Brendan as he landed stomach first on the remaining part of the glass stage, his heart still pounding like a drum. They didn't waste time getting him to his feet and running for the stairs at the back that led down to poolside.

Shaken, Brendan stared at the pool and the sparks that flew from the live wires snapping from the broken stage. Producers yelled out orders and an arm circled his waist. Brendan met Casey's wide, concerned eyes and pulled her closer, swallowing back his residual panic. Nothing like a near death experience to sober the moment.

Crap. He thought he'd *already* met his quota. A phantom pain sliced through his chest as he remembered the searing agony of a collapsed lung and the struggle to get enough air before help arrived. Brendan blinked the memory away when Casey squeezed him tighter.

Crew members ran around in a chaos they hadn't seen since the day the light came down over Casey's chair. So was this just really bad luck that two near-fatal accidents had happened within a span of weeks? Or was it something more? What would someone have to gain in hurting one of them?

"You okay," Casey asked, her hand locked on his waist.

Not counting his runaway heart, sure. Nodding, he met her gaze. "Yeah." He kissed her forehead, and didn't give a shit that cameras were going to catch everything. "Thanks for catching me."

Tipping her head back, she lifted an eyebrow. "I'd say we're even…again," she added softly. Because they'd saved each other twice now. Once in Hawaii and now during the show. "I couldn't have done it without Dante and Jack," she said for the microphones to hear.

"Maybe, but without you, I would've dropped right in. For a second, I thought I was going to pull you in with me." It made him sick to think about it.

"No worries. I would've let go before that happened." She grinned and Brendan smiled back. His chest tightened and a huge realization slammed him like a linebacker. It didn't matter that he didn't know enough about her or that they still had to compete against each other. It didn't matter what his rational brain said, because his heart knew he loved her. Anyone who could joke after the last five minutes deserved a medal.

Or a giant flat screen television as it turned out. Along with Casey's performance, her heroism in racing to Brendan's rescue had earned her the top spot in that week's contest. As far as Brendan was concerned, no one deserved it more.

CHAPTER 15

THE POOL ACCIDENT MADE big news and the show's ratings doubled. To her surprise, Casey ended up winning that week— R&B—with Carrie, while Jack got voted out with Ryan. Carrie continued her winning streak during country week, singing one of Brendan's songs while the show said goodbye to Dante and Rihanna.

Casey couldn't believe she'd actually made it to the end and it was down to her and Brendan. She had plenty of time to think about what she'd nearly lost that night at the pool. It was hard to wrap her head around pursuing something with Brendan after the show, because her brain originally had him wired as the rebound guy. All the signs kept pointing toward him, but she never imagined finding someone so fast. She wanted time to explore, time to grow into her independence. *A good man shouldn't hinder you.* Her mother's words, which under normal circumstances might be true, didn't apply to her ex. A concept Mom never understood.

For Brendan's part, he'd made his intentions very clear. Hell, even the audience knew he wanted to see her after the show ended. Mentally cringing at the idea of the whole country—or at least the twenty million people watching the show—knowing her business, Casey took a deep breath and concentrated on this final week. Pop week. They'd already covered ballads, Broadway, rap, R&B and country so this seemed like a fitting end.

Hyper aware of Brendan following her through the house, she self-consciously glanced at her bronze, long-sleeved silk shirt, dark skinny jeans and heels. She felt pretty confident that no

121

matter how she dressed Brendan had the upper hand when it came to being the favorite. He didn't seem to realize his appeal. But maybe that was what made him *so* appealing. Dressed in a plain white T-shirt, faded blue jeans and tan work boots, Brendan was a god.

With an extra quick step, he opened the door for her and Casey walked outside. A gust of wind nearly blew her back, but she powered through it. A dozen giant palm trees swayed overhead and their fronds seemed to hold on for dear life. She quickly pulled her hair back in a low ponytail to keep it from whipping across her face for the next half hour.

"Wind is brutal today," Brendan said, securing his own long hair in a similar ponytail. His biceps bulged as he wrapped the band and Casey looked away before the cameras caught her drooling. "What do you think they have cooked up for us now?" he asked, taking longer strides to catch up and walk by her side.

"Who knows? As long as it's not anywhere near the pool." Or under a light grid. She found with every new setup that she and Brendan were forced to participate in, she looked for anything that might be considered hazardous. "Or involve any bug eating," she added.

He chuckled and the sound made her warm with awareness. "Hm…sounds like that's where you draw the line. So maybe if I eat a chocolate covered scorpion and write a half assed song this week I could still win." He didn't sound as if he had any suspicions about their close calls, so maybe she was being paranoid.

"You? Write a half-assed song?" The guy didn't know how to do that. Almost every one of his songs landed in the top two every week. "Hey, no one said anything about chocolate." She lifted a pointed index finger. "I would consider that."

He gave her a shoulder bump and the quick connection sizzled through her bloodstream. Lately any kind of touch from him sent a current of heat straight to her lady parts. He curved toward the set on their right—away from the pool, thank God—where a wall with the show logo and two chairs waited. "Looks like that's our spot."

Casey followed his lead and felt some reluctance to see the show end. As much as she despised the cameras, she'd had a chance to get to know Brendan without any sex to muddy her brain. Not that she could forget their kiss or his little exploration on the night he'd made them hot chocolate, but he hadn't come close to anything like that again. Which had been a colossal disappointment.

"Think it matters where we sit?" Casey asked as they approached the two art deco metal seats.

"They don't have our names posted anywhere, so maybe they don't care." So far, almost everything had been scripted to the detail. What time they got in the writing room, the music room, the time allotted alone in their bedrooms or the bathrooms. At times it felt more like a prison than a reality show. Brendan took the seat on their right and Casey sat next to him.

"I wonder if we can still do this out here with all the wind," Casey said over another gust. "Maybe they don't realize how strong it is."

Brendan shook his head. "I think they just like watching us suffer." Then he waved to one of the cameras in the yard since every word they said was being recorded. They had no clue how the producers put the show together around the live portions.

"You excited to finally have Seger this week?" she asked. It was an innocent question, but the second it came out of her mouth, she realized how he might think she was going to pull the rug from beneath him.

To Brendan's credit, he didn't show any sign of nervousness that she might use that card against him here in this final week. "Yeah, you've had him twice already. Did you like him?"

"Loved him. He's awesome. I can see why the girls go crazy over him. He's handsome and he can shred blindfolded." She shot him a pointed stare and went for a little dig since the producers loved this stuff. "He's great for a second place finish." She would know since she'd placed second with him on two different weeks already.

Brendan smiled at the insinuation that she was going to win this week with Carrie. But he didn't let it slide. "Let's see, how many weeks have you won?" He glanced toward the sky pretending to think about it. "One, is it? Oh, did I mention I've won twice?" He cocked his head. His playboy smile was brutally hard to resist as he leaned forward. "Shh, don't tell America," he whispered. "Oh wait, they know."

Casey smacked his leg and felt the sting in her palm. The man was hard-bodied and beautiful. "That's right," she said, rubbing her fingers. "You go ahead and get cocky, and when Carrie and I blow you and your boy, Seger, out of the water, you'll be singing a whole different tune." They were the only ones who knew just how close to the truth she was with the term *your boy*, but once again, Brendan didn't even seem to sweat the idea. He just grinned and made her heart roll over.

Another gust of wind whipped through the yard and something creaked and screeched. Casey looked behind her in time to see the set wall pull up from its supposedly secured spot in the ground. Her heart bolted into her throat and before she could take a breath to warn Brendan, he was diving for her, knocking her to the ground as the wall blew forward.

Casey tried to roll away, but Brendan's weight kept her pinned and she covered his head with her arms and hands, trying to protect him. A deafening crash sounded as the wall hit the chairs and splintered into chunks. Part of the debris landed on Brendan's back and pain shot up Casey's right hand as darkness closed in on them. The chairs had deflected some of the weight, but a big slab still landed on top of them.

Shouts of alarm drifted over the wind and pounding feet vibrated beneath her back as help came running into the set. Pinned in, Casey barely had room to budge.

"Bren—"

"Casey, you okay?" He lifted his head and his warm breath wafted against her cheek.

Her hand hurt and she felt something wet and warm slide through her fingers and down her hand. "I'm okay, are y—"

He kissed her. Check that. He didn't just kiss her. Brendan sucked the breath right out of her lungs and Casey jumped on board bullet fast. She opened her mouth wider to his questing tongue and met his fierce demand with equal abandon. He tasted cool and minty. Sexy and scrumptious. Like paradise and dreams come true. She didn't even care that he was crushing her, she loved the pressure, the heat. She wouldn't mind enjoying this kind of kiss on a regular basis. God, he knew how to set her on fire with only his mouth. She inhaled him for another few seconds until right before the men lifted the heavy wall off them. A fresh gust of wind blew debris into their faces and they flinched and turned.

Breathing hard, Brendan looked down at her, his blue eyes filled with heat and desire and everything she was currently feeling. They would've had each other's clothes off in seconds had they not been in the middle of a crowd. But the lust in eyes turned into something different as he assessed her. Something she hadn't seen in a man's eyes in way too long. Honest concern. "You sure you're okay?"

Casey nodded then noticed the blood soaking the sleeve of her shirt and in his hair. Her adrenaline spiked a second time. "Oh, my God, you're bleeding."

Brendan looked at her arm as crewmembers moved in behind Miles and two other producers. He felt his head for injuries as he moved off her. Wind whipped more debris around them. "I don't think it's me."

Casey finally got a look at her hand. A huge gash between her index and middle finger knuckles bled everywhere and made her instantly nauseous. This was sure to be in the show and only fuel her parents' argument about participating in the first place. On the other hand, there was a better than fifty-fifty chance they weren't even watching the show.

"Get the paramedics here ASAP," Miles yelled over his shoulder.

Brendan whipped off his shirt. The wire for his RF mic snagged at his waist and he stripped the base from his jeans and dropped the whole unit to the ground. He wrapped his shirt around Casey's hand. She tried to sit up, but he held her down. "Keep your hand above your heart. Try and relax," he told her.

Relax? With his six pack abs and crazy broad shoulders staring at her. She almost laughed. "No fair," she groused, trying to ignore her throbbing hand. "Taking your shirt off is going to get you more votes with the television audience."

His straight white smile obliterated any pain she was feeling. "Nothing keeping you from doing the same thing." The only way people heard that was if her mic picked it up.

"Oh, you're hilarious." Her sarcasm lacked bite as she grinned back at him. He was too damn cute. Had she not been bleeding freely—or nearly been killed—she'd have scrubbed any thoughts of keeping her distance, dragged him to a private place, and get hot and heavy for a few hours. She was totally up for trying to recreate Hawaii. "Seriously, are *you* okay?"

He nodded. "I'm fi—"

"How you feeling, Casey?" Miles stuck his head between them and burst her fantasy like a pin in an overfilled balloon. "Paramedics should be here in a couple of minutes." His gelled hair barely moved in the wind.

"I'm okay." She glanced at Brendan who kept pressure on her injured hand. "Thanks to Brendan. Again." She shot a glare at Miles since she was D.O.N.E. DONE with all the accidents.

A scowl darkened Brendan's face as he eyed Miles. "This is the third accident that could've killed one of us. Maybe one accident can happen, but not three. The safety on this set is for shit…unless you're doing some survival reality shit on purpose. We're not continuing until we find out what's going on." Oh, her mic was definitely picking up his volume now, even with the wind howling around them. Even crew members were glancing at each other nervously. Obviously Brendan was as tired of the bullshit as she was.

"Brendan, calm down," Miles said, putting up his palms in surrender. "We're almost at the end so we can't stop now. Look. I get that you're concerned and want—"

"What I want is a full-fledged investigation. I want cops, detectives, something. This is the second time Casey could've been killed and I'm not a big believer in coincidence."

Casey had never seen this side of Brendan before. She never would've pegged him for the conspiracy theory type. But she was glad to know she wasn't the only one with similar thoughts.

"C'mon," Miles said, his gaze encompassing the area, "no one could predict the wind would be blowing this hard. This was a freak thing."

"Like the light falling over Casey's head was a freak thing and the stage cracking exactly where she was dancing a couple of weeks ago? I don't buy it. For all we know, you're purposely setting us up for your fucking ratings! And if that's the case, you can bet your next paycheck that we're going to have a lawyer on your ass faster than you can say *your show is cancelled!* I guarantee whoever is behind this is watching the show, waiting for results that have nothing to do with songwriting."

That statement sent a cold chill down Casey's back? Had she really been the specific target? Sure, she was a little suspicious, but she'd been thinking about the show itself. The ratings had certainly gone up. Good ratings translated to money for the network, for the show. Casey looked over at Miles, who'd turned to confer with Karen and one of the other producers. He didn't seem too concerned that this interview wouldn't happen. Why would he be? He had incredible footage to show the country instead.

FRUSTRATION BURNED THROUGH BRENDAN like molten lava. This night had gone to hell faster than Mach speed. If he had to be honest, he'd enjoyed watching the wind blow Casey's flowing shirt against the sweet curves of her body. Maybe that was why he couldn't keep his lips off hers when she said she was all right. Except she hadn't been all right and he felt like shit. He had to do something more than watch her bleed.

Tired of waiting for the paramedics, Brendan took matters— more like Casey—into his own hands. "Let's get inside and out of this fucking hurricane," he groused. The whole concept of *the show must go on* could go in a dark closet and screw itself. Enough of the bullshit. He was done with these people.

Casey shifted to stand, but Brendan scooped her into his arms. She felt right. Like she belonged there. "Brendan, what are you doing? Put me down. I'm very capable of walking." Her stern face didn't sway him for a second and she seemed to have regained some of her color.

"I know. I just want to be safe. You've lost some blood and I don't want a gust to tip you over." He led the nervous group of executives inside, doing his best to protect Casey from flying leaves. One of the production assistants opened the door and Brendan set her down on the nearest leather sofa and glanced back to Miles, surprised he hadn't issued a few threats of his own. The asshole was probably used to lawsuits. "Are you sure someone called 911?"

The producer nodded. "The studio paramedics should be here momentarily." He'd barely finished the sentence when two uniformed men strode in from the front door. "See," Miles said, "right on cue."

Brendan had to move so the EMTs could work. Both male, they were all business as they took Casey's vital signs and assessed the nasty gash. It didn't take a genius to see her hand required stitches. A massive wave of helplessness washed over Brendan and left his gut queasy. Feeling inadequate and useless made him angry. Brought back memories he didn't want surfacing. They flashed in his head anyway. The beating he'd suffered as two men had used him for a punching bag hadn't really compared to watching his family members suffer a similar fate. He blamed himself. If he'd been more attentive when he'd first gotten into his house, if he'd done a better job of fighting off the initial attack, maybe his family wouldn't have gone through such hell.

Something hit his face and knocked him back to the present. He recognized one of his Bruce Springsteen concert T-shirts and whipped it over his head. The EMTs readied Casey for transport and Brendan insisted on going with them.

Brendan spotted the man in charge in a circle of people around them. "Listen real close, Miles. We don't come back for the last week until we're assured that this set is safe. No negotiations." Brendan didn't care if he sounded like an asshole. He might not have any recourse and he didn't know exactly what Miles would do, but he didn't care. He couldn't stand by and let something else happen to Casey. Aside from having to ride shotgun in the ambulance, he intended to stay glued to her side.

Even an ambulance ride all the way across town couldn't rid them of cameras. Two guys dressed in black with handhelds followed them to the ER doors and burned up the last of Brendan's patience. "I'm done with this shit," he murmured. Lifting Casey's shirt just high enough to unhook her RF mic from her waistband, he tossed it to one of the camera utility guys racing along with the cameraman.

"You're being awfully brave," she said. "We signed contracts saying we'd keep the mics on us at all times with the exception of the bathroom."

"A visit to the hospital supersedes the contract. Your health is nobody's business but yours." He bent toward Casey's ear as they rolled her through the doors. "Let me come in with you to a treatment room. It's going to be the only chance we get to talk without cameras on us."

"Right." Her eyes widened in understanding.

The EMTs rolled the gurney through emergency and Brendan followed as if he had every right to be there. The best part was when the ER staff forced the cameramen to stop at the double doors leading to treatment rooms.

Once in a room, a nurse came in to assess the wound and get Casey's history. The short Hispanic woman whizzed through the questions with a positive attitude and gave Brendan a good feeling about the hospital. Fifteen minutes later, she left them blissfully, finally, one hundred percent alone. After so many weeks of so many eyes on them, he almost couldn't believe it.

Brendan checked the hallway before coming back and sitting on the edge of Casey's bed. He had no clue where to start. Her eyes shone in that beautiful mix of blue and green that always amazed him. Blood stained the material covering her right arm and her ponytail had come out ages ago leaving her hair down and very sexy.

"You look so serious." She scooped her hair off her shoulders and brought it forward in one silky chunk, wincing when she tweaked her injured hand. "What's bothering you?"

A ton, but he went in order of his mental list. Glancing over his shoulder one more time, Brendan hit her with the question that had been on his mind since day one of the show. "Why didn't you tell anyone about my relationship with Seger?"

She canted her head. "Because I didn't think it had any relevance to the show. Obviously neither one of you knew the other was going to be there."

"As true as that is, how do you know for sure?"

She lifted a dark eyebrow. "You guys might be great musicians but you're shitty actors. You both nearly had coronaries when you saw each other."

Brendan took offense. "That is totally untrue," he said. "I stayed completely chill. I already knew he was going to be there after Mitch drew his name."

"Maybe you knew about him, but Seger definitely didn't know about you. His eyes got about the size of my palm, then your eyes bugged out thinking he was going to say something." She chuckled. "I think everyone else probably thought you were star struck."

Blood seeped slowly through the bandage on her hand and Brendan looked out the door to see if he could flag down a nurse. "Even so, you could've said something. We both know that failing to admit my work relationship with Seger could cost my place on the show, even though I do nothing remotely related to music when I work for him. You could win right now, by bringing it to light."

She watched him with her ocean eyes and a grin curved her lips. "What fun is that? Besides I've had Seger twice and this is your first time. It's not like you've even worked together before now. Unless maybe you were working on something together before the show started and—"

"No." Brendan was already shaking his head. "I never went to Seger with my music. Not once."

"Why?" She shook her head. "I don't get it."

Brendan lowered his voice and leaned closer. "Because I didn't want to risk my position, my job. One of the roadies approached him eight or ten months ago with his music and the next thing you know, the guy was gone."

Casey's eyes rounded. "Seger fired him?"

"I have no idea. I wasn't in the loop. I just know the guy was really excited to share his stuff and then he was gone. I never thought that working for Seger was going to be a sure ticket to working in the music industry, so when the opportunity for the show came along I didn't plan on losing it just because I'm his damn assistant. I couldn't tell him for the same reason. I didn't lie to the show about my work because I *am* a bartender. Just not a hundred percent of the time."

Casey exhaled hard and dropped her head back onto the pillow. "You know you're totally going to win, now."

Brendan smirked. "Hardly. You're the one that's going to get all the sympathy, and you might not want it, but this injury is going to get you a sympathy vote."

Casey shook her head and met his gaze, a *what the fuck* look in her eyes. "The way you carried me inside? Shirtless? All the women in America are going to vote for you. You've proved chivalry isn't dead and you did it flashing your chest. I don't stand a chance."

At least she'd noticed. "I did what any guy next to you would've done. I just happened to be the closest." Speaking of close. Brendan took a second to soak her in, knowing he had her to himself. Flashes of their night in Hawaii ticked by in his head like a silent movie. Remembering the softness of her skin, the taste of her mouth. He slipped his hand into her good one. "You have no clue how much I missed touching you. Having you in my arms." A pretty flush climbed up her cheeks. He leaned down, about to dive into a much-needed kiss, a follow up of the spontaneous lip-lock he'd given her while buried under a wall. He got a fraction away from her lips, felt her breath against his mouth and—

"The H is for hospital...not hotel," a voice said from the door.

Brendan pulled away and locked eyes with the doctor. The lean, young Asian man had a tired smile on his face and introduced himself as Dr. Hu, the plastic surgeon on call. The nurse followed him in with all the necessary equipment and he rolled a stool over to Casey's bedside and went to work. The numbing shot clearly hurt like a bitch, but she clenched her jaw at took it like a champ. Fifteen minutes later, the doctor repaired the jagged gash on her hand. Eleven stitches and a big-ass bandage later, she was deemed good to go.

Miles sent a limo to return them to the set, insisting that police had been informed and an investigation was under way. Naturally the car came attached with a cameraman shouldering a camera and sitting opposite them in the back seat. Casey remained especially quiet during the ride and Brendan's patience neared its end.

He squeezed her good hand. Screw the damn camera. "You doing all right?"

She glanced at the camera then back to him, clearly debating her next words. "I can't play the piano with this." She lifted her bandaged right hand. "Or the guitar. Or any other instrument for that matter." She had a point. It didn't seem fair for her to get this far and lose just because she couldn't write or play her music.

So how could he fix this? Simple. "What if I help you compose?"

Her eyes widened again and this time probably all of America would see it since the damn camera was pointed at them from across the seat. "If you do that, when do you work on your song with Seger?"

He lifted a shoulder. "We'll figure it out. I've already got something in mind and Seger's a talented man. It'll be fine."

"Why would you do that? This is your chance to totally win this whole thing. Why help me?"

Because he cared about her? Because no matter how they started and despite being pitted against each other, he didn't want to roll over her. If he was going to win, he wanted to beat her best. "I'm not doing that much. You still have a good hand to work with. I'll just be offering a few extra fingers to help you along." Brendan instantly thought of his fingers helping her along that night in Hawaii. The way he'd teased her clit and primed her with deep strokes. He wanted to get to that exact place now. He wanted to say screw the show and the contract and take Casey to a secluded spot where he could spend the next week touching her and tasting her and making her come.

CHAPTER 16

DISCOVERING THE WHOLE GRIP, lighting and construction departments had been fired while she spent five hours away from the set made Casey feel terrible. Apparently, there had been some massive scrambling to find a new crew on the spur of the moment.

"I'm sorry," Brendan said quietly after Miles left them alone in the production office. In a matter of minutes, they'd be getting new RF mics attached and they had about thirty seconds of privacy before cameras and sound recorded everything for the last week of the show. "I didn't know he was going to fire everyone. I just thought they'd bring in some security or something. Or maybe a couple of extra guys to make sure everything was safe before we got into a set."

"I know." Casey tried not to compare Brendan's compulsion to command the situation to Jeff's controlling nature. After everything they'd been through, he had every right to be angry and demand their safety. They just hadn't planned on so many people losing their jobs. On the other hand, they only had one more week left so it could've been worse. Honestly, if someone on the crew had been responsible for the accidents, then she was glad they had fresh faces working on the show.

Brendan was as good as his word when it came time to work. He totally helped her compose her song that week. Had she been thinking straight, she'd have realized it was a mistake. The audience was going to love him even more. He was proving how talented he was by not only helping her, but by creating his own song afterward.

The week flew by without incident. Once Carrie came into

rehearsals, Brendan spent his time with Seger and his own song. The pressure mounted as the hours ticked by.

Show night arrived and Casey's stomach churned in a mass of nerves. Though she had confidence in her song and Carrie's ability to perform it, she felt out of sorts. Not knowing Brendan's song when he was familiar with almost every note of hers made her as uneasy as a shy child in a room full of strangers. The scales were definitely out of balance.

The live show at the Lexington Theater in Hollywood started with introductions and a video recap of the last week. Because of the drama with the wall crashing down and the paramedics and ER visit, not to mention Brendan helping Casey with her song, the audience seemed more invested than usual.

What Casey didn't expect was the relationship building between them. She never would've thought that her feelings for him were on her face, but she saw it with the rest of America. She also saw that Brendan returned her feelings. It was in the way they looked at each other, the way they laughed with each other, the innocent teasing and flirting. Even in the small touches, and especially in the extra-long hugs.

Cameras had caught it all. Had they been like this from the beginning? Maybe this was the first week their feelings were so transparent because they were the only people in the house. They'd had no one else to talk to or interact with. No one that might've acted as a buffer between their raging hormones.

So much for hiding.

Casey didn't dare look at Brendan. The cameras would only catch that too.

Carrie and Seger both sang hit songs from their own albums to get the audience moving and psyched up for the show.

They'd flipped a coin a couple of hours before and Brendan had won the toss. Casey wondered if it was an omen for the night, but kept it to herself. He opted to go last, which meant she and Carrie went first with their song.

Carrie passed Brendan as he walked off to the side, and she joined Casey. They shared a hug and Casey sat behind the piano that had been rolled onto the stage behind them while the curtains were closed. Bright lights hit her from all angles and for a second she froze. Everything spilled out of her head. Her song, the notes, the words, everything. She glanced up and caught Brendan's gaze from off stage. He canted his head the slightest bit, evidently aware of her panic, but he tipped his chin ever so slightly and narrowed his eyes. Then he mouthed, *you can do it.* Maybe he didn't think cameras were on him, or maybe he didn't care. But that encouragement was all Casey needed to pull her head out of her ass and get down to business.

Screw her dry mouth and wet palms. She had a show to win.

For this performance, she'd stripped off the bulky bandages from her hand and just covered the stitches with a few layers of gauze. She prayed her stiff hand kept up with the song.

With a glance to the superstar waiting to sing her song, Casey played the opening notes and Carrie dove in with the first line.

You think you know me, but you don't.
You think you own me, but you won't.
I'm gonna spread my wings and fly.
Gonna touch the sky so high.

Her enthusiasm sucked in the crowd as they caught on to the chorus lyrics.

Get outta my way, I'm gonna make it today.
I got what I need now that I'm flying free.
I'm soaring higher than ever before.
So don't come knocking on my front door.

When Carrie started clapping her hands over her head, the audience joined in like fans at a concert stadium.

Casey couldn't have asked for a better end to her night. She had a real shot at winning this whole thing and hope flowed in her chest like a cool rushing stream. She wanted to dance and shout. She wanted to tell Jeff to suck it and fuck off.

After playing the rest of the song, she joined Carrie center stage and they bowed as the studio audience cheered wildly. There were definitely hard core Casey fans just as there were Brendan fans and she soaked in the love, relishing the applause because it was possibly the last time she was ever going to hear it.

After they'd left stage, Brendan and Seger took their places in front of the microphones. Brendan didn't seem nervous at all. In fact he looked as rock-star cool as Seger. Both wore black jeans and black boots. Seger wore a sleeveless black top that accentuated his biceps and Brendan's short sleeve rust-colored T-shirt hugged his muscled chest.

The boys were sure to get every female vote in the crowd. They were double delicious.

Brendan stood behind the synthesizer then counted out a four beat and the two of them started playing. Seger sang the first line and drew the crowd in like a funnel cloud, taking all the audience expectation and turning it into a swirling mass of enthusiasm. It didn't take long once Seger got to the chorus and belted it out.

I've got a secret and you've got to keep it.
I didn't know it then, but you grew on me when
We drew the lines in the sand, but you still gave a damn.

The crowd ate it up. Every word, every note and Casey found herself bobbing her head to the catchy beat as the synthesizer worked it's magic along with the guitar. It was a good song. A great song, and Seger knew exactly how to deliver it.

Casey's heart jackknifed as they finished to thunderous applause. Nothing left to do now but wait for the audience and judge's opinions. Her whole future could change in the next few minutes. Her wildest dreams might come true.

The show broke for a commercial break and Brendan and Seger exited the stage while crew cleared the equipment.

"You were great," Casey said as Brendan stopped in front of her. Sweat glistened on his skin and his warm smile drew her in.

"You too." He glanced around as everyone scurried to their places before they came back live. When he met her gaze, his eyes shone with the kind of emotion she'd watched on the big screen earlier. "Hey, whatever happens, just know that I think you're really amazing. I wouldn't have traded the last six weeks for anything." He glanced at her bandaged hand. "Well, maybe I'd trade that." He grinned again and stroked a gentle thumb down her cheek. "You're crazy talented. I've loved being around that kind of creativity."

Casey felt her cheeks flush. She smacked his arm to keep from getting too emotional. "Back at ya, big guy."

"Brendan, Casey, to your marks," the AD said. Randy Hall had been working in variety and live television for thirty years. Nothing seemed to set him off and his calm, positive direction always grounded Casey on show nights.

Brendan slipped his guitar strap over his head and handed the instrument to the prop man. He took Casey's hand and together they walked to center stage to face the music. It was all coming to an end after six weeks. Six weeks of unbelievable pressure, of cameras watching nearly every move, of hearing nearly every word out of her mouth and seeing every facial expression.

Either way, in a matter of minutes, she was going to have a whole new life. It was either live her dreams or go back to her new apartment and figure out a new game plan. With no boyfriend, or fiancé. Maybe making it this far still assured her some type of gig with someone in the music industry. Maybe a producer or singer would give her a shot.

Brendan squeezed her hand and winked. She saw no sign of nerves or anxiety. Just a man happy to be standing in front of millions of people and ready to accept whatever answer came his way. He had a lot more confidence in his future than she did with hers. Of course, if he lost, he still had Seger in his corner, still had a shot at making music his livelihood.

She had to stay positive. Somebody out there might want to work with her. Getting this far had to prove her versatility with music. Worst case scenario, she went back to school another year—provided her job still existed—until she found another route to her dream. Teaching kids wasn't terrible. It just wasn't her dream.

The announcer introduced a return from the commercials and their host, Steve, recapped the past weeks and tonight's songs one more time. He talked about the audience tabulations and the thousands of phone calls that had been taken during the show and then he handed it over to the judges.

Sara Bareilles voted for Brendan. Casey's heart thudded loudly between her ears. The second judge, Garth Brooks also voted for Brendan, and Casey felt the win slip from her grasp. The third judge, Sarah McLachlan voted for her and kept her in the running for a few more seconds. The last judge, Rob Thomas kept them in suspense before voting for her as well and Casey blinked away the sting in her eyes. It wasn't over yet, and knowing the judges were split gave her a little reprieve.

Steve asked for the audience tabulations and as the numbers scrolled on a giant board overhead, the audience cheered wildly for their favorite. They screamed her name and Brendan's name. It was a free-for-all.

The numbers came up and Steve's co-host for the show, Ashley Argota, handed him a piece of paper with the winner's name. Her long dark hair glistened in the bright stage lights and her brilliant smile always brightened Monday nights. They only saw Ashley during the live show at the theater. Casey remembered her on television growing up. Ashley had parlayed her child actor status into a career in network television, films and music. Casey could only hope for a fraction of her success.

Steve smiled as he looked from the paper and glanced between them. "The winner of the first season of *Write Your Ticket*, the one who gets five hundred thousand dollars cash and a record contract is..." The crowd went silent and drums beat a fast rhythm that matched the thump of her heart. Casey thought she might pass out before the winner was announced. She concentrated on Brendan's tight grip on her hand.

Steve held up the paper. "Brendan St. John!"

Casey stood frozen for a second before plastering on a smile. Balloons and confetti streamed from huge containers above them and she barely registered the roar of the crowd and the pounding music as the band played Brendan's song. Brendan grabbed her in a massive hug and held her tight. "It's okay, it's okay," he kept saying it in her ear like it might change how she felt.

Like a loser. But if she had to lose, at least she lost to Brendan. He deserved to win.

Told her she couldn't do this. She made a fool out of herself. Out of me. The words Jeff would be thinking and saying to anyone around him right about now. She knew they weren't true, but they were there anyway.

I'm not taking you back when you lose either. Not that she wanted Jeff back, because she didn't. It was just another reminder that she *had lost.* He'd been right and that made her sick.

A tear flew down her cheek and Casey prayed no one saw it. "I'm so happy for you," she managed. "Congratulations. You deserve it."

"You do too, Case." He pulled away and looked her in the eyes, cupping her face with his warm hands. "You deserve it too."

But she hadn't won. "I expect great things from you." She gave him a watery smile, trying to keep the heartache and failure buried deep, trying to keep positive for Brendan.

Seger closed in and Casey backed up to give him room. The guys bear hugged and Carrie showed up to hug her, then Brendan. In a few seconds, people filled the stage, congratulating Brendan and wrapping their arms around her.

It was over. She had nothing to show for her six weeks aside from the experience itself. Her life wouldn't change the way she wanted. Her dreams weren't coming true. Not yet. A knot of despair lodged in her throat and slowly grew. Fighting back the emotion that strangled her took everything Casey had.

WHEN THE RED LIGHTS blinked off and the live show ended, Brendan found himself in a tornado of well-wishers, including his family, the production staff, the contestants and celebrities who hadn't made it to the end—with the exception of Mitch—and even people he didn't know.

The new sound guy took off his RF mic and although the equipment barely weighed anything, it felt as if a thousand pounds had been lifted from his shoulders. He craned his head, looking for Casey, hoping to have a real conversation with her. Somehow, he ended up in a packed room with people milling about, talking loudly and reliving the past six weeks. Wading through the throng was like swimming upstream in a wild current.

When he finally made it out to the hallway, someone snagged his arm and yanked him sideways through a door. Stumbling into the gray-tiled men's room, Brendan looked up to see Seger, arms crossed over his chest, feet spread apart. The hard look in his eyes didn't match the hug he'd given Brendan on camera a few minutes ago.

"Why the hell didn't you tell me you're a songwriter? A musician?" Seger spread his arms. "Why the fuck did I have to find out like this?"

Brendan winced at his volume. "Have you been this mad at me since day one?" he asked, almost amused at his boss's attitude. He rarely saw Seger this pissed off and he'd never been the recipient of his wrath. "Because I didn't realize what a great actor you are too."

"Quit sucking up. You didn't leave me much of a choice, Bren." Seger ran a hand through his short hair. "So spill. Why the secret?"

There was no way to ease around his fears and at this point he had nothing to lose. "Honestly...I was worried you'd think my songs sucked and you'd let me go. I kind of like my job."

"Liked. Past tense," Seger replied. He leaned against the sink and looked up at the ceiling. "Your life now belongs to Miles Griffith. I don't know what your contract says, but I'm guessing he owns you for about the next seven to ten years." He lifted one dark eyebrow for confirmation.

Brendan nodded. "Ten," he mumbled. Actually it was seven albums, and Brendan doubted his ability to deliver that much music in ten years, which meant he'd be indebted to Miles even longer. Miles also received a portion of Brendan's royalties from every song. Basically, if he was successful, he would pay for his five-hundred-thousand-dollar cash prize. He could make that money go a long way and had no plans to blow it all in a massive spending spree. "But I'll have a career." Please God, let him have a career. If this show was any indication, then he really did have what it took to make a living writing and playing music.

Seger nodded slowly. "Oh, you'll definitely have a career. Miles is going to make millions because of you." Nothing Seger said could've made him feel more validated and Brendan's chest expanded with hope.

"Really? Millions?"

Rolling his eyes, Seger shoved from the sink and all but growled. "I can't believe you didn't come to me first."

"I didn't think you wanted your employees begging you to look at their material." Brendan wasn't sure if he should even mention the roadie, but at this point it didn't matter. "I remember when Cameron approached you with his stuff and the next thing I knew he was gone."

Seger's eyes narrowed. "Cameron?"

"Yeah. That roadie guy last year. Cameron."

"Dude." His boss looked up and shook his head at the ceiling. "You thought I'd fire a guy because he showed me his songs? Seriously?"

Shit. Brendan knew a reality check when it hit him and this one bowled him over faster than that set wall last week. "So...that's not what happened?"

"First of all, I appreciated the bravery it took for him to show me his songs. Not everyone gets to a place where they're comfortable sharing their stuff." He gave Brendan a knowing look. "But ultimately, he didn't really have what it takes. I mean he didn't play any instruments and his songs were more like poetry with never-ending lyrics. He didn't have a catchy hook or decent bridge. The guy just wasn't a songwriter, but I didn't fire him for it. He got a call right after we met that his mother was in a serious car accident and he bolted. I didn't fire him."

Brendan wiped his hands down his face. Why the hell had he listened to the rumors? He could've saved himself months of aggravation not to mention the whole process of this damn show. Although the extra five-hundred grand would hold him over for a long time, so that made it worthwhile.

"Correct me if I'm wrong," Seger said, folding his arms again. "But weren't you ineligible to be part of this because you work in the music industry?"

"I don't work in the music industry," Brendan replied hotly. "I work for you, as your assistant. How is taking care of your VIPs at concerts and bringing you Starbucks and picking up your dry cleaning translate to working in the music industry? That's a stupid rule that doesn't apply to me." Seger opened his mouth, but Brendan cut him off. "They would've held it against me anyway, so

I didn't tell them. Hey, I also work as a bartender. Shouldn't that count for something?" He took a deep breath. "I didn't notice you saying anything to me about the show before we started so I wasn't the only one keeping secrets."

"I wasn't allowed to tell anyone I was one of the celebrities, and that makes no difference anyway since I'm *supposed* to be in the recording industry," Seger said, gesturing to himself.

Point taken. Brendan ran his tongue along his teeth as gratitude eased his temper. "Well, thanks for not rattin' me out. I wasn't sure if you were going to say anything when you saw me."

Seger pointed a finger at him. "I have never been, nor will I ever be a narc."

His boss was loyal to a fault and Brendan always appreciated that. He'd seen him defend his wife when fans had pushed her aside to get his picture. He'd watched him send money when a crewmember had been hurt rigging one of the road shows. He didn't do a lot of talking and tended to let his actions speak for him. "Thanks, boss."

Snorting, Seger shook his head. "I can't believe I have to wait ten years to do a song with you."

Those words totally stoked Brendan and another shot of adrenaline pumped him up. "You don't *have* to," he said. No reason he couldn't convince Miles into releasing tonight's song as his first single.

"Yeah, I do. Being on this show was one thing, but my record label is never going to get in bed with Miles. I'm not giving him God knows how much percent of one of my songs because you happen to be attached to it." He headed to the door. "Just save me a few good ones, kid. I'll be looking forward to it." He stopped and turned slowly, his hazel eyes narrowing. "Shit. I need a new assistant now."

Brendan's affirmative showed in his wide grin.

"Shit," Seger muttered then walked out the door.

Brendan took a second to run a hand through his hair before facing the mob outside. A quick check assured his prosthetic ear had weathered the night so far. Winning meant he'd be wearing this thing ninety-seven percent of the time from now on. Worth it.

Next on the agenda: find Casey. He had to get her alone for a few minutes, but how?

Family.

Pulling his phone from his back pocket, he texted Eric. *Find Casey. Take her to… Where?* Where could they meet and have a few quiet minutes? Outside? No, they'd be found in a hot second. He looked around the men's room and shrugged. What the hell…it worked for Seger. *Bring her to the men's room and stand guard outside while we talk.* He hit Send and waited a few seconds, then saw the little bubbles indicating his brother's reply.

She's talking to her sister. Looks pretty devastated.

"Shit," he muttered. He typed back. *Bring her now! Need to talk to her.*

Don't get ur panties in a wad. Gimme a sec. Be there ASAP.

The longest four minutes of Brendan's life ticked by until the door finally pushed open and Casey peeked inside. Brendan heard his brother's voice. "Go ahead. I won't let anyone in."

Casey saw him and looked everywhere *but* him as she closed the door behind her.

Winning suddenly seemed very superficial. Nothing really mattered except the woman in front of him. He took the few steps that put him closer, reached for her hands and pulled her in, wrapping her up in his arms and holding her tightly against him.

At first she seemed reluctant, but then she held on tight. So tight that fresh emotion clogged Brendan's throat as he buried his face in her neck and smelled the sweet, fresh flowery scent of her. Before he thought too much about what he should or shouldn't do, should or shouldn't say, he pulled back enough to lay his mouth on hers. He meant to kiss her softly. Intended to start slow and ease into it, but the second she opened up to him, he lost sight of what he planned to do. Holding her head steady, he kissed her with all the pent up frustration, happiness and madness that coursed through his veins. He wanted her with a desperation that seized his gut. She stayed with him, giving back as good as she got, stroking her tongue against his, running her hands over his chest and around his neck to pull him even more closely against her. She was lightning in a bottle, fire in his arms.

Someone pounded on the door and shocked them both back to reality.

"Bren," his brother called from the hallway, "you might want to hurry it up in there."

"Are you okay," Brendan asked her, ignoring his brother. He searched her eyes, hoping for a positive answer when deep down he knew she had to be crushed.

"I'll be fine." She stepped back and rubbed her knuckles against her lips as if kissing him might've been a mistake. "I'm really happy for you." She quit looking at him and gestured toward the door. "You should go. I'm sure everyone is looking for you." More pounding on the door confirmed it.

He stepped toward her, hating that she seemed to be putting him at a distance. "Look, I know it's going to be busy and crazy for the next week or two, but I need to see you outside of this circus. You know what I mean?" No way in hell was he losing her a second time. Once had been plenty.

She nodded. "I know. We'll stay in touch. It won't be hard to find you." She gave him a lopsided grin, but still avoided eye contact. It was like jumping out of a plane with no parachute. The writing was on the wall.

Brendan took a few steps that brought them closer together. "I'm serious. You and me. Taking it from where we left off in Hawaii. I want to see you, Case. As often as I can."

More pounding on the door wrecked the quiet conversation. "You're on borrowed time, brother," Eric called from the hall.

"Seeing each other is going to be kind of hard while you're on your victory tour," Casey said, glancing toward the door. Translation: You're on your own.

"I know. But it's only going to be for a week or two. I'm not letting you get away, Case. Just remember that." She might've left him once, but he knew how to find her now.

A ruckus broke in the hallway and the sound of Danny's voice carried through the walls. "Get off him, asshole!"

"Shit," Brendan hissed, heading for the door. Danny wouldn't hesitate to jam his fist into someone's face. He didn't have nearly the amount of patience as Eric did. "Time's up." He looked back at Casey even as he heard the shoving match in the hallway. "I'm serious. We stay in touch." He opened the door to find his brothers holding back a handful of show and network executives alike with security headed toward them. *Great.* "I'm here, I'm here." Two seconds later, the crowd swallowed him like a small fish in a bowl full of piranhas.

THE NEXT WEEK WAS a whirlwind for Brendan. Forced to come out of his comfort zone, he did every talk show known to man. Mornings, midday and late night. He talked to women, men, and tag teams. He answered the same questions until he was blue in the face when what he really wanted was to be spending time with Casey, writing music and getting down to the reason he went through this whole shitstorm.

The show flew him to New York, Chicago and Texas then back to New York before coming home again. Casey hadn't picked up or returned any of his calls and he was ready to call Blake and take advantage of his brother's PI skills to track her down. Yeah, so maybe he'd called her at a few bad times, but the fact that she'd never called him back rubbed him as raw as a road-rash. As each day passed he got surlier and surlier, and winning the damn show hadn't turned into everything it should've been.

He'd just walked into his apartment—exhausted, pissed and hurt—when his phone rang. He hadn't had five minutes of privacy since winning the show and every time his phone buzzed his hopes soared that Casey was finally returning a call.

Nope. Again, it wasn't her and his anger and hurt balled up in his chest like it had all week long. Miles's number flashed on the screen.

"Hey, Miles," Brendan said, tossing his bag toward his room and heading for the kitchen. "What's up?"

"What's up?"

Brendan froze at his tone. He was one pissed off motherfucker.

"I'll tell you what's up, you little shit." The slam hit Brendan like a four ton anvil. "You're out, that's what's up. You lied on your application, which disqualifies you from winning. I can't believe the amount of money I spent flying you across the fucking country, the time my company spent booking you on every fucking talk show that matters and you didn't think we'd find out that you lied about working in the music industry!"

"But I didn't! I—"

"Save it! You're no bartender! You worked for Seger Hughes! That's music!"

Something ripped over the phone and it may as well have been Brendan's heart. He never thought it would happen like this. He'd made a plan this past week. Had a direction and a way to make his life exactly what he wanted.

"That was your fucking contract and the money that went with it. You're back to being a nobody, kid. Congratulations." The phone went dead and Brendan stared at the blank screen. A sick knot filled his throat and his stomach plummeted to the floor. How had Miles found out? Who had told him? Not that it mattered now.

He'd just kissed away a half million dollars and potentially...a future in music.

CHAPTER 17

CASEY PLOPPED DOWN ON her sofa with a big bowl of popcorn and channel surfed on the flat screen television from the karaoke competition. She settled on a rerun of a DIY show. Someone was always getting a brand new house or spectacular new landscaping. No losers on those shows. Nope. Everyone came out a winner. The homeowners got a new place or space and the show got ratings. A win-win. Unlike her experience. She'd been so close to having it all.

For the past week the phone had been ringing non-stop. The first few days, she'd answered, but soon she realized it wasn't producers calling her to make music, it was news organizations asking about how it felt to lose the biggest new show of the year. She hadn't picked up any calls since, with the exception of her sister. She hadn't even bothered listening to a dozen voicemails after hearing the first few. Zoe hadn't lectured her or given her the patented *it's going to be okay* response. Casey waited for someone to want her for her music and no one did. The phone quit ringing and she needed an adjustment period. She needed to let the laundry stack up and dishes sit in the sink. She needed to focus on absolutely nothing, then maybe figure out how the hell she could still realize her dream.

She'd been so focused on the show that breaking up with Jeff hadn't really hit her. Not that she would've changed her mind. But with nothing to look forward to, she felt...lost.

Ignoring Brendan's texts and calls had made her sick to her stomach. She wasn't avoiding him maliciously; it was just hard knowing he was living the life she craved. She stuffed popcorn in her mouth, hating how much she disliked herself and drowning in guilt. She'd tried answering a few of his texts, but nothing sounded right. She either sounded depressed or fake. Brendan deserved better. He had a new life and new responsibilities. Was he loving it? Was he adjusting? Did he miss her as much as she missed him? She could find out if she just answered his damn call. Her chest got tight as the monumental size of her mistake dawned on her. She shouldn't have cut him off. How would she feel if he'd done the same thing to her? God, she was an idiot. She sat up. It wasn't too late. She could fix this. She'd call him right now.

She chomped on a last mouthful of popcorn as she reached for her phone on the coffee table. It rang before she got to it. Checking the screen, she recognized the number from the studio. Why would they be calling? Did they want to do some kind of follow-up segment with the big loser? She mentally smacked herself. She had to quit doing that to herself. It was as if Jeff still occupied a place in her brain and berated her.

That had to stop. Pronto.

Something told her this was one phone call she should take. "Hello?"

"Casey, it's Miles. How are you?"

She swallowed her popcorn and had tons of answers to that question. None of which were appropriate to say. The woman on TV covered her face when she saw her *beautiful new home* and Casey used the remote and lowered the volume. "Getting used to the real world again. How about you?"

"Funny you should say that about the real world," he said. "You won't believe what I'm about to tell you."

It couldn't get much worse than losing the show. She looked around her filthy apartment and pretty much figured this was as rock bottom as it got considering she didn't drink or do drugs. "Okay…"

"Due to unforeseen circumstances, you have just been crowned the new winner of *Write Your Ticket*."

Funny how her brain thought he said she'd won the show. Even her pulse revved faster. "I'm sorry. The line broke up and I didn't hear you."

"Brendan's out. You're in." Casey's brain froze as Miles

rambled. It took a second to hear his words. "...to make the announcement as soon as we get our ducks in a row. It's going to mean you'll be on the road doing most of the shows Brendan did last week, plus a few that he didn't. There's going to be a hell of a shitstorm so the first thing you need to do is come in so we can get our stories straight."

Her mouth went stone dry. "Whoa, whoa, whoa! You're talking way too fast, Miles." Almost as fast as her erratic heartbeat. She switched the phone to her other ear. "Why is Brendan out?"

"The little shithead isn't a bartender. He works in the music industry...as Seger Hughes's assistant, no less. The media is going to be all over us when they find out, but we don't have a choice. There's no way to keep it under wraps and our rules are very clear."

All those weeks Brendan and Seger had been on the show and nothing had happened. Why now? "How did you find out?" Her pulse beat so fast she thought she might pass out if she stood up. What if Brendan thought she spilled the beans? She hadn't and her sister and best friend assured her they wouldn't. Which meant it came from someone else. But who?

"We got an anonymous tip and we checked it out. Good thing we did. I can't imagine how much worse it would've been if the media had found out before we did. This way, we can control the fall out. At least most of it. So... You busy right now? Can you come in and go over the schedule for next week?"

"What?" Cool air hit the whites of Casey's eyes as she stared ahead blindly.

"Have you listened to anything I've said? You're the new winner. You get the contract and the money."

The rush of winning landed like a lit match in a pool. It fizzled out instantly. She'd won at Brendan's expense. She was still second place when it came to talent. How was Brendan right now? He had to be feeling ten times worse, because he'd been handed the prize then stripped of it.

"What did you say to Brendan? Have you told him he's out yet?"

"Hell yes, I told him. That little prick cost me thousands. Hey, don't cry any tears for that asshole. He's going to land on his feet because he's got Seger Hughes in his corner, not to mention half of the country. Back to you. Can you come down? We've got a ton of work to do. We need to set you up with a stylist before we send you out, coordinate schedules, yada, yada."

She looked down at her comfortable holey jeans and stained T-shirt, then at her filthy apartment. A wash of embarrassment heated her cheeks despite knowing Miles couldn't see any of it. "Um...I, okay. I guess I can be there in an hour."

"Great. I'll leave a drive-on pass at the gate. See you then." Miles disconnected before she got another word out and her screen faded to black. She glanced around her apartment. A dream. It had to be a dream. She kicked her coffee table and yelped at the instant burn in her big toe.

Nope. Not a dream.

Someone knocked at the door. She wasn't expecting anyone. Hobbling toward the door, she tossed a discarded sweatshirt and pair of sneakers toward the hallway in an attempt to pick up. She looked through the peephole. Brendan stood in a black and gray baseball jersey and faded jeans, his hands on his lean hips. He looked pissed and put out and her heart shot into her throat. She shut her eyes. No, no, no. Maybe he was a mirage. She opened them again, but he was still there.

"Casey, open up. I know you're in there."

How the hell had he found out where she lived?

Dammit. She may have told him they'd see each other after the show, but how was she supposed to look him in the eye after the phone call she just got? She'd left him without a good-bye in Hawaii, avoided him for the past week and now she'd stolen his win from the show, not that she had any control over that. She'd questioned his right to be there from the first day, but his words from breakfast always drifted in her head. *I'm the whatever guy.* His job had sounded very non-music-like. Obviously just because she didn't have a problem with it didn't mean anyone else did. "I'm coming, I'm coming." God, what was she going to say to him?

She opened the door wide. "Look, I'm really—"

Two shots rang out at the same time Brendan stumbled forward. Blood sprayed her face and something pulled her hair. Casey practically caught him as fear erupted in her chest. A scream lodged in her throat as Brendan's weight took her down to the floor. It all seemed to happen in slow motion.

His weight shifted off her as he rolled onto his back. More shots dinged the floor and flew over their heads. Glass sprayed from her big windows and Casey kept an arm over her head. One glance told her Brendan was in trouble. His wide eyes stared at the ceiling, his breathing harsh.

"Brendan? Bren?" *Shit, shit, shit!* Her pulse hammered faster as bullets continued to spray the room. Casey finally took action by kicking the door shut. They still needed to get out of the line of fire. "We have to move," she yelled. Nothing penetrated his haze. "Brendan! Come on!" She tried to drag him, but he weighed a ton. Finally she grabbed the edge of the entryway carpet and pulled with everything she had. Sweat plastered her T-shirt to her skin as she struggled for each inch. "Help me, Bren! You have to help me!"

Finally, Brendan started using his legs to help propel them back toward the kitchen and away from the bullets. "That's it! That's it. This way." Blood was quickly eating away at the material on his shoulder, but Casey took it one problem at a time. Once on the linoleum, she pulled Brendan's cell phone from his pocket since hers was still on the coffee table, and punched 911.

Every one of her nerves shook with paralyzing fear as she spoke to the dispatcher. The shooting stopped, but not before all her windows had been busted and her front door looked like Swiss cheese. Blood flowed from Brendan's shoulder and Casey crawled to the dishwasher and yanked a dishcloth from the handle. On her way back, she noticed drops of blood splattered on her old beige floor, but Brendan hadn't moved from his spot under the counter separating the kitchen and the den. That could only mean one thing. "Shit!" she hissed when she saw the blood dripping from her hair. "Dammit!" She felt the scrape along her scalp. Couldn't have been too bad since she didn't even realize it was there. "We need help, now!" she told the operator. "Cops, ambulance. All of it. ASAP!" She set the cloth on Brendan's shoulder and applied pressure.

He gritted his teeth and his body went even more rigid. Casey put the phone down, but left the line open. "Bren? Brendan, can you hear me?" Sweat slicked his skin and tears blinded Casey. "Brendan!" She practically screamed his name. "Look at me! It's Casey! Look at me!" She shook his good shoulder, trying to get his attention. He was so pale, so out of it, which didn't make sense with the amount of blood he'd lost. Small tremors shook his body with every breath. "Please, Brendan. Please," she whispered.

Eerie silence settled over the apartment until faint footsteps crunched on broken glass near the front door. Casey covered her mouth, holding back the anguish and fear that bubbled in her chest and threatened to leak out in a terrified wail. She needed to do something besides sit here like a carnival duck. She grabbed the small dining room table and flipped it, creating a barricade in the doorway, just as a new round of bullets whizzed through the front windows.

Brendan glanced up and blinked. Then his eyes widened. "Case?" He barely got the word out and he looked around the kitchen, then at her. "What's—"

Casey reached for him as the wood above her head splintered. She shrieked and ducked. The gunman had to be right at the far window to get that angle.

"Move! Move!" Brendan moved into a low crouch and pushed her deeper into the kitchen, oblivious to his injury. "Stay fucking down!" His brutal grip on her arm scared her as much as the bullets. "What happened? What's happening?"

Casey had no clue other than the obvious. At least Brendan seemed to have gotten past his trance. "He's at the front door. We need to get out of here! My room's that way." She pointed straight across the open living room.

"He'll pick us off in a second. Stay here!"

Casey grabbed him before he moved. "You can't go that way either. It's just as dangerous!"

"I'm going to do what I have to if it means you're safe."

Fresh bullets crashed into the apartment and Brendan covered her. Wailing sirens in the distance got louder. More crunching glass and fading footsteps had them listening intently.

"Maybe he left," Casey said, taking in a ragged breath.

"I'll check."

"No!" Casey grabbed him. "Just wait for the police. They're on the way."

"I'm not going to wait for some asshole to break the door down and shoot us!" He glanced toward the door and took something out of his boot. "Don't move. Stay here."

Frustration and fear tangled in her chest like strangling ivy. She couldn't let him check it out alone and moved to follow him.

"What the fuck, Casey! Did you not hear me a second ago? Stay the fuck here!"

His tone made her jump. It was enough to be shot at, but it was another thing to be yelled out. "Fine. You want to check it out? Go! Go check it out! Be the fucking man!" She sat in her spot, angry, shaking from head to toe, and still scared as hell. Blood continued to drip from her hair and she reached for a clean dishcloth in the drawer overhead and put it against her scalp. A shock of pain exploded like the bullets a few minutes ago. "Shit!" Dammit, that hurt! She took the cloth away from her head to check the amount of blood.

"Keep pressure on that," Brendan ordered as he reentered the kitchen. As if he didn't have his own injury to worry about. No, he had to tell *her* what to do.

First her parents, then Jeff and now Brendan. When would people quit ordering her around? She put the towel back against her head, pissed that the wound required it.

The shooting had stopped, but who knew if the psycho had left for good.

Brendan crouched next to her, blood seeping down his shirt. "I think he's gone."

"You're bleeding all over the place. Would you just sit down. The police will be here any second." Thankfully the blaring sirens made an honest woman out of her.

She pressed the cloth he'd abandoned to his shoulder and he winced. "Sorry," she mumbled. The first of many to be sure. She squashed the urge to ask if it hurt—because of course it did—and searched for something else to say. "So just now…you were kind of zoned out. Was that just shock or something?"

He avoided her gaze as he sat next to her. "Yeah. Shock."

Bogus. He really was a shitty actor… A shitty liar too. Fine, he didn't want to come clean and she didn't plan to press him.

Brendan shifted and winced again. He had very little color in his face and despite the tone in his voice, he didn't look that great. He made it hard to stay mad at him for yelling at her the way he did.

Even though he sounded a lot like Jeff, she refused to compare the two. This was a dangerous situation, and Brendan was clearly beyond stressed. Casey clenched her jaw hard enough to crack a walnut, but said nothing.

A few tense minutes passed before sirens got louder and stopped in front of her building. Cops didn't have too much trouble finding her apartment. The bullet holes gave them away.

"In here!" Casey called as pounding feet got closer. "We need help."

The cops went into rescue mode, making sure paramedics and ambulances were on the way. She explained how quickly it happened. A couple of the officers recognized them from the show, but other than that, no one paid any special attention. A few minutes later more sirens blared outside just before two gurneys rolled over the threshold and they were each strapped into one.

"You sure the coast is clear?" Brendan asked.

"We're canvassing the neighborhood," one officer said. "We've got more units on the way."

"Take me out first," Brendan said. "I want to make sure Casey's safe."

Just like Jeff. No one was allowed to hurt her, but him. The pain in her head intensified. Casey pressed her fingers on her forehead and tried to think clearly. *Be fair. He's not Jeff.* So many things raced in her head and she couldn't make sense of any of it. She was pissed off at getting shot and having to face Brendan with the show mess between them and angry at the way he spoke to her. Still, the sane part of her brain screamed out loud. *I didn't give you away.* She wanted to tell him, positive that was the reason he'd knocked on her door in the first place, but couldn't say a word with all these people around.

They went to the hospital in two different ambulances. Casey psyched herself up for the inevitable confrontation. It seemed as if the shit between them just kept piling higher and higher and she didn't know how to clean it up. Or *if* she wanted to clean it up. At the hospital, they were each whisked into their own treatment room. One of the officers from the scene came in and took her statement. Not that she had much to tell. It didn't take long and he left soon after.

The nurse—Peter, a thirty-something guy in green scrubs and with a dark goatee—actually had to shave a small chunk of her head to treat the wound. Had the bullet been a fraction more to the right she probably wouldn't be alive to talk about it. That news sobered her pretty friggin' fast. So did the mountain of a headache that throbbed behind her eyes. She was pretty damn tired of emergency room visits and white sterile hospital walls.

"How's Brendan," she asked as the nurse readied some nasty looking instruments on a small silver table. A needle and a big syringe made her stomach queasy.

"He the one you came in with? Guy with the shoulder injury?" He glanced at her.

"Yeah. Is he okay?"

"I'll check on him for you as soon as I'm done here. He was alert when I passed by his room. Seems pretty tough."

He was tough. One of the toughest men she'd ever met. He deserved some slack. "He was bleeding a lot." What if the bullet had hit an artery or major vein? God, how often had he tried to protect her, tried to keep her safe in the short time she'd known him?

"Yeah, well, bullet wounds tend to bleed. Not surprising. But he's young and strong. He'll probably bounce back without too many problems." He leaned closer, peering at her scalp. "This is going to sting."

Whatever antiseptic he used on her scalp burned like a lightning strike and Casey gasped and pulled away. "Ouch! Jeez!" She didn't think her headache could get worse. Wrong.

"Sorry about that. Just need to clean this up. Most of the bleeding has stopped, but it's still oozing enough. I think the doctor will probably want a stitch or two in this."

Naturally. Because she couldn't catch a break. "Really? I need stitches?" She'd finally gotten the stitches removed from her hand a few days ago and now this.

"Just a couple. Small ones. Just think of it as something for you to write a song about."

BRENDAN KEPT AN EYE on the hallway, hoping to spot Casey in case she got out before him. Despite being totally pissed that she'd left him out in the cold all week, he was all kinds of whipped because he hated not knowing her condition…almost as much as he hated blacking out after getting shot.

The white treatment walls closed in on him and he squeezed his eyes shut. The same memory assaulted him. *Lying on a cold basement floor with his wrists handcuffed behind his back and his shoulders burning hot from fatigue. He couldn't move, could barely take a breath without fire eating his chest. Pain consumed him from everywhere. The blood caked along his neck and shoulder itched something fierce while his ear throbbed like a relentless drum in his head.*

He wasn't sure what brought him out of it. Casey's screaming or the gunshots…maybe both. But his shoulder pain hadn't mattered once he saw her long hair dripping blood.

The whole thing had been triggered when the bullet had slammed into his shoulder and brought back the same burning agony. Casey probably thought he was nuts. How long had he been frozen like that? Instead of coming to her rescue, he'd folded like a useless puppet.

He also didn't like the way they'd left things when the police came in and they'd been taken to the hospital. It reminded him of Hawaii. The way her gaze hardened and her jaw tightened. She was pissed. Well, that made two of them.

He still hadn't talked to her about the show. He didn't really believe she'd gone to the producers about his job with Seger, but he had to ask. Just because they had some serious bone melting attraction didn't mean he knew her or what she was capable of. The rational part of him understood this, but the part that had serious feelings for her refused to believe she would've outed him at this point.

On top of it all, he really wanted to know who the hell was shooting at him and why? Or was it someone after Casey?

Shit! Of course it was someone after Casey. Whoever had tried to kill her during the show was now intending to finish the job. Had anything been attempted during the week he'd been gone? Was it coincidence that he happened to be there at the same time? Did someone want them both dead?

Just like his brother, Blake, Brendan didn't believe in coincidence. Thinking his brother's name actually conjured the man himself and his twin stepped into the room.

"Dude!" Blake took in the bandage on his shoulder and his eyebrows slanted in worry. "You okay?" His concern went beyond the obvious. The implication was written on his face. He put his right hand out and Brendan clasped it in their usual bro greeting.

Brendan had worked hard to heal from his beating and abduction—both physically and mentally—and the whole family worried about him. He was the baby after all even if it was only by four minutes. He may have taken the worst of it, but the whole family had been traumatized. Convincing them that he really was all right seemed like a never-ending job. "Don't freak out. I'm okay." Or was he? What the hell had happened to him tonight? A flashback? Sure he'd had nightmares about the whole thing, but the whole family did too. He wasn't alone on that. But tonight was something he hadn't experienced before. Like living a nightmare over again.

Blake closed his eyes. After a long sigh, he dove right in. "What the hell happened? I left a message with Mom and Dad, so I'm sure they'll be here as soon as they get it. Eric and Danny are on the way, too, and Jess made me promise to text as soon as I saw you." Blake started punching his phone. Neither one of them wanted the fallout of ignoring their big sis.

Brendan tried to find a comfortable spot on the bed, obviously an impossible feat, since any movement sent pain zinging down his arm. "At the wrong place at the wrong time." He told his brother about the incident—omitting his little episode—and was surprised when Blake pulled out a small pad and started taking notes.

"I'll talk to Troy, see if we can keep apprised of the investigation. The boss will definitely be able to hook us up." It didn't hurt to have the services of one of the best private investigators—and his resources—available at any time.

"That'd be great. We don't know anything yet. If it was one

guy or more than one. I know this has to do with the accidents that happened on set. If there was someone out to get Casey during the show, they may still be at it."

"Speaking of Casey..." Blake lifted a dark eyebrow. "Did you talk to her about the show?"

"Never got the chance. Got shot almost as soon as she opened the door." It made him sick to think someone had been waiting for her. Whoever it was would've had an unobstructed view if she'd opened the door to leave. She'd have been dead before she hit the ground. Brendan's stomach knotted again.

"So what's the damage to your shoulder?" Blake asked, gesturing to the bandage.

"Bullet went in and out clean. I should be fine with some physical therapy." He shook his head. "Fucking pisses me off that someone can just fucking do that. Again." Old anger at being a victim rose up like a rattler waving its ugly tail. Brendan could've sworn he was past the rage, but apparently not.

"Easy, easy," Blake said.

No one knew better than Blake how debilitated and helpless he felt right now. His brother had been through his own repeat of hell over a year ago.

"Can you get out of here tonight?" Blake asked. "Be ready. Mom and Dad are going to want you home, and I'm not talking about our apartment."

"Yeah, I know. The doctor hasn't said anything yet. I think he's on the fence because I lost a decent amount of blood." He worried more about Casey at the moment.

"So I was thinking—"

"So I was hoping—"

They both spoke at the same time. Not unusual for them.

"You first," Blake said.

"I was hoping you could go talk to Casey. Maybe keep an eye out on her for a little while. I don't want her walking out of here without some type of protection. What were you going to say?"

Blake grinned. "That... I wanted to talk to Casey. Maybe try to figure out who might want to shoot her. You too, for that matter. Think on it. I'll come back later. Don't worry. I won't let her out of my sight." Great minds thought alike.

Blake left the room in search of Casey. Brendan wished he could've introduced his best friend and brother to the woman who meant so much to him, but he wasn't nearly steady enough to walk down the hallway. Adrenaline had been the only thing keeping him upright at Casey's place and it was long gone.

So, time to get serious. Was there any reason someone wanted him dead? Or was this the same crackpot who'd aimed for Casey during production? Was someone pissed because they'd gone the distance on the show? The questions kept coming and Brendan had zero answers.

CHAPTER 18

HOURS LATER, BRENDAN'S PARENTS sat with him in the same treatment room. As per usual, his mother took control and his dad stayed out of her way. Not to say that his dad didn't have a backbone, he definitely did. But the whole family pretty much knew his mom ran most everything. Both his parents had asked extensive questions and he'd half hoped that the doctor would toss them out in the waiting room. Apparently this hospital had pretty lax rules when it came to family visits in the ER.

The worst part was having to come clean about freezing up after he went down. Apparently his little blackout had made the hospital's history chart. Casey must have blabbed because he would've kept that info private. He didn't remember a damn thing about Casey dragging him to safety. Honestly, that freaked him out more than getting shot. The men in his family, hell, even his mother and sister, had more balls than a football team hyped up on steroids.

So why had he flipped out? The kidnapping had happened years ago. He was over it...wasn't he? He'd been through enough physical and emotional therapy to last a lifetime, so why now?

Brendan still didn't have the all clear sign to go home, but his mom was putting up a good case for him to leave as long as he went home with them. He'd rather go back to his place with Casey so he could keep an eye on her. Unless. Shit, what if he blacked out again? What if he couldn't help her if something else happened? A fresh sweat broke out under his arms. Not having the answers scared the shit out of him.

He heard voices coming closer and took his first sigh of relief when Casey walked into the room with Blake and another lady right behind her. The anger he'd harbored all week at her ghosting him disappeared when he saw the white bandage around Casey's head and all the blood on her clothes.

Brendan introduced his parents—Jay and Terry—and Casey did the same with her sister Zoe who looked just like her, in a smaller, curvier version with darker, curlier hair.

His brother cleared his throat. "I was going to take Casey home in a few minutes to pack a bag, then follow her to her sister's place." It wasn't like she could stay in her place with the windows out and door full of bullet holes. Besides, the police would continue to investigate, making her apartment a crime scene. Blake lifted a dark eyebrow at Brendan. Code for *there's no way I'm telling her what she can and can't do since I don't even know her.*

Brendan glanced at Casey, then her sister. He was going to have to tread very lightly, especially with his parents here.

She looked a little pale. Blood still laced the long blond streaks in her hair, and Brendan's stomach cramped. Another inch and she'd be dead.

He started at the beginning. "So how's your head feel?"

Casey took a second to consider the question. "I think the stitches hurt worse than the actual wound. What about you? Sorry you haven't been cleared yet."

He shrugged, happy the pain meds had kicked in. "I'll be out of here any minute." Yeah, no way could he do this with all these people here. "I'd like to talk to you for a sec if that's all right." He glanced around the room, a silent plea for privacy. A lot of covert looks were exchanged, but his mom picked up her purse on the back of the chair and started for the door.

"We'll be right outside when you're done."

His dad, brother and Casey's sister followed her out.

He hated the awkwardness between them and he wanted to get something off his chest before he dove into his idea for the next few days. "Look, I don't know what happened tonight at your place." A half lie, but one he wasn't ready to come clean about. "I'm sorry I froze up on you." She probably had a ton questions about it, too, so he barreled on in hopes of breezing by it. "And, I'm pretty sure I know the answer to this question, but you didn't tell

Miles or anyone else at the show about me and Seger, did you?"

A weary look clouded her eyes. "No, I didn't. I had a feeling that's what you came to ask me. The more I thought about it, the easier it was to see why you'd think that. But no, I swear, I didn't. Seriously though...a lot of people know you work for him. I mean Seger's crew and staff. Anyone could've leaked it to the show."

Brendan leaned against his pillow. Stupid, but it was something he hadn't even considered. Had he pissed off someone at work? Made someone angry enough to make a call that would wreck his dream? He thought he got along with everyone on Seger's team. "You're right, of course. Could be anyone. I should've trusted you. I'm sorry." She met his gaze for a whole half second before finding something interesting on the floor.

"I'm sorry too. I should've responded to your calls and texts," she said. "I screwed up." She exhaled hard before looking him in the eyes. "I am really sorry. I just didn't know what to say or how to say it." She said the exact thing he wanted to hear, but it crushed him. She looked totally wrecked.

"I missed you so much last week," he said softly. "Not knowing how you were just about killed me. We went from 24/7 to absolutely zero. It was like someone cut off my leg or something."

She swallowed hard and blinked fast. "I'm sorry. I didn't want that." Swiping at her eyes, she continued, "You should know that Miles called right before you knocked. He told me what happened. He also said I'm the new winner of the show." She shot him a fleeting glance.

It was kind of like having his contract ripped up *again*. He should be happy for her, because at least one of them won. It was just a tough pill to swallow. "Okay, so someone takes away my dream and makes yours a reality. Then the first time we see each other bullets fly like it's bird-hunting season and we're the quail. So which one of us is the target?"

Casey lost the little color in her cheeks. "You were at my place, so I'm guessing me. Unless someone followed you."

He felt the need to remind her of a couple things. "The light fixture fell over your chair during the show. The stage cracked where you were supposed to do your move."

She shifted her stance and shook her head in a way that read like a silent, *I don't know*, and he felt like a tool for mentioning it.

"I can't say as I have too many skeletons in my closet," he said. "What about you? Anybody angry at you lately?"

She shook her head then stopped mid-motion, her eyes rounding.

"What? Who?" Brendan asked.

Casey blinked. "It can't be him. Jeff broke up with *me*. I'm out of his life so he has no reason to try and kill me."

"He's still a person the cops can check out, because someone's out there. Which means you need to take extra precautions." Here went nothing. "I don't think it's safe to go to your sister's place tonight." May as well spit it out before he lost his nerve. "In fact, I think staying with Zoe just puts both of you at risk." Her eyes turned stormy and she clearly didn't like his thoughts, so he hurried on before she said anything. "I think you should come home with me. I'd feel better if you did."

Her eyes got wider, if that were even possible. "Go home with you? What happens if you won't be going home? Did you want me to pull up a cot and sleep by your bed?" She shook her head. "You're being ridiculous."

"Look, if I don't go home, then Blake can take you to my place…the apartment I share with him." At her astounded gaze he explained, "He's all but moved in with his girlfriend, but not officially. She's out of town a lot with work and Blake regroups at our place when she's gone. The point is, he can be there if I'm not."

She sighed and tilted her head. "Brendan, I appreciate the concern, but I'm not staying at your place."

The hallway erupted in noise as a newcomer to the ER—obviously high on something—started screaming every vile word in the dictionary at the top of his lungs. It brought his family and Casey's sister back into the room.

Leading the pack, his mother didn't look fazed at all. "Casey's right," she said. "She's not staying at your place. You're both staying with me and your father." It was the first time Brendan wasn't angry about his mom's bionic hearing.

Casey's quick victory smile dropped. "Excuse me?"

"Brendan's doctor just gave us the okay to take him home." She faced Casey and the height difference didn't mean a thing because

Brendan's mom was a red-headed force of nature at only 5'2".

He didn't know what her argument would be, but Brendan already knew she'd won. Relief speared through him as he watched her work.

"I only heard the end of your conversation, but my son is right. You both should stay with us until the police figure out what's happening."

Casey looked to her sister for help, but Zoe just shrugged.

The screaming lunatic in the hallway finally quieted down.

"We have a gated home," his mom continued. "It's safe. After the day you've both had, I think you deserve the time to regroup without being scared. Besides, Casey, if someone's after you, then they won't find you at our house."

Brendan hadn't really been looking forward to going back home to his old room, but he would if it meant Casey's safety. His parents had installed a mother of a security system and a giant ass gate to keep out any kidnapping, unstable sociopaths.

Too bad they hadn't had that wall three years ago.

Blake pulled out his cell phone from his back pocket. "While you guys are moving into Casa St. John, maybe Troy and I can help the cops," he said, turning to Casey.

"Blake told you he's a private investigator, right?" Brendan asked.

"Whoa, wait. Everyone hold up." Casey put her hands out as if she needed to stop the roller coaster. "You can't just tell me what I'm going to do. I'm an adult. I make my own decisions."

He'd heard that defensive tone before, remembered she had a sore spot on that issue.

"Sis," Zoe said, taking Casey's elbow and leading her out into the hallway. "C'mere." They disappeared around the corner, and Brendan and his family listened to the hushed whispers. The uneasy silence in the room was intermittently peppered with short outbursts from Casey that were quickly cut off by her sister. Until one very clear sentence cut through the air.

"Did you call them?" Casey asked, clearly upset with something.

"C'mon, you know I had to," Zoe said. "They have a right to know. They love you, Case, whether you believe it or not."

"Casey!" A woman's worried voice coincided with clicking heels on the hospital tile.

"I'm okay, Mom," Casey said. "Hi, Dad."

Everyone in the room listened to an emotional reunion as Casey insisted she was all right and answered their questions about the incident. "There are some people I want you to meet," she said. A second later, Casey returned, her cheeks flushed. She introduced her parents—Eugene and Betty Turner—to his family and although Brendan would rather have met them on his own two feet, it was nice being alive to meet them at all.

Casey clearly got her height and build from her father, and her sister inherited their mom's curves. Both her parents had steel gray hair and reminded him of his grandparents.

"We just invited Casey to our place," his mom said, diving in where she'd left off. "Under the circumstances we think the kids are safer there."

"I was just convincing Casey she should take them up on the offer," Zoe explained to her parents. "They have a gated home and security system."

Casey's parents exchanged a look. "Is that really necessary?" Eugene asked. "She can stay at home with us."

"Someone tried to kill your daughter today," Brendan said, working to keep his voice even. He understood how they might want Casey close by, but they didn't seem to understand the danger she was in. "I'm sure you want her to be as safe as possible until the police find whoever is responsible."

Another worried glance between her parents before her mother said, "Of course we want her safe. But can't the police provide protection?"

Brendan looked at his twin. They knew first hand that police had few resources to provide that type of manpower.

"We've learned from experience that security is up to us," Jay said. He wrapped a protective arm around Terry.

Eugene pursed his lips and nodded. "It's generous of you to offer. Thank you."

"You know, I *am* in the room," Casey said, glancing between her parents. "Just because I have a bandage on my head doesn't mean I can't speak for myself." She looked at him, then at his parents. "Thank you for your offer. I appreciate it and I'll take you up on it." Next, she studied Blake. "And it was nice of you to offer your services before, but I can't afford a PI."

Blake gave her a reassuring smile. "Consider it pro-bono. Or a family rate. Anyone who shoots at my brother or my brother's friends gets the deal."

Casey stuffed her hands in the pockets of her tattered jeans and it accentuated her willowy frame. "That's very nice. You won't see me stopping you if you really want to help."

"Good. Great." Blake glanced his way and Brendan read the subtle victory grin, before his brother focused on Casey. "Would you mind telling me what you told the cops? Who do you think might have a grudge big enough to shoot at you?"

"Her ex for one," Brendan said.

Casey's mom gasped. "What? This is ridiculous. Jeff wouldn't do any such thing."

"Jeff wouldn't shoot at me," Casey agreed, shaking her head. "No way."

But he saw her wrestle with the idea.

Zoe's eyes rounded as she turned Casey toward her. "After what I walked in on last month, I wouldn't put it past him."

That sounded bad. "What did you walk in on?" Brendan asked. His stomach took a spin and it wasn't because of all the pain meds.

"We'd like to know that too," Eugene said. "Seems like we're the last to know everything."

Casey looked like she was about to implode, but managed to keep her cool. "Now really isn't the time to get into it."

Brendan remembered the little bit he *did* know about Casey's ex. "You told me he gave you an ultimatum. Makes him sound like someone unwilling to compromise. Obviously something else happened."

"That doesn't mean he decided to shoot at me. Or you. I mean, *he* called off the wedding. Not me."

"He called off the wedding when you didn't play by his rules. What if he's mad enough for something this drastic?" His suggestion freaked her out. He saw it in the widening of her eyes and her slack jaw. Maybe he was getting ahead of himself. "Okay, maybe it's not him. But someone out there is pissed enough to want to kill us both."

"There's one thing you two have in common," Blake said. "The show."

LATER THAT NIGHT, CASEY sat on the St. Johns' comfortable sofa in their den. Her suitcase had exploded in the upstairs guest room, and all her clothes and shoes spilled out onto the floor. This house was beautiful and comfortable and much better than staying with her parents. In one short hospital visit followed by a much longer conversation at the St. Johns' house, her parents had learned more about Jeff than they'd ever bargained for. Their surprise—and ultimate joy—at discovering she'd won the show went a long way in mending their relationship with Casey. They definitely needed time to process all the new information. Just like Casey needed time to recoup from the mental and physical hurdles of the day.

Blindly, she stared at the TV as her head throbbed a merciless beat. The whole day had been a horror of a reality show come to life. Too bad she'd never made it to the studio. She'd spoken with Miles from the hospital and told him about the day's events. She couldn't decide if he was happier that she was alive or that he had more drama to exploit...which he did as soon as humanly possible since the news stations had picked up the story in gory detail. Apparently Miles felt compelled to release the information about the show's new winner, and he'd speculated about Brendan's possible motive for showing up at Casey's door.

It was all more than she could deal with, and TV wasn't helping.

As Casey snuck back to her room, she heard Brendan's mom— who insisted Casey call her Terry—rattling around in the kitchen, talking softly to her husband.

Brendan's parents seemed like the kind of people anyone would want for parents. Terry's fiery red hair matched her personality and Jay looked like an older version of Brendan with the beginning of gray patches at his temples. Clearly the two of them made a great team and relied on each other. The evidence was in the covert looks and constant touching.

Oh, to find *that* for the rest of her life...

She was nearly at her room when she heard Brendan.

"Casey, come back. Was that you?"

She debated backtracking and facing him, mainly because she was tapped out. But Brendan had taken a bullet for her today, so she owed him her life a third time. She pushed his door open wider and leaned against the frame, striving for indifference.

It was a mistake.

Resting against the headboard, with his arm in a sling and wearing only a thin sheet up to his waist, Brendan looked like an Adonis. His sculpted chest and abs only reminded her of what she had—and walked out on—over two months ago.

A tall bookcase loaded with books, trophies and pictures sat against a hunter green accent wall. The navy-and-green duvet folded at the bottom of his bed fit him perfectly. It was all masculine and comforting.

"I was just going to bed." Casey managed to meet his gaze.

Pounding up the stairs warned of someone's approach and Casey stood taller as Terry rounded the hall.

"Jay just told me he put your suitcase in the guest room." She reached the door and stepped past Casey, still carrying a dishrag over her shoulder. "How're you feeling, honey?" She placed the back of her hand on Brendan's forehead and he rolled his eyes.

"Mom, I'm not a baby. Cut it out." But he didn't shy away from his mother's hand.

"Just checking for fever. I told the doctor I would." She glanced between the two of them. "Anyway, like I said, Jay just told me he put your suitcase in the guest room."

The suitcase that had already exploded over the room when she couldn't find the bottle of pain relievers she'd tossed in at the last minute.

"I mean, I realize it's not far, but if you want to move it in here, we can do that now." Terry adjusted the blanket at the bottom of the bed and it took Casey a second to process what she'd heard.

Terry was offering her Brendan's bed? With Brendan in it? Casey opened her mouth, but no words came out, so she shook her head. Vic would've jumped at an opportunity like this, but Casey couldn't do it. Waving a hand between Brendan and herself, she barely managed a reply. "Oh, we aren't...you know, no, no, there's nothing, I mean, no, I wouldn't dream of..."

"Moooom." Brendan's groan was long and pitiful. A flush stained his cheeks as he pressed his eyes shut.

"What?" Terry looked between the two of them like they were dense. "Did I get my signals wrong? Because I swear the two of you were an item during the show. You just tried to act like you weren't." She glanced between them again before picking up a dirty plate on Brendan's bedside table. "Okay, seriously, I'm not stupid. I know sparks when I see sparks."

Casey felt a matching flush crawl up her cheeks.

Terry stepped back and adjusted a picture on the shelf. "Brendan, you of all people should know my feelings on this. I mean, face it, I was pregnant at sixteen, so I know the deal."

"Sixteen!" Casey clapped a hand over her mouth. *That's right...get yourself thrown out of the best shelter you have.* "Sorry," she murmured. It just slipped out. Of course, now she understood why Brendan's parents looked so young.

"Yes," Terry said, without a hint of remorse. "Sixteen. So as far as I'm concerned, if you two want time together, I'm not going to put you in another room. You'll only find your way back here. Or, knowing Brendan, he'll creep out of bed to come to your room. I'd rather not risk it. Although I think you two know sex is really off the table with both of you so banged up." She seemed to realize she was talking about a touchy subject and paused. "So..." She looked between them again and scooped up some dirty laundry from the bottom of the bed. "What's the deal?"

This was the last thing Casey expected. There was no way in hell she planned to sleep in Brendan's bed. Not with his parents right down the hall. Not even if someone paid her money.

"The guest room is perfect," she said.

"Okay. If you're sure." Terry took her dishes and laundry and walked past Casey. "Let me know if you change your mind." She disappeared toward the stairs, leaving Casey in a state of shock and embarrassment.

Casey waited until Terry was out of earshot, then looked at Brendan. "Sixteen?"

He nodded. "Hard to imagine, right? It weirds me out to think my parents had three kids by my age, with me and Blake soon to come."

"Seems like your 'rents have a really good relationship." Her parents did too. They were just extremely uptight. They were also significantly older than Terry and Jay, so maybe that made a difference. "You all are pretty tight, huh?" Casey asked settling back against the doorframe.

"Yeah." Brendan nodded, a half smile on his face. "Come over here. Sit down a minute." He gestured to the end of the bed and Casey suddenly remembered why she didn't want to be here in the first place. She was still massively embarrassed for avoiding him the past week…her default emotion when it came to this man. For a guy who should've been pissed as hell at her, he was acting as if nothing had happened. She sure as hell would've been angry if their roles were reversed and he'd ghosted her. Instead of obsessing on it more, she crept in and sat on the chair in the corner of the room.

"Just for a few minutes. I've got a whopper of a headache and I need to go to sleep."

His dark brows slanted. "Did you take something? We've got plenty of pain relievers in the bathroom. Help yourself."

"I had some ibuprofen. I'll be fine." A very awkward silence settled between them and she couldn't really leave when she'd just sat down. "Thanks again for being there today. That first bullet would've nailed me if you hadn't blocked it."

He avoided her gaze and nodded. "I'm glad I was there for you." His voice got rough and Casey's skin tingled when he finally looked at her. His deep blue eyes made it hard for her to stay focused. The emotion she saw and the fact that he didn't try to hide it scared the spit right out of her.

Definitely time to leave.

Casey stood up and before Brendan could talk her out of it, she said, "My head is pounding. I've got to lie down. I'll see you in the morning."

"Case."

Casey steeled herself against the plea in Brendan's low voice. She sucked up the courage she didn't feel and watched him from the doorway. "Yeah?"

He opened his mouth, but paused as if rethinking what he was going to say. "Sleep well. Good night."

Exhaling her relief, she gave him a quick wave. "Night."

Free…at least for the next eight hours.

CHAPTER 19

A DISTANT RINGING INTERRUPTED Casey as she moved over Brendan's muscular chest. His sling was nowhere to be found and he had both arms around her, one hand palming her head as she lowered her mouth over his, and the other easing down her spine to cup her ass and guide her over him. God it felt perfect. Better than perfect. He filled her completely, hit that sensitive bundle of nerves over and over until she thought she might burst with pleasure. It was similar to one of the many positions they'd experimented with on their one and only night together.

Bzzzt. Bzzzt.

That damn buzzing got louder, but Brendan didn't seem to hear it. He just whispered how good she felt. How he'd never touched smoother skin or softer hair. He made her crazy with desire even as she rode him to the finish. Heat blazed off his body as they broke apart and pushed back together again, breathing each other in as their mouths nipped and kissed. God, she was so close, right there...

Bzzzt. Bzzzt. Bzzzt.

The sound finally penetrated and Casey opened her eyes to a strange room. Light peach walls, crown molding on the ceiling. Peach and gray flowered bed spread. The guest room at the St. Johns' house. Her nightshirt molded to her damp skin and her girl parts roared for satisfaction. Her phone vibrated next to her bed and she glanced at the screen, shocked to see Miles's name and number flashing on the screen. At six-thirty in the morning. What the hell?

Casey sat up—way too fast. She closed her eyes against the

dizziness and punched the screen. "'Lo?" She cleared her dry throat and fought down a queasy stomach.

"Why didn't you call me back yesterday?" The question was half pissed, half whine and all obnoxious. She'd never heard this kind of attitude from Miles before. He didn't sound anything like the always-in-control producer she'd come to know.

Casey ran her hand through her hair and tried to wake up her tired brain and give her hot skin a second to cool down. Her headache had kept her up more than she'd slept. "I'm sorry, Miles." *I was too busy getting stitches in my head after someone used me for target practice.* "I didn't know I was supposed to call you back. I thought we postponed the meeting."

"Let me put it to you this way, Casey, and don't take this the wrong way, but the show owns you. I own you. You signed a contract and that's still in place. Everything you do is relevant to me."

Really? "How?"

"You still don't get it. You're a public figure. Everything you do is newsworthy. Especially getting shot at. That right there could amount to tens of thousands of sales."

What? So he wanted to exploit everything she did, everything that happened to her to make a buck? That hadn't been the reason she'd done the show. She just wanted a leg up in the music industry. His way sounded sleazy and underhanded. She wanted people to buy her music because they liked it, not because she'd nearly been killed after winning the show, even if it was by default.

If her silence bumped him, he didn't mention it. He just powered on. "I need you to get to the studio ASAP. We're already fielding calls and setting up interviews for you. This is great publicity. You can't buy this shit."

"What?" She couldn't manage to keep that one internal and her pulse jumped.

"I'll have a drive-on at the gate. Come to the studio and we'll take a car from here to KLAC for the morning show. Better yet, we'll pick you up. We've got to hurry if we're going to make the last segment."

"Miles, I can't be on TV this morning. I still have blood in my hair from yesterday." She'd gotten most of it out except for the top where the wound occurred, but still… If she looked anything like she felt, the camera was going to hate her. "You know I have stitches in my head, right? I'm not really up for an interview at the moment."

"Sweetheart, it doesn't matter what you're up for. It matters that we capitalize on the situation. It's all luck and timing." He barked more orders to someone near him.

"Are you seriously telling me that getting shot was lucky?" Some very warped people worked in the entertainment industry.

"Not getting shot, per se. Just getting shot after winning the show. You'll need to pump up the production of some songs so we can get them out into the world while this is still fresh in people's minds."

He was crazy. "Miles…" She nearly said it to him, but couldn't get the words out. What if he tossed her out like he'd tossed Brendan? Then she'd be back on the losing side and that sucked harder than a new vacuum. "Miles, I don't have anything to wear."

"Ah…you women are all the same. A closet full of clothes and you don't have anything to wear."

"You don't understand." She pinched the bridge of her nose. "I'm not at my apartment. It's a crime scene. I didn't pack anything television worthy. I just tossed some stuff in a bag and left. I have no idea when I'll get back home."

"Shit. I didn't realize that. Okay. Here's the plan. You'll come here and we'll get wardrobe to set you up. Then you and I will head over from here. It's going to be tight and they won't be happy, but we'll get there in time for the segment. Where are you? I'm sending a car now." Clearly, he didn't intend to back down.

God, she didn't even know the address. "Gimme a second. I don't know offhand." Casey scrambled out of bed, threw on a pair of shorts and hurried downstairs. She almost slammed right into Brendan when she flew into the kitchen.

"Hey, what's got you going a hundred miles an hour?" He looked deliciously rumpled in a pair of shorts…only shorts. His long thick hair hung wild to his broad shoulders and his eyes zeroed in on her. He hardly looked fragile despite the bandage and sling on his arm. No, he looked tall and delicious and very formidable. Her face instantly heated and she forgot what she'd come in here for. "Casey?"

"Casey?" Miles yelled over the phone and brought her back to now.

"I need the address here."

Brendan rattled off the address and Casey repeated it to Miles who said a car would be at the curb in twenty minutes. Casey disconnected and turned to dash back upstairs, but Brendan caught her arm.

"Whoa. What's happening? Talk to me."

"Miles is sending a car for me. He's got an interview set up at one of the local morning shows."

Outrage flared in his blue eyes before he got a word out. "What? That asshole! You got shot in the head yesterday and he wants to parade you around on TV today?" He ran a hand through his hair, then shook his head. "Call him back and tell him no."

Casey bit back the irritation at his tone. "Actually…" She faced him head on. "I'm going. This could mean tens of thousands of sales when I release the first single." She hated spouting Miles's words, but they made for a decent argument. "Besides, he's my boss now and I can't say no." Even if *she* didn't want to go, she wasn't going to let Brendan order her into doing anything.

The man didn't back down an inch. In fact, he got even closer. "Someone shot at you yesterday? Did you forget that already?"

Treating her like an idiot without a brain in her head, he made it super easy to pack her stuff and scram. Casey pulled out all the sarcasm she could muster. "Gee, I got shot yesterday? How could I forget that? I mean, it's not like I still have blood in my hair or a headache that's threatening to blow my face off." She would've shoved him if his arm hadn't been in a sling. Despite hating that he was hurt, she was still pissed as hell. "Here's the deal, St. John. I live my own life the way I want to. If it means I get in the car that Miles sends for me, then so be it. If it means I get a hotel room afterward because I'm not staying here, then that's fine too." Her stomach pitched in another queasy roll. Everything seemed to be spinning out of her control no matter what she did.

Maybe Brendan cared about her, but he had a back-assward way of showing it.

Well, she was done with the days of being bossed around. Absolutely finished. *He's been protecting you, not hurting you, since the first minute you met him,* the traitorous voice in her head reminded her, but she shut it down.

Casey spun and stomped up the stairs, intent on repacking and bee-lining for the front door. She needed time. Time to figure out what she wanted, what she needed. She was going to be a mess when that car showed up. Well, so what. She frickin' got shot yesterday, so Miles deserved whatever he got when it came to her looks. Especially since he arranged this interview without even talking to her first.

Frustration mounted exponentially and made her want to scream. Stalking into her room, she began shoving all her shit back into the suitcase.

"Casey, wait. I'm sorry. God, I'm sorry, just hear me out, okay!" Brendan had been on her heels the whole time, but she'd ignored him. It was kind of hard to do that now with him standing in her way of the bathroom.

She didn't want to "hear him out." She didn't want to look at him because she knew what she'd see, so she spun back to the room to see if she'd missed something. Shit. She was still in her nightshirt and the workout shorts she'd thrown on. Spinning back to face Brendan, she pointed to the door. "Out. I have to get dressed." She grabbed the closest pair of jeans and a shirt.

"I'll get out as soon as you hear what I have to say."

Casey clenched her jaw so hard her headache blossomed to explosive levels.

BRENDAN KNEW BORROWED TIME when he had it, so he rushed ahead. "I'm sorry I pissed you off. That wasn't my intention." His mom had taught him that apologies went a long way with a woman. He prayed she was right. "It's just Miles calls before the sun is even up and you're jumping like he's your fucking master." Oh shit. Wrong thing to say. Casey's face got even stormier. "No, wait. I didn't mean it that way. I just mean, after yesterday you don't have to jump every time he calls."

Her eyes narrowed. "He made it very clear that he owns me, Brendan. I can't really say no to him."

"The fuck you can't! Sorry. Didn't mean to drop the F-bomb. I just want you to stand up for yourself."

Canting her head, she put her hands on her hips. Her long hair hung in a messy sheet down her arm. "Not sure if you've noticed or not, but I am standing up for myself. You're blocking my way to the bathroom."

Brendan barely got out of the way before Casey mowed him down. She shut the door in his face just as his parents arrived. The cavalry! He'd never been happier to see them.

"What's going on?" his mother asked. She wore her blue sweats, which meant she'd been working out already. At least *she'd* talk some sense into Casey.

"Casey's doing some type of morning show. Miles is sending a car for her." That may have sounded a little second grade, but he needed back up ASAP.

His parents shared a look and when Casey came out a minute later, dressed in jeans and a form fitting tank top with her hair brushed to a silky sheen, his mom didn't hesitate. "Honey, do you think you're up for going out?" *Yes.* His mom slipped into parenting mode right on schedule.

Casey dumped an armload of toiletries into her bag and slapped a forced smile on her face. "I'm fine. Thank you, Mrs. St—Terry. Thank you. It's really not a big deal, and I don't want to put you out so I'm just going to find someplace else to stay tonight." She slipped into her sandals.

Terry's brows slanted down. "What? Why?" She glanced at Brendan before focusing on Casey. "Where are you going?"

"Honestly, I don't know yet, but I can't stay here." She shot Brendan a loaded look as she zipped her bag and a second later he felt his mother's eyes on him too.

"Jay…" Terry tipped her head in Casey's direction and Jay nodded. After so many years together the two of them didn't even need words anymore. His parents weren't stupid. They knew the potential danger Casey and he faced after yesterday. There was no way they'd let Casey leave without an argument. "Brendan, come with me," his mother ordered.

What? Dammit! He hated this shit. He was not a baby. He'd moved out of the house almost two years ago. He had two good jobs, he paid his bills on time. He did not need to be lectured by his mother. "Mom," he warned even as he followed her.

"Don't *Mom* me." She reached the end of the hallway and faced him. "What has her so angry? And don't pretend like you don't know."

Brendan went to throw his hands in the air and a shock of pain in his shoulder stopped him fast. "I don't know. Maybe I asked if she remembered getting shot yesterday. Something like that." His mom pursed her lips and shook her head. "She just flipped out on me, okay? She can't go alone, Mom. I seriously doubt she's going to change her mind. Miles has her all jacked up. I have to go with her."

She folded her arms across her chest. "I don't think Miles is going to let you ride in the car with her, honey. You know you're not his favorite person."

"He's probably not even going to be in the car. It's taking her right back to the studio. I'll follow her. I want to make sure no one's tailing her at the very least."

"I thought your brother knew how to do that stuff. Since when did you become a private investigator?"

"Blake and I talk. Besides, I'm not trying to be covert. I just need to see if someone else is following Casey or not."

"So I don't have to remind you that *you* also got shot yesterday?" She rolled her eyes at his deadpan stare and glanced at the ceiling. "Fine. I'm not going to stop you. I know what it's like to do what it takes to keep someone safe." She tipped her head toward his room. "You better hurry and get dressed or she's going to be out the door before you're ready."

Brendan turned to go, his brain already calculating how fast he could get ready.

"Brendan." His mother's voice stopped him. "We need to talk about the way you communicate with people."

Seriously? He communicated just fine. Most of the time. Brendan rushed to his room, eased his arm out of the sling to get a

T-shirt over his head—which hurt like a motherfucker—pulled on some jeans and his boots, slipped back into the sling, and he was good to go. Almost. He rinsed with some mouthwash and made it into the hallway as Casey barreled out of the guest room.

She stopped for a second when she saw him, gave a look to his Dad, who still stood in the middle of the room, then headed off again.

"Look, I know you're pissed and I'm not going to stop you from getting into the car, but I am going to follow you to make sure no one else is." He stayed right on her heels down the stairs.

"I can't stop you," she mumbled.

"But please reconsider..." he stopped when he realized she didn't have her suitcase with her. Had his dad talked her into staying?

She spun at the door. "Reconsider what?"

"Staying here," he said softly. He moved toward her, his heart pounding hard. He wanted to touch her so badly he hurt with it, but he was afraid if he tried that she'd run. Emotion knotted his throat and Brendan swallowed back the gut-wrenching fear of her walking out of the protection of the house...walking out on them. "Case," he whispered. "I'm sorry. I don't want you to be mad at me."

Canting her head, she studied him. "Do you even know why you're apologizing?"

He actually didn't. *"We need to talk about the way you communicate with people."* His mom's words flashed in his head. "Because I need to work on my communicating, I know. I'm really sorry."

She huffed a breath, turned to go, then instantly turned back. "Here's the deal, St. John. I swore to myself that I would speak up when something bothered me. I'm not yours. You don't own me. You can't tell me what to do or when to do it. Understand?"

He nodded. "Yes, I understand, but this *is* your life we're talking about. This is your *safety*. This is me wanting to ensure that some whack-job isn't going to make a move on you without going through me first." He wanted to put his hand on her shoulder, caress her cheek with his thumb. She had the fucking smoothest skin he'd ever seen. They hadn't been this close in weeks and he got lightheaded just from her elusive fresh scent. "I've missed you, Casey."

Emotion welled in her eyes along with confusion, but Brendan kept going.

"You know, I think back to that night in Hawaii all the time." He stepped closer and watched her pulse beat a fast rhythm in her neck. "I replay all those hours of having you next to me. Skin to skin. I remember what's it like to taste you, be inside you."

"Brendan..." She whispered his name, sounded conflicted as hell as she glanced at his mouth.

Encouraged and torn at the same time, Brendan barely managed to keep his hands to himself. "I've missed you so much," he whispered. "You have no clue."

With a subtle shake of her head she said, "What are you doing to me?"

He almost didn't her soft question and he didn't have an answer. *She* was *turning him* inside out. Because he didn't have words, he wanted to show her so he slowly bent his head, taking time to weave a spell, hoping like hell she wouldn't run.

"The car is going to be here any minute. I should wait outside."

He froze. Shit. Okay. No kiss. He could live with that...for the moment. He just needed to find common ground with her. "The driver can ring the intercom. You don't have to go anywhere." They locked gazes again and Brendan suddenly realized that his best offense was space. He backed up a step and gave her room. She blinked, stood taller and he instinctively knew he'd done the right thing.

"Please give me a chance to make things right," he said. Her ex had seriously done a number on her. He had to remember that. "Whatever it takes." He spread his good arm wide. "But please don't walk away from what we have. What we *can* have." They'd had some great times during the show. They'd laughed and talked for hours, mindless of cameras rolling. "We're good together, Case. Give us a chance. Give *me* a chance." He saw the turmoil in her eyes. She couldn't deny all the good times they'd shared both in bed and out of it.

The intercom buzzed—*dammit.*

Brendan yanked the phone from the side table in the living room. "She'll be right out. Give us a minute." He hung up and took Casey's hand. "Just think about what I've said. Please. I'm worried about you." Instead of reading all that indecision in her eyes, he led her through the house toward the back kitchen door. "C'mon, get in my car and I'll take you out."

"Bren, I can walk the distance to the street."

"I know that. I just want you to have as much cover as possible."

"So you're saying that someone followed us here from the hospital last night? That's pretty unlikely."

"Maybe." He opened the back door, walked outside and checked the driveway before motioning her out. "But can you play it safe? For me? Because I'd lose my mind if something happened to you."

"Bren, we need to talk. This thing between us…" She shook her head. "It's not, it can't be…"

"What?" he asked, standing in front of her. "It's not real because of the way we met or the circumstances we've been in since then? It can't be real because we still don't know a ton about each other? Fine, then let's take the time we need to get past all that. There's nothing stopping us, and there's nothing I want more than to see where we can take this." He paused and searched her reluctant eyes. "I knew you were special when we met in Hawaii. I knew I wanted to see you again when we got back to California." The urge was too much and Brendan couldn't stop himself. "Dammit, Case," he said softly, and kissed her.

He wanted to make sure she understood just how much she meant to him and it seemed the only way to do that was by showing her. He stroked his hand through her long, soft hair. It wasn't their first kiss, but it may as well have been. He wanted her even more than he did in Hawaii. He wanted her sweetness, her softness. He wanted the taste of her on his lips, his tongue. He wanted her soft sigh as they came together. He wanted her surrender to the emotions swirling between them like a tornado.

Brendan brushed his tongue across her lower lip and went to heaven when she opened her mouth and invited him in. Their tongues met in a long, full mating of perfection. She tasted minty and clean, hot and delicious. He pulled back before he got too carried away because it was too easy to do with this woman.

"I guess the question is what do *you* want?" he asked.

CHAPTER 20

CASEY DIDN'T KNOW WHAT she wanted, but sitting in the spacious black Town Car heading to a local morning show to do an interview did absolutely *not* make her list. Especially with zero notice and a raging headache. To top it off, she'd caved and kissed Brendan anyway. Even though she was furious at him and confused as hell. One second he was ordering her around and the next, he was the sweet guy who said all the right things and kissed like a dream.

Aside from Jeff and one other boy in college, she had very limited kissing experience. She'd been the odd ball in high school…too tall, shy and gangly, and the boys she'd liked hadn't returned the feeling. She'd expected things to change in college, but one disastrous make-out session with a frat boy had turned her off to the party scene. Meeting Jeff at the gym had changed her life. Through the rest of college, he'd been her one and only. It wasn't that he'd been a bad kisser, he just didn't waste his time on it the last couple of years. Not when he could be doing other stuff, or make *her* do other stuff.

Casey cringed at the way she'd caved to Jeff for so many years. Usually she didn't think about it but sometimes it crept up on her. The way he'd used her without caring about her feelings. The way he'd made her do things assuring her that she'd grow to like it and the important thing was pleasing him. *Pleasing him made their relationship stronger.* What an absolute load of horseshit. How could she have fallen for that for so long? *Why* had she?

Because she kept hoping the man she met at the gym would reappear. He'd been funny and thoughtful and he'd come from a good family. For two years he'd treated her like gold. She'd invested in him...her heart and soul. Then he'd met a group of men at one of his father's fundraisers and he'd slowly changed. He spent less time with her, and when they *were* together, his short temper almost always got in the way. Casey had been sure she could bring back the man she fell in love with. All she had to do was work harder. Make him happy. Jeff was happy to perpetuate that notion. The scales became unbalanced. Jeff made her believe she needed him because he was the whole package. The star quarterback of the football team with a 4.5 grade point average. Then a law school student training to take over his dad's firm, before a political career like his father. He'd whittled away her self-esteem until virtually all of it was gone and she second-guessed everything about herself.

What would've happened if she'd actually married the guy? Casey shivered.

Maybe the other question was how would Jeff react in this situation? She snorted. He'd call her paranoid and stupid for thinking someone wanted her dead. He'd tell her she wasn't worth anyone's time to go to that much trouble. How could she really compare the two men when they were exact opposites? Brendan had repeatedly saved her and nearly died in the process. He thought she had talent and laughed at her jokes. He made her feel special and wanted. The only times he sounded bossy was when her safety concerned him. Could she really hold that against him?

She looked over her shoulder for the tenth time to see if Brendan was behind the car. They both agreed not to say anything to Miles in case the man went ballistic that Brendan was in the vicinity, and Brendan wasn't worried about her once she got through the studio gates. The last minute notice for them probably meant her stalker wouldn't know about it either. Plus Brendan thought the guy had lost them after they'd gone into the hospital and to his parents' place afterward.

At the studio, the stylist at *Write Your Ticket* dressed her in a sleek, muted green dress and gold Jimmy Choo wrap sandals. A speedy quick makeup and hair session gave her face a little color and cleaned the blood out of her hair before Casey was rushed out for the last segment of the morning show. With a deep side part and her hair flipped over to cover the stitches, Casey did the interview robotically. She plastered a smile on her face and answered the questions. It all happened so fast that she barely remembered any of it. The familiar bright lights reminded her of the reality show and the interview process every week after a different contestant got booted out. She kept expecting to wake up from a dream...or nightmare if she included yesterday.

In an "unprecedented" change of plans, Miles had told her he'd rescheduled the rest of her talk show tour, preferring instead to get to the music while she was still a hot topic. So new plan: Today was the day she started writing. Miles wanted songs. A lot of songs. The pressure made her headache throb harder and brought back her queasy stomach.

Casey expected the car to take her right back to the studio or the St. Johns' house, so she texted Zoe, needing a pep talk from her big sis. She looked up when the driver stopped in front of a gray one-story building. Across the parking lot stood another similar building. "Where are we?"

"This is the final stop," he said with a slight German accent. His blond crew cut and ice blue eyes gave her the creeps.

Casey didn't like the way he said *final*, and Miles had left in a separate car after the morning show segment, saying he'd catch up with her.

Peering out the dark tinted window, Casey looked at all the expensive cars parked in the lot. If the driver planned to kill her she'd probably be in the desert by now instead of some ritzy spot in Hollywood.

"You can go in," the driver said. "They're expecting you."

They? She hated that even the driver knew more than she did. It made her feel like the child Jeff sometimes accused her of being. God, she had to get that man out of her head!

The blazing sun smacked her like an oven as she walked toward the main entrance. Each step ratcheted up her anxiety until her headache throbbed with renewed force. She didn't see any handles on the door so she hit the blue neon button on a small panel. A buzz and click sounded and a lady opened the glass door

OUT OF THE BLUE

and continued out. Cool air breezed through Casey's hair as she walked in.

The silence in the building seemed otherworldly. Behind a sleek chrome desk, a receptionist sat typing away at a giant computer. She turned as Casey approached. Her dark hair barely touched her shoulders and her smile displayed a small gap between her top teeth. "Hi!" Her eyes lit up before Casey said anything. "You're Casey!" She stood and smoothed her wrinkled yellow dress. "I'm Annie. We've been expecting you. Follow me."

Questions piled up as Casey followed Annie through a maze of hallways and into a recording studio. Her heels clicked on the tile floor while Annie's flats didn't make a sound. Why hadn't Miles mentioned this earlier? How long was she going to be here? Had Brendan followed her here too? She hadn't seen him once they'd gone past the security gate at the studio.

A comfortable sitting area with a gray sofa and matching cushy chair sat outside the actual recording booth and on the other side of the room a high tech console took up enough space for three people to sit behind it. A stack of notepads and an array of pencils, pens and highlighters sat on a small end table next to the sofa. A small refrigerator nestled in the corner. Budding excitement grew in her chest. She had to admit this setup was as legit as she'd ever seen.

"Have a seat. Everyone should be here shortly."

It seemed as if she was the only one out of the loop and despite the anticipation of creating new music, it sure as hell grated against her nerves.

"Help yourself to anything in the fridge," Annie said, pointing toward to the corner. "The ladies room is farther down the hallway to your right. Let me know if you need anything." She left the door open when she padded out.

Casey took a seat on the chair, not willing to share her space with the strangers she expected to encounter. The clock ticked and Casey fidgeted in her seat. She picked up the pad and a pen and started doodling. Slowly a few words came to her and she began writing.

You're making me wait. You're making me late.
I don't want to be here. I'd rather tempt fate.
I'd rather be out, painting the town.
I don't need fancy or your sparkly gown.

The pen hovered over the page as words danced in her head.

Gimme the freedom to live my life
To break the bonds and—

"Casey!" Miles shocked her with his loud entrance and Casey hugged the pad to her chest as she stood. "There you are," he said. "Sit down, sit down. Get comfortable." He took the spot on the edge of the sofa nearest her as more men entered the room and gathered around. "I wanted you to meet the team," Miles said, glancing at everyone.

"The team?" She didn't know there was a team and didn't immediately sit.

"Yeah. These are the guys you're going to collaborate with to make the next hit record for Griffstar Enterprises. Guys, this is Casey. Casey this is Leroy, Dennis, RJ and Stubby." All of them had varying degrees of tattoos on their arms. RJ and Stubby wore man buns, Leroy had an old-school afro and gold front tooth, and Dennis wore a knit cap despite the heat outside. Miles tipped his chin toward her pad. "Whatcha got? I saw you writing already." He grinned and pointed to the corner of the ceiling where a camera shot video of the whole room.

"I'm on camera?" Casey asked numbly. It was like being on the reality show all over again and she wasn't ready for it. Her knees wobbled, her gut pitched and she finally sat down.

Miles just laughed, his dark eyes twinkling, his smile bright. "Always, babe. Always. So c'mon let's hear it. What'd you write so far?"

Casey kept the pad against her chest. "It's nothing. Just scribbling. It's not anything I can share."

"It better be." Miles lifted an eyebrow. "Everything you write, everything you come up with belongs to me, which means I get to see it whether you want me to or not."

It was like an ice bucket challenge no one warned her about. She wanted to run away screaming, but the shock of his words stunned her silent.

"What?" Miles asked. "You look like I killed your dog."

And yet, that seemed to amuse him. Casey resisted the urge to shiver. "Not everything I write belongs to you, Miles. We live in the U.S.A., remember. I'm a free human being."

"You might be a free human being, but any songs you write belong to me. That's the contract you signed to do the show. It's the exchange for half a million dollars and a contract for multiple albums."

Half a million dollars. The reminder made her giddy and nauseous at the same time. Signing that contract and winning the show made her a very wealthy woman. Now she had to live with the pressure.

Fine. Anything she wrote belonged to Miles. But if she recorded something on her phone with no one around, then how was he ever going to find out about it? This contract wasn't going to last a lifetime. She had ten years to be at Miles beck and call before she could launch her own career, and she sure as hell planned on making that happen. If she could get this far, she could make it through to the other side.

"How long is this going to take?" Casey asked. She wouldn't mind lying down with a couple more ibuprofen to knock out this headache. "By the way, why didn't you tell me you had this planned?" How often did he intend to surprise her with spur of the moment songwriting sessions?

"Not long," Miles said. "Maybe an hour. I just want everyone to get acquainted. Can't write hits if we don't get along. I wasn't sure the guys could make it and they called right as you were leaving the show." He sat back in the sofa and grinned like a lunatic.

That must have been the phone call her driver took when they left the studio.

Poor Brendan. What if he was outside, waiting for her in the sweltering heat? That wouldn't be good for him after yesterday. Casey excused herself to the ladies room and texted him.

Where are you? Not sure if you followed the car or not.

Her screen lit up immediately and Brendan replied, *Yes. Followed you. What's up?*

Admittedly, she liked knowing he was close by, not so much because she thought someone might bust through the door and kill her, but because of the uncertainty in a strange place. Brendan gave her some security. She wished he didn't, but there it was.

Impromptu songwriting session, she texted. *Might be here for at least an hour. Surprise for me too. Sorry.*

Thanks for the heads up. All good, he typed back.

Her relief turned to frustration, because now she was going to worry about him the whole time. Seriously, what if the heat was too much for him? What if his shoulder hurt as badly as her head?

Screw it. He was a big boy and he made his own decisions. She doubted anything she said would change his mind anyway.

Casey strode back to the studio. RJ sat behind the console while the other three played in the recording booth. Leroy played bass, Stubby sat behind a keyboard and Dennis riffed on his guitar.

"What do you think of this sound," RJ asked. He flipped a switch and a beat pumped into the room via two massive speakers placed behind him.

It was too much bass for Casey's taste, but she waited for Miles to say something. The three guys jammed and the edgy sound crawled up Casey's spine and weighed on her every last nerve.

"Let's put some words to this sound," Miles announced with a glance to Casey.

"What?" Casey stomach nearly dropped to the floor. She didn't work like this. She started with the words and let the music follow suit. How could she find the rhythm if she didn't have the words? Sweat dampened her palms.

"You're the songwriter. Let's make it happen, babe. You're in the real world now."

BRENDAN WAITED. THEN WAITED more. After Casey's text, he'd run across the street to the corner market and loaded up on water, energy drinks and power bars. He just hadn't expected to go through everything he bought. He baked in the car like a side of beef in the broiler. The wrap and sling on his arm made him twice as hot and his shirt stuck to his skin as if someone had glued it on. Intermittent intervals with the AC didn't much help either. At the two hour mark he texted her, but got no response. Closing in on hour three, he'd had enough. He didn't care about running into Miles. He planned to pull Casey out of there. She'd been frickin' shot yesterday and had stitches in her head for God's sake. What the hell did Miles think he was doing?

He got halfway across the parking lot when the door opened and Casey came out. She didn't just walk out...she ran. For a split second his heart soared as she bee lined toward him, but then his adrenaline spiked and his senses heightened when he saw the angst in her eyes.

It took a few seconds to realize she didn't plan to stop and Brendan braced himself for contact. Like a linebacker, she ran into him, almost knocking him back, but he caught her in his good arm even as pain ricocheted in his bad one.

"What happened? What's wrong?" He held her as close as he could, considering one arm was immobile against his chest. He pulled away to look into her eyes, easing her hair back with his right hand. An overwhelming urge to hurt someone on her behalf whistled through him. "Talk to me. What happened?"

Glancing up at him, she shook her head. "Can we get out of here, please? Like, now. Please." She looked over her shoulder and grabbed Brendan's good hand, leading the way to the truck.

"Yes. Yeah. But do I need to go back in there and kick someone's ass?" He hung back, leery to leave in case this gave him a chance to confront Miles.

"No, no. Just c'mon please. Before any of them come out."

Them? "Who's coming out?" The need to beat the shit out of someone burned through him like fire. He'd fought feelings like this for years, but now he didn't want to work through the rage, he wanted to pound somebody. Ultimately the desperation on Casey's face changed his mind. The last thing he wanted was to add to her clear agony.

She didn't say anything until they were in the truck and Brendan had pulled into traffic. Then she put her head in her hands. Her shoulders shook and Brendan wished to God she was laughing, but he knew better. Her tears tore him up.

"Case, talk to me. What happened in there? Are you all right?"

She nodded and sniffed. Pulled a tissue out of her purse and blew her nose. "I'm okay. I just need to lie down. I have a killer headache." He didn't like the look of her pale skin. "Miles wanted me to write songs. Like I could just sit down in a strange place with strange people and bust out a hit. He brought in musicians, a producer...he had the studio ready for a whole session. He didn't even warn me about this."

It clearly freaked her out. "Not your process, huh?"

"Not even close." She told him about the session. About how the words didn't come. How she hated the music they played and it was nothing like she imagined. "I thought Miles wanted what I brought to the show. I mean how am I going to write songs for music that isn't my own? Doesn't he realize that's going to be a problem?"

Apparently not, but Brendan didn't say it out loud.

They reached the house and Brendan was glad Casey could take it easy. He was pretty wiped out himself. He wouldn't be surprised if he'd sweat off ten pounds today.

They made a stop in the kitchen where he grabbed ice water for them both.

Casey's phone vibrated on the counter and she checked the screen. "It's the police," she said, glancing at him before accepting the call. "Hello?" She paused. "This is Casey. Did you find something?"

Brendan watched her face as she listened. Watched what little color she had drain away.

She looked at her watch. "Right now?" She glanced at him, the exhaustion in her eyes as clear as the day outside. "No, I totally understand. I'm on my way. I should be there in less than an hour." She disconnected and took the glass of water from his hand. After guzzling half the glass she sighed. "I have to go to the police station. They found something, but they won't tell me over the phone."

"Fine. Let's go." His shoulder hurt like a bear. He'd been looking forward to a cool house and soft bed, but no way was he letting Casey out of his sight. "After you eat something." He opened the fridge and found a couple of turkey sandwiches his mom must have made for them. "We can take these for the road." With all the crap he ate in the car, Brendan wasn't starving, but he knew she had to be.

Casey didn't argue with the fact that he planned to come with her. Maybe she figured he deserved to know the information too since he'd been a victim as well. After she changed out of her dress and heels into a pair of white capri pants, flats and a navy tank, they trudged back to the car and drove thirty minutes to the police station. She wolfed down half her sandwich and a bottle of water during the drive.

The closer Brendan got to the building, the more his stomach cramped in anxiety. After opening the door, a burst of cool air wafted over them, but Brendan still got the heebie-jeebies from the place. It reminded him too much of the aftermath of his kidnapping. Going through mug shots after his release from the hospital, the nauseous feeling in his stomach because his ribs hurt so badly. Now he was back and he still felt sick this many years later.

They waited ten minutes for the officer who called to meet them at the front desk. He introduced himself as Officer Ramos and ushered them to a back bullpen filled with desks. After pulling an extra chair over for Brendan, they all sat down.

"Miss Turner, can you tell me if you've had anyone in your apartment lately?"

Casey's eyes narrowed. "I'm not sure I understand the question. I mean, I was gone for six weeks doing the show and no one came over once I got home." She shot a glance to Brendan. "I kind of needed some time to regroup." After she lost. She didn't say it out loud, but the implication was there.

"What about before the show?" the officer asked. "Did you have any kind of party or send off?"

"No." She glanced at Brendan again. "We had to keep it confidential per the contract. My parents and Jeff knew, but they weren't going to advertise it. No one was supposed to know except the two people who were the outside interviews and they had to sign confidentiality clauses, too, since they were on camera."

The officer tapped his pencil. "So no one was at your place for any period of time without you being there?"

"Absolutely not. No."

"Why?" Brendan finally asked. Enough with the bullshit.

Officer Ramos looked Casey in the eyes. "Your apartment was bugged."

Her shock registered with wide eyes. "What? Where?" He understood how violated she felt. Understood it with a clarity that tightened his chest.

"It was under the table in your dining area. Just about the exact center spot of your apartment, not counting your bedroom. Any conversations that took place in your kitchen or den would've been picked up by it. The question is how long was it there?"

Color drained from Casey's cheeks. "I have no idea." She shook her head. "So you're saying someone broke into my apartment without me knowing? How is that even possible? Wouldn't I have noticed a broken lock or broken..." Her eyes widened even more. "Oh my God."

"What?" Brendan asked.

"Zoe was watching my apartment when I was in Hawaii, just stopping by every couple of days to make sure everything was okay and bring in my mail. One day she got there and a window near the door was broken. She went in and found a baseball. She checked my jewelry box and everything was there. No electronics were missing and she figured some kids had been playing catch and busted it. She had the window replaced and told me when I got home. I checked and nothing seemed to be missing so I forgot about it."

"Son of a bitch," Brendan seethed.

The officer nodded his head. "That was our guy. So he planted the bug while you were gone and listened to everything when you got home." He pulled a pad of paper over. "Did your sister tell you when that happened?"

"It was midway in my trip, I remember that. I can call Zoe and ask. She'll remember."

Officer Ramos nodded. "Good. Do you remember any phone conversations you might have had in your living room that might have been overheard?"

"Zoe came over, but that was it. I talked with her and my parents on the phone when I got home, but..." She froze again and looked at Brendan. "Oh my God. That's how the show—how Miles—found out."

"Found out what?" the officer asked.

Casey ignored him and turned fully to Brendan. "I told Zoe about meeting you in Hawaii and she put the pieces together after watching us during the show. She knew we'd met before. I told her your name and that you worked for Seger. She knows me inside and out, and she totally saw the surprise on my face when you walked in the first day of the show. So when I got home we talked about it. Whoever bugged my place heard the same conversation. That was right before the news came out. Oh my God, Bren, it was my fault after all. I'm so sorry."

The anguish in her voice killed him. Brendan leaned forward and wrapped an arm around her. "It's okay. You didn't know you were being recorded. Don't blame yourself." He turned to the officer. "Any chance you picked up a print when you found the bug?"

"We picked up two sets. My guess is they belong to Miss Turner and her sister, but—" he glanced at Casey, "—we need to get your prints and hers to verify. Do you think she'd come down for that?"

"Of course. Anything to help. I'll call her."

The officer nodded. He asked a few more questions and ten minutes later Brendan was driving Casey back to his parents' place.

With her fingers massaging her temples, Casey looked to be in about as much pain as he was. Once at the house, with the security gate closed and their safety assured, Brendan took Casey's hand and walked her upstairs to his old bedroom. He gestured to the bed. "Get comfortable. I'll be right back."

"Bren, I have my own room. I'm not going to sleep with you."

"I know and I know. Can we just lay down next to each other for a minute and give some pain relievers a chance to take away your headache and my shoulder ache?"

She dropped her chin to her chest. "Yes, yes, I'm sorry. I'm just..." She blinked back emotion. "I'm just a little overwhelmed right now."

Brendan backtracked and pulled her close. "I know, Case. Me too." He breathed in the sweet smell of her flowery shampoo and ran his hand up her arm until he cupped her nape. The more he touched her the more he wanted her. "Let me get those ibuprofens. I'll be right back."

Four minutes later, they were lying next to each other on top of the blanket, staring up at the ceiling. Brendan turned just in time to see a tear streak down Casey's temple. He took her hand and squeezed. "It's going to be okay. I'll make sure of it." He didn't know if could make good on his promise, but he damn well intended to try.

CHAPTER 21

CASEY SLOWLY OPENED HER eyes to a strange bedroom. Brendan's bedroom to be exact. She lay alone on the bed, but the indent of Brendan's head still showed on his pillow. The sun was setting outside and turned the partly cloudy sky into a mix of pinks and oranges.

Sports trophies and books lined the oak bookcase on the sidewall with framed family pictures dotting open areas. The hunter green walls kept her in a relaxed haze and her headache had mostly disappeared with the exception of a tiny reminder where the stitches pulled at her scalp.

Like a knife to her chest, instant pressure built at the thought of creating songs to music she didn't connect with. A knot lodged in her throat and her eyes stung. How was she going to handle another day like today? Would every songwriting session be this painful? She should be happy that her dream was coming true, except she knew the reality of winning the show wasn't the reality of her expectations.

Miles didn't want her music. He wanted her words. He expected lyrics to fit in with the music provided by RJ and his bunch. How long would he give her to write lyrics and what happened if she couldn't come up with anything? Or what if he hated what she *did* write?

The door eased open and Brendan came in with a tray balanced in his good hand. He'd changed out of jeans and into black nylon basketball shorts and fresh white T-shirt. A light dusting of auburn hair covered his legs. "It's the early bird dinner," he said, setting the tray on the bed. "Pasta salad, fruit and..."

"Is that lemonade?" she asked, fluffing a pillow behind her before taking a sip of the pink liquid in a clear glass.

"Yep. Hope that's okay."

"My favorite." He clearly remembered that from one of their conversations during the show. Her heart thawed. "Thanks." She picked up the closest bowl and dug in. "Mmm, so good," she said around a mouthful. "How'd you know I'd be starving?"

He lifted a dark eyebrow. "Because you've been going since early this morning and you only had half a sandwich in the car this afternoon."

He was right. She'd been too sick to her stomach before the morning show to eat anything. Then she'd been thrown into a writing session with complete strangers and hadn't even thought about food. What should've been a few minutes of *get to know me* turned into a three hour horror show of edgy music and zero creativity on her part.

"Besides, I'm starving too." Baking in the sun today had obviously given him an appetite. He took his own forkful and closed his eyes in satisfaction.

There was something about watching a sexy man eat. The way his jaw moved. The way his Adam's apple bobbed and his neck muscles worked when he swallowed. Brendan had his thick hair pulled back into a ponytail and Casey noticed his disfigured ear.

"When did you quit wearing the prosthetic?" she asked, taking another bite.

Brendan looked up as if she'd mentioned something taboo.

"I mean, I get why you wore it during the show, but I didn't know…" Shit, she was making this worse. She already knew it was a sore spot with him from their time in Hawaii. "Forget I said anything. Sorry."

He finished chewing his bite and washed it down with lemonade. "I don't usually wear it, but I didn't want the whole world scrutinizing me in case someone noticed," he said quietly.

"I get it. It's a private thing." She hesitated before asking, but figured what the hell. "Why not just wear it all the time if it bothers you so much?"

Shrugging, he took a sip of his drink. "I don't know. I thought maybe I needed to just be me, and me is a guy with a disfigured ear. The reality is harder to handle when people notice and want to talk about it."

Casey couldn't help herself. "*Do* you ever talk about it?" The hard look in his eyes answered her question. "Okaaayyyy. I guess we'll move on to another topic." She took a bite of her pasta and maybe it was a bit more forceful than she expected because she bit the side of her mouth, barely holding back a gasp.

"Look..." Brendan set his bowl on the tray. "I... Honestly, I rarely talk about it. It's just..." He clearly struggled to find words as his gaze darted to hers. "Did you ever see the movie *Payback* with Julie Frazer?"

Casey snorted. "Who didn't? How often does a movie get box office and critical success?" Her sentence ended abruptly when she thought about the movie. About the family kidnapped and used as leverage so that a crime lord could exact his revenge on someone else. One of the brother's ears had been sliced and sent to his sister to ensure her cooperation. "Oh my God. It was *your* family that was kidnapped?" Casey set her bowl down. "*You* were the one..." She couldn't even say it out loud.

"The one who had most of his ear sliced off and mailed to his sister. Yeah," he said, his voice hard, but barely audible. "That was me." It explained the high tech gate in an otherwise gate free community. It explained how overprotective he was when it came to her safety.

The pasta turned in Casey's stomach. "God, Bren. I didn't know. I didn't realize." She wanted to hug him or comfort him somehow, but his straight spine and hard eyes said back off. Not to mention the tray of food between them.

Bits of the movie flashed in her mind. The fight when the first two brothers were taken. The brutal violence of the scene. If Casey remembered correctly and if the movie was true to real life events, which she'd read that it was, Brendan had been the one most injured during the kidnapping. He'd suffered multiple broken ribs, a concussion, a severed ear and by the end, a collapsed lung.

He nodded, picked up his bowl and continued eating, so Casey did the same. They finished their meal silently until Brendan made a move to take the tray.

Casey stopped him. "I've got it," she said. "You brought it up. I can take it down." She grabbed the tray before Brendan argued. As she went downstairs, her brain processed all this new information about Brendan. He'd been through a horrifying experience and come out the other side. Though he appeared to be mentally and physically healthy, he definitely carried scars. God, this could explain why he'd frozen up on her apartment floor. Maybe he'd had some sort of flashback.

Casey washed the dishes and stuck them in the drain board next to the sink. She was about to open the freezer to see if there was anything she could surprise Brendan with for dessert when the back door opened and Terry entered.

"Hi!" Terry's hair gleamed burnt orange in the setting sun and her cheeks were flushed. "How are you feeling?"

"I'm okay. Thanks." A nap and food had worked wonders for her mood.

"Good." She moved to the desk in the corner of the kitchen. "Look, I didn't get a chance to talk to you this morning. I know you were in a hurry, but I'm really glad you didn't leave."

Casey remembered the earnest concern in Jay's eyes as he'd convinced her to stay. Presenting the facts as if he'd been in court, using logic without making her feel small or stupid, and doing it all in a matter of minutes. He'd spoken with respect and without a trace of condemnation. Knowing how young he was explained why he seemed less of a parent and more of a peer. If genetics were any indication, Brendan was going to remain as gorgeous as his dad. "Your husband is very persuasive."

Terry's smile and nod lit up her face. "I know, isn't he? He's one hell of a lawyer. Not a bad husband either." She winked then paused. "Brendan is a lot like him. A little stubborn, a lot macho." Her grin faded. "They're both very fierce when they want to protect something important to them." She picked up an envelope from the desk. "I hope you'll give Brendan the benefit of the doubt. He's a good man and he means well. Sometimes, his fierceness gets in his way." She lifted her hand with the envelope and flashed her bright smile. "I knew I left these here. Jay and I have tickets to the Ahmanson tonight. You guys are okay, right? Or should we cancel?"

"No, don't cancel!" Casey said. The instant change of subject left no room for a rebuttal, not that Casey had one. "We had a long day, but we're fine. You should go and have fun."

"Okay. I'll check on you when we get back." She gestured outside. "Jay's waiting, so I'll see you later." She got to the door then turned. "Oh, I almost forgot. Here," she lifted the lid on a cake plate that Casey hadn't even noticed on the counter. A huge chocolate cake made her mouth water and answered her dessert dilemma. "I made Brendan's favorite. Take him a slice. He'll be in the palm of your hand all night." Terry winked again, replaced the top and headed out.

"Thanks," Casey called after her as the door closed. "Bye."

A whole night with Brendan to herself.

BRENDAN RAN A HAND over his head. "Shit," he muttered. He should tell her...not that she didn't already know the basics since the movie was pretty damn close to the real thing. His sister—Hollywood's newest "It Girl"—had made sure the movie stayed true to actual events. Since she'd directed and produced the whole thing with her husband, she'd held total creative control. That was a feat mostly unheard of in Hollywood. But if anyone deserved the success, Jess did. She worked damn hard to make that film and the success had gone hand in hand with her personal happiness as well.

Still, the event that she had so willingly shared with the world was something he'd tried to hide. Close family and friends knew he didn't like to talk about it, so they respected him and didn't. Rarely did the subject come up any other time and Brendan *never* brought it up. He hated relieving that event. Despised the helplessness and fear that made him sick to this day. The pain had almost been secondary to the horror of watching his family members repeatedly trying to divert the physical abuse to themselves. He didn't think he'd ever get past the guilt.

Now he felt as if he owed Casey an explanation. She'd done as he requested, had come to his parents' place to regroup while the police investigated. The least he could do was be honest about his history.

Casey returned with a plate in one hand and glass of milk in the other. The smell registered a half a second after he realized what she had. His heart took an extra thump watching the most beautiful girl holding his favorite dessert. One of life's perfect moments.

"Holy shit. No way." Brendan sat up, staring at the decadent chocolate cake with vanilla ice cream. He blinked to make sure he wasn't dreaming.

"I heard it on good authority that this is your favorite."

The smile on Casey's face lit his fuse as much as the chocolate. "You heard right. Did my mom bring that home? I didn't see it on the table when we walked in."

"She had it covered, pushed in the corner on the counter. I wouldn't have seen it if she hadn't popped in. She and your dad have tickets for a show tonight. She asked me if they should cancel and I told her not to."

Brendan's heart took a few extra hard beats. The thought of having assured alone time made his blood run hot. Sure, they were both less than a hundred percent, but he craved skin time with her. He wanted to touch her so bad, kiss her without the threat of interruption, without worrying about anything but just being with her. Screw the cake, he'd rather devour Casey.

She sat next to him and offered the plate and fork.

It was too hard to resist. "Don't you want any?" he asked, taking the first bite. The moist, rich chocolate nearly melted in his mouth. "Oh my God, my mother knows how to bake a fucking cake. This is unbelievable. Here." He sliced a piece and lifted it to her lips. Casey opened her mouth for the chocolate-and-vanilla combo. She closed her eyes and moaned, and the sound went straight to Brendan's dick. "Why didn't you get some for yourself?"

"I didn't think I wanted any. The pasta filled me up."

He shook his head. "Trust me. You'll always want my mom's cake. Have another bite." Brendan fed her another piece. Their eyes locked as she chewed and it was the sexiest thing he'd seen since that first night when he'd stripped her of clothes. They finished the slice with Brendan giving Casey a bite for every few of his. He chugged the milk, then put the plate and glass aside when he finished.

"Wait, c'mere," she said, leaning closer. "You've got a little chocolate right..." She leaned over and swiped the chocolate off the corner of his mouth with her finger.

Brendan caught her hand, held it, stared into her eyes as he slowly sucked the chocolate off her finger. Her eyes widened; her breath froze. Most of the blood in his system rushed south. She licked her lips with that luscious pink tongue and Brendan lost what little control he had left.

He shifted, pulled her closer with his good arm, and tilted his head, his gaze never leaving hers. Slowly, he brushed his lips over hers, loving the sweet smoothness of her amazing mouth. God, he wanted more, wanted her closer.

He'd taken the edge off the pain with a couple of pills so his arm didn't bother him as much as it could have. In fact...screw it. He pulled back and eased the sling off completely.

"Brendan, don't." The dreaminess faded from her voice. "What are you doing?" Now she sounded like his mother, all business and no pleasure.

"Making things easier." He didn't let her get another word out because he had new leverage and at the same time he closed his mouth over hers, he took her down, forcing her back right where she sat until her head rested at the foot of the bed. The zinging pain in his arm, had nothing on the pleasure of feeling her under him.

"Brendan," she breathed. "You're going to hurt yourself. Cut it out." But she didn't fight him when he dove in for another sheet melting kiss. She tasted like warm chocolate, like heaven, like perfection. Her little sighs only added fuel to the burning fire in his veins.

He leaned on his good arm and caressed her with the other, grazing the curve of her waist and gentle slope of her breast. "I've missed you." He went in deeper, swept his tongue around hers in total conquest and she matched him, giving what she got with all the passion he remembered from Hawaii.

She moaned and revved Brendan's blood hotter, but then both hands framed his face. "Bren. Hold up. Wait." She held his head and looked into his eyes. "We're not sleeping together now."

He blinked a few times, tried to make sense of the words that didn't match their action. "What?" Maybe someone had come home. He listened to the silent house, but didn't hear anything. "We're alone—really alone—for the first time since Hawaii. No interruptions, it's all good." He moved to kiss her again, but she stopped him.

"Bren, it's not that I don't want to, I just—"

He kissed her before she said anything else and the fact that she kissed him back gave him hope. Nothing topped Casey when she gave herself heart and soul. Brendan loved the way her hands moved over his shoulders or splayed against his chest. She lit him up faster than a match to dried twigs. Except after another scorcher of a kiss she pulled his head back again and wiggled away, leaving him cold and alone.

"Seriously. I can't do this. I thought I could, but I can't. I'm sorry." She stood up, breathing hard, her cheeks flushed.

Brendan lay sprawled on the bed, keeping his arm across his chest and fighting the pain. Not the pain in his arm, but the hurt that she didn't want to be with him.

"I'm in a weird place, okay. Hawaii was amazing, but I didn't think I'd ever see you again. I just needed to break free. I needed something to help me find my way. Something to give me confidence and start on a fresh road."

Brendan finally looked at her, at the emotion in her eyes. She looked as wrecked as she had earlier that day. It was the last thing he wanted.

"I didn't mean to push you just now. It's just…when you kissed me back, I thought…"

"I know, I know. I take full responsibility and I'm sorry. I thought the same thing when your parent's left. I thought we'd get a few hours to reconnect. To recreate Hawaii, but we can't. I like you. A lot." She swiped beneath her eyes. "Probably too much."

He sat up. "How is that a problem? I like you too." A big fat lie because he more than liked her, but wrapping his brain around the other *L* word didn't seem possible.

"I know." She nodded, but the frown on her forehead spoke volumes. "I just have to be honest. There are things about you that I'm not sure of."

That cut deep. Especially after everything they'd been through together. Yeah, they'd had their moments, but for the most part, he felt a real connection with her. "What things?" he asked and he was damn proud of the even tone of his voice when inside he was howling.

"You just...sometimes you say things and it makes me feel like my ex did. I won't go back to something like that. I can't. I have to feel like I'm a partner, not someone less than, and it's way too soon for that anyway for us." She glanced around the room before meeting his gaze. "Hawaii really screwed things up."

"I don't believe that," he said. "I mean, that Hawaii screwed things up. Meeting you..." he trailed off, trying to find the words that expressed what he felt. "I've never connected with anyone the way I did with you."

She scoffed and rolled her eyes.

"I'm serious, and I'm not talking about the sex. I had a great time with you before the sex. You're funny. Sexy. You're creative as hell." He sat up and reached for her hand, relieved when she didn't pull away. "And I'm sorry if I've ever made you feel 'less than.' It was never my intention. My mom has mentioned on occasion that sometimes I lack finesse. I'll work harder on that...on communicating better." He patted the spot next to him because he wanted answers. "Sit? Please?"

She hesitated only a few seconds before sitting next to him and twirling the ring on her finger.

"Okay, so I know your ex was a douchebag. But to what extent? I mean...did he hurt you? Physically?" Because if he did, the bastard was going to hear from him.

She pressed her lips together and the fact that she didn't give him an immediate *no* answered his question.

"The fucker hit you?" He stood up, couldn't keep the anger out of his voice.

"No," she said. "He never hit me, per se. A couple months before we broke up he wrapped his hands around my neck and gave me a good scare."

Brendan wanted to hunt the asshole down and break him apart piece by piece.

"Mainly he was very good at breaking things and verbal assaults."

"What kind of verbal assaults?" Brendan reigned in his emotions and sat next to her.

"I don't know. Like I should wear a certain dress he bought me because the new one I bought made me look like a whore. Or…here's a favorite. I should never wear heels because they make me freakishly tall." She snorted and flicked some hair over her shoulder. "He was big on apologies, too—from me. Didn't matter if something was *my* fault or not. If he thought I should apologize, then I was in the shit house until I said, I'm sorry.

"Look, he and I are over. It's done. I'm trying to put it behind me. I'm getting my confidence back."

She was. He'd seen it and he was proud of her for it. Some of his anger dissipated. "FYI," Brendan said. "You rock in a pair of heels."

Her sheepish grin and slight flush arrowed a direct hit to his heart.

He wanted more. More of her smile, her light. "Heels make you a fucking cover model. I mean, we're talking 'Vanity Fair' beautiful." Brendan snorted. He had a good idea why her ex had a problem with heels. "I have to ask, how tall was this joker?"

"Six feet."

"So heels made you taller than him. Of course he didn't like them. Fucker."

Casey looked away and Brendan realized that talking about him wasn't helping. He took her hand. "Okay. Enough of the Fucker Douchebag. What do you want to do? My parents are out and it's just the two of us."

She met his gaze, hope in her eyes. "You really want to know?"

"Yeah. Of course. Name it."

CHAPTER 22

CASEY DIDN'T WANT TO push too hard, but she wanted to know about Brendan. It seemed fair considering she'd told him about herself. Sure the movie had shown what the family had gone through physically, but how many scars did Brendan have internally? What if she was right about him freezing after he'd been shot because of some kind of traumatic reaction to his past? Casey didn't want to keep him at a distance. She wanted to understand him. "Can you just hold me for a little while?"

He nodded, gave her a half grin. "Yeah. You don't have to sound like it's a jail sentence. I am very down with holding you." He moved toward the headboard and motioned her next to him.

"Will you tell me about yourself too?"

His face darkened; even his muscles tensed. "You're talking about the kidnapping."

Maybe it wasn't fair to ask this of him. But if he really wanted her, wanted to build something solid, then she needed more. "I guess I'm just so amazed at how...how..." She couldn't find the words she wanted to describe him. "How together you are. I mean, you're talented, smart, fun—you don't seem jaded or cynical."

"I am, though," he said, giving her a side glance. "I'm cynical as hell. I don't trust people anymore. I snap. I don't have the patience I used to have." He leaned back against the pillow. "And now I know I'm useless in stressful situations." Bam. There was yesterday in the blink of an eye and he looked miserable about it.

"I disagree." Casey scooted next to him until she rested against his chest. She felt safe nestled in the strength of his arm. "I think you're forgetting the stressful situations of saving me in the ocean and all those other times during the show. You got knocked around too."

"Not really the same thing, but thanks." He stilled completely and Casey looked up at him. "Yesterday—the fact that I froze—scares the shit out of me. Because what if I do it again?"

She sat up, her heart twisting as she studied his tortured eyes. "Look at all the times you didn't freeze. Yesterday was an anomaly. A person isn't supposed to be attacked in their own home or anyone else's. I think the surprise and the pain just put you in a different zone."

He snorted then sighed, as if resigned to an idea. "Are you sure you're not a shrink. Because that sounds very shrink-like." She smiled at the teasing tone of his words. "It's also possible you're a hundred percent right." Her pulled her down next to him again. "Would you believe I was a total egghead before the kidnapping?"

"What? No." She looked up at him. The five o'clock shadow made him uber sexy. With the amount of muscles defining every inch of skin, he could've easily been a professional model or athlete. "I don't believe you. You mean a computer geek?"

Nodding, he stroked his hand along her hair and brought goose bumps to her skin. "Totally. I always thought I was going to design some kind of app or something to revolutionize the world, but after the...after I got out of the hospital, I was a different person. All I wanted was to get strong. I vowed that something like that was never going to happen to me again. Blake and I talked about it a few times. We started pushing each other at the gym. We both carry protection."

Casey leaned on her elbow. Her heart opened up a little bit more. "You do? You mean like a gun?"

"Not a gun, no. A knife. It's tucked in a sheath inside my boot."

"I wondered why you were wearing boots in this heat. You always wear them?"

He nodded. "The next time someone comes after me, I'm going to be prepared. Bullets notwithstanding, obviously." He lifted his hurt arm and winced.

She nestled next to him again. "So did everything happen exactly as it did in the movie?"

"Pretty much."

Casey shivered. "I couldn't even watch the scene when the twins—when you and Blake—came home. The music itself scared the crap out of me. But the violence. I hate violence." Knowing four men awaited them as the twins entered the house had the audience on the edge of the seat.

"Makes two of us," Brendan murmured. He rubbed her arm and brought her closer.

Shifting, Casey canted her head to see his face. "I have to ask this question." He looked into her eyes and nodded, so she continued, "Why did you keep fighting? I mean there were two of them and they were much bigger than you. I don't understand why you didn't stay down."

Brendan shrugged. "I couldn't quit. They were in *my* house. I just assumed Blake and I busted in on a robbery in progress and I had it in my head that no one was going to take any of our shit. Period."

"But your brother was screaming at you to stop, to stay down." Blake had been overpowered by two men as well.

"I never heard him." He shook his head. "I didn't hear anything, but my heart pounding between my ears. It was like this white noise in between every time they hit me. My chest hurt so bad, it felt like it was on fire."

Casey absently stroked her hand across the soft cotton over his rock hard abs. "That's what happens with broken ribs and a collapsed lung."

He shook his head. "My lung didn't collapse until my brother-in-law tossed me over his shoulder to get me out of the basement at the end. I was in bad shape before with a couple of broken ribs, but at that point, I didn't think I was going to make it. I couldn't breathe."

"Oh my God, I totally know which part you're talking about." Her heart had been racing, her palms drenched with sweat at the climactic ending. "But if he hadn't done that—"

"If he hadn't done that, I probably wouldn't be here today talking about it. I doubt *any* of us would be here today." A sobering thought.

"So you recovered and got strong."

He nodded. "I did. Blake always had more muscle than me. I mean, we were mostly the same build, but Blake worked out. It took me some time to catch up, especially after so many weeks recovering. I lost a ton of weight and what muscle I did have atrophied. It took me forever to get as strong as him."

"Why didn't you go back to your computer stuff?"

He thought about it for a moment. "Basically, I couldn't sit still anymore. If I stayed in a chair too long, I got fidgety. I kept looking over my shoulder, looking out the window. I needed to do something different. I couldn't concentrate long enough anymore to do that kind of work. Bartending was a good way to keep moving and make a few bucks." His calloused fingers stroked along her arm and created more goose bumps. "My dad had introduced us all to music at a young age, but I never took it seriously. After the kidnapping I had all this shit in my head, all these emotions that kept twisting around and eating at me. I ended up going back to the music. Lyrics became my outlet. Putting the lyrics to music just followed. Music was physical. I didn't have to be still. Hell, I *couldn't* be still."

"Then you fell into the job with Seger."

He nodded. "Exactly. It was perfect because I'm always moving for him. Running errands or giving people tours at different venues, helping to coordinate his schedule or whatever. I guess I've done a little bit of everything for him."

"You know, I never did ask, what did he say when you two were finally alone after the show...when the cameras were gone?"

Brendan chuckled. "He was a little bent out of shape that I hadn't said anything to him about my music beforehand."

"Because he likes it, right?"

He nodded, a half grin kicking up his lips. "Yeah, yeah." Brendan stalled before glancing at her. "He wants to work together on his next project. He wants to make a duet album."

Casey's jaw nearly hit her chest. "Are you kidding me? That's better than winning the show. But, don't you have to get permission from Miles, or give him a cut? Wasn't that in the contract we signed?"

"Yeah, Miles was so pissed at me, he shredded the contract. I'm pretty sure he wasn't thinking about what I might do next, he just wanted to make sure I knew I wasn't getting the half million. The guy did me a favor."

Huffing a laugh, Casey clapped a hand over her mouth. "Oh, my God. I can't believe he did that. Hey, didn't I read that Seger's starting his own record label?"

"Yeah. He wants this album to be the first one on the label."

"Wow! Brendan, that's great. That's so great." Casey hugged him tight, her heart full. The little bolt of pride turned into a giant ball of euphoria. She couldn't have been happier for him. One second she was in his arms, then she was looking into his gorgeous eyes, laughing her relief. She didn't know how it happened but in the next instant they had their lips fused together. The laughter abruptly ended and turned into pleasure...and heat.

BRENDAN WAS PRETTY SURE he hadn't initiated the kiss, but it didn't stop him from going with it. He didn't care if they weren't going to have sex. Sap that he was, he was happy to take any fucking morsel of attention she wanted to give him. He was in *that* deep with her. It scared him a little to be so emotionally attached to someone who didn't feel the same way. And why would she when she still had all those walls she'd built after being dumped by her ex. She wasn't jumping into anything emotional and Brendan couldn't blame her.

Still, as far as kisses went, this one was about as hot, heavy and sexy as any before it. Scratch that. It was hotter, heavier and sexier.

Casey poured herself into this kiss. It was slow. Wet. Deep.

Completely breath-stealing.

Brendan couldn't control the swift uprising of his dick or the hot blood that surged through his veins. He loved the weight of her on his chest as she eased on top of him. He ran his fingers through her hair and cupped her head with his good hand, hoping to keep her close, to absorb all the attention she put into that kiss.

God, the way she made him feel... Like he was king of the world. The warrior in him wanted to take control, wrap her hair around his hand, drag her beneath him and take her body in primitive need. But sanity prevailed—albeit by a thread—and Brendan let her lead the way.

She killed him with her mouth, with the slowest, deepest and sexiest kisses they'd shared yet. Hawaii had been mostly fast and hard. Deliciously dirty and unplanned. The newness had stoked the flames and kept the fire between them burning brightly all night.

But now. This. This slow seduction had Brendan on edge. Casey rubbed herself against his erection and Brendan sucked in a hard breath. Shit, that moan belonged to him.

He should stop her if only for his sanity, but her silky hand slipped beneath his shirt, trailed down his abs and stomach sending electric streaks right to his dick. Just as he was about to say something, she shifted and placed her hand on his package. He moaned again. Couldn't help himself. "Case," he breathed. He didn't know if he wanted to stop her or beg for more.

"Shh." She kissed him again as she eased her hand beneath the waistband of his shorts. Had she changed her mind?

"Casey?"

"Shh," she said again. Seconds later she had her hand wrapped around his dick and Brendan lost all train of thought. Nothing registered but the pressure of her palm, the way she stroked him with a tight fist. He could only thrust into her hand, seeking the release of all his pent up frustration from the past two months.

The slow kiss turned desperate...at least on his part. He couldn't get enough. He gripped her head tighter, consumed her as she pushed him closer to the edge. Heat nearly incinerated him. Flames licked up his gut as every muscle tightened and his control frayed. Over and over she pumped him, stroking him harder, faster. Sweat broke out from every pore.

"Case," he growled. "I can't... I need..." He didn't want it like this, but he couldn't tell her stop either.

"Do it," she whispered. "Let go. I've got you. I'm right here."

Dammit. Just those words, her encouragement, sent him over the edge. He growled, tried to hold off a little longer, but failed. Two more strokes and he lost it. He came hard. Stars flashed behind his lids and each pulsing beat of his heart pounded like the climax blazing through him. Her hot breath wafted across his cheek, the soft noise in her throat heightened his orgasm.

When the tremors stopped. When Brendan lay there completely tapped out and weak, he opened his eyes.

Casey stared down at him, her eyes bright, a near smile on her face, but not quite.

"Why'd you do that? You didn't have to." He'd been positive that any kind of sex had been removed from the table a little while ago. Unless…was this a pity hand job? His brain had been too busy dealing with the pleasure to think about her motives, but now Brendan walked a tightrope between anger and relief. Any kind of sex with Casey took their relationship in the right direction, with the exception of sympathy sex.

"I did it because I wanted to."

"But before you said—"

"I know what I said, and I meant it. We didn't have sex. At least not the intercourse kind. This was just…I don't know. I just hated hearing that story and then I was really happy about the Seger news and I wanted to make you feel good. Sue me."

Maybe he hadn't been too far off the mark. He eased her off him and sat up before stripping his damp shirt over his head. He used it to clean up the mess on his stomach then threw it in the corner before standing up.

"What?" she asked. "You're pissed." She sat up in the middle of the bed, her hair rumpled, her lips red from his kiss. She sounded completely baffled and his anger faded.

"Casey, look…" He grabbed a fresh black T-shirt from his old stash in the drawer and eased his beat up arm—yeah, it hurt—through a hole before pulling it over his head. "You want to know the truth. I'm getting serious mixed signals from you. You know I'm into you. It's not a secret. I don't know what kind of emotional shit your ex put you through, but I'm not him. I need you to realize that. You just have to be honest with me. Tell me if I do or say something that freaks you out."

Her forehead creased and she looked as if he'd punched her. Brendan felt like shit. He moved toward her, but she stopped him, her hand out. "No. You're right. I'm sorry. I said one thing then did another. Kind of." She shook her head. "It's just, sex is one thing. Making you feel good is something else."

"Case, sex is sex. I already like you. We've been through this. I like you a lot." He wasn't ready to tell her how much, mostly because it scared the hell out of him which meant it would probably send her running the other direction as fast as an Olympian. "Every time you touch me I like you that much more. But if this," he gestured between them, "is only a pity situation on your part, then tell me now. Because I can't do that. I'm either in this with you or I'm out." She moved away from him, but Brendan snagged her hand and brought her back. "Hold up. I'm just being honest. I think it's time you're honest with me." He sat next to her.

"I've been totally honest with you," she replied, her words laced with attitude.

"Okay, okay," he pulled her back when she tried to leave again. "Right now. What's going on right now? Why are you mad?"

"Because you won't let me go. It's something Jeff would've done."

Brendan immediately released her and put his hands up. "Sorry. Not my intention. I'm just trying to talk to you."

Casey stood and wrapped her arms around her middle. "I'm mad because I'm so fucked up because of him. Because I want to have sex with you, but I'm scared. You were supposed to be the rebound guy, Bren. You were supposed to be in and out of my life in one day. I didn't expect this. I didn't expect to feel this much when we're together." She paused and met his gaze. "I thought I was going to get comfortable in my own skin before I met another guy. You kind of blindsided me."

He laughed at that. "*I* blindsided *you?* How do you think *I* feel? You were so bold that first day. Turning breakfast into time at the pool. Then dinner. Then after dinner." He smiled at the blush on her cheeks. "I'll never forget that night as long as I live, Case. Never." Brendan stood and faced her. He eased some hair behind her ear. "You and I found each other. I don't care when or how it happened. I just know that we met and we click. I don't care what we've been through. I care about where we're going. Am I making sense so far?"

She nodded, her eyes still skeptical.

"Besides, Hawaii seems so long ago at this point, I don't even know that it pertains to now. Let's call ourselves old friends who've reconnected and go from there. How's that sound?"

"Old friends?" That got a smile out of her and Brendan grinned.

"Yeah." He leaned down and kissed her lips softly. "It so happens that *this* old friend owes *this* old friend an orgasm."

The sound of her laugh went straight to Brendan's heart.

"Funny, I don't remember getting an IOU for that," she said.

"No worries. All that matters is that I remember." He leaned in and brushed his lips across hers, a soft caress that had her sighing into his mouth, but she pulled back a second later.

"Brendan, you don't have to. Seriously, I just wanted—"

"Sh," he whispered against her lips. Just as she'd done with him. "I know I don't have to. I want to. Just like you wanted to for me." He kissed her again, teased her with his lips and tongue. Since she seemed set on avoiding intercourse, Brendan decided to reciprocate by matching her seduction. He worked the button and zipper of her tight capri pants and eased his hand beneath her tiny lace thong. God, just thinking about that little piece of material started his blood pumping south again.

Casey wrapped her hands around his neck and dove into his kiss.

All aboard. This train wasn't stopping until Casey's engine ran out of gas.

Brendan took her down to the bed—ignoring the hot sting of pain in his shoulder. His technique was limited, but he still had his mouth and one good arm.

Shit. It only took a second to discover he needed his weight on his good arm, which put his injured arm to the test. Lifting her shirt, he pushed her bra cup beneath her breast and sucked on that sweet nipple begging for attention. She moaned, arched into his mouth and got rid of the top completely when she whipped it over her head. Hell yes. The sounds she made, the utter abandonment set his blood on fire. Next, he settled his hand on her stomach and eased it down to the opening of her pants. Damn, he wanted to see her. He pushed one side down and she helped him with the other side. Finding the small dark racing strip of hair between her legs was like finding the Holy Grail. Apparently she was a woman who experimented, since last time she'd been baby smooth.

"I love this little patch, Case. Very sexy. It's like an *X* marking the treasure." He adjusted, kissed her mouth as he pushed the tip of his finger inside her heat. She moaned again and lifted her hips to take more, but Brendan held back. "Easy there. I've got you." He teased her more, stroking along the wet seam of her vagina and alternately dipping inside for more of her hot cream to ease his way. "I love that you're so wet for me, Case. Also sexy."

"Brendan, you're killing me. Hurry. Please." She squirmed under his touch and Brendan smiled against her ear.

"Patience is a virtue, remember?"

"It's overrated," she huffed, taking his head in her hands and guiding his mouth toward hers. She kicked her pants off the rest of the way. "If you don't finger me in the next two seconds, I'll do myself."

Brendan froze, because picturing Casey taking the reins of her own pleasure nearly gave him a heart attack. It also sent a fresh surge of lust coursing through his veins. "That sounds like a show I could get into."

"I'd rather you stick with your original plan because—" She gasped when he hooked his finger deep inside her and hit a bundle of nerves. "Oh, God, yes, please. Just like that." Her hips moved, seeking more and he battled the urge to do more than use his hand.

Brendan circled her clit with his thumb while he pumped a couple of fingers into her tight heat. Casey arched, moaned, squirmed, bucked. "God, Brendan, yes, yes, yes." She kissed him again as if her life depended on it and Brendan picked up the pace, mesmerized by her total abandonment, and loving her passion.

Casey palmed her breast, squeezed it. "Right there." She cried out and Brendan felt the contractions of her climax pulse around his fingers. His dick was solid stone again just from watching her response. He would've moved over her if he thought his arm would support him, but his shoulder throbbed like a bitch.

When she finally came down, he pulled his fingers from between her legs, cupped that sweet, wet spot and whispered in her ear. "That would make us even."

She shook her head, still breathing unsteady. "I don't think so. I think after that, I probably owe you again." She opened her eyes and met his gaze, a slow smile spreading across her lips. "That was pretty amazing. Who knew you were so talented one-handed?"

As he searched for a glib reply, squeaking sounded out front and Casey stiffened in his arms. Her eyes widened. Someone was coming through the front gate.

Shit. Brendan rolled off the bed and peeked out the window. His dad's black Mustang eased up the drive. "Weird. It's my parents. I thought—"

"Oh my God! They're early!" She bolted upright and scrambled for her clothes. "This room totally smells like sex." She waved her hands all over the place after getting her shirt on. Then she ran to his dresser and sprayed the cologne he'd left behind when he'd moved out.

Brendan was pretty sure nothing would fool his mother, but he eased the sling back over his shoulder to at least give the appearance that he hadn't just had the best hand sex of his life. They heard the door open downstairs while Casey struggled to get her pants right side out.

"Oh, my God, Oh my God, your mother is going to hate me," she whispered frantically, hopping on one foot as she yanked on the capris. Commando style. His dick perked up again.

"No, she's not." Brendan picked up his shirt from the floor and stuffed it under his pillow then eased the door open all the way.

Just as Casey slipped into her sandals, his mother walked in.

She looked up from her phone and glanced between them, her observant blue eyes soaking in everything. "Hi? How are you guys feeling? It was a long day. Everything okay?"

The blush crawling up Casey's face might've been a dead giveaway, but his mother didn't let on. "Yes, we're good here. Did the show end early?" she asked.

"We never got there. The car battery died and we stalled. Had to call the auto club for a jump. By the time they showed up we'd have missed the first half, so we bailed and got a new battery before closing time."

Brendan noticed Casey's thong on the floor partially under the bed and stepped on it as he neared his mom. He kissed her cheek. "Wow. Sorry about that. Hey, thanks for the cake, Mom. Delicious as always."

"You're welcome." She looked between them a second time and Brendan knew she knew. "Well, it was a long day so I'm going to bed. Just wanted to check on you two. See you in the morning."

She left and they heard the door close to his parents' room.

He really did have the coolest mom on the planet. One day he might even tell her.

"She totally knew," Casey said, dropping her chin to her chest. "She's going to hate me."

Brendan grinned as he wrapped his arm around her and pulled her close. Maybe it meant something that she wanted his mom to like her. Maybe it was another crack in that wall she'd built between them. Hopefully that wall was about to topple for good. "Stop it. No one could ever hate you."

CHAPTER 23

HE HATED HER.

Apparently he wasn't the only one.

He couldn't concentrate anymore and shoved the papers back as he swiveled the comfortable leather chair toward the windows. Cars zoomed by on the busy street.

So who wanted her dead besides him and how could he make it work to his advantage? Sitting in his office he replayed the attack in his head for the fiftieth time. It was all he could think about. In hindsight, he realized he should've gone after the man who'd sprayed the bullets. At least then he'd have a clue who to focus on.

Not that he worried. He had plenty of resources.

A grin slid across his lips as he thought about a bullet sailing into Casey's new boyfriend. Brendan St. John deserved to die as much as she did. Anyone who got in his way deserved to die as far as he was concerned.

Maybe that was why he'd stuck around yesterday…to see how they survived. He'd been surprised when they'd both been wheeled out on gurneys. He'd been sure St. John had taken all the bullets and protected Casey, but clearly not.

He'd considered striding into her hospital treatment room for a half second just to see the look on her face when she saw him. But he obviously couldn't have done that. Still, it had been fun to fantasize about.

How close were those two anyway? The show had the country believing they were a hot item, but it wasn't as if they'd shared some kind of dramatic reunion when she'd opened the door. He'd seen tension in their body language, not attraction.

Flipping a pen through his fingers, he stared at the palm trees lining the street. It might be fun to cause Casey even more pain by way of hurting the people around her. He hadn't really considered that idea before. After all, she was now shacking up with St. John. That much he knew.

So now what? For starters, he had to keep an eye out for the shooter. He couldn't let him take all the fun. Although as long as the guy took the heat, everything would be fine. He just had to make sure that no matter what happened to Casey—or St. John—that the bozo with crappy timing took the fall.

He picked up his phone.

"Yes?" Stacy's cool voice came over the line. She was a beauty just like Casey. She was hoping their one-night stand would turn into a permanent situation. Not in this lifetime. He might fuck the secretaries, but he never shacked up with them.

"Hey, it's me. I'll be taking off the rest of the day." He had an appointment with a man. "I think I ate something bad at lunch, so I'm heading home. I'll check in tomorrow morning. Later." Hanging up, he grabbed his sunglasses off his desk and headed out.

Time to refill his stash… And find some information.

CASEY RAN A HAND through her hair and the stitches tugged against her scalp. They itched as bad as the poison ivy she got as a kid during a hellish camping trip. The only good thing to come from that vacation with cousins was the bonding she'd done with her big sis, Zoe. Camping turned out to be their favorite thing to despise.

The four stooges—as she secretly referred to RJ, Leroy, Stubby and Dennis—had gone to lunch, leaving her alone in the studio. The quiet should've helped her come up with words to some type of tune, but so far she had nothing.

She'd convinced Brendan to drop her off and go home. Believing she was safe in a securely protected studio, he'd complied. She'd also convinced him that she needed her car so when he picked her up, he was going to drive to her apartment. Obviously the guy couldn't be at her beck and call every day and she didn't want him to be. It was tough enough being so close to him most of the day—and night. She needed space.

Her thoughts drifted to yesterday. To the few minutes they'd shared in Brendan's bedroom. Jeff was in decent shape, but he didn't hold a candle to Brendan. As far as making her hot...Jeff never took the time to please her the way Brendan did.

Yes, Brendan and Jeff were fundamentally different. So why was she putting the brakes on with Brendan? Why couldn't she let go and see what might happen between them?

"Because you're chicken-shit," she mumbled aloud. Afraid to get back in the saddle and commit to another man...especially the man who was supposed to be strictly her rebound guy.

The door flew open and Casey jumped from the chair.

Miles bounded into room, his mouth a straight line across his hard face. "RJ said this whole morning was a bust. What's the problem, Casey? We're here to write songs, not twiddle our thumbs all day."

"I tried to tell you yesterday that this isn't my process. I need a quiet place. Maybe one instrument." She gestured around the studio. "This is too much. I don't work like this. If you want my music then I need some time. Quiet time," she stressed.

The four guys picked that moment to enter the room, laughing, swearing, smacking each other and generally acting like junior high school delinquents. Casey lifted her brows in a *see what I mean* look.

"Fine," Miles relented, shaking his head. "Go home. You have the weekend. Two days. But in two days you're back here and we put whatever you have to music. Got it?" He stormed out of the room instead of waiting for an answer.

Casey pulled her stuff together and texted Brendan with the news. She hadn't expected the early out and figured she'd have to wait twenty or so minutes for him to get there, but when he knocked on the glass door three minutes later, she realized he'd never gone home. "I told you not to wait for me," she said, following him to the car. The sun blazed down with the same intensity as the day before. Brendan's sweaty shirt stuck to his chest and outlined the contours of his muscles.

"I heard you." He unlocked and opened her door. Something Jeff had never done.

"But you chose to do otherwise." She closed the door before he could, not sure if she was angry that he didn't listen to her or perturbed that she'd lost control of her life in general.

He opened his door and sat behind the wheel. "Look, Casey, if I left you alone and something happened to you, I wouldn't forgive myself." His deep blue eyes begged for understanding. "I'm sorry if I'm smothering you. I just need to know you're safe and until we find more information on whoever wants to hurt you, then you're mostly stuck with me."

She didn't see how that was possible. "What about Seger? Your job? Doesn't that play a factor here?"

He cranked the engine and his truck roared to life. "Seger just came off a huge tour. He's taking some down time, which means I have more leeway with my schedule. It's the upside—or downside depending how you look at—with my job. If my arm worked, I'd probably be behind the bar for a month or two, but that's not in the cards until my shoulder heals more." He slipped his sunglasses on and backed out of the spot.

She sighed and shook her head, but he made it really hard to be angry with him. "I still need to pick up my car," she said. "I'd rather have it in case I need wheels and you're not around. Besides, if I don't start it every few days the battery will crap out."

"That's fine. You can keep it at my parents' place. There's plenty of room." He was so damn accommodating and it only made her feel shittier.

At the apartment, crime scene tape blocked her small patio and her boarded up front door sent a chill down her spine. It made Casey sick to think someone had camped out across the street and waited until they had a shot. Pushing the nasty thought aside, she headed to her car. Brendan scanned the area as he followed her.

"I doubt someone's going to try shooting at us again so soon," Casey said.

Brendan grunted.

Casey ignored him and hit the unlock button on her key fob. The Chevrolet chirped, but made a different sound than normal. "That's weird." She opened the door.

"What?" Brendan stopped next to her.

"The alarm sounded funny. I wonder if the battery is already dying." Her ass barely made contact with the driver's seat when Brendan grabbed her arm and pulled her out, his focus on the ground. "Hey! What are you doing? I need to make sure—"

"*Sh...run!*" He bolted away from the car, dragging Casey along as she stumbled over the pavement. He shoved her behind the industrial sized trash bin sitting ten feet away, yanked her down and covered her with his body.

A whole lot of silence followed...along with the stink from the garbage next to them.

Breathing hard, her pulse racing, Casey resisted the urge to roll her eyes. What was he thinking? Yes, she appreciated his desire to protect her, but this was ridiculous. She pushed at his chest, but he only got far enough away to look into her eyes. Not a spec of humor in his gaze.

"Um...false alarm?" She made it a question to lessen the blow. "I think everything's fine." Except now her clean jeans were dirty. Nothing sounded but chirping birds in Magnolia trees lining the street.

He eased off her, his eyebrows slanted and his mouth a hard line. He stood and pulled her next to him before scanning the neighborhood. "I would've sworn—"

A giant explosion ripped through the air. The heat and force shoved the bin into both of them and knocked them back on their butts. Shrapnel and hot embers rained down and Brendan scrambled to cover Casey as another explosion rocked the ground beneath them.

Casey's heart pumped a river of adrenaline. Tremors shook her from head to toe. Fire roared next to them and heat radiated from beneath the bin.

"It's okay. It's okay. I've got you. You're okay." Brendan kept up the chatter as he looked into her eyes and scanned her for any injury. "You okay? Did anything hit you?"

"Just you," she squeaked out in a shaky voice. Her palms burned where she'd hit the pavement, but that seemed like a small price to pay. "I'm okay." As okay as she could be considering someone nearly killed her. *Again.* She was seriously sick and fucking tired of it.

"C'mon," he said, helping her up. "We need to get clear. It's too hot." He flinched as she took his hand.

"Bren, are you okay? Did *you* get hit?"

He adjusted the sling as they backed up toward the street. "I'm okay. Just tweaked my shoulder." He pulled out his phone, at the same time sirens blared in the distance. "That's probably coming here."

Probably so, since the raging ball of fire that used to be her car wasn't going to put itself out. "Dammit!" Anger quickly took over from the shock and fear. "That was my freaking *car*, dammit!"

Neighbors filtered out of nearby apartment buildings as orange flames licked all around her car and shot high into the air. Thick black smoke billowed beneath the long carport and the noxious fumes climbed up her nose. The cars around hers had been damaged as well. Her insurance company was going to love this.

Fire trucks screamed around the corner and stopped at the curb. A team of firefighters dressed in their bright yellow gear went to work, dragging the hose and attaching it to the nearby hydrant.

Casey's legs felt like noodles so she sat on the curb under the shade of her favorite Magnolia tree and rested her head in her hands. The accidents on set had been bad enough. Yesterday's shooting seemed like the pinnacle, but this? This sealed it for her. One close call too many. She swallowed back the urge to cry. What if the man doing this was watching her right now? What if he wanted to see her weak and afraid?

Brendan sat next to her. His hand warm on her back as he soothed her frayed nerves without saying a word. Where would she be without him? *Dead*. The answer hit her like a brick. She leaned into him, drinking in his comfort like the parched earth during rain.

"Thanks for saving my ass. For the eight thousandth time," she added under her breath. She shook her head, dazed. "We should just stop keeping track and I'll be your indentured servant for the rest of my life. This is ridiculous." He didn't say anything. "How did you even know something was wrong?" She finally met his gaze.

His brows quirked in concern. "First, you said the alarm sounded different. Then when you opened the door I saw a bit of wire under the car. I just connected the dots. Honestly, I wasn't even sure, but I figured it was better to play it safe." He shook his head. "For a second I thought maybe I was overreacting, but..."

"But you weren't." Her chest constricted and her eyes stung as she stared across the street. "I don't know what I'm supposed to do," she whispered. She didn't aim the question directly to Brendan, but he was the only one there to field it.

"You just keep going. Write a few songs and kick some ass." He gently squeezed her nape. "You're the fucking winner of *Write Your Ticket.* You're going to write the most amazing songs we've ever heard."

She scoffed. Yes, the winner by default, so how much weight did that carry anyway? "Yeah, no pressure. Thanks." She should've put a lid on the sarcasm, but couldn't manage it. Her stomach twisted knowing she'd have to go back to Brendan's place and somehow write music after this.

The police arrived along with two news vans and a helicopter overhead. Casey called her parents before they saw the news and texted Zoe that she was fine. It was just another shitty day in a pile of shitty days for Casey. From the minute she'd found out she'd won the show, her life had gone downhill faster than a luge at the Olympics. With the exception of Brendan. He'd been her savior countless times.

Maybe God was trying to tell her something and she needed to listen.

THE SUN BEAT DOWN relentlessly adding to the heat and smoke from the explosion. Brendan was tired of the bullshit. Tired of constantly being one step behind. Tired of fighting the ghost of Casey's ex. It seemed he had too many mountains to climb where this lady was concerned. The biggest—and deadliest—being who the hell wanted her dead so badly and why?

More police showed up along with the bomb squad and more reporters. The chaos grew. Brendan and Casey didn't have any information to share so they ended up leaving the scene when the tow truck drove off with Casey's burnt out car over two hours later.

"Goddammit!" Casey growled, clicking the seatbelt across her lap. She stomped her foot on the floorboard of his truck. Brendan had never seen her this pissed.

"I only had a few more payments on that damn car!" She looked around the neighborhood, at the few remaining people who'd come to watch the excitement. She closed her eyes and sighed. "But I'm alive, so I'm going to keep my eyes on the big picture. Now I just need to figure out how I'm going to write songs all weekend after this."

A motorcycle screamed past his door and Brendan flinched, his senses too on edge. He didn't know how to answer her. Creativity was a fickle thing. "You'll find a way. Life is full of material, right. You've got a ton of material going for you."

She shook her head. "Pfft. This is shitty material, my friend."

He'd have reached for her hand if he didn't need it to steer the damn truck. Words of wisdom escaped him and the rest of the drive continued in silence. His primary goal consisted of getting her home and safe. When he turned the corner to his parents' house he immediately noticed the black Hummer parked in front.

"Oh my God," Casey breathed.

Not welcome words. "What?" Brendan checked out the guy who got out of the monster truck as they drove up. Dressed in a gray power suit, the man leaned against the back with his arms crossed. "Who's that?" Although he had a suspicion.

"Jeff. It's Jeff. How did he find me?" She'd gone completely pale, her blue eyes wide. Because nearly getting blown up today just wasn't enough, now she had to deal with her douchebag ex.

Brendan pulled in front of the gate and got out. He wished he didn't have his arm in a fucking sling. "Can I help you with something?" His pulse quickened and his muscles tensed, ready for the unexpected, which he'd had way too much of already in his lifetime.

The dude stood up straighter and Brendan took satisfaction in being taller than him, although the guy beat him in bulk. He looked civilized enough, but Brendan had learned a couple years ago—by way of his brother-in-law—not to judge a book by its cover.

"I'm here for Casey. Need a minute of her time."

Over Brendan's lifeless body, maybe. "You're not going to get it. What can I do for you?" The words *before I throw you back in your ride* might have been implied.

"You can get out of my way, shithead. I'm here for Casey."

Ding, ding, ding. Major Asshole Alert. Brendan was ready to shove the guy's balls down his throat and he took a step toward him when Casey grabbed his arm and kept him next to her. Standing tall, she faced the creep with complete composure. Brendan had never felt so much pride for another person.

"I don't have anything to say to you, Jeff. You shouldn't have come here."

Hell, how'd he even find them? That issue was enough for Brendan to be doubly suspicious of the guy. The smile he gave Casey made Brendan's skin crawl…and it took a lot to make that happen. "C'mon, Casey, just a few minutes of your time."

"Anything you have to say to me, you can say in front of Brendan."

"Really." Jeff took a second to look Brendan up and down, not bothering to hide his disdain. "I see you had no problem jumping from my bed into someone else's. Guess my mom had you pegged right."

A red haze slowly filled Brendan's vision. He took a step toward Jeff and crowded the asshole against his car. Casey grabbed his arm to hold him back, but he barely registered her touch. "I think you need to get in your truck, drive the hell away and *stay* the hell away."

Jeff stood up to his full height and got chest to chest with Brendan. "You don't get to tell me what to do, asshat. Now move out of my way or meet my fist."

"Bring it, you little—"

"Stop!" Casey plowed between them as tires squealed behind Brendan. She pushed him back, but only because Jeff had nowhere else to go. "What do you want, Jeff? Make it fast."

Jeff's gaze went over his shoulder and Brendan caught sight of Eric and Danny closing in fast. He had no problem with a little backup, but only because he wasn't a hundred percent. If he didn't have the damn sling, it would be another story.

"I know who took those shots at you yesterday and who planted that bomb today." Jeff's cocky attitude was enough to make Brendan puke, but then his words landed like another bomb. He knew who was trying to kill her, yet he'd done nothing about it?

Brendan snapped. "You fucking son of a—" He made another move toward Jeff, but his brothers held him back. The pain in his shoulder only fueled his anger.

Casey crossed her arms. "If you know who did it, then why didn't you go to the police?"

"I didn't know his name until just now and I thought you should know before I went to the cops."

Brendan wasn't buying this shit for one second. "Who?" he asked, because obviously this joker had a plan. Why else would he wait this long when he knew Casey was in danger?

"Mitch Constantine." Jeff kept his gaze on Casey. "The guy you knocked out on the first night of the show."

She watched him carefully. "I don't believe you. How would you know this?" She paused and her body stiffened. "You've been following me, haven't you? Or more likely you had someone follow me."

It would explain how he knew where to find her. Brendan's anger simmered hotter and his brothers felt it because their hold on him tightened.

"So you've waited until now to tell me?" Casey said, a new level of calm to her voice. Brendan had never seen her like this: poised, but on edge.

"Like I said, I didn't know he who he was until just now."

She tilted her head to the side and her hair fell in a long sheet across her arm. "But you couldn't go to the police and give them a description either, could you?" Oh yeah…she was way too calm.

"Look, for all I knew, the guy watching you was another dick you blew." He shrugged and lowered his voice. "I do miss that sweet mouth of yours on my—"

Wham! It happened before Brendan blinked. Casey punched the guy right in the face. Fist plant straight in the kisser. His head snapped back and blood sprayed on his shirt and tie. She went after him again and this time Brendan and his brothers jumped in to separate them. He held her back while his brothers kept a wall of muscle between them.

Jeff gave her a deadly glare as he wiped blood from his nose. "You fucking bitch. You are so going to pay for that."

"Okay," Eric said, grabbing his arm and shoving him inside the door that Danny very graciously held open. "This is you getting in your truck and driving away." He closed the door then smacked the frame at the open window. "This is also you never looking back. You're not talking to her again, you're not looking at her again. You got me?"

The bastard had the balls to smile at Eric. "What do you think you're going to do about it if I don't give a fuck what you just said?"

"I think we'll have a restraining order out faster than that right jab Casey just nailed you with. Then maybe a little call to the news stations so they know who's been harassing the winner of America's hottest new reality show. You hearing me?" Eric backed away from the Hummer and tipped his head toward the road. "Hit it. Don't come back."

Jeff cranked the engine and peeled rubber out of the spot. Brendan took his first look at Casey. She was shaking from head to toe. Shit, what a fucking day from hell.

"C'mon," he said softly, taking her hand and leading her toward the gate. "Dano, catch!" he called over his shoulder and tossed the keys to his truck. "Pull my truck in would you?"

"You got it," Danny said, snapping the keys from the air.

"Case, let's get you something to drink, okay." She was probably dehydrated from the sun. They'd been outside for hours dealing with the fire department, police and dodging reporters, then this mess with Jeff. Brendan wished he'd been the one to knock the guy senseless. Although Casey probably needed to get that out of her system and he totally understood.

Once in the kitchen, he sat her at the table and got her a glass of ice water. "Here." He knelt in front of her, trying to gauge her mood and her health. He waited until she drank most of it and set the rest on the table. "How's your hand?" he asked.

"Hurts!" Oh she was definitely still angry.

Brendan almost smiled, but it wasn't a laughing matter. Instead he got her some ice wrapped in a thin dishtowel. "Let's put this on your hand." He lifted her wrist, shocked when he saw her raw knuckles. "Aw, Case." It must have hurt like a bitch. He set the ice on her hand and sat next to her. "You know I'm kind of pissed too."

"Why are you pissed?" She had that same attitude in her voice and Brendan liked it better than fear.

"Because *I* wanted to hit him! I've been practicing my moves, see." He did a couple dodge and weaves next to her and brought a reluctant smile to her beautiful lips although it only lasted a second.

She sat for a minute, staring at nothing. "I don't know whether to believe him or not," she finally said. "I mean, I think he was probably following me or paying someone to follow me. So it's possible they spotted whoever shot at us and blew up my car. Or..."

"Or he did it himself?" Brendan asked. Either way they needed to call the police and share this new information.

She shook her head, hooked some hair behind her ear. "I just can't picture him doing it. His dad is too high profile for him to do something like that."

Brendan sighed. Dealing with someone high profile only meant more red tape along the way. "Who's his dad?"

"Senator Bauer."

Brendan's eyes widened. "What? Get out of here. The guy who was just indicted for blackmail and extortion?" Apparently the good senator had blackmailed a colleague when he'd discovered the man was having an affair. The whole thing had blown up in his face after he learned the other woman was really the man's wife. Apparently the two liked role playing. Needless to say, things hadn't gone well for Senator Bauer when he'd doubled down with his threat and it was all caught on film.

Casey nodded. "A great role model, right? But that's my point. Jeff wouldn't put his dad in bigger trouble by doing something this stupid."

Leaning against the table, Brendan scoffed. "I don't know... Guy seemed pretty clueless to me. I mean, who says shit like that to a woman with a right jab like yours?" He was pretty sure he won her over with that comment because she kissed him.

CHAPTER 24

CASEY POURED ALL OF her anger into the songs she wrote for the next two days. The words flowed out of her, and the edgy tunes playing in the back of her head sounded nothing like her norm. She felt violated and abused and it came out in the music. Plus her damn knuckles and palms hurt and made it hard to play any instruments. Her battered hands reminded her of everything she'd been through the past couple of weeks.

Brendan had shown her the family's studio—formerly the garage. The soundproof walls, new Berber carpeting and a dozen instruments made the perfect spot to create new music. The words kept coming and she just wrote them down, arranged them in a way that made sense. Aside from bringing her meals, Brendan and his parents left her alone for the most part. If anyone understood working through a traumatic experience, the St. Johns did.

The shooting, the car bomb and her confrontation with Jeff all took a toll. Not to mention the pressure from Miles to get *his* songs written.

On Monday, after a summons from Miles, Brendan drove her to the same recording studio in Hollywood. The day seemed especially bright and glare off the dashboard blinded her even after she got out of his truck. Casey walked in, shoulders back, head high. If Miles didn't like what she had, then he could kiss her ass. If only. He held all the cards and they both knew it.

She'd dressed up a pair of skinny jeans with the only pair of black heels she'd tossed in her bag. Her black, capped-sleeve shirt, gathered at the waist, flowed around her. She wanted Miles to see someone worthy of the win.

229

Though she was buzzed into the building, no one sat at the front desk. The quiet hallway seemed like a long bubble of doom, and each step took her closer to something unknown. She found Miles in the same studio as before. Dressed in all black, he'd kicked his feet up on the console so she set the sheet music near his heels. His slicked back hair had enough product in it to grease an engine.

"Here you go. Fifteen songs. It was the best I could do in two days." It was unheard to write that many songs in that amount of time and Miles knew it.

He studied her with narrow eyes. "Fifteen songs? How the hell'd you do that? A little artificial stimulation, babe?" His smile showed his glaringly white teeth.

There was a time when she liked this man, but that had been very short lived. "No, Miles, no artificial stimulation. Just pure emotion." *You might want to try it sometime.* She didn't have the balls to say it out loud.

"Why didn't you answer any of my calls?" he asked. "That car bomb was big news, and when the reporters started calling, I had nothing to give them because you didn't call me back. You know that's breach of your contract, right?"

Fresh anger swamped Casey. "Let me get this straight, you gave me two days to write songs, but you're still allowed to make me do interviews during *my* time?"

Miles stood up. "Casey, you don't have any *me* time. You're on Miles time. From the moment St. John handed you the win to the moment your contract ends, I own you. When I tell you to write songs, you write songs. When I tell you to put on a pretty face and answer some reporters' question, then you do that too. If I ask you to suck my dick in between sessions, you'll do that too."

Casey stomach heaved and she thought she might puke. She ran out the door only to be faced with Jeff. The sick smile on his face looked distorted and grotesque. She turned and raced toward the back door, her heart pumping, her legs straining, when a man came out of the last studio and blocked her way.

Mitch. The evil in his eyes matched the snarl on his lips. Casey backed up. Sweat popped from her pores and her heart bounced off her ribs like a medicine ball.

"You can't run from me, Casey. You never could," Jeff said.

Miles stood in the doorway, a hand on his button. "Your fiancé tells me you know what a man likes. Come on over here and show me."

Fear bubbled up like bile in her throat and Casey made a break for it, slamming into Mitch to get past him, but he grabbed her arms and held her tight. "Casey, Casey," he said. Over and over. He kept saying her name as she struggled in his arms. He pulled her closer and closer back to Miles until all she could do was scream.

Brendan, she needed Brendan!

"I'm here, I'm here! Casey, wake up! Wake up!"

Casey's eyes snapped open. Brendan sat next to her on her wrecked bed, holding her arms. Light filtered in through the blinds and sweat glued her shirt to her skin. She glanced at the clock on the night table. Still Sunday, not Monday. Breathing hard, she sat up and ran a shaky hand through her hair. She'd fallen asleep over her sheet music. Obviously working on the bed had been a bad idea.

Brendan stroked a gentle finger down her cheek and eased some damp hair off her face. "You scared the shit out of me. I couldn't wake you up." He waited and when she didn't say anything he went on. "Must have been a hell of a nightmare."

She nodded. "It was." She scooted against the headboard then reached for the glass of water near her phone, pissed when her shaky hand nearly upended the contents.

"Want to talk about it?" he asked.

God, the guy was adorable. She gulped a long swallow. "I can't seem to get past that little confrontation with Jeff from the other day." She set the glass down and straightened the papers on the bed.

"You know I'm not going to let that asshole near you again, right?"

"Bren, you're sweet, but you can't be around all the time. One of these days I'll go back to my apartment. You're not my bodyguard. You have a life, too, remember?"

"What if you're part of my life?" He looked so damn serious. "I mean it. What if I want more with you, Case?"

"I don't know." She shook her head. "It's so soon. We just met."

"We didn't just meet," he countered. "We met over two months ago. Then we spent six weeks together in the same house." He snorted. "That was like…what…three dates times seven days a week is twenty-one times six weeks is…" His eyes squinted as he calculated. "A hundred twenty-six dates right there. We totally did not just meet."

When he put it like that… "Okay, so maybe we didn't *just* meet, but you have to admit we had a very unorthodox beginning."

"Unorthodox? When did you suddenly become eighty-seven years old?"

She smacked him, but laughed…and laughing made her chest tight and brought a knot to her throat because he was so adorable on top of sexy and he wanted her and she'd been a total idiot for too long. Swallowing the huge lump, she pressed her lips together and tried to cap her emotions.

"What? What?" God, he always read her so well.

"You keep…" She sniffed. "You keep making me feel better."

His eyes widened then narrowed. "That's a bad thing?"

"No, no." She shook her head. "It's a good thing." She met his serious gaze. "But it scares me a little. I told myself I'd take time— a lot of time—to be with me. To find myself before I shared myself with someone else. Emotionally," she added, since she'd obviously shared herself with him the night they met. But that had been the first step to her freedom. Her breakaway moment. It had worked wonders for her confidence and self-esteem. He'd been exactly what she needed that night.

But what if he was exactly what she needed period? What if God said, *you know what? I think you've been stuck with enough bullshit and it's time you get some good stuff in life*. What if Brendan was the good stuff?

"Instead of a lot of time, I had like a week and then bam, I met you and, and…" Fell way too deep in a matter of hours. How was he so sure of her, of them? "You're not freaked out about it?"

"About what?" he asked. He set his hand beneath her hair on her nape and he felt strong and warm. Like a security blanket of mega-proportions. No sense of being smothered or trapped. She felt how much he cared and worried.

"About us? About what you're feeling?" she asked.

"Honestly…I'd be freaked out if *I* were the only one feeling it. But I don't think I am. I think you're not sure and I respect that. But I'm not freaked out because I think we have something really special." He stroked his fingers along her neck in a mini massage. "Look, what we did in Hawaii… I don't do that. I don't fall into bed with someone I barely know." He shook his head, a half smile kicked up his lips. "That day was amazing. I loved every second. Well, excluding the near drowning and the getting mowed over by a bus. I could've lived without those parts."

She snorted and met his gaze, saw all the emotion in his beautiful eyes.

"So my timing probably sucks," he said softly. "But after everything we've gone through and knowing how we feel about each other…can we call ourselves official?"

Official? Her brain shut down for a moment. Why was she hesitating? He was an amazing man. He'd been through so much and he was clearly a special guy. If she didn't get over her issues with Jeff now, then when would she, and what happened if Brendan moved on and some other girl snapped him up.

"Yeah." She nodded. "I'm good with official."

His reaction surprised her. He didn't make a big deal about it. He nodded and that same half smile kicked up his lips again. "So I can officially call you *my girl, my one and only. The light of my life*?"

She shoved at his chest, careful of his arm, but she had another dopey grin on her face. "Only if you put it in a song and sing it to me."

His grin stretched a mile wide and filled her heart. He was so damn gorgeous when he looked at her like that. Like she was important to him. Like he needed her. Like she was more than just a pair of breasts and lips.

He searched her eyes and stroked her cheek with a gentle thumb. Instead of saying anything, he leaned in and kissed her. Gently. His lips gliding along hers whisper soft. "I know he did a number on you. I'm going to undo it and you're going to see what it's like to be treated the way you should be treated." He kissed her again and Casey opened her mouth for more of him. He gave it, stroking his tongue against hers and reminding her again what it felt like to be appreciated, and dare she even think it, loved. Instead of thinking how her meeting with Miles was really going to go, she let Brendan kiss her senseless. His hand stroked down her side and Casey guided him to her breast. She arched into his touch, wanting nothing more than to drown in the wave of heat and tingles he created with his hands, his mouth.

She shifted lower on the bed and pulled him over her, holding him to her, kissing him frantically and hoping to show him that she appreciated his patience. She wanted him for a completely different reason than in Hawaii. She stroked her tongue against his and slid her hand over the very hard bulge in his jeans.

"Case, Casey," he said, holding her head and slowing them down. "I'm happy to put a sock on the doorknob and continue this, because this is blowing me away on so many different levels, but you need to know the whole family is downstairs. Anyone could—"

She laughed. Of course his family was downstairs. Smiling, she kissed him softly. "Thanks for telling me." She kissed him again because he was there and would continue to be there. "You'll remind me where we left off later, right?"

His eyes gleamed and his grin melted her heart. "You can count on it." After one last kiss he lifted up and straightened her shirt.

"I need to finish these songs anyway, so…" She tipped her head toward the door as Brendan stood.

"So I need to scram." He bent forward. "You have no idea how hot it makes me when you take control."

Casey felt the heat in her cheeks, beyond happy that this amazing man wanted her. She smacked his ass. "So you'll explain it to me later. I'll be looking forward to it."

With one last kiss hot enough to melt steel, Brendan left her alone.

THE PHONE RANG AS he stared out his office window, watching the sun climb higher in the sky. He liked the Sunday quiet, happy to have the office to himself. He wondered if the dickhead would answer. He'd been debating all morning whether to call, or give the idiot one more try to get it right. In the end, his gut told him to quit wasting time.

"Yeah?"

His pulse jumped. "Hey, buddy."

There was a pause as the guy tried to place his voice—and couldn't. "Who is this?"

"Just a pal looking out for you." He flipped a pen between his fingers and kicked his feet up on the windowsill. "I've got some information you might like."

"I'm not interested in anything you're selling. Take a hike."

"Not so fast, my friend. Let's just say, I'm aware of the lengths you've gone to in attempt to rid the world of a certain reality star. Do I have your attention now?"

There was another pause as the dickhead considered this information. "Who is this?"

"What if I told you where she was going to be tomorrow morning, and what if I made sure there was nothing standing in your way of getting that sweet revenge you want for all that embarrassment she caused you?"

"I'd say, what's in it for you?"

He laughed. "Not much, actually. I'm just as anxious as you are to make her a page in the history books."

"Why are you so willing to facilitate this when it sounds like you could do it yourself?"

A very good question. Maybe this guy wasn't as dumb as he looked. "Let's just say that I'm willing to let you have the fun. We'll chock it up to me doing you a favor. One day you can repay me."

"I don't even know who you are. How would I ever repay you? Besides, I don't know if you're full of shit."

"Fair assessment. Let me put it this way. I have information that links you to the shooting." He waited for that bit of information to sink in. "Yes, that's right. I've got some sweet video of you working on her car before the bomb went off. It's crystal clear. The camera loves you." Another silence told him he had the man's complete attention.

"She'll be at the recording studio on Sunset at nine-fifteen. That's forty-five minutes before anyone else arrives. You'll be there a half hour before her. I'll have someone there to let you in. That should be plenty of time to do what you need to do."

"Who is this?" he asked again.

"Your guardian angel…looking out for your best interests." *And mine.* "Eight forty-five. Don't be late." He hung up the phone before the man got another word out. This was too big a carrot for him to pass up.

He looked out his office window. Another beautiful California day just got a little brighter.

CHAPTER 25

SUNDAY NIGHT, SITTING IN the cozy chair in her room, Casey was as fried as an Oreo cookie at a fair. Her brain felt fuzzy around the edges as she stuffed her notebook and sheet music into a beat up manila folder and stuffed *that* into her black leather case. She could go for a nice cool margarita right about now. The weekend had been a songwriting marathon and she'd produced eight songs. Not the fifteen in her dream, but eight songs in forty-eight hours was still an unbelievable accomplishment and personal best by a long shot. Now that it was over, she was completely wiped out. She stretched, popping a few vertebrae back in line.

Her phone vibrated next to her. She didn't recognize the number, but it was a local call and since she'd been thrown into the spotlight, she'd had all sorts of calls from production assistants to producers trying to schedule her for things.

"Hi, is this Casey?" a man asked.

She didn't recognize the voice and a tickle of unease skated down her spine. As usual, she debated confirming. "Who is this?"

"My name is Charlie. I work for Miles. He asked if you could come in at nine-fifteen instead of ten tomorrow morning. He wanted to talk to you privately before the band arrives."

Miles had two full-time assistants and neither were named Charlie. "How come I haven't met you before?" She would've remembered him from the show.

"Oh. Oh, well I'm new. I just took over for Sam. I was supposed to start a week ago, but I had a family emergency, so Sam stayed on a little longer." He laughed. "Sorry. TMI. Anyway, can I tell Miles you'll be there early?"

She knew Sam, so Charlie must be legit and she couldn't really say no. A quick flash of her nightmare gave her shivers, but she shook off the feeling. "Sure. That's fine. I'll be there at nine-fifteen."

"Great. Thanks. I'll let him know."

Casey disconnected the call and reset her notifications since she always silenced them while she wrote. She headed downstairs in search of Brendan. The house seemed exceptionally quiet and that sliver of unease snaked through her a second time. "Brendan?" she called. She waited, but got no reply. Her phone dinged and she looked down to find a text from her sister. That's when she noticed all the other texts she'd missed. Including one from Brendan. *In the garage if you need anything.*

Casey strolled out back and breathed in the honeysuckle bushes along the house. Birds chirped in the twilight and the clouds looked like giant purple cotton balls in the setting sun. A very faint bass played a rhythm as she closed in on the studio/garage. She peeked in the window of the door before going inside where she saw Brendan, his older brothers and his parents. His mom waved her in as she finished the end of an old Bob Seger song. Dressed in black skinny jeans, high heeled, brown boots and matching brown shirt with intricate black stitching, Terry could've been a rock star.

The room had been sound proofed with thick padding on all the walls and an extra heavy door. Brendan's father, Jay, played drums in the corner while Danny jammed on the bass, Eric played keyboard, Brendan played guitar and his mother sang. The familiar—and much loved—"Rock and Roll Never Forgets" filled the garage. The song took Casey back to her fondest memories as a toddler. She clapped at the end, then gave a sharp two-fingered whistle. Good music deserved appreciation.

"Did you even know that song?" Terry asked. She set the microphone back in the stand and moved the whole thing into a corner. "That was a serious oldie."

"Are you kidding? I grew up on Bob Seger. My aunt loves him. I think he was her first concert." Thank God for a normal aunt who understood her love of music and introduced her to everything besides her parents' classical collection.

"Sounds like your aunt is our kind of people."

"Definitely." Too bad her parents weren't. It still surprised Casey how different her mom was from her aunt. Two sisters with two completely different mindsets. Zoe and she definitely had differences, but growing up in the same stifled household had bonded them.

"We've got to jam out of here," Eric said, covering his keyboard while Danny set his bass in a case and shoved it high on a shelf. All the brothers had the same long-legged build and broad shoulders. Casey was surprised that only Brendan's twin had a steady girlfriend.

"Us too," Jay said as he covered the drum set. He picked up a nice camel sports coat hanging on a peg behind him. "See you guys," he called after his oldest sons as the door closed on their backs.

Terry checked her watch. "Are you ready? We're supposed to be at the restaurant at six-thirty."

"Just give me a minute to grab the car keys and we can go." He took Terry's hand and they moved toward the door.

Casey's parents had been married almost forty-five years. They rarely touched and seemed more like roommates. Casey wanted more. She wanted what these two had. "Where are you off to?" she asked. They looked adorable, like they might be headed on a first date. That kind of long-lasting love was seriously rare.

"Dinner and a movie with some old friends. We'll be home late. Don't wait up." Terry grinned, the sun glinting off her red hair before the door shut behind them.

"Your parents go out a lot," Casey commented. Her parents rarely left home.

"Yeah, they're dating fools," Brendan said, grinning at what must have been the look on her face. "My mom's words, not mine. After raising five kids on a strict budget, mom decided they were going to party when we all left the house."

Casey nodded, loving the idea of dating after so many years of marriage. She strolled around the space as Brendan picked a slow tune on his guitar. He had amazing dexterity despite his injury. She could watch him play for days, loved the way his hands worked the guitar. He was a master, and the soulful sounds he came up with constantly awed her. "That's pretty," she said, when he stopped playing.

He put the instrument down and put his arm back in the sling. "Eh... I'm just messing around with something new." He walked toward her and Casey's stomach fluttered with nerves. "Did you finish or are you going back to work more?" Maybe she imagined the hope in his eyes.

"I'm done. Pretty fried, actually. Don't think I could write another word if you paid me."

He wrapped his good arm around her and pulled her against him. He felt strong and solid and smelled like heaven. "You mean I finally have you to myself? I was beginning to think that was never going to happen."

"Sorry. But I didn't have much choice." She settled against his chest and breathed him in.

"Hey," he said softly and waited until she met his gaze. "Don't apologize. I understand the pressure, okay? I don't ever want you to feel pressure from me. I don't ever want to do something that reminds you of whatshisname. That's important to me." Any teasing tone or gleam in his eyes was long gone.

"I know." And she did. Fundamentally he was the exact opposite of Jeff.

Brendan bent his head and kissed her softly. A fantasy kiss. His lips brushed over hers, back and forth until she opened for him. He always kissed her so gently to start, easing her into the mood with a skillful tongue and masterful hands. Kisses that dreams were made of.

Thinking of dreams, Casey pulled away. "Before I forget, I have to be in a little earlier tomorrow. Nine-fifteen, not ten."

"Oh yeah? Did Miles call?"

"Kind of. It was Charlie, his new assistant. Miles wants to talk to me before the band gets there. I'm sure he's going to spring something else on me. Can't wait."

Brendan's grin was infectious. "Not a problem. I'll have you there." He kissed her again, nibbled her lower lip and made her insides tingle with anticipation. The guitar wasn't the only thing he knew how to play.

"I really do hate that you think you have to be my driver," she said against his lips. "My insurance will pay for a rental until I get a new car."

He shook his head and leaned back a fraction. "I'm not leaving you alone. Not until I know you're safe."

"Look, I appreciate it. I really do. But what happens if they don't find this guy? You can't do this forever."

BRENDAN HATED THE LOOK in her eyes, the guilt on top of guilt. He cupped her neck, ran his thumb along her jaw. "With all the man power on your case, I'm sure something will give soon. You know, you've got more than just the LAPD working on this thing. You've got my brother and his boss on it too. They're the best private investigators in the city."

She nodded, but didn't seem completely sold. Instead of talking about it more, he wanted to distract her, take her mind off the case.

"So you've been working for two days straight... I think that deserves a reward. How about a little celebration?" he asked.

She gave him a half smile. "I like celebrating. What did you have in mind?"

Good question. He had no idea. "All depends on what you feel like. We can stay here and cook dinner. I'm sure there's something in the fridge. There always is. Or we could go someplace and—"

"Here." She wrapped her arms around his neck and moved in all close and personal. "I don't want to share you tonight."

He leaned his head back and said a silent thank-you to the powers that be before meeting her gaze. He stroked his hand down her back until it was precariously low, just on the slope of her ass, and Casey stepped in closer and rubbed against his growing erection. "I'm totally on board with that idea." Before he lost the small amount of control he had, he pulled away, took her hand and led her back into the house. "Food. We need food." Once inside, he opened the fridge door, hoping the cool air might counter the heat building in his blood.

"Food sounds good. I'm kind of hungry."

He was starving, and not necessarily for food. But first things first. He needed to feed her before they worked off all the calories.

241

He spied a casserole plate and lifted the lid. *No way!* "Hey, my mom made enchiladas." His mouth watered. "Please tell me you like Mexican food. This is one of my favorites. My mom is a mean cook."

"Is there anything your mom *doesn't* do?" Casey asked, pulling out the dish since he was limited.

"Not really." He thought back to all the years growing up in this household. "She was always the one who wanted to try something new. Always encouraging us to go out of our comfort zones. I think that's why I ended up working for Seger. I mean, I liked messing around with technology and computers, and bartending can be hectic, but it's fun. I liked talking to people and finding ways to make a favorite drink better. I just think my mom realized that there was part of me that needed a more creative outlet. How many do you want?" he asked, after removing the glass lid.

"Two is good. So can you pinpoint when you knew music was *it* for you?" Casey asked.

Brendan cut six enchiladas from the dish and scooped them onto a plate. "Honestly, I think my mom saw it before I did. I mean, I loved sitting down with my dad and jamming in the garage, coming up with new tunes. It wasn't like he had that much free time or that I was living in the garage and only playing music, but when we did, when I did, it just..." He shook his head. Couldn't seem to put his thoughts into words. "...It just clicked." He found some Spanish rice in the fridge and added that to the plate, then slid it all inside the microwave and set the timer.

"I get it," she assured him. "It was the same with me. I love teaching, but it didn't give me the time to create my own stuff." Casey grabbed two glasses from the cabinet. "After school, I always had private lessons, so the little time I had to devote to music was precious time." She sniffed the enchiladas before returning the lid and replacing the dish in the fridge. "Mmm, these smell wonderful." She took out a pitcher of tea and poured two glasses.

"Trust me, you're going to love them." It only took a couple of minutes to reheat their dinner. They sat at the kitchen table and dug into their meal. The chilies added the perfect amount of spice.

"Oh man, sometimes I wonder why I moved out," Brendan said around his first bite. Melted cheese, moist chicken, green chilies all wrapped in a flour tortilla and covered with his mom's enchilada sauce. *Perfecto.*

Casey shook her head and swallowed her bite. "I so didn't have that problem. I couldn't get out of my house fast enough. Oh my, God, this is good."

He grinned. "Told ya. So what had you scrambling to get out?" They'd never talked about her family life before and he'd missed the conversation with her parents after the shooting since he'd been in rough shape.

"You met my parents. They're older and conservative. Crazy conservative." She sipped her tea.

"Politically?" he asked.

"Every which way you can imagine. My mom is old fashioned. She sets the woman's movement back sixty years. She thinks men and women have different jobs. It's the man's job to provide financially, and it's the woman's job to take care of the house and kids. Never shall the two meet."

"Isn't that kind of archaic?" Brendan asked before taking another mouth-watering bite of his dinner.

"Kind of? Try extremely! It's not like I begrudge her opinion. I just don't get how she can expect all women to think her way. I swear her only motivation for sending me to college was so I'd meet a guy and get married."

"You almost did," he reminded her.

She nodded. "Almost." She shivered. "What a colossal mistake that would've been."

"What about your sister. Does she have the same issues with your parents?"

Casey laughed. "Oh my God. Zoe is like a force of nature. She's a lot like your mom in some ways. Very adventurous and strong. She knows her own mind. I can't tell you how many times my mom used to cry about her once she went to college. Mom was sure she was going to end up in jail or worse. They fought constantly and I was always the one trying to calm everyone down."

"Not into confrontation?" Brendan asked. With the exception of Friday, of course. Her right jab still made him grin.

"Not at all. Sure, I have limits, but I'm usually the one trying to make peace. When Zoe moved, the house got a lot quieter. I think my mom thought she'd have more control over me, but..." Casey shook her head. "You can't force your beliefs on other people. She's never realized that. After the shooting and before we had that conversation here, I think she was still hoping I would make things work with Jeff."

"No fucking way? Are you serious?" He shoveled in a bite of rice.

"Very. My folks are way older than yours. It's a different generation. I think even if my mom knew that Jeff tried to—" She took a jagged breath. She took a bite of food as if that might end the conversation, but Brendan wasn't done.

"That he tried to what?"

"Nothing. Forget it. It's not important." Her hair fell and shielded her face.

"Case, what'd he try?" Brendan put his fork down, suddenly not very hungry for his favorite meal.

She hooked her hair behind her ear and pushed some food around her plate. "The morning before the show, I was expecting Zoe to pick me up. I opened the door without checking and Jeff was there. He barged in, tried to convince me to bail on the show. He got a little physical, but Zoe got there in time and nothing happened."

Brendan stood up from the chair as fresh anger coursed through him. "That fucker. I really wish I'd hit him the other day." He turned to her. "You told me he never hit you. When you say physical, are you talking sexual assault?"

She sighed and looked him in the eye. "Yes."

CHAPTER 26

BRENDAN CLENCHED HIS JAW and fought the rage pounding through him.

"Look, he knows how to push my buttons, knows...what I'm not a fan of. I don't know if you've noticed, but there are some things in bed I'm not very comfortable with," Casey said.

He hadn't noticed anything of the kind. "Casey, we spent one amazing night together. You totally rocked my world." He sat in his chair again and after she took a drink, he tipped her chin to face him. "You're amazing in bed... Out of it too. Look, I'm not going to pressure you to do anything you don't want to do. Ever. You know that, right?"

She nodded slowly, her eyes soulful. "I know. It's one of the reasons I like you so much. I know you won't hurt me. Like I said, Zoe got there and nothing happened. Nothing else to tell."

Brendan tamped down the fresh jolt of fury that boiled his blood. He really did want to teach that asshole a lesson. Clearly, Casey didn't want to talk about this subject, so he moved on...for now. "Tell me more about Zoe. How much older is she?"

"Two years." Casey smiled. "She used to sneak out of the house and I'd lie in her bed and pretend to be her when my parents checked on us before they went to bed."

"But didn't they check on you? You couldn't be in two beds at once."

"I stuffed pillows under my blankets. Sometimes, I'd go to sleep with my hair wet and wrapped in a towel, so I'd just stick a stuffed animal in the towel and pull the sheets up and my folks never bothered to look. Besides, I was the good child. I grew up and got an honorable job teaching music to kids. Although my mom hated that I worked at a *hippie* school."

"Hippie school?" Brendan asked.

"You know, the private schools that teach critical thinking and don't judge a child's intelligence on standardized testing. I would've loved a school like that when I was growing up, but we couldn't afford it. Anyway, I think my mom figured that if I worked around kids I'd want to get pregnant faster. I don't know. They didn't start worrying about me until the whole reality-show issue came up. Before then I was the model daughter. I had good grades, I went to college, I found a guy, got engaged. All of it was according to their plan. Then I went off-roading." She glanced at him. "Why are you grinning like that?"

"Because, I love that you broke away. I love that you realized you needed to live your life the way you want and not the way anyone else wants. I'm lucky in that my parents always stressed individuality. They wanted us all to explore life and try different things before we settled on what might fulfill us."

"You are very lucky." Her smile faded and Brendan felt how the loss of her parents' relationship hurt her.

"I'm lucky I met you." He gave her a sidelong glance before taking another bite of his dinner. If he kissed her now he wouldn't be able to stop.

"Well, now you're just sucking up," she said, also diving back into her dinner.

"I've been told I'm good at it."

She laughed...and his heart rolled over. He loved the sound, hadn't heard it much since Hawaii.

"Okay, so your sister, the wild child...has no fear. I'll keep that in mind."

"I always wanted to be more like her. I was just too chicken to try. Then she left for school and I was alone with my folks." She shook her head. "I think when Jeff met them he realized what he had in me. A total puppet. Because that's what my mom is. Not that my dad makes her, but because it's what she chooses to be. It kills me. It's funny how Zoe is the exact opposite. When she walked in on Jeff that day... I thought she was going to murder him. She has no fear. Me...I'm scared of everything."

He shoved her shoulder. "No you're not. You went into a crazy ocean and nearly drowned. You auditioned for and participated in a national reality TV show. Those things sure as hell didn't scare you."

She shrugged and took a long drink of her tea. "Okay, now you know about my family, tell me about yours. You guys have a nice vibe."

He nodded. "We are very tight. We were close before the kidnapping, too, but after that, we got very protective of each other. Most people don't realize how everything can be gone in an instant. Be it accidental or premeditated. We've been through it all. We don't take each other for granted."

"Your brothers were pretty awesome in getting rid of Jeff."

"That's the one good thing about big brothers. They don't let anyone outside the family pick on me."

"Oh my, God. Zoe was the same way. She could beat me up, but no else could."

He laughed. "Your sister isn't even close to your size. How could she beat you up?"

"I told you, she's tough. Much tougher than me. Size doesn't matter as much if you got the attitude."

He loved her adamant statement and the sparkle in her eyes.

"You're smiling at me again," she said.

"Because I like talking to you." He liked doing other things with her, too, but he promised not to push her, so he wouldn't. They finished eating and he picked up their dirty dishes and rinsed them in the sink.

Casey loaded them in the dishwasher. The simple domestic chore had never been more fun. "Blake is the private investigator. Your sister is a filmmaker. What do your other brothers do?"

"I'll tell you everything. Come with me." He took her hand and led her into the den. "Eric is the oldest. Named after my Dad's mom, Erica. He went to law school and graduated, but he's having second thoughts. My parents are not thrilled, but at the same time they want him to be happy, so they're dealing with it." He sat her on the sofa, turned on the TV and crashed next to her. "Danny is the wildcard of us all. He takes after our mom. He wants to do everything and he wants to do it on his terms. He's pretty funny.

He's got a big head, but we know him and love him anyway. He's one of those guys that grows on you after you meet him." He put his arm around her shoulders and brought her close against his chest, loving her warmth and softness.

"Is your sister working on a film now?"

He nodded. "Yep. I think Tanner—that's her husband—and she are in Hawaii scouting locations."

"Must be nice," Casey mumbled.

He squeezed her arm. "You know you can afford a trip to Hawaii now. You did win half a million dollars."

"Money I won't see until Miles has all of his songs. Who knows how long it will take?" She ran her finger over a burgeoning hole in his jeans, and the innocent caress sent his blood simmering hotter. "My nightmare is that he vetoes all of them just to keep his money."

"It's not his money," Brendan said, forcing himself to concentrate on the conversation. "I'm sure it's budgeted into the show. It has to be."

"Apparently, that doesn't matter to Miles."

"We need to find you an agent and maybe a lawyer, and I'll bet my big sister and Eric can help you with that." It was a good opportunity to adjust their positions because if he didn't stop her from touching his thigh he might totally pounce on her. "I'll give Jess a call." Brendan wedged his phone from his back pocket.

Her eyes widened. "Wait! You're calling her now?"

"Sure, why not?"

"I didn't think you meant this minute."

"Why? Did you have other plans for me?" Again, Brendan's mind went to a very dirty place. He'd have to get better at that.

She flushed. "Actually... I did." Casey plucked the phone from his hand and tossed it on the other side of the sofa. "I've got some voicemails from agents and managers, but I haven't had a chance to follow up with anyone." She straddled his lap as she spoke and Brendan's pulse jacked up accordingly. She towered over him like a woman on a mission. "Maybe Jess can help me narrow it down. Do you mind?" she asked as she eased the sling over his head and Brendan raised his arm to help.

"Don't mind at all," he rumbled.

Casey rocked against his growing erection and he sucked in a rough breath just as her lips closed over his.

He couldn't help but move his hands over her thighs and around to her ass. He did not give two shits about his sore shoulder. Her long legs trapped him to the sofa in the best possible vise. Her hair fell over them and created a silk canopy. Their lips and tongues tangled in wet synchronicity and only proved to Brendan how good they were together.

Casey's gentle hands roamed from his hair down to his chest and kept going, blazing a trail of warmth even through his T-shirt. Brendan sucked in more air when she grabbed his package and squeezed.

"You don't mind if I..." She unbuttoned his jeans and slid the zipper down. "...do that, do you?"

"Ung, uh." The loss of blood in his big brain made him dopey. "Naw. G'ahead."

She bunched up his shirt and her lips continued their assault down his chest as she worked her way south. "Tell me if you don't like something," she said.

"Don't see that as an issue," he gritted out.

She smiled when she lowered his boxer briefs. She ended up holding his very erect dick in her hand and watching him with aqua eyes. Brendan thought his heart might bust through his rib cage.

"Believe it or not, this is more for me than for you," she said.

He laughed at that. Shook his head. "Not sure I belie— Ah!" She squeezed the base and licked the tip at the same time and Brendan nearly lost his mind. Every nerve ending came alive in a massive rush. "Whatever you say," he managed. He fisted the couch cushion in a white knuckle hold.

She smoothed the drop of moisture at the tip around and around before licking it off. The sparkle in her eyes almost set him off. The way she watched him absolutely destroyed him.

"I'm not going to last two minutes if you keep this up."

She licked the entire length and Brendan dropped his head back into the cushions, holding off on the urge to push...or beg. There was something about having a beautiful woman on her knees, between your legs, her mouth doing unbelievable things... He definitely needed a distraction before she undid him. Leaning to his right, he scooped her up at the waist and pulled her on top of him upside down.

"Don't mind me," he said, making quick work of the button and zipper on her jeans. He only got them partially down, just far enough to get to that sweet spot he wanted so badly.

She moaned as he licked into her. He groaned as she sucked him into her mouth.

Casey strained against the denim pinning her legs together, and all that taut muscle drove Brendan closer to the edge. She was too sexy. Since he wasn't going to last, he worked extra hard to make sure she went over the edge when he did. He lashed at her clit over and over alternately sucking and nibbling, working her up until she detonated. Her internal muscles clenched at the same time she moaned and the vibration ran through his dick like an electric current. His muscles tensed and his balls tightened up. The suction was too much to fight and his climax hit him like a sledgehammer. He groaned, felt the heat of Casey's mouth as he unloaded. Stars blinked behind his closed eyes and he barely managed to suck air into his fried lungs.

He had no clue how many minutes they lay there, breathing hard. He just knew he loved the intimacy. "Mother of God," he whispered against her thigh. It didn't get much better than that. He gave one last kiss over her tight little nub and she gasped before moving off him.

After fixing her jeans, she sat in front of him on the floor, their faces close together since he was still laid out on the sofa. "You surprised me." She licked her lips before giving him a gentle kiss.

He chuckled. "You're the one doing the surprising. That was pretty fucking amazing."

She nodded. "It was, but not in the way you're thinking."

That stumped him.

A smile curved her lips and a blush stained her cheeks. She bit her bottom lip and closed her eyes. When she met his gaze, he saw the same confidence he'd seen during their night together in Hawaii. He wasn't sure what just happened, but he liked it.

"You taste good," she whispered. Brendan didn't think anything could get him hard any time soon, but that statement did it. "You have no idea what this means," she added.

Maybe not…but a guy could hope.

CHAPTER 27

HE WATCHED THE GUY pull up and walk down the street to the studio. He had an unexpected confidence about him. Maybe this thing would go off as planned. Depended on how capable this man really was...and just how badly he wanted Casey dead.

The man he'd hired to break into the studio and disable all the video cameras was waiting by the garbage bin out back. At this point, the only thing left to do was to climb the fire escape and enter from the door access on the roof. Much easier to do that than risk people seeing them on the street level. It was nice of the owners to build a deck up there. Probably made it easier to watch the yearly Hollywood Parade. *Idiots.*

Now he just had to hope the guy did as he was told. Get into the building and remove Casey from the building. Simple. Whether Casey was dead or not before he got her out was a non-issue, as long as the guy got *dead* done.

The dude disappeared around the building right on schedule at eight forty-five. So far so good. Time ticked by and seven minutes later he got a text from his guy: *He's in. I'm outta here. Will expect payment in my account by tonight.*

He texted back: *Count on it.*

Now all he had to do was make sure Casey showed up on time, then he was gone too. No sense in getting spotted. He reached for the glove compartment and took out a little bit of something to celebrate the occasion. He checked the street for cops then poured a small line on the back of a clipboard he had stashed behind his seat. He sniffed the line then repeated the process on the other side. He wiped his nose and leaned his head back, taking a second to let the drug work its magic.

Perfect. Just what he needed to pass the time.

Twenty minutes later, Casey did show up, towing her idiot boyfriend. She looked hot in tight jeans and heels and his groin tightened. His reaction pissed him off. Too bad the boyfriend wasn't part of the deal today, but bad blood with the producer kept him at a decent distance.

They said good-bye at the truck and Casey buzzed the door to get in.

He held his breath, waiting to see if the idiot had followed directions and knew how to let her in. She hit the buzzer a second time and his pulse spiked. If this asshole fucked up—

The door opened. Finally. His pulse picked up.

Showtime.

STILL RIDING HER BRENDAN high on Monday morning, Casey enjoyed the warm sun as she strode toward the studio and thought about yesterday. It hadn't taken long to discover that Brendan had overdone it on the sofa and his shoulder was killing him, so she'd played nurse all night and made sure he was comfortable. And because she still didn't have enough balls to sleep in his bed in his parents' house, they'd said goodnight in the hallway and went their separate ways.

It had been a night of revelations for her. Vic would probably pass out from shock if she ever found out Casey participated in a sixty-nine. Casey hadn't intended to do what she did to him on the sofa. But seeing how much he loved her touch and how much he needed her absolutely lit her fuse. She'd wanted all of him…and loved getting him. The experience had been completely new and totally earth shattering. The intimacy astounded her…as had her orgasm. She kept replaying those few minutes in her head before finally going to sleep. She couldn't wait to do it again.

But if she planned to get any work done today, she needed to get Brendan out of her head and focus on the music. Hopefully whatever Miles had to tell her wasn't going to interfere with the songs she'd written over the weekend.

She buzzed the door and looked around, didn't recognize the

lone car parked in the lot, but it was in front of the other building thirty yards behind her. For a second, she wondered if she'd gotten the time wrong, but someone finally let her inside. She walked in with a quick glance to the man. "Thanks. I wasn't sure if anyone was here or not. Are you Charlie?" He wore a baseball cap and sunglasses. His scraggly beard was probably in fashion, but Casey wasn't a fan of the look.

"Right this way," he said, avoiding her question.

Whatever. People seemed to be getting ruder and ruder. She followed him into an office she hadn't been in yet. A big oak desk and leather chair sat off the left and dark blinds shaded the room from bright morning sun. She turned in the middle of the room and faced the man.

"Is Miles running late?" she asked.

He closed the door and locked it. The snick was like a switch to her heart. The tiniest sound that meant the biggest trouble. She quit breathing, her pulse skyrocketed and hair prickled on her nape.

TROUBLE! PANIC!

NO!

Stay calm. Get out! She didn't recognize this man, but he wasn't as big as Jeff, which gave her more confidence.

It all happened in a split second and before he turned around, she advanced, shoved him sideways as hard as she could, unlocked the door and ran like hell down the hall. Air barely flowed into her lungs and she gulped it in as she ran, her heels slowing her down. She got to the door and tried to yank it open, nearly dislocating her shoulder when the damn thing didn't budge. That's when she remembered the large green button she had to hit on the wall to open the lock. A security precaution that just might get her killed.

Casey heard him behind her as she slammed her palm on the green disk on the wall. She just got the door opened when he crashed into her, knocking her full force into the door. The whole glass panel shook and for a second, Casey thought the thing might shatter, but it stayed intact. Kept her trapped.

Air whooshed from her lungs as he pinned her hard against the glass and twisted her right arm hard behind her back. Pain shot up her shoulder. "Don't make this tougher than it has to be," he growled in her ear, his breath hot and rank against her cheek.

She didn't know how to get free and not break her arm, and he forced her back down the hallway. Her heart banged against her ribs and fire ripped through her arm. "Why are you doing this? Who are you?" She had to buy time somehow until Miles showed up. Unless… Oh God. "This was a lie to get me here early. Miles isn't coming, is he?"

"You're smart for a dead lady."

She struggled against his hold, tried to slow his momentum. "Stop! Stop!"

He threw her into a back studio, where she stumbled and landed on the ground. He stood at the door and fished out a phone from his pocket. He'd lost his glasses in the struggle and something about his eyes looked familiar.

"Mitch," she whispered. Jeff had been right. "What are you doing? This is crazy!"

He glared at her with nothing but hatred in his eyes. "I've got her," he said into the phone. He pulled a knife from his back pocket and every bit of spit in Casey's mouth dried up like the state of California. She stood on wobbly legs and looked around for something, anything that might work as a weapon. A microphone stand was only a few feet away. Better than nothing.

Mitch grunted some response over the line then disconnected. He advanced two steps toward her.

"Why are you doing this, Mitch? The show is over. It's done."

"You fucking stole my dream, that's why? You took me out before I even had a shot to show those assholes what I can do! I was the best songwriter on that show and I never got the chance…" His face turned red and rage distorted his features.

"I didn't do it on purpose," she yelled. "Besides, I didn't even really win. Brendan St. John won. You never went after…" But he did. He'd shot them both at her apartment. "Look, Mitch, just because you got knocked out the first night doesn't mean you were going to win the whole thing. I wouldn't have won if Brendan hadn't been disqualified."

"You're not listening to me! I could've won it! I should've won it! My whole life, people have been telling me I should be writing music. I should be singing my songs! But no one *heard* my songs!

That's your fault! No one else's, just yours!" He came toward her.

Casey bolted for the microphone stand. Instead of trying to pull it back, she used her momentum to swing it around. She nailed Mitch in the shoulder and knocked him off balance. Making a run for the door, she got as far as the hallway before he was behind her again, tackling her full force to the ground.

The knife? Where was the knife? It was the only thing her brain could focus on. She needed a miracle in the next five seconds or she was dead.

BRENDAN'S MOBILE RANG AS he waited outside the studio, and Blake's name flashed on the screen. "Yo," he said, answering the call. "What's up?"

"We got something...found a link between Mitch and one of the crew members on the show," Blake said, by way of greeting. "Turns out one of the day checkers is an old schoolmate of Mitch's. We found a withdrawal from Mitch's account for two grand that very conveniently coincided with a deposit for the same amount on the exact date of the first accident with the lighting rig. Same with the set wall. Kevin Andrews is our suspect. We called the police so they're checking him out now. It also turns out that Mitch is a mechanic by trade, so he's a good bet for the car bomb. We should have more info later today."

"Wow. Nice job, bro." Finally! Maybe the end of this whole fiasco was near. Of course, the police just had to pick up both men, but he had faith that Blake could find either one of them if they tried to run. "Looks like I owe you big."

"Music to my ears." Blake laughed. "Catch you later, I need to run." He disconnected before Brendan got a word out.

The relief rushing through Brendan fizzled out as he checked his watch. Miles was late. For a guy who lived by his clock and insisted on a schedule, it seemed very out of character. Five minutes late for Miles was like an hour late for anyone else.

An uneasy feeling settled in Brendan's gut. He glanced at the building just in time to notice the door open, then slam shut hard enough to shake all the glass in four front panels. For a second, Brendan thought it was a trick of the sun's glare, but instinct kicked in. He cranked the engine, pulled into street traffic and made a hard right up the inclined driveway. Casey had told him about the security in the building. Dark tinted windows made it impossible to see through the glass.

Brendan's motto when it came to Casey and her security was Act Now, Ask Questions Later.

Instead of even attempting to get in the front door the old fashioned way, he used the only sure fire method of entry. He laid on the gas and drove through. It only dawned on him a second before impact that Casey might be standing at one of those dark windows so he slammed on the brakes at contact.

Glass shattered in a huge explosion. His air bag blew up and smacked his face. Pain shot up his chin, and white dust temporarily blinded him. He heard Casey screaming as he ejected from his seat and tore through a smoky haze. Spotting her struggling with a man in the hallway, he sprinted forward, ditching the sling as he ran. A second later, he yanked the guy off her and threw him into the wall. Hot pain roared through his shoulder.

The glint of a knife flashed a second before Brendan got his hand on the man's wrist and stopped the momentum. Every muscle strained as he fought the guy. If he'd been using his good hand, it wouldn't have been an issue, but his bad arm was still weak and not nearly ready for this type of action. The guy swiped his leg and caught Brendan off balance and they both toppled. Brendan never let go of the guy's wrist and the knife loomed inches from his face. Sweat popped from every pore as he struggled, his jaw clenched tight. Fear roared through his veins along with adrenaline. He didn't have any leverage, didn't have—

Somehow Casey was there, adding her weight to the guy's arm and forcing his hand back. The guy—shit, it *was* Mitch—screamed and fought harder, his eyes wide and wild as the odds shifted.

"Drop the fucking knife," Brendan warned through gritted teeth.

Casey shifted and did something, because Mitch screamed and dropped the knife. He threw the same arm back and connected with Casey's stomach hard as he rolled off Brendan. She went down with a gasp and a second later, Mitch came up with a gun. Brendan pounced before the guy could aim, then he grabbed Mitch's hand and shifted the barrel of the small gun away from him.

"Casey, run!" Brendan yelled, wanting her gone. But she didn't leave him; she got to her feet, ready to help as she had with the knife. Slowly the gun turned, and Brendan strained to get it out of Mitch's grasp. "Drop it, asshole. Drop the g—"

The gun went off. Exploded in an instant and took most of Mitch's head with it.

Casey recoiled, landed flat on her ass and Brendan, too, jumped back and off the guy. Blood was everywhere...the walls, their clothes, the floor. Brendan's heart beat so hard he thought he might puke from the pressure.

Sirens sounded from a distance and he finally looked at Casey.

She was as pale as the white sands in Hawaii. Blood streaked her clothes and face, just like him. With her eyes wide and panicked, she visibly shook.

"Case." Brendan didn't know what to say, what to do. Mitch lay between them. "Are you okay?" Such a stupid question, but he needed to know if she was injured aside from the obvious shock.

"He opened the door for me, but there was never any meeting." She sounded miles away. "It was a setup. It's Mitch. From the show. Just like Jeff said. It's Mitch."

Brendan stood up on rubbery legs and stepped over the body. He pulled Casey into his arms and held her so she couldn't stare at the gore. "It's okay. It's okay now. It's over. He can't hurt you anymore." She nodded and it ripped Brendan in two to feel her shaking in his arms. "You're safe now."

Police stormed the destruction with guns drawn. Brendan had no choice but to let Casey go and they raised their hands to show they had no weapons. They made their way outside where an ambulance had pulled up along with two fire trucks.

Too bad the cavalry hadn't gotten here before the gun went off. The only thing Brendan knew for certain was that his finger never touched the trigger.

Police separated them to take their statements so Brendan still didn't know what Casey had endured before he got there. He noticed a nice bruise forming on her cheek and fresh rage burned him up inside.

At least it was over. That was the only good thing about this whole day. Casey was safe.

CHAPTER 28

CASEY GENTLY PATTED HER face dry before hazarding a glance at her reflection. She didn't have much color in her skin...with the exception of the giant bruise on her cheek. She wasn't even sure when that happened. Maybe when Mitch tackled her in the hallway? Or when he slammed her against the glass door. Didn't really matter. It was only another in a long line of aches and pains from Monday.

This was her last night at the St. Johns' house. She could finally get back to her apartment tomorrow and Brendan said he'd drop her off at the rental car agency so she'd have her own wheels.

Monday had been too much. She'd never forget it as long as she lived. Never forget the horror of watching a man lose a chunk of his head or the sticky warmth of his blood on her skin. Life was fragile. It could end any second. She knew it, but seeing death so up close and personal gave her a new prospective. It was time she took control of the life she had.

Someone rapped on the door.

"Case, it's me. You okay?" Brendan had been so attentive the last two days. He hadn't let her out of his sight. He hadn't said too much, but he was dealing with the same thing so she knew he was doubly freaked out since he'd had his hand on the gun when it went off.

Casey hadn't realized Brendan's father worked as a defense attorney. Not that any charges would be brought up because it was clearly a case of self-defense and their stories corroborated each other.

It didn't change the horrifying circumstances or the fact that she was once again—or still—in the public eye. Miles was in publicity heaven. He even took the news of temporarily losing his studio in stride. He'd told her to work on more songs while he searched for a studio to record at. Casey didn't know how much time that would take, but with the threat gone and her apartment cleaned up, she could go back home.

"Yeah," she said, setting the towel on the bar and opening the door. The Jack and Jill bathroom adjoined her room to Brendan's. "I'm good." She studied the red scratches on his chin from the airbag and tried not to ogle his six pack abs or the light trail of hair that disappeared beneath the waistband of his nylon shorts. She didn't stand a chance when the guy went topless. "How about you? How's the shoulder feel?"

"Sore." He adjusted the sling. "I'll be glad when I'm out of this stupid thing." He licked his lips. "So are you sure about tomorrow? Sure that you're ready to go back to your place. Because you're welcome to stay here for as long as you need."

"Bren, I can't stay at your parents' house indefinitely."

"I didn't mean indefinitely. Just until you're ready to go home."

"I'm ready. The threat is gone." A quick picture of Jeff storming her apartment two months ago flashed through her brain, but she shoved it aside. She'd be sure to keep her eye out for him in the future. "Although I might have to come back if your dad ever barbeques again. That was a pretty awesome dinner tonight." She couldn't remember the last time she'd had as good a meal. Actually, dinner with Brendan in Hawaii had been pretty amazing.

"Yeah, my dad grills a mean salmon. You know they'd love to have you over whenever you want."

His parents had welcomed her with open arms. The whole family had treated her as if she was one of them. It made it doubly hard to leave, but she had to. Her parents had asked her to come home on Monday, and Casey actually considered it, until her mom made a comment about the trouble she got into because of the show. Though she didn't doubt her parents' love, she also knew she couldn't live under the same roof with them. Not even for two days.

"Are you as wiped out as I am?" Brendan asked.

She hadn't slept much the past couple of nights. Every time she closed her eyes she saw Mitch's head blow off. "I think the dark circles under my eyes can probably answer that," Casey mused.

He took her hand. "Come on."

"Where are we going?" she asked, following his lead. "My bed is behind me."

"I want to spend the night with you."

She stopped, forcing him to stop. When he turned, she shook her head. "Bren, I'm not comfortable with that. Not with your parents down the hall."

"I didn't say we were going to screw around. I said I want to sleep with you. I want you in my arms. I want to reach over in the middle of the night and feel you next to me, know you're safe. C'mon, Case, my parents are cool with it. You know that." He laughed softly and pulled her close. "I'll tell you a secret if you promise not to tell Blake I told you." His eyes sparkled with a mischievous glow.

He piqued her interest. "What?"

"Blake was hurt a year ago and his girlfriend Abbey was here. Mom and Dad were on the way out for the night, and Mom took Abbey aside and told her if they had sex that she needed to be on top because Blake needed to take it easy."

Casey's jaw dropped open. "No way. She did not say that. I don't believe you."

"Cross my heart. Swear to God. My mom knows the deal. But like I said in the beginning, I'm not going to do anything you're not comfortable with." He tugged her along with him. "We're only sleeping...and possibly cuddling."

"Cuddling? Did you just use the C word?" He laughed again and the sound filled up every vacant part of her heart. "Seriously," she went on, "I've never met a guy who had too much interest in cuddling. You have to understand my skepticism."

He took her the last few steps to his bed. "I do. Look, I may not act like it most of the time, because I can't seem to get Hawaii out of my mind and I want a replay of that night desperately, or even Sunday night for that matter, but I'm good with sticking it out until you're ready." His smile faded as he placed her hand around his neck and put his arm around her waist. "When I woke up in Hawaii and found you gone..." He shook his head. "I was crushed, Case. I wanted to hold you so bad. I wanted to feel you against me, breathe you in."

He was mesmerizing when he spoke to her like that. All of her insides melted into a giant puddle at his feet.

"So please. Sleep with me. Lay your head next to mine. Let me hold you or your hand. Let me breathe you in like I wanted to that morning in Hawaii." His blue eyes nearly killed her with their longing.

"You make it really hard to say no," she whispered.

He grinned and touched his forehead to hers. "That was the idea."

She didn't have much of a choice. He made a very solid argument. No better time than the present to start living her life the way she wanted. Not the way her parents wanted. Time to reach for a life that made her happy on her terms. "Okay."

That gorgeous smile returned and almost blinded her with its intensity. His optimism was absolutely contagious and just what she needed. He stepped back and gestured to the already opened bed. "Ladies first."

She climbed into Brendan's bed and lifted the light blanket over her nightshirt and shorts.

Brendan got comfortable next to her. "C'mere." He put his arm out and coaxed her against him. Not a bad place to be. He was so solid. So sexy. His sculpted chest made a perfect pillow and it took every ounce of control not to reach out with her tongue and taste him.

She traced a finger along the indent of his abs and shared her fear. "I guess I keep waiting for the other shoe to drop."

"What shoe?"

"I'm already high maintenance because of Mitch and Jeff. I figured you'd realize that I'm not the girl you met on the beach and you'd cut and run."

He shifted and looked down at her. "What do you mean? Of course you're the same girl."

She shook her head. "That girl doesn't exist. She *rarely* exists," she amended when he opened his mouth to argue. "That girl wanted to live life and be someone else for a night. She wanted to break all the rules she'd ever lived with and cut loose. She wanted to go for something she wanted and not have any regrets."

Brendan didn't answer at first. "Okay, so what I'm getting is that you never break rules and have never gone after something you really wanted. I have to disagree with that." This time he went on before she could respond. "You gave your douchebag ex the heave-ho. Rule—"

"Actually, he gave me the heave-ho," she cut in.

"Bullshit. I think you knew that non-compliance was going to be a deal breaker and you did it anyway. As I was saying...rule number one obliterated. You went into the ocean when you probably shouldn't have. Rule number two, snapped like a twig. You found a stranger and seduced him—which by the way made that stranger a very happy man. I don't know about you, but I have zero regrets from that night. I loved every minute and I'd do it again in a heartbeat. That makes rule number three, toast. You went against your family's wishes and auditioned—and made—a reality show, which you won. Rule number four, history.

"So if you're telling me you're not that girl, I'm going to disagree. Your confidence that night sucked me in. There is nothing sexier than a confident woman. Nothing more appealing than a woman who knows what she wants."

"What if that person is gone?" she whispered. "What if I can't find her again after all this?"

He squeezed her closer. "She's not gone. She's right here in my arms."

Casey swallowed back her response. She noticed the bulge in his shorts and felt guilty for leading him on in some way. "I'm not so sure about that, Bren. I mean, it sounds good in theory, but the reality is I don't feel like the same person."

"You've been through a life changing experience. Hell, several of them. Give yourself time to figure out who you are now and who you want to be in the future. Either way, I'm here for you. I don't plan on going anywhere." He kissed her forehead. "We're official, remember? Don't forget that."

Official girlfriends didn't leave their boyfriends hanging.

Footsteps sounded in the hallway and Casey tensed waiting for

Brendan's mom or dad to walk past the door. She pulled away from him just as his mom stuck her head in.

"Good night, you two. Don't stay up late. You're both still recovering. Get some sleep." She smiled and continued to her room.

Casey had never known anything like it.

"Why do you look so shocked," Brendan asked.

She pointed out the door. "Your mom. She just...she didn't even... My mom would've blown a gasket if she caught me with a boy in my bed."

"I told you my mom is cool with that. We're adults."

"I know, I know. I was just raised by old-fashioned people." She sighed and snuggled next to him, letting his warmth and strength lull her to sleep.

BRENDAN LET THE COOL water wash the soap off his skin. He'd tried to coax Casey into the shower with him, but she'd given him big eyes like he'd obliterated commandment number twelve. Thou shalt not shower with thy girlfriend in your parents' house. It had been worth a shot since he was getting massively tired of cold showers. Sharing a bathroom with her only fueled the fire. Seeing all her girl paraphernalia—the lotion that made her skin so soft, the shampoo that made her hair shiny as silk—smelling her when she wasn't there, gave him a false sense of commitment that he knew she wasn't feeling.

He didn't know how he managed to fall asleep with the biggest hard-on of his life, but he ended up with one of the most peaceful night's rest since the kidnapping. A full night of sleep was something he'd taken for granted. Now it was rare for him to go a night without a bad dream waking him up with his heart pounding out of control and sweat slicking his body.

Finally, he had Casey next to him. He was glad she'd confided in him about that night in Hawaii. It made it easier to understand where she was coming from. The girl had a lot on her plate.

He wasn't mentally ready to take her—bags and all—to get her rental, but he didn't really have a leg to stand on when it came to excuses and keeping her with him. The threat was gone. Nothing kept her from living her own life. He just hoped like hell he was still going to be part of it. Their conversation the night before enlightened him, but didn't particularly spark confidence when it came to Casey's feelings about him.

He'd pretty much emotionally blindsided her. He got that. Not that he could help it. He'd fallen for her like an avalanche, so he understood her reluctance to go with those feelings—especially after coming out of a long-term relationship. So yeah, he had to move slowly, build her confidence and gain her trust. He was cool with that. Sunday night had been a giant exercise in trust. In his eyes, that kind of intimacy only bonded them closer. He just had to give her time to realize it.

Brendan shook his head under the spray, remembering Blake's journey with Abbey. How many times had he told his twin to cut his losses and bail? How many times had he wanted to wring Abbey's neck—not literally, but figuratively—for screwing with his brother's heart? But Blake had insisted she was the one. He'd been intent in finding a way into Abbey's heart and he had. To Brendan's amazement, Abbey had blossomed into a confident woman. None of them knew her history, hell, Brendan still didn't, but Blake had assured him that Abbey's fears had been based on something horrific and to cut her some slack, so he had.

Brendan shut down the water, dried off and pulled on jeans and a T-shirt. His cell phone rang as he put his boots on. "Yo," he said to his big brother. "What's up?"

"I need advice," Danny said.

Brendan rolled his eyes. Danny rarely asked for Brendan's two cents and when he got it, he never listened to it. "Go ask Eric. I'm heading out in a few minutes."

"No! Wait! Seriously. Eric's not answering and I need help before she calls back."

"Before who calls back?" Brendan asked.

"Nikki."

"Who's that?"

"A girl I met a month ago at a bar. Her hair kind of reminds me of Casey's. Hey, speaking of Casey, how is she? Recovering okay?"

"Yeah, Casey's good."

"Good. Okay, so back to me. This girl Nikki is a total

whackjob. We had a one night thing and all of a sudden she thinks she owns me."

"Yeah, one-nighters bite." It was why he quit doing them.

"She won't leave me alone. First she did the *left behind*. You know, when a chick leaves something at your place after a crazy night so she can come back again? She was totally rocking a tight skirt, fuck me pumps and had red lipstick. You know how that kills me. So we did it again even though I know she planned the whole thing. I couldn't stop myself. How do I get rid of her?"

"Sometimes one night things turn into more and they suck, right?" He hoped his brother caught the sarcasm. "Why are you calling me?"

"Because you're the only one who answered the damn phone. Help."

"Look, she seems pretty insecure to me. Any time I feel crowded like that, I put the brakes on. Life's too short to deal with that kind of shit. Tell her to back off and for fuck's sake don't sleep with her again. You have a real problem keeping your dick in your pants, you know that?"

"Fuck you, little brother. You're just saying that because you have someone to fuck."

"Shows how little you know, Dano. Casey isn't what she looks like." Because she looked like a very modern woman with confidence when in reality she was leery of the real world.

CHAPTER 29

CASEY NEARLY KNOCKED ON the bathroom door to see if Brendan was almost done when she heard him say, *"Casey's good."* She didn't know who he was talking to and a second later he said, *"Sometimes one night things turn into more and they suck, right?"* Her cheeks flamed. Eavesdropping wasn't something she did under normal circumstances, so when he said, *"Look, she seems pretty insecure to me."* She turned around, picked up her small suitcase and headed downstairs as quietly as possible.

Emotion clogged her throat, but she refused to cry. She knew it was too good to be true. Maybe there were no good men left, because so far the ones she'd dealt with were full of nothing but bullshit. Well, she wasn't sticking around for it.

She pulled her phone from her bag and texted her sister. *You around? I need a ride ASAP. I'm at Brendan's parents' house in Larchmont.*

Her sister texted back. *I'm a solid twenty minutes away at work. Uber is faster than me.*

Good idea, Casey texted back. She found the app on her phone and called for a car. ETA four minutes. Perfect. She scribbled a quick thank-you note for Brendan's parents and left it on the kitchen counter, then she quietly walked out the kitchen door, moved her ass down the driveway and out the front gate. The car pulled up and she closed the gate behind her. She gave the driver the address to the rental car agency and three seconds later they were off.

So long, Brendan. Sorry to be so much trouble.

He'd had her so convinced that he cared about her. Why go

through everything he had if he didn't care about her? *Because he wanted a repeat of that night in Hawaii,* her inner voice said. *Or he wanted a piece of your fame.* God, she really didn't know why he was pursuing her if he thought being with her sucked.

Good thing she was getting out now before she fell for him even harder. Tears pricked her eyes and she had to face it…she'd already fallen *so* hard. "Dammit," she mumbled swiping at her eyes. She refused to be crushed by this.

Songs. She had to put the emotion into her songs and get over it. Goodbye, Brendan; hello, hit single.

Yeah, that's how she had to look at it. This was ammo for great music.

Minutes later, she arrived at the rental car agency and picked up the new wheels. A silver compact. One day soon she wouldn't have to worry about money. One day soon her songs were going to be blasting on the radio and she'd be traveling in style in a stretch limo and she'd have her choice of any guy she wanted.

Brendan.

No, she told her pitiful self. Not Brendan.

Casey drove home, dreading walking into her apartment alone, but knowing she'd have to face it. She couldn't stay away forever. Zoe had assured her that she'd taken care of the apartment. It had been cleaned and repaired. There was something to be said for big protective sisters. They took care of their siblings.

Casey parked on the street since a section under the carport was still blocked off due to damage from the explosion. She pulled out her bag and trekked to her front door. A very creepy tingle whispered along her neck and she turned around, looking at the surrounding neighborhood, the cars, the trees, but nothing seemed remotely suspicious. She shook off the feeling, unlocked her door and went inside. She bolted the door and faced her apartment. Everything seemed normal. No more bullet holes in the walls. Zoe must've ridden the building manager's ass to get it fixed so fast. Or she'd gone to the trouble and expense to fix it herself. She'd even replaced the white slipcover on her sofa with a new red one that popped in her subdued color scheme. A new standing lamp replaced the one that was destroyed.

Her big sis had spent significant dough to repair this place.

Casey owed her a chunk of change. Knowing Zoe, she'd wave her hand and say, *"I'll put it on your tab."* Her big sis made serious money working as a realtor. She'd tapped into the neighborhoods of the mega-famous and her portion of any sale equaled hundreds of thousands of dollars at one pop. The fact that she sold multiple houses a year made her a very wealthy woman. A fact she worked hard to hide from the average eye. She lived in a nice condo in Brentwood and invested her money to make even more. Casey was proud of her big sis, but it was hard to accept her constant generosity when Casey couldn't pay her back. Although now, she had the opportunity. All she had to do was write a hit song. Or two. Possibly more if the gods were looking down on her kindly.

The opening notes of Bob Seger's "Old Time Rock and Roll" played and Casey reached for her phone in her bag. Brendan. It was only a matter of time before he called. She stared at his name and number on the screen, debated answering. She'd have to face him one of these days.

He knew she was fine. He'd probably seen the note on the counter to his parents. The threat was gone with Mitch being dead, so she didn't have anything to worry about... Unless she counted Jeff, which she didn't. She had no plans to open the door blindly anymore. He wouldn't catch her alone in her apartment unless he broke in and she didn't see that happening.

Still, after everything they'd been through, she couldn't ghost him again. She swiped the screen. "Hello."

"Hello?" He sounded way too calm as he matched her tone. He was royally pissed. Good. So was she. "Is that all you have? Just hello?"

"Look, I'm fine Brendan. I'm at home. I'm about to start working, so..." She took a deep breath. "Thanks for everything the past few days. I mean it. But it's time I got back to the real world."

"Are you blowing me off?" She'd never heard him so upset and a piece of her crumbled inside. "What the hell happened? One minute we're about to get your car and the next you've fucking disappeared. Gone. Not a word, nothing. *Again.* What the...what am I supposed to think, Casey?"

What was *she* supposed to think after what *he* said? "Look, I heard your conversation on the phone. Not all of it, but enough to know that what you've said and how you really feel are two different things. Okay, maybe you felt sorry for me. Whatever. You don't have to see me again. I'm trying to make it easier for you."

"Easier for me?" He sounded incredulous. "Ripping my heart out is what you call easier?"

There was a knock on the door and Casey jumped a mile as she spun around.

"It's me," Brendan said in the phone. "I'm at the door. Would you please open the door?"

Casey's cheeks burned. Numbly she disconnected the phone and opened the door. She wished she was stronger, wished she didn't have her heart in her throat or on her sleeve. But looking at the same pain on his face only hurt worse.

"What are you making easier for me, Case?" he asked softly. He shoved his phone in his pocket.

"I know how you really feel," she said just as quietly. "I heard you on the phone. I'm insecure. It's not attractive. Relationships after one night stands suck. I heard it all."

He dropped his chin to his chest and exhaled before meeting her gaze. "May I come in?"

She shook her head. "No. We should just say good-bye right here. Right now." Even though it was going to rip her heart out.

"You know what you didn't hear when you listened to *my* half of the conversation?" Some of his anger returned. "You didn't hear my brother on the other end of the phone! You didn't hear him ask me for advice on getting rid of a one-night stand who won't stop tailing him."

"But you said my name. Then you started talking about me."

"Bullshit, I did." He looked around. "Can we finish this conversation inside? The last time I stood in this spot I got shot."

Oh, God, she hadn't even thought of that. "Yes, I'm sorry. Come in." She stood aside and closed the door behind him, her heart slamming against her ribs.

He reached the middle of the room and turned. "I can't believe you left without a god damn word, Case. That kills me. You have no idea how much that hurt."

"I didn't think you wanted me around af—"

"After hearing my side of a stupid conversation with my brother, who by the way has serious issues with keeping his pants zipped. *He* had a one-night stand that won't leave him alone, so he called me for advice. He thinks because I work for a rock star, all I do is have one nighters and dump them afterward."

Casey's chest got tight and a sliver of hope sent a ray of light through her dark heart. "Really?" She barely got the word out.

He ran a frustrated hand through his thick hair. "Yes, really. You seriously have not been listening to a word I've said, have you? I care about you, Casey. A lot. A whole fucking lot. And I thought you cared about me. When you care about someone, it means you talk things out. You don't run away."

"I know." She covered her face with her hands before meeting his gaze. "This is all new to me. I just heard you and I ran." She shook her head, terrified that she screwed it all up.

Brendan glanced at the ceiling and exhaled. "I'm trying to tell you that I love you, Casey. I love you. I don't want you to run away from me. I want you to come to me. I want to talk things out. I want to hold you. I want to console you when you're sad or upset."

What? A knot lodged in her throat and she swallowed it back. "You love me?"

Brendan opened his mouth then shut it. "Shit," he hissed. "That was not how I envisioned telling you that." He met her gaze, his eyes soulful. No trace of anger there. "Yes, I love you. I think I've loved you since that first day in Hawaii. I fell hard for you, Case."

She swallowed again. "But I told you I'm not that person, remember?"

He nodded. "I remember. But I think you're wrong. You are that person. Deep down, you're strong. You're capable. You fight for what you want, for what you believe in. You stand up for yourself and the ones you love."

This was nothing like Jeff. This was the reason she'd fallen so hard for Brendan in the first place. He said stuff no one had ever said to her before. Her eyes stung and her chest tightened.

A few steps brought him right in front of her. "So yes, I love you, all the parts of you, even the screwed up parts that don't trust what we have. What we *can* have if you give me a shot, if you trust me." He took a tear away with a gentle swipe of his thumb.

She was totally screwed up. She knew that. "I thought I knew what love was," she said, trying to make him understand. "I thought I was in love, but I wasn't. With Jeff, it was about doing things right and getting acceptance. It was about pleasing him all the time and being good and doing the right thing."

"I know. I'm not him." His soft words tore down the last bit of wall that she'd been holding up.

"I know." She closed her eyes, nodded. "I know." She had to quit comparing him to Jeff. Time to pull her head out of her ass and see him for the man he was.

BRENDAN WAITED FOR CASEY to decide. She looked completely torn up, with her eyes shut tight and her forehead furrowed. The answer came now, as far as he was concerned. She either trusted him or didn't. She wanted him or didn't. He'd have to accept whatever it was. He didn't think he had the fortitude of his twin brother. Didn't think he could hold out for a year or more waiting for Casey to work through her issues. Maybe it made him a dick. But honestly, he was only human. She'd caught his attention and held it from day one. He loved her humor and her creativity and couldn't help but be floored by her beauty too.

He took her non-answer as her reply and his heart never felt heavier. He would give his life for her...hell he nearly had. The sad truth stared him in the face. She didn't feel the same way. Maybe she never would. Maybe she was right in the first place when she said she needed to get over the douchebag before moving on. Who knew how long that would take?

Instead of waiting for the rejection he saw on her face, he brushed by her and headed for the door.

"Brendan!"

He stopped and forced himself to face her. "What?"

"Don't go. Please don't go."

He clenched his jaw. Didn't dream that her stopping him was a good thing. "Why? Give me a reason to stay." That's all he needed. One good reason.

She stared at him and the agony in her eyes turned to

something else. Something Brendan didn't dare hope for. "Because you're the best thing that's ever happened to me. You, your whole family has supported me more in the last few days than my parents have in years. I was stupid for staying with Jeff for long. I'd be even stupider to let you walk out the door."

Brendan let her words penetrate his tattered heart and slowly, second by second, she reeled him in.

"After everything you've done for me, I shouldn't have run out the way I did. I should've asked you about it face to face instead of letting my imagination run wild." She closed the distance between them, her steps tentative. "I'm sorry."

"Don't apologize." He stepped closer too. "I don't want you to apologize." That was a sore spot for her. She'd told him as much. How she'd end up apologizing to Jeff for shit that wasn't her fault. Maybe she had made some mistakes, but she realized it and that was all he wanted. "As long as you won't run again. As long as we agree to talk everything out, it doesn't matter."

Here they were. Face to face. A new beginning? He hoped so, but she still hadn't reciprocated with the three little words that had spilled from his mouth.

"It's okay. I can say I'm sorry when I'm wrong," she said quietly. "I was wrong to run. Apologies worked for whatshisname because I fed into it. It's what I thought I had to do for him to love me. But I won't go back to that again," she hurried to say when he began shaking his head. "Unless it's required. Like now. I'm sorry." She moved even closer. Close enough to bring her mouth inches from his. "Do you forgive me?"

With barely a shake of his head, Brendan did. His brain was starting to short circuit with having her so close. The flowery scent of her shampoo and lushness of those irresistible lips fogged his senses.

"That was a yes, right?" Her words whispered over his mouth and her aqua eyes sparkled with hope.

"Yeah." He barely choked the word out.

"Okay, good." She wrapped her hands around his neck and got even closer, bringing them tightly together. "Can I seal it with a kiss?"

Fuck it. It wasn't what Brendan wanted. He wanted the words, but he wouldn't turn this down for a million bucks, because it was a start. Maybe she didn't love him now, but he didn't need now as long he had hope for the future.

Brendan sealed it for her. He bent the inch needed to put their lips together and kissed her. He didn't attack. He loved. He brushed his lips over hers, wanted her to feel how much this moment meant to him.

CHAPTER 30

CASEY SOAKED UP HAVING Brendan so close. She loved the way his lips teased hers with feather-light strokes and sweet seduction. But she wanted more. She wanted him to know she meant what he said. She *was* sorry and she wanted another chance with him.

How many people got a second chance like this? A chance for that once in a lifetime thing that seemed so elusive. She'd thought she had to compromise to find love. To be someone she wasn't to find a man who loved her. Brendan knew the woman she was and the woman she wanted to be and he loved *all* parts of her. The realization opened her heart.

She took his kiss a step farther and darted her tongue across his lips, requesting entry. When he opened his mouth to her, she met his tongue in a sweet dance of sin. He tasted warm and minty. He tasted like Brendan. Sweet, brave and all hers.

He loved her! The longer they kissed the more she realized what she had, what she'd nearly lost, and she wanted to make sure he knew she wouldn't take him for granted anymore.

What was the quickest way to get her point across?

Show him.

Then tell him! God, she hadn't even said the words. He'd put everything out there and she'd just glossed right over it.

That night in Hawaii had been magical. Hours of skin time. Kissing. Touching. Rolling together on a king-sized bed, giving and taking... That's what she wanted now, and all day. Screw songwriting. She'd come up with a song later. Now belonged to Brendan.

Casey slowly edged him backward, easing him around the furniture toward her bedroom.

"What are you doing?" he asked between long, soul-destroying kisses.

"Taking you to my bed for make-up sex."

He pulled back before she laid another kiss on him. "Casey, I didn't mean for this...for my coming here today...to be about sex."

"You talk way too much." She snagged his lips and he didn't argue. He palmed her head and kept her sealed to his mouth. They made it right next to the bed, but the second she came up for air, he jumped in where he left off.

"Look, seriously. If you need more time to process, I understand. I just wanted to clear the air with you."

"I think we're crystal clear," she murmured, taking a nibble from his neck. He shivered. She hid her smile before meeting his gaze. "Unless you don't want to have make-up sex."

He looked so serious with eyebrows furrowed and his blue eyes full of concern. "That's not it." His stroked his hand down her side and her lids got heavier. "You know how much I want you. But I don't want to rush you into anything either. I know Hawaii was a turning point and I know what I said about recreating it, but we can't." He shook his head. "I mean we can, but we can't, because we can't go back to that night. It won't change that we'll always have that night though." His lips lifted in a grin. "It was amazing. One of the best nights of my life."

That same damn knot lodged in her throat again. She brushed her thumb along his scraped jaw and smiled into those serious sweet eyes that melted her. "Hawaii was great, but what's about to happen here is going to be even better. You know why?" He shook his head, but didn't interrupt her. "Because we didn't love each other in Hawaii, and we do now." Her words registered in on his face. "You heard me." She stroked her lips across his. "I love you." She held his head and looked him in the eyes. "I wasn't even thinking about meeting someone new. Someone who might be the one, but you showed up anyway. You snuck under my skin. I've been so busy pushing you away that I wasn't taking the time to realize that maybe I met you for a reason. What if there is no time frame on when you're supposed to meet the right person or fall in love?"

He blinked and she saw the emotion she felt mirrored in his eyes. "I love you. Right now, I want to show you how much. I want to thank you for being patient with me. For understanding that I had to work through some stuff to get to this point." She ran her bottom lip through her teeth. "Want to know a secret? I haven't been able to get Sunday night out of my head. I'm so crazy hot for you, I feel like I might implode."

The heat in his eyes made her flush. "Are you done talking yet?" he whispered, a smile creeping back onto his lips. He eased the sling over his head and Casey's heart chugged along faster.

She played it cool, canted her head and looked up as if considering something she might have forgotten. He laughed and pulled her against him in a giant hug. A Brendan hug with both arms wrapped around her tight. Casey let her happiness shine through as two fat tears leaked down her cheeks.

"I love you," he whispered fiercely.

She pulled back and looked into his eyes. "I so feel a song coming on." She kissed the grin right off his face at the same time she eased her hands beneath his T-shirt and stroked her palms up his abs to his chest. His groan rumbled through her. He didn't need any coaxing as he helped her remove the shirt completely.

"Are you sure your shoulder is up to this?" she asked.

"It's not my shoulder that's up for this, trust me," he breathed, reassuring her with a joke. "Make-up sex, huh?" he said between deep, hot kisses.

"Oh yeah," she breathed. "Lots of it."

He groaned again before taking her mouth a little harder, crushing his lips over hers like a starving man. She loved his intensity, his strength. He pulled back quickly and had her shirt over her head in seconds, then stopped, looked her in the eyes and let his gaze roam lower to her chest. He stroked his thumbs along the edge of her lacey bra, sending darts of need straight between her legs and making her nipples press against the thin material. "I could stare at you forever," he said softly.

"You want to take it off, or should I?" Casey asked, hoping to find that brave girl from Hawaii.

His gaze drilled into hers. "I want to." Taking his time, he unclasped the front closer and slowly let the cups pull away to reveal her breasts. The erotic scratch and slide of the material rubbed against her protruding nipples and Casey closed her eyes, imagining his mouth and hands on the same spot. "You're so sexy like that, Case." He nuzzled her neck and his warm breath fluttered over her skin. "I want to make this last forever."

God that sounded good. To block out everything else. To forget everything they'd gone through the last few weeks and concentrate on each other.

He pulled back, and looking into his eyes she saw regret. "I only have a few hours," he said. "Seger called after my brother and I need to do a few things for him later today."

"Oh." That jammed a pin in her bubble of love.

His dark brows furrowed together. "But I've got a couple hours now and I can come back tonight. How's that sound?"

"Sounds perfect." Maybe while he was gone, she might be able to capture some of this emotion and put it to paper.

His breath-stealing smile when he fumbled for his wallet in the back pocket of his jeans made her heart ache. He found the condom he was looking for and tossed the wallet behind him. His grin faded when he moved in and kissed her. Casey let all her troubles slip away. She let the sureness of his touch as he skimmed her bare back take her to a heavenly place where nothing mattered but Brendan and the way he treated her. His gentle hands stroked down her arms and back up her ribs to cup her breasts. He made her feel fragile, like she might break if he didn't take care. He licked one nipple into his mouth as he rolled the other between his fingers, and it was like yanking an invisible line between her legs.

He fumbled with the button on her jeans and she helped him slide them down her legs. His jeans went next and she loved seeing just how much he wanted this moment. Not that she had too many doubts, but the proof was there, jutting out and eager for attention.

"That bad boy is ready to party," she said around another kiss. The bad boy in question was now pressed tightly against her lower stomach.

Brendan's answer was to yank the blanket all the way back, lift her and toss her onto the bed.

Casey shrieked and laughed as he pounced on top of her, but in the next second, the serious man returned, kissing her softly, thoroughly, until her need to have him overrode any other thoughts.

He wanted this to last, but she couldn't wait. Grabbing his good shoulder and anchoring his leg with her own, she flipped him to his back.

He didn't seem to mind. In fact, his *"God, yes,"* made her think he was pretty on board with the whole change of scenery.

"Where'd that condom go?" she asked, her breath already coming out in short pants. She'd never wanted anyone this desperately before. Not even in Hawaii had she been this ready to be with a man. Her thighs were slick from her own arousal and he'd barely touched her.

Maybe he understood her need because he ripped the packet open with his teeth and handed it to her. "At your service."

"I love a man who's prepared." She rolled the latex over his erection and he sucked in a breath as she gave him a few extra strokes for good measure. "I know it's not the same as Hawaii, but..." She straddled him. Before she could adjust herself over him, he pulled her down, kissed her like he might die if he didn't get her mouth.

"I love you so much, Casey. I love you."

She kissed him again, with all her heart and soul. She loved the way he palmed her head, the way he stroked his hand down her back and circled that erogenous zone right at the base of her spine. She rubbed against him, slicked them up with her arousal. This time when she adjusted to take him, he was right there, helping her, until the tip of his erection kissed the wet seam of her entrance.

Slowly, inch by inch, she took him in. He stretched her, filled her, made her whole as they became one. Casey sat astride him, didn't move. She closed her eyes and let the joy of being connected to Brendan heal her. It had been so long. Too long. How could she have gone so many months without this feeling?

His hands caressed her sides, then her ribs until he had each one under her breasts. She arched into his palms as he finally claimed her and that's when she began moving, taking her time, rising and falling. Each delicious stroke sent fiery pleasure arcing through her.

Finally, she opened her heavy eyes and seeing the love on his face, the desire in his eyes, she knew what love was. It was this. Now. It was Brendan, looking at her exactly like that. It was his touch, his patience, his understanding. Love was the man beneath her, taking her to new heights and new beginnings.

"C'mere." His voice was rough, full of passion, full of heat. When she lay over him and kissed his lips, her whole world came together in one crystalized moment.

"I love you," she breathed. "I love you." She couldn't stop saying it, over and over between every kiss and with every move that took him deeper inside her. The slow, deep penetration turned into a frantic, almost desperate attempt to bind him to her forever.

She rode that line of pleasure where every move had her balancing on a precipice. Every in and out kept an invisible string taut with need. When he grabbed her ass and squeezed tight, when he thrust up and pushed her down, she went over the edge. A foreign cry sounded in her throat as her internal muscles clenched and waves of bliss rolled in with each rapid heartbeat.

With a final thrust, Brendan froze beneath her. His muscles tightened into rock hard cords as his climax pounded through him. His long hair was as damp as hers when she finally collapsed on top of him, breathing hard, her body limp and sated.

"Holy hell," he breathed, skimming his fingers along her slick back. She shivered in delight at the caress. "I didn't think it was possible, but that was better than Hawaii."

She smiled against his chest, had never felt so free yet so connected with someone. "Told ya so," she mumbled. She shrieked when he rolled and tickled her, but a minute later his lips met hers again. She hated that he had to go. "Whatever you have to do for Seger, make it fast, okay? I want you back here, just like this later."

His smile killed her. "Oh you can count on that." Staring down at her with his long beautiful hair framing his face, he got serious again. "Make no mistake. Tonight there will be no sleeping. Have I made myself clear."

"Crystal." She couldn't have held back a grin if her life depended on it.

BRENDAN COULDN'T REMEMBER EVER being this happy. Before the kidnapping, he'd had good times, sure, but since the kidnapping, he'd been in a different place, a much darker place. He'd held himself off, become less accessible to strangers and acquaintances. He'd hid behind his hair.

Breaking through Casey's defenses felt like winning the lottery. Hearing her say the words and back them up simultaneously with her kiss, with her smile and that sparkle in her eyes, freed him of any doubt, any worries that she loved him.

For the first time in years, his ear was a non-issue. He realized he never even thought about it when he was with her because she made him feel whole. For that alone he'd love her until the end of time.

Of all days for Seger to finally need him. Dammit.

Brendan kissed her again, because he couldn't stop himself. The way she smiled up at him, the joy in her eyes, made him the happiest man on earth. She wove a spell with her tongue as they kissed. Just like Hawaii, being with her reduced everything else to the peripheral. Nothing mattered but her now, and the connection they shared.

Given another few minutes, he could very well show her again how important she was to him, but the job niggled in the back of his brain.

"You should go now so you can get back sooner," she breathed, spreading kisses along his jaw.

"I was thinking the same thing." He stroked a lock of long damp hair off her cheek and brushed his lips across hers one last time. "Should I bring back dinner later or should I take you out for a real date." Something they never even had a chance to do since Hawaii.

She thought about it for a second. "Let's save the date for another time. I want you to myself tonight."

"Dinner in then. I'll surprise you with something delicious."

"*You* are my something delicious," she whispered before lifting her head and kissing him. God, she made it hard to leave. He kissed her again, stroking his tongue along hers, loving the warmth of her mouth and the sweet sigh in her exhale.

"I'm not helping, am I?" she murmured at his lips.

"Not one bit."

She laughed and pushed him back. "Fine. I can be strong. Go. Do your thing. I'll see you back here later."

He gave her one last quick kiss and gently moved off her, instantly missing her heat and the warmth of her smooth skin against his. After tossing the condom and cleaning up in her bathroom, he returned to find her in a giant white T-shirt and not much else. "Damn, that's sexy," he said, wrapping her in his good arm since he had the sling back in place.

"It's even sexier when I take it off." She leaned up and kissed him then pulled away. "I'll see you later?"

"Nothing's going to keep me away," he assured her.

She held his hand all the way to the door. "Love you. Drive safe."

He smiled at the wifely order and nearly choked on the adjective. God, was he so far gone that he was ready to think of her as a wife? It seemed crazy, but not in a bad way...more like an unexpected way. "Lock the door behind me." It was probably smarter than getting down on one knee and proposing on the spot. That might really freak her out.

"I planned on it," she said. He liked that even though the trouble was over, she planned to be smart.

"See you later." He kissed her, one last long deep one for the road. Something to keep him going for the next five hours or so. "Write something pretty," he said, knowing what the rest of her day would consist of. Then he was out the door, jogging to his truck so he could get back ASAP.

CHAPTER 31

JEFF WATCHED ST. JOHN drive off and a wave of relief and determination coiled together in his chest. The day was still early and this checked off a giant item on his *to do* list. Reaching into his glove compartment, he pulled out a small baggie of coke then tapped out a line on his finger. He inhaled, then repeated the process on the other side. It was just the thing he needed to make this party perfect.

"Time for a little reunion, Casey," he murmured as he exited his rental car and moved down the street. His Hummer was too identifiable in this neighborhood, so he'd been smart and kept it at home. He didn't need much time here. Maybe fifteen, twenty minutes at the most. Since St. John had been here for a while, there was a good chance he left behind a decent amount of DNA, enough to pin him for murder, especially with the way he hauled ass out of the apartment to his car. The guy had nearly bowled over one of Casey's neighbors in his rush.

He hadn't been able to make the *Mitch kills Casey* plan work, but at least that idiot was gone and one less worry on Jeff's shoulders. If he set this up right, he could definitely turn an investigation back to St. John. The cops would have to consider the animosity between Casey and St. John with the way things went down with the show.

The idea swirled round in his head as he got closer to her apartment. He checked the area around her complex...no one coming or going, no one watching him as he moved up the sidewalk closer to her door.

His blood pumped faster the way it did when he was about to win something.

Didn't she understand that he always won? Always. This time was no exception. No one left him or made him look like a fool. If Casey thought to get away with those things, then she was about to be set straight.

CASEY BREEZED BACK TO her bedroom, a silly smile on her face. Nothing…no one made her happier than Brendan. It seemed almost a crime to be so happy, to feel so loved and wanted. Maybe it was the newness of those feelings that had her flying so high.

Taking one look at the wrecked bed made her blush. Then she twirled in her spot, her heart overflowing with love and joy. After her little love dance, she picked up a blanket from the floor and tossed it to the bed. Something dropped on the floor.

Brendan's wallet. "Uh oh." She picked it up and set it on the bedside table as she continued making the bed.

Someone knocked on the door a few minutes later and she grinned as she snatched up the wallet and headed through her apartment.

She didn't bother looking in the peephole, but she kept the chain across the door because she knew if she just opened it, Brendan would pitch a fit. Her heart thumped along wildly. It didn't matter that he'd be leaving again in five seconds, just the thought of seeing him again so soon made her happy beyond reason.

Opening the door a crack, she held up the wallet. "Forget some—" Her words died on her tongue as Jeff loomed on the other side. Her pulse exploded. She didn't wait for him to say anything, she just slammed the door closed.

He was too fast. He got his hand inside near the chain and his foot over the step.

Casey lost every bit of spit in her mouth. The wallet bounced out of her hands, forgotten as she repeatedly slammed the door on Jeff, trying to get him back, get him out.

"Open up, baby," he said, still working his fingers on the chain, using that sickly sweet voice that promised retribution. "I know you miss me."

"Get out." It was all she could manage. The oddest sounds came out of her throat as she struggled with the door, a cross between a moan and a scream. He put his shoulder into it and the chain pulled from the door. Sick fear coated Casey's throat. If he got in here she was dead. The sudden certainty made her sick. With new adrenaline, she pushed the door with her own shoulder and slammed his wrist hard.

"Motherfuck," he yelled. "You're going to pay for that, Casey. You're going to pay hard." With another solid jolt of his shoulder, the chain popped off the wall, taking bits of wood with it and the door bounced open.

Casey flew back into her apartment and landed on her ass. Jeff stood over her, his face a mask of cold hatred. He slammed the door behind him and glanced around the place. Her limbs shook and sweat prickled along her back.

"Casey, Casey, Casey. Why do you always make life so difficult?" His eyes looked a little wild and wigged out. She didn't dare ask if he was high on something. As nervous as he made her in the past, she'd never known him to be this violent, this enraged. He advanced on her and Casey scrambled to get her wobbly legs beneath her. Jeff's brows lifted on his forehead. "Did you think you were going somewhere, baby?" He shook his head. "'Cause you're not."

Phone or knife, phone or knife? Casey didn't know which way to go. The kitchen for a weapon or her bedroom for the phone? Easy choice since she'd never get as far as her bedroom and get a call off before Jeff got his hands on her.

She bolted for the kitchen, keeping the wall that separated it from the den between them, but Jeff quickly cut her off and stood at the opposite end right near her knife block on the counter.

"I can play this game all day, baby." His smile made her sick. "You know I'm going to win. I always win, Casey. How many years have I been telling you that? I always win."

"Get out, Jeff." Casey hated the way her voice shook. Hated how much she feared this man. "Go win somewhere else with someone else."

He shook his head again. When his gaze trailed from her bare legs up to her eyes, Casey's skin crawled. "You've got that just-

OUT OF THE BLUE

fucked look to you, baby. I remember that look. I miss it." He reached over and pulled a knife from the wooden block. "Were you looking for this?"

Casey scrambled for anything she could think of. "You should leave now, Jeff. Brendan's on his way back. He's going to find you."

"That's right... Brendan. I forgot his name for a minute." He twirled the knife in his hand. "I can just set him up the way I did Mitch. That won't be a problem."

Casey reeled with that information. "What? What are you talking about?"

"Mitch was easy to manipulate," Jeff boasted. "He was so fucking eager to take his pound of flesh that he hardly questioned anything when I called him. I saw him take those shots at you. I pretty much had him nailed to the wall. Not that he understood that. Plus he told me he arranged those accidents on the show. He had a friend in the grip department. I thought that was pretty fucking convenient, but we all know it's a small town, right." He wiped his nose with the back of his hand. "Never thought the guy would end up dead, but it saved me the trouble of doing it. Still, it would've been easier if he stuck to the plan and got you out of there. I practically fed you to him on a silver platter and he still couldn't get it right."

Mitch had a made a call after he'd shoved her into the studio. She'd completely forgotten about it. He'd called Jeff. It was too much information for Casey to process under the circumstances. The fact that he was telling her this only made it clearer he planned to use the knife in his hand.

"C'mon, Casey, I thought you knew me better than this." His gaze settled on hers after another trip up her legs. "I think it's time we relive some old memories."

Casey didn't wait for him to come closer. She ran for her room, a roaring pounded in her head as she heard Jeff closing the distance behind her. Time seemed to slow, then fast forward all in the same breath. One second she was on her feet and the next second, two hundred and twenty pounds of man slammed her to the floor in the hallway.

Air whooshed from her lungs and pain tore through her hands

and knees when she landed on the hardwood. She struggled beneath him, trying to get a breath in her parched lungs.

"Don't move, Casey," he grunted on top of her. The knife came into her vision, the meaning very clear and she stilled. "That's my girl," he said. He pushed his growing erection against her ass, then grabbed her hair and yanked her head up. Tears pricked her eyes. "You think I don't know you've been fucking this loser since Hawaii? Yeah," he said when he saw her surprise. "I went to Hawaii too. You thought you'd just fly over and enjoy a trip I paid for?" Her scalp burned as he pulled harder. "Remember when your boy nearly took a header in front of a bus? You have me to thank for that. You felt me there, baby. I know you did."

The surprises kept coming. The more he revealed, the more she understood just how crazy he was. She needed help. Would Brendan realize he forgot his wallet? She couldn't count on it.

Maybe if she had Jeff believing she'd cooperate she had a shot at freedom. Panting hard, she tried to get a breath. "Put the knife down, Jeff. I'll do whatever you want. Please, just put the knife down."

"I love when you beg for it, baby. You know how hot that gets me." He licked her ear and she nearly gagged. "Beg for it," he whispered.

Bile rose in her throat and her heart continued to pound so hard she thought she might stroke out. "Please, put the knife down."

"Beg me to fuck you, Casey. Go on. Do it. I know you want it." He loosened the grip on her hair, but slammed her face into the floor and pain ruptured in her cheek. Her vision blurred.

"Let me turn around so I can see you," she said. She had no way to defend herself on her stomach. She needed her hands, her knees, anything to lay a blow. She'd hurt his right wrist, too, so she had to aim for that first. Or his eyes...or that tiny dick in his pants.

He lifted up and she turned, but he grabbed her wrists and held them above her head in one meaty hand. Stupid. She hadn't counted on him pinning her like this. The knife clattered somewhere out of her peripheral vision and his free hand roughly roamed her body.

Casey held back the revulsion and wiggled beneath him. "Let

go, Jeff. I can't touch you without my hands. You know how much you love my hands on you." She used his strategy against him.

He laughed. "You're right about that, baby. I do love those hands of yours. I love your mouth even more. You know what you're going to do with that mouth?" He rubbed against her harder and Casey's T-shirt rode up her stomach. Slowly, straddling her, he inched up her body, using his free hand to unbutton his jeans.

No, no, no! This couldn't be happening. There had to be a way out of this. "I need my hands, Jeff. C'mon." What would convince him? "You know I'm not strong enough to hurt a guy like you."

The vile intent in his crazy eyes went hand in hand with his conceit. "I'll make you a deal, baby. You suck my cock like a good girl and I'll let go of your hands when I'm done with you. The second you do something I don't like is the second I use that knife to cut your throat. You understand me?"

She swallowed back bile.

"Take the zipper down with your teeth," he told her.

Not in this lifetime. She was dead no matter what, but she sure as hell wasn't going to let him rape her before he killed her.

His face distorted with a nasty frown as he cupped her jaw and forced her mouth open. That was all she needed.

Quick as a snake striking its prey, Casey jerked her head, latched on to his nasty thumb and bit down with everything she had.

Jeff screamed and she tasted blood. He released her wrists, which was what she needed. She grabbed his dick with one hand as she poked at his face with the other, aiming for his eyes, but having a hard time because of the way her head was angled. Instead of trying to deflect one of her attacks, he punched her hard on the side of her head. The explosion of light and pain nearly crippled her. She didn't know how, but she managed to keep her teeth clamped and her hand tight on his crotch, twisting even harder. If she let him go, she was definitely dead.

He screamed at the top of his lungs as he pulled his fist back about to hit her again. Casey closed her eyes, and waited for impact, biting down even harder while she still could. If he broke her jaw she'd have zero leverage with her mouth. More noise filled the room, a roaring different than the drums pounding in her head and chest. A split second later, Jeff's weight disappeared.

Casey scrambled back at the same time she realized Brendan had returned. Relief barreled through her like a locomotive, but it quickly disappeared as the two of them struggled in the den. Jeff didn't seem as if anything fazed him. Not the bite to his thumb or the pain that had to be emanating from his tiny pecker.

The men traded nasty punches until Jeff landed a blow to Brendan's shoulder that sent him to his knees.

She had to do something! There, on the floor, she spotted the knife she'd wanted so badly. Casey crawled toward it, dizzy and sick to her stomach as Brendan got to his feet. Before she reached it, the guys crashed and rolled over the coffee table. Watching in horror, Casey could do nothing as Jeff landed on top and went after Brendan with a viciousness and strength she'd never seen before, hitting him over and over.

Enraged and terrified for Brendan, Casey jumped on Jeff's back and wrapped her arm around his neck, choking off his air and screaming in his ear, doing anything and everything she could to distract him. The ploy worked...maybe too well.

Jeff got to his feet, trying to force her off him, but she stuck to his back like a monkey on its mama. He slammed her against the bookshelf and pain exploded in her back. Everything on the shelves fell around them. She tried to tighten her hold, but he slammed her one more time, sideways. Blinding pain burst in her side. She wouldn't be able to hold on much longer. There had to be a weak spot.

Jeff struggled against her, choked on the little air getting to his lungs.

"Brendan!" she screamed. Brendan slowly got to his feet and stumbled over to them, his face bloody and swollen.

Jeff attacked him even with her still attached to his back. Casey adjusted her grip and climbed his back enough to get leverage. She brought her elbow down hard on the side of his head at the same time Brendan let loose with a massive right hook to Jeff's cheek.

The combination stunned him. Like a darted animal, Jeff collapsed in slow motion... First to his knees—where Casey jumped off him—before he fell sideways and rolled to his back.

Sirens wailed outside.

"Sure, now the cops come," Brendan mumbled, wiping blood from his lip as he landed on his knees. Casey joined him on the floor, every part of her in pain.

"You...okay?" she asked, shaking and out of breath. The stitches had burst open and blood seeped through his T-shirt. His face was a mess with a cut lip and cheek, his nose bloody. On the upside, Jeff looked just as bad.

"I'm okay," Brendan said. He inspected her cheek. "What about you? That looks nasty."

Her cheek throbbed with every heartbeat. "I'm okay." She studied his concerned eyes. "I'd be dead...if you hadn't come back." She leaned forward and reached for the ever elusive knife, making sure it wasn't anywhere near Jeff.

"I forgot my—"

"Wallet," they said at the same time.

She turned to him, still trying to catch her breath. "I know. I found it when I was making the bed. I hoped to hell you'd realize it and come back."

Brendan looked at the front door. "He just busted in?"

She nodded and swallowed, her heart still racing. "Pretty much. I have no idea how long he'd been watching us. You won't believe what he told me about Mitch."

The cops stormed in, weapons drawn at the same time an unholy sound rumbled from Jeff's chest. Out of nowhere he jackknifed forward and flew toward Casey like a missile. Bullets popped in the air, blood blossomed on his chest, but nothing stopped him. Without thinking, Casey gripped the knife tighter in her hands and lifted it straight into Jeff's oncoming chest. Brendan's block shoved him off before his dead weight collapsed on her. Blood covered her trembling fingers and splattered across the floor and her clothes. Casey stared in horror at the knife lodged in Jeff's chest and the multiple bullet holes that bled profusely.

In the next instant, she was in Brendan's arms as he pulled her away from the gruesome sight. "It's okay, it's okay," he soothed softly in her ear. "It's over. It's all over. I'm so proud of you, Case. You kept fighting. You never gave up. You never gave up."

Yet she'd almost given up on Brendan. Casey squeezed him as hard as she could, considering her side throbbed like a bitch. Her knees shook so hard, she didn't think she could stand up. "Thanks...for coming back," she whispered and she didn't plan to let him go anytime soon.

EPILOGUE

Three months later

A WHISPER SOFT STROKE along her spine woke Casey. She shifted, letting her legs slide between the cool sheets as Brendan glided a calloused finger down her bare back. "Mmm," she purred. Not a bad way to wake up. She cracked a sleepy eyelid and saw Brendan's oak dresser in the darkness and a stack of moving boxes that hadn't been emptied yet. His bedroom in his apartment. Actually, *their* bedroom in *their* apartment. She grinned. "You're horny *again*?" she mumbled into the pillow. They'd already fooled around enough to make her sore. Not that she was complaining. Nope. Not her.

He moved closer, tucked her next to him and she felt the undeniable answer to her question growing between her butt cheeks. "Can't help myself. You're too sexy." He brushed his lips over her hair, searching for her ear. "Mmm." He found it and awakened all those little sex gremlins previously asleep.

Casey rolled over and smiled at him. "Can't sleep, huh?" Their excitement was the reason they'd exhausted themselves with sex. At least they'd tried to. Clearly it wasn't enough for Brendan.

He shook his head and played with a lock of her hair. "Nope. Too nervous."

A couple hours ago they'd downloaded their respective albums from the Internet. They'd been traveling like crazy, performing, doing interviews and generally promoting their music. Casey never would've imagined that they'd release on the same day. That was an accidental happening and it conspired to keep them apart. They'd both arrived back in town yesterday after three brutal weeks apart.

Three weeks of texting, Skype and phone calls. Three weeks of some of the most fabulous phone sex Casey had ever had. But it didn't compare to the real thing. She wrapped a leg over his thigh and snugged up tight, loving the warmth of his skin, the way his strength made her feel secure.

Seger had come up with a plan and approached Miles with it. To Casey's shock, Miles actually agreed, so starting tonight, Casey was opening for Seger's new tour. Headlining with Seger was none other than Brendan St. John.

"This is crazy, right?" She eased a hand through his long, thick hair. "Just a dream? I'm going to wake up any minute and realize it's all just a dream."

His grin brightened the darkness. "It's a dream coming true maybe, yeah. I have no problem with it."

She didn't either, but the reality scared her. "It's going to be really hard," she said. He rubbed against her and she felt exactly what was hard. She laughed. "Not you, you big goober. Juggling all this is going to be hard." Her fears reared up and smacked her in the face. "This is just the beginning. What happens when we're apart for three months at a time or longer?"

His smile faded and he pulled her closer. "First, we make a deal that no matter what, we'll figure our schedules so that we won't go that long without seeing each other. Seger and Ashley make it work."

"Yeah, but she's not a musician on her own tour."

"No, but she's a famous artist and someone's always commissioning her to paint a mural on some massive wall somewhere. She doesn't travel with Seger as much as she used to." He nibbled her lips then leaned back, his grin returning. "The best part is the next six months on tour with you." He flopped to his back. "I could kiss Seger for making this happen."

Casey rolled onto his stomach. "You'd better not. You do not want to see me jealous. The only person you'll be kissing i—" His lips shut her up. Then he rolled her to her back and continued to keep her quiet. Well, unless someone counted the sighs, moans and all those *yeses* coming out of her mouth.

At this rate, their stash of condoms wasn't going to last very long.

Casey gasped as Brendan pushed in to the hilt with one smooth glide and didn't budge...with the exception of his mouth. He devoured her lips with single-minded determination, exploring with seductive forays of his tongue. His weight felt delicious as he pressed her to the bed. Wrapping her legs around his waist, she urged him to move, but he didn't.

"A little while longer," he whispered. "Just like this. Want to be inside you for as long as possible."

Oh, God, he made her so hot when he talked like that. Feeling him inside her, stretching her, hitting all those sensitive spots made her crazy. Seconds turned into minutes and still he didn't move. He just drugged her with long slow kisses that decimated her. Every bit of attention focused on the spot where they connected. She felt every throb, every twitch of him inside her and it built the need to a breaking point. "Brendan, now. Need you so much," she said, against his mouth. "Can't wait."

"A little longer," he whispered back and kissed her again. More minutes ticked by until Casey thought she might explode with wanting him.

"Now? Please?" His devious smile wrecked her. He rubbed against her without pulling out and the slide nearly brought her to orgasm. "Oh, God, Bren. Please. I'm dying." She rubbed against him, silently begging for more.

A low growl rumbled in his chest and he finally pulled out and pushed back in. Casey came in a blinding rush, the intensity of the orgasm surprising the breath right out of her. She froze as each delicious wave powered through her. Brendan tensed above her, groaned and she felt the undeniable throbbing of his climax deep inside her. Wrung out, Bren collapsed over her for a heartbeat before he shifted to his side, pulling her with him. They lay there, sweaty and satisfied, in a sex haze.

When Casey's brain started working again, she adjusted her pillow and got eye to eye. "I feel a little weird. I mean it took Blake a year to move in with his girlfriend and here I am moved in after only a few months. Your parents must think I'm super easy." *Her* parents sure did. Although they had definitely warmed to

Brendan, so there was still hope for them. The fact that she'd actually released music that the general public seemed to like had, sadly, astonished them. But they were finally seeing their youngest daughter in a new light and Casey didn't mind that at all.

"Want to know a secret?" he asked, rising up on his elbow and looking down at her.

"Sure. What?"

"Blake proposed to Abbey last night."

Casey sat up, a wave of happiness bursting through her. "No way! And? What did she say?"

"I'd have heard from him if she'd said no, so I'm guessing they're in good shape over there." Brendan's smile beamed bright. "I mean he did move in, so I imagine she knew this was coming one day."

"That is so sweet. I'm so happy for them." Casey had met Abbey right after Jeff died.

The St. Johns had arranged a press conference where Casey and Brendan both made statements and answered questions from the press. Their bruises verified much of the tale. News outlets had already reported the stash of cocaine in Jeff's Hummer and the rental he'd driven to Casey's apartment. It was the last straw needed to crumble the political life of the Bauer family. More interesting to Casey was discovering that Jeff's drug problem started two years ago. Exactly the time he started his personality change.

Casey's parents, sister and all the St. Johns had been at the press conference, including Abbey. Casey had heard a lot about her, but hadn't realized she was *the* Abbey Washington from *Dance 'Til You Drop*, a dance show competing with *Dancing With The Stars*. Abbey's star had been burning brightly the past year. She'd actually parlayed her dance job on the show into a big part in a new dance movie due to be released next year. Blake and she were obviously in love. It was evident in the way they looked at each other, and the way they laughed and touched each other.

It baffled Casey that she hadn't noticed all these things missing when she was with Jeff. But she berated herself less and less as time wore on, and she soaked up Brendan's love like a dry sponge and gave it back with her whole heart.

"You know Blake and I have always kind of run on the same clock," he said, sitting up and running a hand through his long hair.

"You mean because of the twin thing?" she asked, adjusting to rest her head on his shoulder. She loved running her hands along his chest. It was nice to have him healthy and strong again with no sling and no movement issues. He was back to a hundred percent.

"Probably. Don't know. I mean, it's not like we do everything together anymore obviously, but we still tend to think alike."

"That's nice." Casey yawned, hoping to sneak in a few more hours of sleep before the day started. They had to be at a local morning radio show to promote the new album. In a marketing risk, they'd combined efforts to promote themselves and each other so even though they spent so much time apart, now they'd get to spend even more months together as they promoted and toured their music.

The duet Seger and Brendan released as the first single had debuted at number one and already the buzz was high for the record. Brendan's future was all but sealed.

Casey's single was still climbing the charts, but she realized she didn't have a name like Seger Hughes attached to her, so her success wasn't as guaranteed as Brendan's. Not that anything was guaranteed in this business, but he had a leg up since he'd initially won the show and had Seger in his corner.

Brendan shifted under her and clicked on the bedside lamp. Light busted in on her much needed darkness. "So, Case, I need to ask you a question."

"Mmm." She kept her eyes closed against the light, figuring he'd shut it off after he found what he needed in the nightstand.

"You know how much I love you, right?"

"Mmm-hmm. I love you too." Casey heard a little pop. A tiny sound, but for some reason it made her heart thump harder. She squinted her eyes open a fraction to let in some of that light and see what Brendan was up to.

"Because I love you, and I know beyond a doubt that you're the one for me, I want to make it official."

Casey rubbed her eyes as she sat up, forcing her fuzzy brain to wake up. "We made it official months ago, remember?"

"Not like this." He paused for a fraction of a second. "Case, will you marry me?"

Her eyes flashed open, wide awake now. She met his gaze then looked down at the unbelievable sparkly diamond ring sitting in a black velvet box. Her heart lodged someplace in her throat.

"You're proposing *now?*" She wiped her hands down her face then through her messy hair. "This is happening *now?*" She needed a brush, makeup. She needed to look better when he proposed. "I've got pillow lines on my face." She wiped at her chin. No doubt she had dried drool there.

He took her hands, stilled them. "Sweetheart, you couldn't look any more beautiful than you do right now." He leaned in and brushed his lips along hers. "I love when your hair is kind of messy. I dig those pillow lines, too, because you got them sleeping next to me. There isn't anything I don't love about you." He pulled the ring out of the box. "So will you marry me?" His shocking blue eyes stared into hers and in them she saw everything she wanted in a man. She saw love, acceptance and respect. She saw someone who'd champion her causes and be her biggest supporter.

"Yes," she said. Her eyes stung as he slipped the ring on her finger. "Brendan this is gorgeous. How could you afford this?"

"Let's just say Seger gave me a little advance on the royalties he's expecting."

She shook her head. "That must be some advance." She hadn't received her winnings from the show until just last month. After cuts went to her new management and agent, the rest had gone into the bank...with the exception of a small splurge on some clothes and things she hadn't been able to buy because of Jeff's taste and his hang-ups.

Every now and then it hit her that he was dead. The autopsy had shown that her knife wound hadn't killed him. The bullets had. But still, it was as if a dark cloud covered her when she thought of it. Though she hadn't been happy with him for a long time and his mood swings had grown worse, she still remembered the man she fell in love with. The guy who smiled at her and treated her well in the beginning. Her first mistake was not looking for something behind his personality change and leaving sooner. Her second mistake was pretending to be someone she wasn't to make him happy.

The square-cut diamond sparkled on her finger with stunning brilliance and it reminded Casey what she had now, right in front of her. Brendan loved her for everything she was and everything she was going to be. That was something no one could put a price tag on.

"Do you like it?" he asked. His forehead crinkled in a cute pucker. "You're a little quiet. I know you think I might be rushing this, but I'm not. We can stay engaged for as long as you want. If you need to get used to the idea, that's cool. I totally get it. I just want you to know that I'm in it for the long haul. Like the fifty or sixty year haul. I want you next to me when we're both old and gray, you know? I want to laugh with you and make music with you, confide in you, and I want you to do all those things with me."

Casey wrapped her arms around his neck, straddled his lap and set her lips on his. "I can see why you have a hit song out of the gate," she whispered at his lips. "You're very good with words."

"Yeah?" He grinned. "That's a compliment coming from you, Miss Eight Songs in Two Days."

She shrugged. "What can I say. I had my muse close by." She kissed him again and it wasn't long before he had her spread on those cool sheets, calling his name and coming apart at his touch.

Lying next to each other sweaty and exhausted, Casey reached for his hand. "What if I said I wanted to marry you sooner rather than later?"

His eyes widened? "No shit?" He looked like a puppy with a new toy. "I mean, I said all that because I didn't want to pressure you, but I'd marry you tomorrow, Case. Just say the word."

She laughed. "I think we're a little booked tomorrow." She glanced at the clock. They only had a couple more hours until the alarm went off. "What about after the tour? That's only six months away."

He nodded and chuckled.

"What's so funny?" she asked.

"Blake was shooting for six months with Abbey. That'll be

during her hiatus from the show and before she starts shooting the movie."

"Oh, so then we should make it a different time."

He shrugged. "Unless we had a double wedding." He lifted an eyebrow. "My parents could get it done in one shot. But obviously it's up to you and Abbey and what you and your parents want. I'll do whatever you tell me."

Casey snuggled in his arms. It didn't matter what her parents thought. Whatever everyone else wanted suited her fine. All she cared about was taking care of the man next to her for the rest of her life.

"Bren," she murmured as he gently stroked his fingers down her arm. "Thanks for rescuing me that day on the beach."

He kissed her temple. "Smartest move I've made my whole life. You're the best thing that ever happened to me, Case. You still don't believe me, but I fell in love with you that first day." His chest huffed. "I nearly had a coronary when I saw you that first night on the show, but I knew then. I wasn't letting you go."

The urge to come clean about that first day on the beach overwhelmed Casey. She didn't want to start a life with Brendan without being completely honest. "I have a confession to make," she said, pulling back so she could see his eyes. "That morning in Hawaii wasn't exactly accidental. I'd been watching you jog in the mornings and I decided that on my last day, I wanted to meet you."

His brows slanted in equal lines as he sat up. "You're telling me that you got into the ocean on purpose, hoping I'd rescue—"

"No!" She sat up too. "I just wanted to meet you. I never realized the water was going to take me out. That was definitely an accident. But I am glad you saved me." His brows stayed slanted and Casey's heart slammed harder against her ribs. "Please don't be mad at me. Bren, I love you with all my heart, you have to know that." She swallowed, terrified that she'd made the biggest mistake of her life.

"So you came down at the butt crack of dawn to meet me and thought you'd casually take a dip in the water to look natural? Do I have that right?"

"Um…" Casey flashed her brightest smile. "Yes?"

The next few seconds seemed to last a lifetime, but slowly Brendan's face morphed, his brows lifted and a grin kicked up his lips. He pounced and she shrieked. "The next time you want my attention," he said, covering her with his significant muscle, "all you have to do is smile. That's all you needed to do that morning."

"So you're not mad at me?"

"Case, if you hadn't come out of your room, I wouldn't have met you until the show. I'd like to think that we still would've connected, but that day—and night in Hawaii—that was a turning point for me too."

Casey's heart melted and she glanced at the clock again. Any hope of sleep was long gone so she eased her palm down Brendan's side, making little circles with her fingers.

"Now who's horny?" he said around a chuckle.

"That would be me," she said, cupping his tight ass. "But you can't blame me. Anytime you start talking like that you know it makes me hot."

"Damn, I'm glad I write songs for a living now."

Casey rolled him, loved the way his strong arms encircled her. "That's *hit* songs for a living." She stopped before kissing him again. "Hey, so we're not going to let any of that shit get in the way right? We're just going to write our songs and be supportive of each other?"

His brows furrowed. "Of course. I think there's room for both of us in the business, don't you?"

"I do. So here's the deal. Whoever sells the most music has to make dinner."

He laughed and the rumble in his chest sparked her own laughter. "Deal." He rolled her fast and set his lips on her neck. She opened her legs to accommodate his weight. "And whoever's wearing the engagement ring has to have an orgasm."

Her giggle bubbled from out of nowhere. "Well, if you insist. I don't want to be difficult."

"I knew you were a smart woman." Brendan proved to her two more times just what a smart decision she'd made and Casey knew without a doubt that she'd found the perfect man completely out of the blue.

The End

ALSO BY DEE J. ADAMS

THE ADRENALINE HIGHS SERIES

DANGEROUS RACE

"High Octane Awesomeness!"
5 stars – Laura Wright, author of *Mark of the Vampire* and *Bayou Heat* series.

"Really, really fabulous read. The mystery / suspense subplot is interesting and keeps you on your toes, the main and secondary characters are all great and likable, there is sizzling chemistry in both the primary and secondary romances, and it's well-written."
4.5 stars – The Fiction Vixen

Taking high octane romance and suspense to a whole other level, Adams goes green flag with a prologue that left me shaken and a story that both thrilled and chilled.
4 stars – One Good Book Deserves Another

DANGER ZONE

"Okay, I'll admit it. I'm a sucker for romances set in the world of movie-making. But in Danger Zone, *Dee J. Adams not only uses her years of experience in Hollywood to create a delightfully gritty and authentic world filled with insider insights; she also creates a cast of very real and likable characters. I especially loved stunt-woman Ellie Morgan's kickass, take-no-prisoners attitude, and her long-time friendship with her best-friend and roommate Ashley. As for the book's hero, Quinn Reynolds? I'm in love. This one's on my keeper shelf."*
New York Times Bestselling author Suzanne Brockmann

"Highly recommended for romantic suspense fans, especially those who like stories with complex relationships."
Marlene Harris, Reading Reality LLC
Starred Review from *Library Journal*

DANGEROUSLY CLOSE

"Witty dialogue and unyielding suspense make for another great story in the Adrenaline Highs series. The hero and heroine are fully developed and emotionally rich, and the best part of the novel is the developing relationship between them from strangers to friends to lovers. Readers will enjoy spending time with these memorable characters."

4 stars – *Romantic Times*

*"*Dangerously Close *is hands down my favorite book in this series thus far and it's easily one of my top picks for 2012. I was completely and utterly drawn into this story. The strong romance balanced out perfectly with the suspense element."*

5 stars – The Book Vixen

LIVING DANGEROUSLY
Winner: 2014 Gayle Wilson Award of Excellence

"It has everything from the glitterati of Hollywood to a high-speed cross-country getaway—even a bit of bondage. Narrow escapes are the norm in this action-filled novel."

4 stars + Scorcher – *Romantic Times*

IMMINENT DANGER

"Loved it! Lots of romance action mystery and sex! Love the series."

5 stars – Happy Amazon Reader

"Adams never fails to deliver a fast-paced plot filled with unexpected twists and 'whoa…I can't believe that just happened' moments. Abbey & Blake's story is as deliciously sexually charged as it is suspenseful."

4 stars – Goodreads reviewer

A LITTLE DANGER

"This is the type of book where you'll want to clear some time and just sit and read it. You won't want to put it down. But be warned, it's like riding a roller coaster of emotions."

5 stars – Happy Amazon Reader

"Adams expertly writes the earthquake as a formidable villain that appears determined to keep Elena and Bill apart."
5 stars – Happy Amazon Reviewer

ALWAYS DANGEROUS

"Dee J. Adams does a great job at mixing just the right amount of excitement in with the romance and the pace of the developing relationship between Kim and Leo was perfect. They're sexy together and have great chemistry."
4 stars – Under the Covers Book Blog

"Miss Adams has a new fan in me after this, and I'm definitely planning on going back and reading all the previous titles in this series. If the final book is anything to go by, I've been missing out."
– Dirty Girl Romance

HIGHS STAKES SERIES

AGAINST THE WALL

"When it comes to romantic suspense, Dee J. Adams delivers!"
New York Times Bestselling author Suzanne Brockmann

This was an action-packed and pulse-pounding read with some surprising, gasp-worthy twists and turns. I was caught off guard more than once by developments I hadn't seen coming and moved by characters who left an impression.
4 stars – One Good Book Deserves Another

OVER THE TOP

Another great read by Dee J Adams! Love her style of writing. Her books have a little of everything I love in a book.
5 stars – Happy Amazon Reader

I can't believe how much stress <Dee J.> packed into such a short book… Awesome!
5 stars – Goodreads reviewer

ABOUT THE AUTHOR

After graduating high school in Texas, Dee J. moved to Los Angeles to pursue acting. For twenty years, she acted in television and worked behind the scenes as an acting/dialogue coach for sitcoms. Writing happened accidentally after a vivid dream and the urging of her husband to "Just write it down." Three weeks, fourteen hours a day, and four hundred and fifty (long hand) pages later, she had her first novel. Dee J. loves writing books filled with action, mystery and love. (Not necessarily in that order.) Her experience in show business led to her narrating many of the books in the Adrenaline Highs series for Audible.com. She is the wife of a wonderful man and mother to a fabulous daughter. She's a dog lover all the way, with a fondness towards Boxers and Pit Bulls. She is a member of several organizations, including Romance Writers of America and SAG-AFTRA.

For more information on Dee J.'s books please visit:
www.deejadams.com

Dee J. can be found on
Facebook: http://www.facebook.com/DeeJAdamsAuthor

Twitter: https://twitter.com/DeeJAdams

Goodreads:
http://www.goodreads.com/author/show/5107047.Dee_J_Adams

Amazon: http://amzn.to/MuznPw